SWEET TEMPTATION

"Sizzle, sex appeal and sensuality! Maya Banks has it all . . . This book is on the inferno side of hot, and it shows on every page . . . You will not want to miss out on this story."
—*Romance Junkies*

"An enjoyable tale of [a] second chance at life."
—*Genre Go Round Reviews*

SWEET SEDUCTION

"Maya Banks never fails to tell compelling tales that evoke an emotional reaction in readers . . . Kept me on the edge of my seat."
—*Romance Junkies*

SWEET PERSUASION

"Surpassed all my expectations. Incredibly intense and complex characters, delicious conflict and explosive sex scenes that fairly melt the print off the pages, *Sweet Persuasion* will have Maya Banks fans, new and existing alike, lasciviously begging for more."
—*RT Book Reviews* (4½ stars)

"Ignites the pages . . . Readers will relish Maya Banks's exciting erotic romance."
—*The Best Reviews*

"Well written and evocative."
—*Dear Author*

BE WITH ME

"I absolutely loved it! Simply wonderful writing. There's a new star on the rise and her name is Maya Banks."
—Sunny, national bestselling author of *Mona Lisa Eclipsing*

SWEET SURRENDER

"This story ran my heart through the wringer more than once."
—*CK²S Kwips and Kritiques*

"From page one, I was drawn into the story and literally could not stop reading until the last page."
—*The Romance Studio*

"Maya Banks's story lines are always full of situations that captivate readers, but it's the emotional pull you experience which brings the story to life." —*Romance Junkies*

FOR HER PLEASURE

"[It] is the ultimate in pleasurable reading. Enticing, enchanting and sinfully sensual, I couldn't have asked for a better anthology." —*Joyfully Reviewed*

"Full of emotional situations, lovable characters and kick-butt story lines that will leave you desperate for more . . . For readers who like spicy romances with a suspenseful element—it's definitely a must-read!" —*Romance Junkies*

"Totally intoxicating, *For Her Pleasure* is one of those reads you won't be forgetting any time soon."
—*The Road to Romance*

Berkley titles by Maya Banks

FOR HER PLEASURE
SWEET SURRENDER
BE WITH ME
SWEET PERSUASION
SWEET SEDUCTION
SWEET TEMPTATION

THE DARKEST HOUR
NO PLACE TO RUN
HIDDEN AWAY
WHISPERS IN THE DARK

WHISPERS IN THE DARK

MAYA BANKS

BERKLEY SENSATION, NEW YORK

THE BERKLEY PUBLISHING GROUP
Published by the Penguin Group
Penguin Group (USA) Inc.
375 Hudson Street, New York, New York 10014, USA
Penguin Group (Canada), 90 Eglinton Avenue East, Suite 700, Toronto, Ontario M4P 2Y3, Canada
(a division of Pearson Penguin Canada Inc.)
Penguin Books Ltd., 80 Strand, London WC2R 0RL, England
Penguin Group Ireland, 25 St. Stephen's Green, Dublin 2, Ireland (a division of Penguin Books Ltd.)
Penguin Group (Australia), 250 Camberwell Road, Camberwell, Victoria 3124, Australia
(a division of Pearson Australia Group Pty. Ltd.)
Penguin Books India Pvt. Ltd., 11 Community Centre, Panchsheel Park, New Delhi—110 017, India
Penguin Group (NZ), 67 Apollo Drive, Rosedale, Auckland 0632, New Zealand
(a division of Pearson New Zealand Ltd.)
Penguin Books (South Africa) (Pty.) Ltd., 24 Sturdee Avenue, Rosebank, Johannesburg 2196,
South Africa

Penguin Books Ltd., Registered Offices: 80 Strand, London WC2R 0RL, England

This is a work of fiction. Names, characters, places, and incidents either are the product of the author's imagination or are used fictitiously, and any resemblance to actual persons, living or dead, business establishments, events, or locales is entirely coincidental. The publisher does not have any control over and does not assume any responsibility for author or third-party websites or their content.

WHISPERS IN THE DARK

A Berkley Sensation Book / published by arrangement with the author

PRINTING HISTORY
Berkley Sensation mass-market edition / January 2012

Copyright © 2012 by Maya Banks.
Excerpt on pages 337–339 by Maya Banks copyright © by Maya Banks.
Cover art by Craig White.
Cover design by Rita Frangie.
Interior text design by Laura K. Corless.

ISBN: 978-0-425-24610-8

BERKLEY SENSATION®
Berkley Sensation Books are published by The Berkley Publishing Group,
a division of Penguin Group (USA) Inc.,
375 Hudson Street, New York, New York 10014.
BERKLEY SENSATION® is a registered trademark of Penguin Group (USA) Inc.
The "B" design is a trademark of Penguin Group (USA) Inc.

PRINTED IN THE UNITED STATES OF AMERICA

10 9 8 7 6 5 4 3 2 1

For Telisa,
who was a fan of the KGI series even before
she knew I was the one who wrote it

ACKNOWLEDGMENTS

Sometimes writing is very solitary, but in the end, I'm always reminded of some very special people who go the extra mile to help make my books the best they can be. Valerie and Natalie, you have my utmost appreciation for always dropping everything to read for me. Lillie, not only do you read, but you reread and read again. And you give awesome book talk, not to mention all the spoilers you provide me. I don't have adequate words to express my gratitude to you all.

Research can be daunting and overwhelming, and separating good and accurate information from the pack isn't always easy. My sincerest thanks to my sources who are only too happy to discuss fun stuff like our mutual love of guns and things that go "boom." Not to mention the helicopters and our love of New Mexico and Colorado. Your help is invaluable, and any errors are solely my own.

To my editor and the team of copyeditors and proofreaders who work hard to make sure my book is the best it can be. Thank you. Any errors, typos, or issues with continuity are strictly mine.

As many people as I have to thank and acknowledge, it's you, the reader, who I owe the most to. Without you, I wouldn't be able to do what I love most: write emotional stories of love and family and life. You've made it possible for the KGI series to continue and for me to be able to continue the stories of the

Kelly family. I sincerely hope I'm able to do them justice for you.

Love,
Maya

CHAPTER 1

SHEA Peterson's eyelids flew open as she came instantly and fully awake. Her breath escaped in soft pants as agony crushed through her body. She went tense and her fingers curled into the tangled sheets at her sides.

She heard him again. Felt his despair in black, suffocating waves. She closed her eyes as his pain mingled with hers, lacing intricate patterns through her veins until they were merged, she a part of him.

Tonight more than any other time she felt his will to live dissolve. She felt his shame. The thought that he was a coward and didn't deserve to die with honor.

Tears burned her eyelids. How long had she felt him suffer in silence? His strength had always amazed her, and now she could feel it crumbling under the weight of his despair. She hurt with him. She hurt *for* him.

She could no longer remain still. She could no longer remain silent despite the awful risk to herself and her sister, Grace. She couldn't turn her back on this man. Not when his need was so great.

She drew in a deep breath, afraid and yet determined. She closed her eyes and reached out, following the trail of pain until she became hyperaware of the hell that he lived in.

The smell was pungent. She sucked in her breath as the scent of blood, dirt, sweat and *death* filtered through her nostrils.

Her instinct was to flee this place, break the link between her and the suffering man. Fear lodged in her throat, and pain was raw, sawing over her nerves.

In the distance, cries, grunts, muttered curses, a foreign language indecipherable to her. The man put a hand to his head. He knew something was different but he put it off as evidence of a losing battle for his sanity.

She huddled there, completely still in his mind, cautiously examining the surroundings through his senses.

He was imprisoned. A soldier. She caught fleeting images as they flashed through his head. His capture. The endless days of torture, starvation and misery.

He sat in a corner, his face in his hands, feelings of loathing and rage firing relentlessly through his brain. He hated his weakness, hated that he wanted to die. Hated that he wasn't able to help the others who suffered with him.

He thought of his family. They brought comfort to him and yet he worried what his disappearance was doing to his parents and to his brothers. He thought constantly of his twin. Joe.

His name floated in Shea's mind, spelled out in a flash of color before gradually fading away.

No one had come for him in two days. He felt a mixture of relief and dread because he knew that his reprieve would soon be over and he would suffer terribly once again. He wasn't sure he had the strength to survive more. And he hated the weakness that made him question whether he preferred death to his continued existence. Caged like an animal.

He'd never felt so alone in his life.

Tears slipped down Shea's cheeks, and she knew she could no longer be silent, no longer pretend she wasn't connected to this man.

You aren't alone. I'm here.

He went still, his head coming up as he stared through the piercing darkness. Despite his weakness and his broken-down spirit, the warrior within him immediately came to life. His muscles tensed and he turned, his nostrils flaring as if to scent the intruder.

"Who's there," he uttered in a cracked, hoarse voice.

Shhh. You don't want to alert the others. Talk to me in this way. With your mind. If you think it, I will hear you.

"Jesus," he whispered. "It's finally happened. I've finally lost my goddamn mind."

A chill stole over his body and he hunched farther down, wrapping his arms around his legs and rocking back and forth. He buried his face against his knees and closed his eyes. Weariness and sadness crept over him. And acceptance of his fate.

No. You mustn't give up. I'm with you. I won't leave you.

"Who are you?" he muttered, not picking up his head from his knees.

Why do you persist in talking? They'll hear you. Don't do anything to draw their attention.

It doesn't matter whether I draw their attention or not.

The weary thought drifted into her mind, and the knot grew in her throat at the resignation so heavy in his consciousness.

You're not alone. She pushed the thought at him again. More forcefully this time. Then she cradled him against her, imagined her arms sliding around him to give him what comfort she could.

She stroked her hands over his body and murmured soothing, nonsensical words in his ear. She pressed a kiss to his brow, ignoring the smell of sweat and blood surrounding them.

She didn't know this man, but she could no more deny him comfort than she could deny anyone who suffered so much.

What she was about to do was dangerous. But how could she not do what she could to give him relief when she had the ability to help him just for a while?

She merged more fully with him, sent herself inside his very soul. She bit her lip to control the cry of agony as his pain swamped over her, through her. His pain became her own.

Tears ran freely down her cheeks as the full extent of his suffering blew over her like a scorching wildfire. It took all her strength and concentration to maintain the link between them.

What are you doing?

His quiet question was full of bewilderment. She could sense his disbelief, even as his body relaxed in brief respite from the discomfort tearing at him. He thought this was some bizarre dream that was a manifestation of his growing insanity. He thought she was a coping mechanism. Something his shattered mind had conjured as a way to cope with his horrific reality.

It took her a long moment before she was able to respond. She lay on her bed, shaking, her nerve endings shooting little jolts of fire through her body as she absorbed the pain from him.

Are you there?

There was hope in the uncertain question. She saw his battle between truth and hallucination and then his acceptance that he didn't care. No matter whether she was real or not, he desperately hung on to the notion that he was no longer isolated.

I'm here.

Her voice was fainter in his mind now, and he frowned even as he raised his head and stretched his arms above and then around him.

What did you do?

She didn't respond. It took all her strength to maintain the bond between them, but she could still feel it fading.

What did you do? His question became more strident. She felt a surge of strength through his body as he tested his arms, his hands and then his legs. *How could you have done it? Who are you?*

I'll return to you. Her thought was a mere whisper in his mind now. *I won't leave you alone to face this. I swear it.*

She caught traces of his frustration just before she let go and retreated from his mind. For a long while, she lay on the bed gasping and shuddering as she tried to process the waves of pain, both physical and mental.

She rolled to her side, pulling her knees to her chest in a manner reminiscent of his own posture in his filthy, dark cell. She rested her forehead on her knees and sucked in breath after breath until finally the pain began to recede.

Her cheeks were damp. The tendrils of hair over her ears were wet from her tears. She staggered to her feet and walked clumsily toward the bathroom, where she splashed cold water on her face.

Who was he? Why was she drawn to him? Why had she heard him amid the millions of other cries in the night? Her gift was so random. Her fist pounded down on the sink. She couldn't control it. Not like the people who hunted her and her sister wanted.

Shea couldn't heal others like Grace could. She could only ease suffering for a little while. She could hear people's thoughts. Talk to them in the same manner. What use was that to anyone?

And yet she was pursued ruthlessly. As was Grace. The two sisters had made a pact. As painful as it was to be away from each other, they'd gone in separate directions, hiding, not contacting each other.

If either sister were found, one would be used to draw the other out. Shea wouldn't allow that to happen. She wouldn't be responsible for Grace's capture.

Grace was special. She was vulnerable and her gift was as much a curse as it was a true gift. She could not survive in the hands of people determined to use her gift with no regard for the cost to Grace. They'd kill her because they didn't understand Grace's abilities. They wouldn't mean to. They wouldn't want to. But they'd force her to use her skills, and the result would be Grace's death.

"I won't allow it to happen," Shea murmured fiercely.

Grace was *good*. She was tenderhearted to her detriment. She couldn't bear to see anyone suffer, and as a result, Grace often suffered pain beyond Shea's imaginings. Shea's temporary agony of tonight was nothing compared to the days when Grace would be gripped by the very illness she took from others.

Shea hastily tossed her toiletries into a large case and then stood in front of the sink, her hands braced on the surface, eyes closed as she battled the weariness that beat at her.

She'd hoped by reaching out to him that she might somehow gain relief. But now sorrow blanketed her. She couldn't leave him to suffer alone. He was so very close to giving up all hope. She could sense his desire to die and slip away from his awful reality.

She shook her head in denial. She wasn't going to let him go.

NATHAN Kelly sat quietly in the corner of his tiny cell and stared broodingly into the darkness. He had no idea if it was night or day. For all practical purposes, he was in a box. A tiny, airless box. How long had he been here?

For the first weeks, he kept meticulous count, sure that rescue would come at any moment. Not only did he have the U.S. Army to count on, but his brothers ran a top-notch military ops group. They were a private organization that took jobs nobody wanted or had the means to complete. They often contracted with the U.S. government, but they just as often took assignments from the private sector. No way they'd let him stay imprisoned in some hellhole. Not after what had happened to Rachel. They would question everything. They wouldn't blindly accept his death, no matter what they were told.

He closed his eyes and thought about his fragile sister-in-law, Rachel, who was married to his older brother Ethan. Then he shook his head. She wasn't fragile. A fragile person wouldn't survive an entire year imprisoned in hell.

Nathan couldn't have been here for more than a month and already he was losing his grip on reality—and his sanity.

He moved again, waiting for the fresh resurgence of pain. But it remained at bay. It wasn't that he was numb or that he'd finally gone beyond the parameters of pain. He was aware—hyperaware—of his surroundings. He could feel each bead of sweat that rolled down his chest. The pain was simply gone.

After he'd lived with agony for so long, having every waking moment be one of intense suffering, it was unsettling to suddenly feel nothing.

How had it happened? Was she an angel? The voice in his mind could only be a hallucination. Sweet. Warm. So soothing that he wanted to drown in the sensation.

For one brief moment he knew peace. His mind was empty, and calm had descended, wrapped around him like a warm, fuzzy blanket.

It was absurd to think that there was any peace in hell. It wouldn't last, but he was grateful for even a moment's respite.

He eased down onto the rough floor and curled into as tight a ball as he could muster. He was nearly lost in the corner, a mere shadow in darkness.

Fatigue held him in its relentless grasp. But then he felt the faint touch of another. It was as though someone stroked a hand over his hair. Whispers, like a gentle summer breeze, drifted through his ears.

I'm here.

He closed his eyes, determined to rest, to regain his strength. Whatever had happened today, whether he'd finally broken from reality or not, he felt a renewed determination to live. To fight.

He focused on his family. He'd live for them. This would pass. He would survive it.

Yes. You'll live. I won't let you give up.

The angel whispered, and he felt some of the horror in his mind recede. If he could, he would grab on and wrap the angel around him.

He felt her smile. It was like a burst of sunshine in his shattered mind. And then he felt her arms surround him and hold him close. Just as he'd imagined her doing.

Sleep now, she gently urged.

"Stay with me," he said even as he drifted into healing sleep.

CHAPTER 2

SHEA stepped into the crisp morning air and inhaled deeply in an effort to clear her mind. Flashes of her encounter the night before and the weight of emotion still haunted her. She'd tried to go back to sleep after she'd reached out to the man being kept prisoner, but she'd been too on edge to relax.

She pulled her jacket tighter around her body and stared down the street as the sky lightened around her. It was still relatively quiet, but in an hour or so, the hustle and bustle of early-morning rush hour would replace the calm. She only had one house to clean today and it wouldn't take her long. She had never dared to find a job where she was required to give any personal information. She took what jobs she could find that would pay her cash and she moved on after short periods of time. Staying too long in one spot made her nervous, and she was determined to stay ahead of those who pursued her.

Already her gut was screaming that she'd remained too long here. It was time to go.

She bent as if tying her shoe and casually looked left and right, as if simply preparing for her exercise regimen.

In truth, she hated jogging. She was in shape out of necessity, not out of any love for exercise. She used the routine to carefully scout her surroundings, always looking for any change, anything out of the ordinary. She watched for those who hunted her.

You're pensive this morning, Shea.

Shea frowned as she rose and began to stretch.

You can't ignore me. I know you hear me. Talk to me, Grace begged softly.

Shea sighed. *You know we shouldn't communicate, Grace. It isn't safe. I don't want to know anything that could be used against you. You don't need to know anything about me. If I know nothing, I can hardly be forced to tell what I don't know.*

It isn't your job to protect me, Grace reprimanded.

The hell it isn't. You have a gift, Grace. I won't allow those bastards to use it or you. I want you safe. Are you all right? Do you need something?

Shea could feel her sister's exasperated sigh.

I felt your pain and your fear. I worried for you. I . . . I miss talking to you.

Shea's heart twisted and sadness welled in her throat. *I miss you too. Now go away before I see more than I should.*

Grace went silent for a moment. *You have a gift too, Shea. You sell yourself short. What you give to people is priceless. What you give to me is priceless.*

I love you, Shea said fiercely. *We'll be together again. I swear it.*

Shea felt Grace's sadness and she slowed in her run so that she could mentally wrap her arms around her older sister just as she'd done the night before to the soldier who so desperately needed comfort.

The sensation of her sister returning her hug was so warm and powerful that Shea closed her eyes to savor it.

I love you too, Shea. Be careful.

Always.

As always when she communicated with her sister, when they broke contact, Shea was left with an emptiness so keen that it ached. Her sister was her best friend in the world, and she hadn't seen her for a year.

Tears blurred her vision as she pushed herself on, lengthening her stride until the muscles in her legs began to tremble and protest.

A year ago, she and her family were living a normal life. As normal as any family could live when she and Grace shared remarkable abilities. They lived with their parents mainly because her father and mother had feared for the two women to live out on their own.

Shea and Grace had complied good-naturedly, although they'd always believed their parents too paranoid. Their abilities were secret. No one knew what they could do. Their parents were adamant that they never used them. It was as if they wanted to eliminate them by ignoring them.

And then one night their home had been broken into despite their state-of-the-art security system. Their parents had been gunned down, and the only reason Shea and Grace had escaped capture was because of the safe room their father had meticulously constructed, complete with an escape route that led into the dense woods surrounding their house.

Their father had shoved them into the safe room, set the locks, and the two girls stood there in frozen horror as they listened to their parents being murdered just feet away.

Their parents hadn't been paranoid. They'd known the very real danger their daughters faced. Maybe if Shea and Grace had taken their fears more seriously, their mom and dad would be alive today.

Her fists clenched in rage and she slowed to a walk, cursing the fact that she'd gone much farther than usual. She turned in a half circle and began to walk back the way she came.

Halfway back to the tiny duplex she rented, she noticed a dark sedan with tinted windows parked on the opposite side of the street. It hadn't been there before. She would have noted it. Nor did it belong to the owner of the house.

She was meticulous in her recon. She knew every vehicle for every house in an eight-block radius. She'd even memorized license plate numbers. She glanced casually over, never letting her gaze stop its progress. Quickly committing the plate to memory, she picked up her pace just a bit.

At the end of the block, she turned right instead of continuing straight ahead toward her street. She swung her arms, rotating as if working the kinks out, like she hadn't a care in the world.

But she glanced back to see the vehicle slide from its parking space, execute a quick U-turn and then crawl down the street in the direction she'd gone.

Shea held her breath and forced herself to remain calm and not bolt. Not yet. She needed a few more feet before she'd have a few moments where she wouldn't be spotted.

As soon as she was out of view, she put on the speed and ran through the yard and in between two houses. Everyone on the damn street had privacy fences, which made them a bitch to get over.

She flew over the top and landed in a heap on the ground on the other side. She picked herself up, fled toward the back of the lot and pulled herself over the top of the fence again.

She hoped the car turned down the street she'd taken and hadn't headed directly toward her house. She needed just a few minutes to get home, grab the bag she always kept packed, and then she'd get the hell out.

Through it all, she kept her mind tightly shielded so that her sister wouldn't sense her fear and agitation. The last thing she wanted was Grace to come out of hiding because she worried that Shea was in danger.

And she would. She'd do anything if she thought it would keep Shea safe. Just as Shea would do for Grace. If Shea allowed herself to get caught, Grace would be a sitting duck.

Well, fuck that.

She wasn't going down without one hell of a fight.

By the time she reached her backyard, she was winded and sucking some pretty heavy air. Instead of going balls to the wall inside her house, she took stock of the surroundings, listened for the sound of a vehicle and then quietly crept to her back door.

The very last thing she needed was to run headlong into a bad situation.

She cracked the door open and listened intently for any sound coming from within. As she stepped inside, she immediately looked toward the front picture window, which gave her an unimpeded view of the street.

She breathed in a sigh of relief and bolted into action. She ran for her bedroom, took the already packed bag out of the closet and then went for the handgun in her nightstand drawer.

She popped the clip in, thumbed the safety and then

jammed it into her shorts. Wasting not a single glance at the things she was leaving behind, she hustled to the front door.

Her car was parked as close to the house as possible, but not so close that she couldn't execute a sharp turn and drive away without having to back out of the drive.

It sucked to have to live this way, but the alternative didn't bear thinking about.

She shoved out of the door, ran for her car and threw her bag inside. She jammed the key into the ignition, started the engine and then roared out of the drive.

As she pulled onto the street, she glanced in her rearview mirror. Fear slid up her spine and around her neck until it had a stranglehold on her.

The sedan she'd seen on her run was pulling up the street just past her house.

It was pointless to try and play it cool. As if they hadn't seen her. She blew the stop sign at the end of the street and hauled ass.

SHEA was somewhere in Colorado, her eyes peeled for a place to stop for the night, when she was seized by unimaginable pain. Her entire body went rigid, her vision blurred and her mouth went horribly dry. She was too exhausted from days spent on the road with little to no sleep to fight off the onslaught of her soldier's suffering.

She barely managed to pull to the side of the road before another wave of agony bit through her flesh and burned her from the inside out.

Oh no. *No.*

She leaned forward, resting her forehead on the steering wheel as she battled for control. Then she reached for him, sliding into his mind and body. She hadn't meant to leave him alone for so long. Guilt flooded her. The last days had been spent running and looking over her shoulder until she was sure she'd shaken her pursuers.

I'm here. Be strong. Please be strong. Don't let them defeat you.

She could feel the tears on his face. Felt the helpless wave of despair that hit her so strongly it knocked her back against the seat. She forced herself to see through his eyes and then gasped her horror, tears squeezing her own eyes.

Another man knelt in front of her soldier. He'd been removed from the tiny, dark hole they kept him in. When they hadn't been successful in gaining what they wanted from her soldier, they'd dragged another man into the room and forced him to his knees so that he had no choice but to look at him.

Shea closed her eyes to the atrocities committed. But it was no use. She saw through her soldier's eyes. Felt everything he felt. Knew what he knew.

Rage built. Horror. Fear. Loathing. Pain.

He wanted to kill them. For a moment he considered giving in, but he knew it wouldn't alter the fate of the other captive. These were animals with no honor.

And then a single gunshot rang out, echoing first through the soldier's mind and then bleeding into Shea's consciousness. She blinked and stared glassy-eyed through the windshield as she watched the other captive fall forward to the floor, blood streaming from his head.

Grief welled, though she wasn't sure if it was her own or her soldier's. There was self-condemnation and guilt. He considered that the other captive was better off because he at least wasn't suffering any longer.

Why were they keeping him alive? Why didn't they just kill him and end it all?

His emotions bombarded her, a mixture of determination to survive and the desire to be free of his pain. He hated that he was so weak, and self-loathing was sharp and bitter in his mind.

It wasn't your fault. You can't blame yourself for his death. Turn your hatred to the animals who deserve it. Not yourself.

Who are you?

The demand was strong. He was still in the grip of a terrible rage. It consumed him, even more so than his pain. She could feel it sizzling through his veins and into hers. It was white, nearly electric and blinding in its intensity.

Someone who wants to help you.

How can you possibly help me?

The weary question slipped into her mind. She knew he expected no answer. He didn't even think she was real.

She went completely still when he was suddenly hauled to his feet and roughly dragged from the room where the dead man lay. It was silly. They couldn't detect her. And yet she was afraid to move, afraid that anything she did might make the soldier react and draw more abuse from his captors.

When he was thrust back into his cell, he hit the floor hard and then crawled toward his corner, the same corner he huddled in day after day. Night after night.

Unable to resist, she wrapped her arms around him and held him as he shivered violently in reaction to the torture he'd endured. The air around them was stale and warm and yet he quaked as chills raced up and down his body.

She closed her eyes, drew in a deep breath and then focused on her task of ridding him of his pain.

This time she didn't make a single sound. Her jaw was too locked, her body too rigid. She didn't think she could have cried out, though in her mind she was screaming at the things he'd endured.

When she was done, she lay limply to the side, her head tilted sideways as she struggled to regain her senses. She sensed his question, knew his brow was furrowed in confusion as he mentally took stock of his painless state.

He rubbed the marks on his body, ran his hands over his wounds, testing, poking, baffled by the fact that he no longer felt anything.

Do you know where you are?

She tried to inject strength into her question. Confidence. But she failed miserably. The inquiry came out as a faint whisper, barely audible in his mind.

Immediately his frustration was strong and a sense of help-lessness gripped him, as strong as any pain he'd previously felt.

No.

There has to be something we can do. You can't continue like this. Is there anyone who can help you?

She felt his sigh. He rubbed his head tiredly and then pushed both palms into his eyes and curled his fingers over the top of his skull.

My brothers are looking for me. I know it. They won't give up until I'm found. Dead or alive.

I could contact them.

The offer spilled out before she thought better of it. Regret was instant. How could she place herself and Grace in danger? How could she trade themselves for this unknown man?

And yet as soon as the question rose, she knew that she had no choice. She wouldn't leave him to die. His survival had become all-important to her. She didn't even know why exactly. Or how they'd forged the connection they had. It was just another random aspect of her gift. As random as everything else when it came to her abilities.

He laughed. It was hoarse, cracked and ugly sounding. His voice was rusty from disuse. He rubbed his eyes again.

How can you help me? You aren't real.

She wasn't going to argue her validity to him. She barely had the strength left to maintain her connection to him, but now more than ever, she sensed that he couldn't bear to be alone. He was inching ever closer to the edge.

Assume for the moment that I'm real, that I'm standing in front of you and yet no one else can see me. I can move in and out without detection. What would you tell me that could help you? How would I contact your brothers?

He shook his head. *I can't believe I'm having this conversation with myself.*

Damn it, talk to me! She pounded her fist against the steering wheel in frustration. *Stop with the denial. What have you got to lose? If I'm not real, then no one will come. But is anyone going to come anyway? Tell me what I need to know to help you. There has to be something I can tell them.*

He went silent as he weighed her words. Hope slid through his mind, but he extinguished it as soon as it came alive. He refused to descend into fantasy. He believed it was the final straw, that if he allowed himself this hope, he would truly be checking out.

Tell me your name. Tell me who you are so I can help you.

Nathan . . . He drew in a breath and then let it out. *Nathan Kelly.*

She dragged herself upward in her seat, worried that if she remained on the side of the road for too long, she'd draw unwanted attention.

Wearily she pushed her hair from her face and fumbled with the keys as she attempted to start the car again.

Nathan.

She hadn't realized she'd sent the name out until he responded.

If we're making introductions, I'd at least like to know what the insane part of me calls herself.

She bit her lip as she maneuvered back onto the highway. Exhaustion dragged at her, pulling relentlessly until she could barely keep her eyes open.

He frowned and put a hand to his head. *Are you . . . Are you all right?*

He was irritated that he'd ask, that he'd accept that she wasn't his own crazy manifestation, and yet he could feel her just as she could feel him, and he sensed her weakness and pain, especially now that his was gone.

She smiled faintly at his reluctant concern for her.

I'm Shea, she finally said after battling over whether she should even divulge that much.

CHAPTER 3

NATHAN leaned his head back against the rough stone surface of the cell wall and stared sightlessly into the dark. His pain was gone. Sort of. He could feel it hovering on the fringe, almost like he was catching *impressions* of pain from someone else but not exactly feeling it in his body.

Was she real? It wasn't possible.

But then did it matter if his imagination got him through this ordeal?

Shea. She'd said her name was Shea. And she wanted to help him.

Was he crazy? Was this some cruel trap hatched by his captors as a way to drag information from him? How could they get into his head? He'd heard of subliminal shit, but he'd never given it a thought. Besides, how the hell did someone subliminally talk to you? Shea—whoever she was—wasn't planting ideas. She'd taken his pain and she was *suffering*. Because of him.

She'd been silent for several long seconds now, and panic grabbed him. His pulse sped up, and a knot formed in his throat that remained no matter how hard he swallowed. Regardless of whether she was real or imagined, he didn't want her to go.

Shea.

He tested her name in his mind, liking the way it sounded. The way it felt.

I'm here.

She sounded weak. He frowned. *What did you do? How is it you can take my pain away?*

That's not important. You have to tell me how to help you. Isn't there anything you can tell me about your location? Who is holding you? What branch of the military are you with? Surely there's someone I can contact.

He could sense the hundred questions bursting into his mind from hers. She was frustrated and impatient. She needed information fast because she feared not being able to hold their link.

He frowned again and felt the beginnings of a throb in his head. He was feeling *her* pain.

Every one of his instincts told him that this was crazy. That this was some bizarre manifestation brought on by endless torture. He'd broken from reality.

But if that was true and he was merely imagining this entire conversation with Shea, then it couldn't hurt to tell her how to contact his brothers.

Hope flickered and he angrily called it back. He wouldn't put stock in this insanity. He knew that any disappointment could finally break him completely.

Nathan, hurry.

He palmed his temples and pressed, closing his eyes. *Sam Kelly. He lives in Dover, Tennessee, with the rest of my family. Garrett, Donovan, Ethan and Joe* . . . God, where was Joe? The idea that his twin could be in a similar hell sent fear crashing through him. No, Joe wasn't here. Nathan would know. He would have heard. Joe wasn't even on the same team. He'd be home by now. Maybe even discharged already. Nathan had to believe that because he couldn't bear any other alternative.

He felt her stir again, and he got the sense of her stepping out of a car. Had she been driving? She drifted farther away and alarm slammed into him again. Sweat covered him and he swallowed rapidly.

Then she touched him. The sensation of her hands on his shoulders, soothing and warm. A gentle brush of her lips against his temple.

Give me a moment. I have to make sure I'm safe. I won't leave you. Not yet.

The next moments were the longest of his life as he sat in the darkness. There was . . . nothing. No distant cries. No sounds of violence. It was so quiet that unease slithered down his spine until he was gripped by panic again.

They wouldn't come again. Not so soon.

He licked his dry, cracked lips. He'd sell his soul for water. Food, he'd long since lost the desire for. But water. He could make himself ill on it if only he had it.

He thought of his brothers. His mom and dad. Imagined himself at home in the loving hold of his family. Where were they? Were they looking for him now? What had the army told them about his disappearance?

But even as he thought of rescue and of going home, he wondered if he'd ever be the same Nathan Kelly again.

He didn't feel like a man. He felt like an *animal*. Less than an animal. His mind didn't even work the same as before. He was reduced to basic survival. He coped from one hour to the next, locked in hell.

As a soldier he lived with the reality that each day could be his last. Death wasn't something he could afford to be in denial over. It wasn't what happened to other people. It happened to his fellow soldiers on a daily basis.

And now he realized that there were some things worse than death. Death meant peace. It meant rest. It meant relief from unimaginable conditions. Even animals were afforded more dignity than he was. Sometimes simply enduring was worse than death.

He didn't fear it. A part of him welcomed it.

He slid a hand over his bare chest and down to his gaunt belly. He could feel each rib. Dirt and blood covered his naked body, but he'd long since gotten over the outrage of being stripped of his clothing.

Imagine that you're in a hot bath and that food surrounds you on all sides.

Startled by the soft intrusion, he laughed softly at the image she painted in his mind. *Are you safe? Where are you now? Why do you think you're in danger?*

She was bone weary and pain beat relentlessly at her head.

She was curled into a ball. On a bed? If she was in danger, she was extremely vulnerable. Had she locked the doors? Did she have means to defend herself?

It's you we need to concern ourselves with, she murmured in a drowsy voice that hummed like sweet honey through his head. *Tell me more now. I can't . . . I can't just call your brother up. It's too risky for me. But I can send him a letter. Or . . .* She huffed in frustration and closed her eyes as she tried to gather her senses. Her battle confused him. He had no idea how any of this was possible. *I don't know. I'll figure something out.*

Though there was fatigue and resignation bleeding from her, he sensed steely resolve. She was determined to help him.

You could email Van. He's always on the computer. He'd see it right away. It was out before he even thought about what he was doing. He was giving out his brother's email address to his imaginary friend. Then the rest of what she'd said caught up to him. *Why is it risky for you? What kind of trouble are you in? My brothers could protect you. They'd be in your debt if you helped them find me.*

I'm not safe. I'll never be safe.

The soft words slipped through his mind. They were tinged with regret but said matter-of-factly. Whatever her situation, she absolutely believed that she was in danger. She accepted it without hesitation.

Think, Nathan. Think about where you could be. Where were you when you were captured? Were you transported far? Were you conscious at the time? There has to be something I can pass on to your brothers.

He sucked in his breath and tried to calm his thoughts. Every time he thought back to that day, his mind became a jumble of gunfire, explosions, mixed shouts. Some from his men, some from the enemy.

He and his team had pulled a recon. Nothing complicated. They weren't expecting to be engaged. The area had been quiet. The hot zone was to the south. They'd split off from Joe's team, one going farther north, Nathan and his team taking the immediate area.

Then all hell had broken loose.

It was hard to piece together that day. An explosion close

to him had knocked him unconscious, and when he'd come to, he was bound and in the back of a shoddy-ass cargo truck. Three of his team members were there. One had died soon after. The other had died today. Only Swanny remained. Alive in hell with Nathan.

Grief overwhelmed him. Emotion knotted his throat. He'd kept his word, his pact with his team. They'd vowed not to be broken, not to cooperate no matter the cost. And now Taylor was dead.

His last words to Nathan had been, "Don't do it, Kelly. Don't you fucking do it."

Nathan had remained silent and Taylor had died.

Was it worth it? Was any of it worth it?

Never before had he questioned his dedication or his resolve. He was a soldier. His job was to serve his country. It was a duty he'd embraced.

But here in the dark, alone, without hope, he doubted everything that made him who he was.

Nathan.

Her voice so full of understanding. Caring. How could she care so damn much? She didn't even know him.

I can't maintain the link between us much longer. You have to tell me what you can about your location. I'll write it down. Word for word. I'll do what I can to help you, and I won't leave you if I can help it. I'll stay with you until they find you.

The promise in her words ignited a spark in the darkness of his soul. He wanted it to be true. He wanted this miracle. Was it God talking to him? Was she an angel?

His email is Van@KGI.org. Tell him . . . Tell him to talk to Joe. Tell him . . . Nathan strained to get his bearings. To remember. He'd been dragged from the truck. It was daylight. He remembered looking down. *Tell him Korengal Valley.*

Can you rest now? You have to preserve your strength. Is your pain better?

He felt the stroke of a hand over his cheek. So soft and soothing. He closed his eyes and leaned into empty space. Even with her strength nearly gone, she gave the last of it to offer him solace.

He reached up as if he would capture the hand on his face but his fingers found only his own dirty, blood-crusted skin.

But still, he palmed his cheek, savoring the idea that he held her hand in his.

Rest with me. I can feel your weakness. My pain is gone, but yours isn't. I would take it away if I could.

He felt her smile, and warmth spread through his veins.

Silly, she murmured. *No point in me taking your pain if you take it back. Sleep now. I'll be here if you need me. Just call for me.*

CHAPTER 4

"IT'S been two goddamn months, and we've got nothing," Donovan Kelly bit out. Rage consumed him. He wanted to take apart the newly constructed war room with his bare hands.

His brothers didn't look any happier.

Sam Kelly hunched over the table where the map lay. On it were thumbtacks noting all the places where KGI had already gone in search of Nathan. Garrett stood next to his brother and Ethan was on the other side, his hand curled around his nape as he stared down in frustration.

They were tired. Their resources stretched thin. They'd already spent so much time away from their family. Their wives. Sam's daughter. Nathan's disappearance had taken a toll on them all, and yet no one was going to give up until he was found and brought home.

"This is bullshit," Donovan continued. "You can't tell me they're doing everything to find him."

Sam held up his hand then let it fall to the table again. Donovan went silent but still simmered with fury. He turned away and paced toward the window that overlooked the Kelly compound.

Construction in varying stages was going on all over the

grounds. In the distance, the plot of land he'd picked out for his own house stood, still unblemished and thick with trees. How the hell could he think about a damn house when his brother was still missing?

How could any of them think of anything else?

Everything had come to a halt in the Kelly family. Garrett and Sarah weren't marrying until they had news of Nathan one way or another. There was little cause for celebration when their family wasn't whole.

The KGI teams had gone in search of Nathan four times already, the first two without permission by Uncle Sam. Not that they gave a flying fuck. Resnick had dragged his heels, not wanting any part of a potentially sticky situation between a private rescue operation and any U.S.-sanctioned rescue operation, not to mention the fallout when KGI kicked the shit out of whoever held their brother.

By the time official permission had been given, KGI was already staging their third mission to the Middle East. It hadn't surprised any of them that while Uncle Sam was willing to not kick their asses over it, they sure as hell weren't giving official support either.

"You're on your own," Resnick had grimly stated.

Yeah, what else was new?

Not that Donovan thought Resnick was a total asshole. His hands were tied. It wasn't like in the past when the government had a personal stake in supporting one of KGI's missions. There was no CIA most wanted this time. No criminal or threat to national security. Just a brother Donovan had no intention of relying on others to mount a rescue for.

Joe was still laid up and casted and he was one pissed-off motherfucker that his twin was out there and he couldn't go after him. He wasn't even officially out of the army yet, so whether he was good to go or not, Uncle Sam still had a tight leash on his ass.

It didn't mean he was shy about busting the rest of his brothers' balls over going in to get Nathan out.

If they only knew where the fuck to find him.

"Van, get me the latest satellite imagery. Maybe we'll get lucky and see movement," Garrett said.

Donovan turned to the computer they called Hoss and

leaned over to call up the map. They'd only been back a few days. They couldn't remain in Afghanistan indefinitely. It was too risky. They had to get in and out and make their recon stealthy. But he was itching to go back. He hadn't wanted to leave. Nathan was there. Somewhere. And he needed them.

He printed the map so they could compare it to the last captured image and started to walk away when he saw the new email alert in the lower-left-hand corner.

He clicked to pop up the message, frowning when he saw the recipient. It wasn't anyone he was familiar with and it was one of those obviously fake Hotmail addresses that usually meant SPAM.

Then his gaze dropped to the message and he froze.

Nathan said to talk to Joe. He's not far from last coordinate. Said to tell you Korengel Valley. He needs your help. He won't last much longer.

That was it? Dear God. Donovan stared in helpless fury at the vaguely worded message. Ask Joe? Like they hadn't already grilled their brother mercilessly? Like Joe hadn't told them everything he knew?

"Son of a bitch!"

Was this how Ethan felt when he'd received information about his wife, Rachel? How the fuck was he supposed to take something like this seriously? How could he not? Especially when the information about Rachel had led them right to her?

"What's up, Van?" Sam demanded.

Donovan slowly turned around to face his brothers. "You have to see this."

NATHAN lay in the dark, willing himself to rest, but every muscle in his body was tense. Pain had crept back in hours past, but he'd remained silent, not wanting to say her name. He hadn't allowed himself to even think it.

It was agony because he wanted her there in his mind. He wanted the reassurance of another human being. He ached for the comfort only she could give him. But he didn't want her to take his pain. He didn't want her to suffer again.

And so he lay there and endured both physical and mental anguish.

His thoughts were consumed with escape, revenge, hatred, hopelessness, but mostly escape. He closed his eyes and imagined himself back home with his brothers having beer on the lake. Ma's home cooking. His dad's steady presence. Rachel's sweet smile. Even Rusty's smart mouth.

Would he ever see them again?

He couldn't bear to think of the pain his family was going through. They'd already endured so much with Rachel's captivity and then his mother's abduction. How much more could they take?

He shook his head. It wasn't a matter of what they could take. The Kellys were unshakable. He worried more about his own sanity and, if he did get back home, how much he would be changed.

You'll go back home, Nathan. You have to believe that.

His pulse rocketed and he sat up. Relief made him weak. His hands shook and his knees wobbled. She was back.

I sent the email to your brother. It's not a lot of information, though. Have you been able to think of anything else that might help them locate you sooner?

Nathan hunched over and wrapped his arms around his legs, resting his chin on his knees. He hated that hope fluttered deep inside him. Like a coal in a dying fire that still had some heat left.

Nathan, talk to me. You can't lose hope. You aren't going to survive without hope. If you give up now, there'll be nothing for your brothers to find.

Tell them . . . Goddamn it, I don't know! I haven't seen daylight in I don't know when. I've been in this shit hole, and when I'm not here, they're working me over in some dank, moldy room. I'm so damn disoriented most of the time that I have a hard time separating what's real and what's not.

Something clicked in his mind, and he closed his eyes for a moment as he brought back the image of them killing Taylor.

Cave. I'm in a fucking cave.

What hope he'd briefly entertained dwindled to nothing.

They'll never find me here. There are caves all over these mountains.

Then you have to escape.

He tried to laugh but the sound came out as a harsh rasp.

You make it sound so easy. Don't you think I would have escaped already if I could? I've tried! God knows, I've tried.

You didn't have me before.

The resoluteness of her words brought an abrupt halt to the pity train.

Do you have some other kind of powers? Besides being able to talk to me in my head and hear my thoughts?

Unfortunately no. But we'll work with what we have.

I was being an ass. You've taken my pain and that's no small thing. I don't know how you do it or why, but I'm grateful. I don't think I've ever even said thank you.

You're hurting now.

It was on the tip of his tongue to deny it but then he realized the absurdity of denying what she already knew.

Before he could respond, warmth spread through him. To his very core. He couldn't even describe the sensation of comfort sliding so deeply into his heart and mind. He wanted to tell her to stop, that he didn't want her to hurt in his place, but he was overwhelmed and nearly shattered by the instant relief that swamped him.

And then he became aware of her huddled, wrapping her arms around her body, her soft moans sliding through his mind. Without thought as to how to accomplish it, he simply reached out, imagined holding her to offer the comfort she so selflessly offered him.

She went still, suddenly alert and wary. And then as if realizing who it was who held her, she relaxed.

He was immediately assailed by the feel and smell of her. Her scent drifted through his nostrils, a sharp and welcome contrast to the odor of sweat and blood and death.

The sensation of holding her was so keen that he closed his eyes and imagined himself in a place far away from his present reality.

She was warm in his arms, though she still trembled from the aftereffects of taking his pain. Her hair was soft against his cheek, and he rubbed up and down, feeling the tickle of the strands against his nose.

He inhaled sharply, taking in the scent of her shampoo. Honeysuckle danced through his nostrils, reminding him of summers in Tennessee.

Tell me about you. You said you were in trouble.

She tensed and he panicked, thinking that she would withdraw. His link to her had become the single most important thing in his existence.

Tell me anything, he hastily amended. *Just talk to me. Who are you? How do you have this ability to talk to me, to take my pain and hear my thoughts?*

She laughed softly. *You don't ask for much.*

We can talk about anything. I just hate the silence.

He felt the soft explosion of air against his neck as she sighed.

I don't know how or why I have the abilities I do. I've always had them, at least for as long as I can remember. My mother always knew I was different or so she said. She told me a story of when I was a toddler and she burned her hand cooking. She cried out and I grabbed her hand only wanting to take the pain from her.

She said I started to cry the longer I held her hand, and when she pulled it away I had an identical burn mark on my palm. She said her pain was completely gone but we both had a blister.

He went completely still as he grappled with what she'd just told him. Dread gathered in his gut. *Are you telling me that when you take my pain from me, you actually take on the wounds as well?*

She was quiet for a moment.

Tell me, he said fiercely.

What do you want me to say, Nathan? Yes, I take the pain and the marks or wounds, but it isn't permanent. They don't last as long as yours will. They often begin to fade within a few hours.

Son of a bitch. I don't want you to do it anymore.

It's my choice.

Why? Why, goddamn it? You don't know me. I could be a complete asshole. Why would you do something like that for me at such a risk to yourself?

Because you need me.

Because he needed her. It was an explanation he couldn't even wrap his mind around. It was so simple and yet baffling.

Did anyone ever just do for someone because they needed it? It wasn't like she was helping a hungry child, or giving money to a homeless person. She was taking on unimaginable pain. Because she didn't think he could bear it any longer.

You were so close to giving up. I was in your mind, Nathan. I knew what you were thinking. What you were feeling. It broke my heart. I couldn't not *help you.*

Shame slid through his chest. Guilt that he'd been so weak to even briefly contemplate giving up. Because of that weakness she'd taken far more than she ever should have. And yet, could he have survived if she hadn't?

He knew the answer. It ate at him that he was so dependent on this faceless woman, just a whisper in the dark. Now that the connection had been made, he'd go insane if it was broken.

There's no shame in needing someone, she offered softly.

He considered her words for a moment. *No, I don't suppose there is.*

You just have to hold on until your brothers come for you. I know how you see them, that you have absolute faith in them. Hold on to that and you'll be home soon.

You're a fucking miracle, Shea. I don't know what the hell I would have done if you hadn't spoken to me when you did.

You would have endured.

You have more faith in me than I have.

I see who you are, Nathan. The heart of you. You can't hide that from me. A weaker person would have already given up. You didn't.

Her words filled him with determination. Her faith humbled him. It made him *want* to be the man she saw, the one she believed him to be.

You're going to escape. I'll be with you the whole way. We just have to wait for the right time. We can do this.

Maybe it was the way she said it with such conviction. Or maybe it was that she said *we* in every instance. Like they were a team. It was a promise never to leave him and it heartened him in a way he hadn't been able to do for himself since his captivity.

Whether she was real or imagined, he thanked God for her. His own personal angel in hell.

SHEA left the comfort of Nathan's arms when the link became too much to maintain. Her body still quivered with lingering pain, but the marks on her skin were gone.

She stumbled into the shower and ran the water as hot as she could bear it and stood under the spray, her forehead resting against the cool tile of the stall.

What the hell was she doing? She couldn't afford to weaken herself as she had done with Nathan. Just maintaining the link for so long was taxing enough, but the pain took it out of her when she had nothing to spare.

What if she were found again? Would she even have the strength to run?

But she'd made him a promise and she wouldn't break it. She couldn't bear the thought of him not making it back home to his family.

The only solution for her was to keep moving. Preemptive run. If she kept constantly on the move, then she would lessen the risk of her being caught at her most vulnerable.

She almost reached out to Grace. She bit her lip to prevent herself from saying her sister's name. Her heart grew heavy until the ache crawled up her throat and into her jaw.

"I miss you," she whispered.

Maybe it was why she'd reached out to Nathan. His desolation matched her own. They were both lonely and desperate. Perhaps she saw in Nathan someone whose situation was worse than her own and she'd been unable to turn her back even if it was what she should have done.

When she was through with her shower, she dressed and picked up the bag she hadn't yet unpacked. She stepped from the hotel room and shivered as the cold mountain air sliced through her T-shirt.

She'd battled her decision to continue westward. But she'd already traveled extensively over the United States. Would her pursuers expect her to double back? She hoped not. She hoped she was making the right strategic choice. Wouldn't it be the very last place they'd expect her to hide?

She climbed into her car and for a moment she sat there, hands curled around the steering wheel. She was tired. So tired. Of running. Of being separated from her sister. Of worrying that nothing would ever be the same again in her life.

At what point would it all end?

Nagging doubt crept in and her nostrils flared in anger. She'd just given Nathan a rah-rah speech about not giving up, about not being fatalistic and about having hope. She could use a healthy dose of her own advice.

She keyed the ignition, slammed the vehicle into gear and said good-bye to Colorado.

CHAPTER 5

NATHAN awoke when the door of his cell flew open and he was blinded by white light. He flung an arm up to cover his eyes but he was hauled to his feet and dragged out.

This time he took closer stock of his surroundings as they forced him into a chair and tied his arms behind his back. A chill pervaded the air, making the sweat on his body blow cold. It was damp and the scents of unwashed bodies, urine and blood made his nostrils flare in distaste.

Silver flashed in front of his eyes. One of the men waved a knife as another began shouting the same questions they asked every time he was interrogated. Maybe they meant to kill him today. Or maybe they were altering their torture methods.

Strangely, calm acceptance settled over him, and he fixed them with a cold stare.

"Go fuck yourself."

Even if they didn't fully understand the expression, they could certainly ascertain the sentiment.

Fire exploded down his arm. He flinched and then glanced down to see a thin cut opened, blood streaming down his flesh.

His lip curled. "Is that the best you can do? Untie me, asshole. Let's even the odds a little."

This time the knife slashed across his chest in a measured cut meant to inflict pain, but not mortal damage.

He ground his teeth together and focused on breathing in and out. He could endure this. He'd suffered far worse already.

Then warmth crept through his body and he felt sunshine fill his mind. Instead of welcoming it, he screamed a silent *no*.

Get out, Shea! Get the hell out of my head. I don't want you here, damn it.

Do or say nothing to further anger them, she said in the voice he'd already associated with everything good in the world.

He felt her flinch, and it took him a moment to realize that he'd been cut again. He stared down in horror as blood trickled down his chest. But he felt nothing.

She wrapped herself completely around him, holding him, offering her warmth and caring and all the while he could smell *her* blood from the wound given to him.

Never, *never* had he felt more helpless as he sat there being slowly carved up by a knife that he couldn't even feel. He couldn't even feel her pain. She was working hard to keep it all from him.

Tears ran freely down his cheeks, not because of what was being done to him, but because she suffered in his stead. It was more than he could bear.

His fingers dug into the ropes binding him and he clawed relentlessly, trying to break free so he could kill the sons of bitches who were causing Shea so much pain. He'd die before he allowed her to continue hurting.

Just be still, Nathan, and maybe they'll leave you alone. Don't do anything to anger them. Please. It will all be over soon. It's only temporary for me. You know this.

As much as he wanted to rage, he willed himself to quell the hatred and fury that burned so hotly within him. For her, he would do it because it was she who was hurting. Not him. Not him, goddamn it.

She was slick with blood and it threatened what little control he had left over his sanity.

Get the hell away from me, Shea. I don't want you here. This isn't yours to take for me.

It nearly broke him when she raised her hand to softly touch his cheek. A simple gesture of comfort. She was comforting him when she was taking the brunt of his torture.

Please, Shea. Don't do this. God, don't do this. Not for me. I can take it. They won't break me. I'm not giving up. I swear it. Just please go. Break off.

She merely wrapped her arms around him and pressed her body close. He hugged her back as they both endured hell.

His focus was so great on her that he hadn't realized they'd stopped and his hands were free until they yanked him to his feet. His knees buckled and he went down, his palms hitting the floor. Again, he was hauled to his feet and forced back to the cell. He'd never been so grateful to go back to that dark hole.

He collapsed into the corner, and he ran his hands down his body. They came away with blood, but he ignored his wounds. His concern was for Shea. Her presence was faint now, and he had to concentrate hard to bring her back into focus.

She was huddled in a corner weeping softly. Blood smeared her body and her mind was filled with pain.

His eyelids burned and his heart splintered. He gathered her gently into his arms and rocked back and forth.

Why, Shea? Why?

Despair was a never-ending cloak of black that furled over him until he was consumed with it. This had the power to break him as nothing else. That she'd sacrificed so much for him was unfathomable.

He stroked her hair, not wanting to touch any other part of her for fear of hurting the wounds. *His* wounds. The knot in his throat threatened to choke him.

You don't need to be so horrified. Her voice was shaky but there was a thread of steel infused into her words. *It isn't as bad as you think. The pain is already receding. The wounds will disappear soon.*

How could she be so calm about it? She'd just had a knife taken to her body because she was protecting him. Who the hell did that for someone they didn't even know?

You shouldn't have interfered, he said fiercely.

She smiled and put her small hand to his chest. *You have to be strong if you're going to escape. I'm going to keep you strong. There's nothing you can say to change my mind.*

I'll never be able to repay what you've done.

You going back home to your family is payment enough.

Are you feeling better yet? He couldn't keep the anxious note from creeping into his voice. Her pain was still very much present in his consciousness but it seemed more distant. He didn't know if it was because he wanted so much for it to be gone or if she was in fact recovering.

I'm better. I told you it wouldn't last long. I'll be weak for a bit, but it's nothing for you to worry about. I want you to concentrate on getting stronger so you can escape.

You're a bossy little thing.

She smiled again. *My sister says the same thing.*

As soon as the mention of her sister echoed through his mind, sadness came right behind.

Where is your sister? Are you both in trouble?

Again he sensed her withdrawal. It frustrated him that she was so tight lipped about whatever difficulties she was having. She was very alone. He sensed her loneliness—and her fear. He wasn't mistaken about that. He should be helping her but instead he was stuck in this hellhole with her taking the brunt of his torture.

She's safe, Shea finally said. *We can't be together right now, but she's safe and that's all that matters.*

And are you safe? Are you taken care of? Or are you completely on your own with no protection and no help?

I'm doing what I have to do.

And what is that, Shea? Talk to me. What are you running from? Why are neither you nor your sister safe? Damn it, I can help you just like you're helping me.

Your family's focus has to be on helping you. They can't help me. I can't afford to trust anyone. I don't even know for sure who is after me and my sister.

Nathan blew out his breath. His helplessness was pissing him off. It was obvious that she absolutely believed she was in danger, and it infuriated him that she was helping him, which made her even more vulnerable.

You seem to be focused on protecting an awful lot of people, Shea. Me, your sister. What about you?

I'm only doing what needs to be done. Grace is special. I can't allow her to be exploited.

Does she have your abilities? Is that why people are looking for you?

He latched on to the implication in her statement and felt her immediate regret that she'd been too careless with information.

She can do far more than I can.

Shea went silent after that announcement, refusing to offer more.

More than Shea could do? Nathan couldn't imagine anyone being able to do more than Shea had done for him. She was able to talk to him, touch him, take his pain, bear his torture for him. What the hell else was there?

But he sensed the truth in Shea's words. Whether her sister could do more or not, Shea believed it. She grew fiercer when she thought of Grace, and Nathan had already learned that Shea was nothing if not intensely loyal to the people she chose to protect.

Are you still bleeding?

She stirred and then shook her head. *No. The marks are disappearing. It doesn't hurt much anymore.*

You should rest.

As should you. Whether you feel the pain or not, they made cuts to your entire body. You'll be weaker and now you risk infection. You have to stay strong, Nathan. Don't let them defeat you. Not when escape is so close.

Then rest with me. I'll sleep better if I know you're here with me. I may not be able to protect you, but at least I'll know you're safe.

She yawned and he pulled her a little closer, liking the way she fit so well against him, even if it was all in his mind.

For the space of a few moments, he could forget that they were thousands of miles apart, that he was imprisoned in hell and that she was somewhere he couldn't protect her.

Just for now, they were together, her much smaller body curled into his.

As ridiculous as it sounded, he could forget his present

circumstances. He could forget the endless pain and suffering because holding her was like holding a ray of sunshine.

She gave him hope when nothing else had been able to penetrate the dim world he'd descended into. And so he hung on with all the fierceness he could muster, because now that she'd found him, he wasn't going to let her go.

CHAPTER 6

"**SON** of a bitch, this is pissing me off." Donovan stared down at the email message on his phone and let loose another string of expletives that had his brothers wincing.

"What's going on, Van?" Ethan demanded.

Donovan looked up to where his brothers were packing gear and loading up their packs for the trek into the Afghani Mountains. There was grim acceptance of their possible fate. Each of them knew there was a good damn chance they wouldn't come back, but there wasn't an alternative. Not for them.

"He's in a cave or so the latest email says. A fucking cave. Like there aren't a million of those in these mountains?"

Garrett frowned. "But are there that many capable of holding prisoners? There are a few here that have been used as outposts for the Taliban."

"We'll question the locals and hope to hell we can buy information," Sam said. "Our guide should be here soon then we'll take out."

Behind him, Rio stood quietly talking to his team while Steele and his team stood to the side, waiting. They were all mostly silent, their faces impassive.

A few moments later, a young man dressed in tattered pants

and shirt appeared out of the dark. He wore a Western-style hoodie, but it was thin and holes riddled the sleeves and back.

"You are Sam Kelly?" the boy asked.

Sam took a step forward. "Yeah, that's me. Are you Aamil?"

The boy nodded solemnly. "We must hurry. It is too open here. I'll take you into the mountains."

"Whoa, wait a minute," Donovan said.

The boy turned, a slight frown on his face.

"What do you know about caves around the Korengal Valley? A big enough cave to house prisoners."

Aamil swallowed nervously. "I know of a few, but they are heavily guarded. It's too dangerous."

"To hell with dangerous," Garrett said. "P.J. and Cole can take them out with their hands tied behind their backs."

"Glad you're so confident in our abilities," P.J. said dryly. "Do the rest of you plan to do anything or are Cole and I going in alone?"

"Smart-ass," Cole muttered.

"I want to question the locals," Sam said to Aamil. "I need to know where those caves are and what kind of activity is around them."

Aamil hesitated. "It will cost you double what we agreed upon."

"I don't give a damn what it costs," Sam growled. "Just take us there."

"We should go then. It's better to travel in the dark."

"Fall in," Sam called softly. "Let's get this show on the road."

As they melted into the night, Donovan adjusted his rifle and stared into the darkness. He hoped to hell they weren't getting jerked around. It pissed him off that this asshole emailing him obviously knew enough about Nathan's family and situation to send a fucking SOS email but he couldn't supply more than Nathan was in some cave in Korengal Valley?

It didn't make any goddamn sense. Why not be more specific?

And if he knew so damn much about Nathan and had obviously talked to him, why wasn't he doing more to help than just sending an email? For that matter, how the hell did he have the ability to send an email from here? He'd obviously talked to Nathan. Either he was one of the assholes holding Nathan captive and was helping him on the sly or . . . or the entire thing was a damn setup.

The more he thought about the situation, the more he didn't like it. Now the entire KGI organization was on the ground in Afghanistan. In the most dangerous area. No backup. No help from Resnick. No way to guarantee that any of them would get back home.

Donovan glanced over at his brothers. They had no business coming on this mission. They had wives. Garrett had a fiancée. Sam had a daughter. They should have let Donovan come with the rest of KGI and stayed their asses at home.

"Quit looking like you just got a hand job from a drag queen," Garrett muttered beside him.

"How the fuck do you know what I look like?" Donovan asked irritably. "It's dark as shit out here."

"Don't need to see you to know you have that pinched, tight-ass look on your face. You weren't coming without us. No way we'd let Nathan rot in some goddamn cave any more than we let Rachel stay in that shithole in Colombia."

"Yeah, I know," Donovan said in resignation. "But I don't have to like it. You and Sam and Ethan have families back home. You're needed."

"Nathan is family and so are you. No way we'd leave either of you without as much protection as we can muster, so shut the fuck up and let's go blow the fuck out of those goatherding motherfuckers who have Nathan."

Donovan cracked a smile. "Yippee ki-yay."

"Fuckin' A."

"Sarah's been on you about the language, huh."

Garrett snarled in response and then muttered a few more F bombs for good measure.

"Yeah, you better get them all out now because when you get back home, no more F words for you."

"Fuck you, Van. Just fuck you."

SHEA spread the map out over her bed and studied the highways intently. She chewed absently at her bottom lip as she tried to decide where to go next.

If only she knew more about the people after her and Grace. She didn't dare go to the police. What was she supposed to tell them? That she and her sister were telepathic and some maniacs were after them but, oh by the way, I don't know who they are.

For all she knew, it could be the government. It could be the police or the FBI or the CIA or whoever the hell would be interested in Grace's powers.

What she did know was that she wasn't going to allow them to take her or Grace and she damn sure wasn't going to let them use her to get to Grace.

A foreign country sounded nice if she could get out of the United States undetected. She had a passport, but of course, it was in her real name and going to an airport and getting on a plane was like holding up a neon sign that said, "Here I am! Come get me!"

She shook her head in disgust. The only thing she could do was keep moving, at least for now. Until . . . until when? Without a plan. Without someone to help her, how was she ever going to feel safe again? Whom could she trust?

The million-dollar question. The short answer was no one.

She sat on the edge of the bed for a moment to collect her thoughts. She stared at the map again and mentally traced the path she'd traveled for the last year. The longest she'd stayed in one place was a couple of months.

At first she and Grace had run together, but Shea had quickly surmised that the only smart thing to do was split up. They were too noticeable as a pair. Grace drew enough attention on her own. The contrast between the two sisters was striking. Shea was petite, blond, paler skinned. Grace was taller, darker skinned with long raven hair.

The hardest part had been convincing Grace that not only did they need to split up, but that it was imperative that they not know where the other was at any time.

Grace had been infuriated, much like Nathan had been, that Shea sought to protect her. In the end, Shea had forgone trying to make Grace see the logic behind Shea's idea and had simply taken off.

It had hurt her to leave her sister, but she knew that to keep both of them safe, it had to be this way.

You do realize that thinking of me so much is just like talking to me.

Grace's amused voice slid through Shea's mind, bringing a smile to Shea's lips.

Are you all right, Shea? I sense that some heavy shit has gone down with you, but you're working hard to keep me from seeing what you've been up to. Why is that? Are you in trouble?

Grace, I'm fine. You would know if I wasn't.

Grace snorted. *I do know and I know that everything is not fine. What the hell is going on with you? Why are you talking to other people?*

Let it go. I'm okay. Getting ready to move again.

You just moved.

How the hell do you know that?

While you're working so hard not to see or hear me, I can read you easily, or at least what you aren't closely guarding. What happened in Colorado? Why did you leave Kansas?

Fuck.

I heard that.

I had a narrow miss in Kansas and I don't want to stay in any one place for a while. It made me jumpy.

Grace swore. *Damn it, Shea. Enough of this being apart bullshit. We're safer together. Why can't you get it through your head that I don't need you to protect me? I'm bigger and stronger than you are. Could you even kill someone if you had to?*

Yes.

Grace went silent as the forceful word slipped from Shea's mind into Grace's.

Hell yeah, she could kill someone. Maybe she'd been known as the sweet younger sister. The baby. The coddled one in the family.

That was all in the past. Seeing your parents murdered and fearing for your sister's safety had a way of hardening even the softest heart. She'd changed a lot in the last year. She'd learned to protect herself, and she had no compunction about doing whatever was necessary to make sure nothing happened to her or to Grace.

I don't like what this has done to you, Shea.

The sadness in Grace's voice left a shadow in Shea's mind. *You are all I have left, Grace. I'll do whatever it takes to make sure you're safe. I've learned a lot in this past year. I might surprise you in the butt-kicking department now.*

Grace laughed but it was strained and sad. *Just don't be so intent on saving the world that you fuck up and get yourself caught. Don't think for even a minute I won't do everything I can to keep you safe.*

I won't. Be careful, Grace. I love you.

I love you too, sis. Be safe. While you're out trying to save me and whoever else you're suffering for, I'm doing some investigating into the assholes who killed Mom and Dad.

Fear bolted through Shea's chest, squeezing until she was breathless. *Don't. Grace, you have to be careful. We have no idea what they're capable of. What if it's some secret government agency?*

You've been watching too many over-the-top television thrillers. I suspect this is some private organization, one of those crazy-ass cult-type things. If it was the government, don't you think we would have been found by now? They're being way too careful, like they're as worried about being caught as we are.

Damn it, Grace, just leave it alone. Stay low.

Until when? You want to run forever? When are we going to come up with a solution? Your solution is to run and keep me safe by refusing contact, fearing you'll know where I am and the information can be tortured out of you. Well, fuck that. We aren't doing anything to solve the problem. We're running like two sissies and waiting. For what? For Superman to swoop down and save us? How can we solve anything if we don't know who is after us? When we know who, then we'll know who we can and can't trust.

Shea blew out her breath in frustration. *I get it, okay? But here's what you're not considering. Say you find out it's some private off-their-rocker group who know what we are and what we can do and they want us for their own nefarious purposes. So you figure this out and go to the police or the government or whoever.*

What's to stop them from deciding they want to exploit you? You could very well be trading one enemy for another, and if it is some private half-ass group who's afraid of discovery, then good. That gives us an advantage. But if we go to the authorities and they decide they want to use us, what the hell do we do then?

Grace sighed. *Damn it, I hate when you start making sense. That's supposed to be my job as the older sister. Still, it doesn't hurt to learn as much as we can about these assholes. We have to trust someone at some point, right? Or do we plan to spend the rest of our lives running?*

Shea closed her eyes. *I hope not. We'll figure something out.*

Grace touched Shea's cheek and then pulled her into a fierce hug. *We'll beat this, Shea.*

For once it was Grace offering comfort and encouragement.

CHAPTER 7

THERE was something to be said for big cities, but they still made her nervous. After ditching her car after the near miss in Kansas City, she'd decided to go with something a little more rugged. Just in case. Four-wheel drive. Something that could handle rough terrain if it came to that.

She'd really wanted to stay in Colorado, lose herself in some remote mountain area, but if she was tracked there, her escape possibilities were slim. And she knew little to nothing about roughing it. Her idea of camping was a nice hotel with room service and a spa.

Until Nathan was rescued and no longer needed her, she absolutely had to keep to areas that swallowed people up. Afterward, she could hopefully find a place that was quiet, big enough that she wouldn't garner too many questions but small enough that she would know if her pursuers showed up.

And yeah, she'd prefer a place with an actual roof, working utilities and a bathroom so she wasn't forced to do her thing behind a bush.

She'd start in California. Work her way up the coast, closer to where it all began. Maybe Grace was right in that they needed more information. If she could eventually get back to her parents' house undetected, she could access the surveillance footage from when her parents were killed. Maybe by then it wouldn't hurt quite so much. Maybe the distance would enable her to view the act with a critical eye.

She shuddered and squeezed her eyes shut at the idea of ever being able to be that analytical when it came to the monsters who'd killed her family.

That would come later. For now she had to concentrate on remaining safe and undetected.

First she checked into a dive motel, giving a fake name and a story about her purse being stolen with all her ID. The clerk hadn't cared about anything other than her ability to pay, and when she produced cash, he gave her a key without question.

The next item on her agenda was to walk into a salon and undergo a radical change in her appearance. The hairdresser had been dubious about her decision to dye her honey blond hair dark brown, but she'd shrugged and done the job.

It wasn't the first time Shea had dyed her hair. She'd changed her appearance every few months. Since she'd been back to blond in her last close call, she chose dark and she'd switch to the brown-colored contacts.

In other circumstances, it would have amused her that over the last year she'd been a redhead, a blonde, several shades of brunette, and her eyes had been a range of green, blue and brown.

She'd go back to blond the next time she moved. The important part was that whenever she left an area, that same woman didn't appear somewhere else.

Back at her hotel, she took the handgun out of her bag and placed it on the nightstand so it would be within easy reach. The rest of her things she left packed in case she needed to make a fast getaway.

She was starving, but she was more exhausted. She sank onto the bed, grimaced at the hard lumpy mattress and closed her eyes.

It was automatic to reach for Nathan. She'd checked on him frequently as she made the drive to Southern California. Part of her fatigue was from maintaining such constant contact.

To her surprise, he was alert, intensely so. Rigid, crouched in his cell, rage so prevalent that it rolled through her like fire.

This time there wasn't a hesitation. He'd grown used to sensing her as soon as she brushed against his mind. He no longer questioned her presence.

They're working Swanson over, goddamn it.

Fury hit her like a tornado. Nathan boiled with it. Helpless fury. He clenched and unclenched his hands, and hatred clawed at Shea until she flinched from the negative wash that poured from him.

She did the only thing she felt capable of doing. She wrapped herself around him and held on, offering him whatever comfort she could.

You'll be free soon. Believe that, Nathan. Swanson too.

Damn right. I swear to God, I'll get him out.

She sensed strength in him that hadn't been there before. Renewed determination. An iron will that was nearly tangible. Thank God. He was ready to fight. He was refusing to give up.

This time there was no pain for her to take. He'd blocked it out himself with the uncontrollable anger that rocked his body. His focus was on his teammate.

Part of her wanted to shield him from the sounds of his teammate's suffering, but she knew that it was what was feeding his rage and determination. So she sat there with him, holding him as he shook with fury.

The door of his cell burst open. Nathan shot to his feet, startling Shea and sending her sprawling on the bed. Two guns were pointed at him as he was yanked forcibly to his feet.

This time they didn't bind him. They dragged him out of the cell, down a dim hallway that must have been a pathway in the cave. A moment later he was thrust into blinding sunlight.

Shea winced and blinked as Nathan threw his arm over his ravaged eyes. Her sight was distorted because he couldn't see. All she saw were flashes of light, the ground. The air was cold. The wind bit at Nathan's naked body as he was shoved to his knees.

Gradually he blinked and squinted enough that he could see, and she sucked in her breath at the sight before her.

Swanson was standing a few feet away, bloodied and bruised, his eyes bleak. The left side of his face was a mess. There was a ragged cut that ran from his temple, over his jaw and lower to his neck. The flesh lay open, blood streaming. There was panic and defeat in his eyes.

"Don't you do it, Swanny. Don't you fucking do it," Nathan said, echoing words from the teammate who'd been killed in front of him.

Shea gasped when the barrel of a pistol was jammed into the back of Nathan's head. Oh God, they were going to use him to break Swanson because Nathan had been unbreakable so far.

They no longer had use for Nathan. Maybe they'd grown tired or bored or frustrated with their efforts.

Now, Nathan. You have to fight now. You have your hands. They aren't expecting you to fight. Oh God, you have to try.

Tears poured down Shea's cheeks. She couldn't allow this. She'd never felt more helpless in her life.

Nathan lifted his gaze so that he stared straight back at Swanson, and Shea caught her breath at the silent exchange. It was do-or-die time for both of them.

I'm with you, Nathan. I won't leave you.

The men holding Swanson began barking a series of questions in broken English. Swanson stood there like a stone, his expression impassive. Then he seemed to crumble.

"All right, all right, I'll talk. Just leave him alone."

Don't freak, Shea. He's acting. Get ready. I need you for this.

She sat up on the bed, her focus razor sharp.

And suddenly Nathan whipped around, ramming his fist into the knee of the man holding the gun. The pistol hit the ground, and Nathan had it before she could think to tell him it was there.

One shot. Then two. Three more in rapid succession. The world tilted crazily, and she struggled to keep everything in perspective as Nathan exploded into action.

Swanson had managed to disarm one of his captors but the other pointed a gun at Swanson's head.

No! Shea screamed.

Nathan dropped the man with a shot just as Swanson slit the other captor's throat.

Nathan grabbed another gun, a knife and then rushed toward Swanson.

"Let's go!"

Bullets exploded past Nathan and Swanson as they ran for cover. Dirt blew up beside them. Shea could hear the thud as bullets struck trees on either side of them.

Oh God, why couldn't she have telekinesis as a power? Or be able to set shit on fire? Blow them all to hell?

Grace didn't think Shea had the balls to kill anyone. Right now she'd set the entire world on fire and burn the bastards straight to hell.

Already she was exhausted but Nathan needed her now more than ever. She drew pain away from him, his fear, absorbed every emotion except his anger and determination to escape. And she infused him with every ounce of her own resolve.

The two men ran through the trees, heavy brush, over a stream, never stopping. The gunshots grew more distant. The shouts of alarm went silent.

Keep running, she begged.

After an hour, Swanson went down, but this time he didn't get back up. He was bleeding heavily and his face was ashen. His breaths were labored.

"Get up, Swanny. Come on, man. We've got to keep moving. They'll be tracking us and we've been sloppy as hell."

"I can't do it, Nate. Go on without me. Don't let me drag you down."

"Fuck that! We go as a team. I'm not leaving you. Even if I have to carry your ass out of these mountains."

"Don't think I'm going to make it anyway," Swanson said in a raspy voice. "They broke something inside me. Pretty sure I'm bleeding internally. You know you have to leave me."

Nathan's fist tightened in frustration. *Shea, help me. Please. I don't know what to do.*

I don't have a connection to him. God, I wish I did. I hate how random my abilities are.

Try, Shea. Do it for me. Use me. Do whatever you have to do.

Shea, what the fuck is going on? What are you doing?

Shea wanted to scream in frustration as Grace broke into her thoughts. She sensed her sister's panic and worry, but oh God, not now!

Not now, Grace. Please. I have to figure this out.

Shea's own panic was rising, and she tried valiantly to keep it from spilling over into Nathan. He didn't need this. She had to be strong for him.

Go to him, Shea. Grace's calm voice penetrated the haze. *Quit trying to shut me out so I can help you help him.*

No! Grace, no. I won't let you do this! You know what it does to you.

Shut the fuck up and quit fighting me. Get your ass over there so we can save him.

Nathan, I don't have a connection to him. You have to be near him. Touch him. Put your hands on him so my sister can help.

This was never going to work. How could it?

Nathan dropped down and put his hands on Swanson's chest.

"Nate, what the fuck? Get the hell out of here. What are you doing?"

"Shut up, Swanny. We go together." *Do it now, Shea. Hurry!*

She opened herself fully to her sister for the first time since they'd last been together. She was bombarded by so many emotions she was staggered.

Keep it together, Shea. I know this is hard maintaining both links. I can do this.

Sweat beaded Shea's forehead. Her breathing went shallow and she teetered precariously on the edge of the bed.

Hot white light flooded Shea. She felt Nathan's surprise as he, too, felt the effects of her sister's healing energy.

Don't go overboard, Shea said fiercely to her sister. *Just do enough that he can move. We don't have the time, and I won't have you suffer more than you have to.*

Swanson's eyes snapped open. Color flooded back into the one undamaged cheek and he drew in deep breaths. "Holy fuck."

Shea worked at pushing all of the energy she received from Grace into Nathan. She was fast weakening and she knew there was still a long way to go before Nathan and Swanson were safe.

Then Nathan broke suddenly away.

That's enough. His voice was harsh and laced with worry.

Stay with me, Shea. I know you're weak, but I need you. We need you.

Shea retreated and focused solely on her sister. *Grace. Are you okay? Talk to me, Grace.*

Her sister's soft moan of pain splintered Shea's heart. Oh God.

Stop it, Shea. I'm not dying, for fuck's sake. I may feel like it, but your guy broke the link before it got too involved. I was at least able to fix his lung.

Shea closed her eyes in relief. *Thank you, Nathan.*

Now break away, Grace demanded. *I can't believe I'm the one telling you that this time, but I can feel how weak you are and I have no idea what the fuck kind of mess you've landed yourself in, but be careful, and as soon as this is over, you better talk to me because you have a lot of explaining to do and I want to make damn sure you're all right.*

I promise.

And then Grace was gone. Shea feared that it was worse than what Grace was letting on. She could be in bad shape right now and she wouldn't want to worry Shea.

Shea, are you still with me?

Nathan's worried voice cut through the anxiety she felt for her sister. She sucked in a fortifying breath and focused all her attention back on Nathan.

I'm here. Get Swanson up and get moving. We've already wasted too much time.

Nathan reached down, pulled Swanson to his feet and half dragged, half carried the other man farther into the trees.

"I can walk," Swanson ground out. "I have no goddamn idea what went on back there, but I can make it. Let's get the fuck out of here."

Swanson gripped a handgun in one hand and a rifle in the other. He didn't grimace when he walked and his step had quickened.

Shea breathed a sigh of relief and concentrated on helping Nathan.

They cut a path through a narrow gulch, and in some places it was so narrow that they had to turn sideways to edge through. Rocks cut into Nathan's feet, but she shielded him from the pain. It was doubtful he even knew that the soles of his feet were dripping blood.

The terrain leveled out when the gulch opened up into a wider valley. The men kept to the edge, moving stealthily through the brush.

Just before they could slip into another dense path of trees, the whine of a bullet reached Shea's ears and pain exploded through Nathan's leg.

He stumbled and went down.

Oh God, oh God. He'd been shot.

Without thinking, she used every bit of her flagging strength to draw the pain. Agony pulsed down her thigh and blood seeped into the material of her pants.

She flooded him with hope, determination. She took away the pain, gritting her teeth against the urge to scream out as fire coursed through her veins.

Get up! You're okay, Nathan. Keep going.

This time it was Swanson who reached down and pulled Nathan to his feet.

Shea. Thank you.

She closed her eyes as she began the slow slide into oblivion. She had to hold on. She had to keep him strong. She couldn't falter. Not now. She'd made him a promise not to leave him until he was safe. She wouldn't fail.

They charged into the wooded area and then both men took cover behind a tree as they pulled out their guns.

Shea sensed Nathan's grim determination that they wouldn't take him alive under any circumstances. He would die fighting them and take as many of the bastards with him as he could.

Blood ran more freely down her leg and the pain had become unbearable. She was further weakened by the fact that not only was she shouldering his pain, but she was also shielding him from picking up on *her* agony.

Her head pounded. Nausea rose in her throat and the walls of her hotel room spun in rapid circles.

Shea, my God. You have to stop this.

Get the hell away from me, Grace. You're distracting me.

At once warmth and strength poured into Shea, bolstering her when she so badly needed the reinforcement.

Don't bother trying to hold our link. I'll do what I can. Focus on your guy. I need to stop your bleeding.

Shea didn't argue. She didn't have the strength and she couldn't afford even the tiniest slip where Nathan was concerned.

"Make your shots count, Swanny. When we run through this ammo, we're SOL."

Swanson nodded, a fierce scowl etched across his face. "Bring it on, motherfuckers."

More bullets slapped the trees and ground around them. Nathan ducked behind the broad tree and looked over at Swanson. "They're still a good distance away. Don't shoot until you're sure you've got a good shot."

Swanson nodded.

The valley went quiet. Wind whistled eerily through the trees. Leaves rustled. Chills raced down Shea's arms. She was Nathan's only barrier to the cold. His only protection from pain that should have had him unconscious on the ground.

In the distance, the bastards crept forward, drawing closer to Nathan's position. He held a finger up to tell Swanson to hold off.

"Wait," he mouthed.

Swanson nodded and tightened his grip around the rifle.

They were about four hundred yards away when the world exploded in a series of gunfire. Several of the men who'd been pursuing Nathan and Swanson hit the ground. Others broke and ran, shooting wildly left and right, completely away from where Nathan and Swanson stood.

"What the fuck?" Swanson demanded.

As Nathan stared, mystified, the valley swarmed with soldiers. Holy fucking hell. *American* goddamn soldiers.

His heart raced and damn near beat out of his chest.

"Oh my God," Swanson breathed. "They've come for us."

CHAPTER 8

NATHAN had never been so happy to see someone in his entire life. It was all he could do not to run out, waving his arms, but he remained in his position and told Swanny to do the same.

It was clear by the number of Tangos hitting the ground that snipers were picking them off on either side. What was left was taking heavy fire from the swarm of soldiers coming at them from all sides.

A few Tangos got close enough for Nathan and Swanson to squeeze off shots. In a matter of minutes, what few remained turned tail and hauled ass back the way they'd come.

Swanson let out a whoop and hoisted his rifle into the air. Jubilation filled Nathan as well. *We did it, Shea!*

Nathan waited for the reassuring response from Shea but she was silent. Dread gripped him until finally he felt her stir and warmth traveled through his body again.

I knew you'd do it.

Her confidence imbued him with the strength to walk out from behind the tree. He staggered from cover just as Swanson started out as well. The two men helped each other as they went to meet the approaching soldiers.

As they drew closer, Nathan's pulse ratcheted up and tears

blurred his vision. Donovan? Sam? Ethan? Garrett? Holy shit. It was KGI, not the army.

"It's my brothers," Nathan croaked.

"I don't give a fuck if they're your sisters," Swanson said as he hoisted Nathan's sagging body. "I'll kiss them just the same."

Adrenaline left him. Even Shea's unwavering support couldn't hold him up any longer. Nathan sagged, going down to his knees.

It was like a breaking dam. Pain flooded him. Fire burned through his limbs, his muscles, even his veins.

He realized that Shea's strength was gone. She could no longer shield him. She'd shielded him far too long already.

He glanced up to see horror written on his brothers' faces as they ran toward him. Then he looked down, realizing what they saw. He was gaunt, completely naked, and blood ran in rivulets down his body from all the cuts. It streamed down his leg where he'd taken a bullet.

He looked like he'd been to hell and back. He could feel the fires of hell licking up his body until he was consumed in agony.

He pitched forward, bracing his palms against the cold earth as his brothers surrounded him.

You're safe now, Nathan.

Shea's weak voice reached him just as he sensed her withdrawal. Only it felt final this time. Not like the others when she'd always promised to come back.

Please, please don't tell anyone about me. Please keep my secret safe. My safety depends on it.

And then she was gone, leaving a giant, yawning hole in the pit of his soul. His fingers curled into the dirt. "No! Don't leave! Goddamn it, don't leave!"

"Nathan, my God. It's me, Donovan. You're okay now, man. We're here. We're not going to leave you. We're going to take you home."

As his brothers tried to roll him over, Nathan went ballistic. Here, when he was surrounded by his brothers, he'd never felt so alone in his life.

"Don't go! Oh God, don't go. Please don't leave me," he whispered brokenly.

Garrett palmed Nathan's face with both hands and lowered

his face until they were mere inches apart. "Nathan, we're here. We're taking you home. Everything's okay now. We're going to get you out of here."

"Swanny. Take care of Swanny," he managed to gasp out.

"I've got him," Ethan said. "Don't worry. We've got him."

Tears streamed down Nathan's cheeks as he stared up at the sky, so brilliantly blue. It ought to be red for all the bloodshed and yet it was pristine and soft.

"Don't go. Don't leave me, Shea."

The words broke painfully from his raw throat. He hadn't realized he'd been screaming just a moment ago. He closed his eyes as pain engulfed him.

"Who the fuck is Shea?" Sam demanded.

"Mine," Nathan murmured. "Mine."

Donovan knelt to wrap Nathan's leg to stop the bleeding. He didn't even flinch. There was simply too much pain, too much loss.

Shea. Don't go.

He caught a vague image of her curled into a tight ball, suffering alone. It was more than he could bear. And then his mind went blank. No Shea. It was as if she'd never existed.

"Get that fucking helo here!" Garrett yelled.

"Down! Down!" Sam hollered.

None of what they said made sense but suddenly Nathan found himself covered. Donovan pressed him to the ground.

"They're American!" Ethan hollered. "Hold your fire! Hold your fire!"

Donovan pushed himself off Nathan and then stared down at his brother. "Looks like Uncle Sam decided to come along after all."

Nathan turned his head, squinting into the sun. The valley was swarming with soldiers. It was too much to take in. He'd been on the verge of giving up all hope of ever returning home.

Thanks to a faceless woman with the voice of an angel and the strength of a warrior, he'd survived.

CHAPTER 9

NATHAN hammered a nail into the two-by-four and then leaned back and wiped the sweat from his forehead. His hands shook and it pissed him off. He was still weak. Not fully himself. But then it was doubtful he'd ever be one hundred percent again.

He'd gained some of the weight back, but he was still whipcord lean and a good twenty pounds lighter than his normal size.

His house was framed. It could already be built by now, but he'd shunned a contractor. He couldn't explain his drive to build the house himself, but it had become all-important for him to drive every nail, to create the refuge exactly as he envisioned it.

These days, it was all that kept him sane.

The mere idea of small, closed-in spaces made him break out in a cold sweat.

Weeks in a hospital had in some way been as hellish as his captivity. He'd felt helpless and he fought a daily battle over whether or not he'd imagined Shea. And worrying about her if she did in fact exist.

After having her as a shadow in his mind for so long, his head was frighteningly quiet. No comforting presence. But at other times, while he slept, he could swear he felt her. Warm and soothing, easing his pain and anxiety. When he awakened, she was never there. Still, he couldn't discount the fact that the agony that should have incapacitated him simply didn't exist.

The medical staff marveled at his ability to withstand and block out pain. What could he tell them? That he'd imagined a savior with the ability to take his pain as her own? They would have carried him away in a straitjacket. He'd probably still be locked up in some damn institution for psychiatric evaluation.

So yeah, he'd kept his mouth shut. During debriefing he'd kept to the facts. He'd been captured, tortured, and he'd managed to escape when they intended to kill him. Swanny must have kept his mouth shut too, because the incident where Shea and her sister had helped Swanny had gone unmentioned. Maybe Swanny himself didn't even remember what had happened. Or maybe, like Nathan, he thought he was crazy.

Not as easy was answering his brothers' questions when he was well enough and lucid enough to face them. They'd all hovered in his hospital room. His parents had flown in. The whole damn Kelly clan had gathered and had stayed in shifts until he was finally discharged.

One night when his parents had gone to eat with Rachel, Sophie and Sarah, his brothers had remained behind in his hospital room and they'd asked about the person who'd emailed Donovan. They asked who Shea was and why Nathan had screamed her name.

It was against his nature to lie to his family. He hated lying. But neither was he going to delve into his experience with Shea. She had to be real. How else would Donovan have received the emails he'd gotten? Van had even showed them to him.

He merely told them there was a sympathetic guard who'd promised to contact Nathan's brother on Nathan's behalf. Nathan had seen the disbelief in his brothers' eyes. Questions that burned on their tongues, but they didn't press. It probably damn near killed them.

As for Shea, the moment they mentioned her name, he refused to respond. He had no ready explanation, no easy way to explain away why he'd screamed for her not to leave him.

So he said nothing, and his stony silence became a source of frustration for his brothers.

Nathan sighed as he hammered another nail. He knew his brothers worried. Nathan had changed, but hell, how could he not? How could anyone go through what he'd endured and not be fundamentally a changed man?

It wasn't like he wanted to be different. He'd love to have his old life back. The same confidence. His resolute belief in his abilities. He'd give anything not to go to bed at night in a cold sweat because he couldn't bear to close his eyes in case he woke up and was back in that cave being cut into ribbons again.

He hated the panic attacks. The loss of control. His sudden, unexplained fears at the most inopportune times. He'd come a long way since being   ed, but he still battled his demons on a daily basis. There were times, even though he was only six months out from his rescue, when he wondered if he'd always battle them. They seemed as much a part of him as breathing.

As much as he'd feared never seeing his family again, now that he was home, he preferred to spend most of his time alone. They loved him and he loved them, but their worry and concern weighed heavily on him. He couldn't pretend he was normal. He couldn't pretend to be the man who'd left them all those months ago to go on another mission. He was changed, and he was still dealing with the effects of that change himself. How could he expect them to accept the change when he hadn't accepted it?

He didn't want to push them away—it wasn't what he consciously did. But he found himself seeking solitude more and more and spending less time in the ranks of his noisy and boisterous family. He missed them and avoided them in equal measure.

He reached for another nail and wiped the sweat off his brow with the back of his arm, freezing for a moment as the crisscross pattern of still healing scars flashing in front of him.

He looked and felt like a damn patchwork doll.

Raising the hammer, he started to drive another nail, when a sound behind him stopped him. He turned, expecting to see one of his brothers. They checked in on him daily, whether he wanted them to or not. But it wasn't one of them standing a few feet away.

He dropped the hammer. "Swanny! What the hell are you doing here?"

Nathan strode over to his former teammate and gripped him in a tight hug. He pulled away, taking note of Swanny's appearance.

Like Nathan, he hadn't regained the weight he'd lost in captivity. He, also like Nathan, was heavily scarred. The wound on his face had been deep and long and it snaked over the entire left side of his face. Lines were grooved into his forehead and around his eyes. There was even a smattering of gray at his temples. Hell had aged him and he hadn't recovered. Maybe he never would.

"I had to come see you, Nate. I had to thank you in person."

"Come sit down. Want a beer?"

Nathan gestured toward two large boulders that overlooked sprawling Kentucky Lake. While Swanny went to take a seat, Nathan dug into his cooler for two beers. Then thinking better of it, he dragged the entire ice chest over to where Swanny sat.

"How the hell are you?" Nathan asked as he tossed a can in Swanny's direction.

Swanny was quiet for a moment. "I'm good. Making it. I thought I was more than ready to get out when my tour was up, but now I have too much time to think. It sucks."

"Yeah, I hear you."

"Nice place you have here. I wasn't sure they were going to let me through the gates."

Nathan's lips quirked into a half smile. "My brothers are pretty serious about security."

Swanny sipped at the beer and stared out over the shimmering surface of the lake in the distance. Then he turned his gaze on Nathan. His eyes were dark and haunted. Tired.

"What happened out there, Nate?"

Nathan looked away, his shoulders rigid.

"I've tried to rationalize it. I've tried to explain it away, say it didn't happen, but I didn't imagine it. I did not imagine you putting your hands on me. I didn't make up how injured I was before and the immediate sensation of relief. The x-rays showed no internal damage, but I know I was bleeding. I know I was hurt. Hell, I was coughing up blood. I couldn't breathe. So you explain it to me, Nate. Tell me what the hell you did."

"I didn't do anything," Nathan said honestly. "Swear to God, I didn't. I have so many what-the-fuck moments about that entire ordeal. Some days I think I lost it back there and I'll never get it back. Some part of my mind just broke during captivity and I imagined all sorts of things."

"Yeah," Swanny muttered.

Nathan picked up another beer and popped the tab. He took several long gulps and then directed his gaze toward the lake and let the blue swallow him.

"Someone or something helped us," Nathan said. "It was like the most fucking beautiful thing I've ever encountered. I worried I was dead or dying because I was sure I felt the presence of an angel."

If he closed his eyes and thought hard enough, he could still feel the brush of Shea's fingers on his face, the warmth of her soul as it merged with his. It was inexplicable. He didn't want to examine it too closely, because he wanted it to be real. He wanted *her* to be real.

"Angel. Yeah, that about covers the feeling. It was warm. Like the warmest, most soothing sensation I've ever experienced in my life. My panic and fear just melted away. I just can't wrap my head around it. I've never really had a firm belief in God one way or another. I mean I suppose there has to be some higher power out there, but was that what it was? Was God helping us?"

Nathan's hands shook and he set his beer down so he wouldn't spill it. "I've asked myself that a thousand times. I don't have an answer. Maybe I never will."

The idea that he'd never talk to her again, never feel her inside him, destroyed a part of his soul that she'd claimed for her own.

There was so much more he could tell Swanny. But he wouldn't ever divulge just how close to surrender he'd been in those darkest hours. Shea had saved him. Not just him but Swanny too.

Shea.

He couldn't help the soft call. Her name echoed through his brain, making no connection. She simply wasn't there.

Was she in trouble? Had she sacrificed her safety in order to help him? He wished to hell he knew.

He glanced back up at Swanny, who seemed as content with the silence as Nathan was.

"What now, man?" Nathan asked softly.

Swanny grimaced and absently fingered the puckered scar marring his face. "I wish to hell I knew. What about you?"

Nathan blew out his breath. "I've been working on that." He gestured over his shoulder. "Haven't made a whole lot of progress, but it gives me something to do. My brothers alternate between wanting to commit me to a long-term rest facility complete with psych ward and wanting me to start training with them. Joe's doing well. He's already training with a team."

The ache inside his chest intensified. There was a gulf between him and his twin. Joe wanted to rush in, make it all better. Bully Nathan into taking action. Joe was impetuous, but it served him well. Nothing got him down. He'd blown through physical therapy for his busted leg and had started training the moment he got the okay from the therapist.

He expected Nathan to be able to do the same. Shake it off. Physically heal and then get back into the game. It wasn't that Nathan didn't want to join KGI. He did. It had always been his and Joe's plan. Once they served their last tour in the army, they were going to work with their brothers.

He'd only been a few weeks away from that goal when everything had gone to hell.

Now . . . Now he wasn't willing to commit unless he could be sure he'd give his brothers one hundred percent. He couldn't guarantee anyone that. Not yet.

He also knew that his brothers were urging him to "join" simply so they could take care of him, stay on his ass to take care of himself, but they had no intention of letting him go on missions. They wanted to give him a purpose.

He wasn't sure what his purpose was these days. It sounded fatalistic. He wasn't. But for so long his purpose had simply been survival. Now he had to regroup, pick up the pieces and decide what the hell he was going to do with the life he'd been granted. A life that Shea had given him.

Somehow sitting here talking to Swanny brought Shea that much more sharply back to him and convinced him that he hadn't imagined her.

"I'm not sure what I'm going to do next either," Swanny said. "I honestly never expected to make it back. I thought I was going to die in that shithole cave."

Nathan nodded because he'd been just as convinced as Swanny had been.

A cool breeze blew in from the lake, and Nathan turned his face up to catch the sweet scent of honeysuckle. He loved it here. To experience such peace after being in such unimaginable stress was disconcerting almost.

"Well, what do you say we don't make any life decisions for the next day or two at least," Nathan said with a smile. "You got a place to stay? I'm thinking the biggest decision we need to think about is what beer we want and whether we're going to run out."

Swanny grinned. "Now you're speaking my language. I booked a hotel in Paris and drove over the lake to find you."

"Cancel the hotel. I've got better accommodations here." He gestured at a tent toward the edge of the cliff overlooking the lake just beyond the frame of his house. "If you don't mind rustic, plenty of fresh air and all the beer you can drink. Ma has made it her mission to make sure I never starve, so we can count on routine deliveries of food."

"Home-cooked food and beer? And they say you can't get to heaven without dying."

Nathan sobered. No. But you could certainly go to hell without dying. He shook away that thought and then stood.

"Let's go get your stuff and check you out of your hotel. We'll stop by the store, get what we need, and we'll spend a few nights under the stars."

Swanny got to his feet. He stared out over the lake for a minute and then turned his gaze to Nathan. A smile softened the harsh lines around his eyes. "Yeah. Sounds like a plan."

CHAPTER 10

SWANNY sat back in his chair with a groan. "That was the best meal I've had in a long time, Mrs. Kelly."

Nathan's mom beamed as she got up from her seat to start clearing the table. She stopped by Swanny and patted him on the cheek.

"You have to call me Marlene. Or Mom. Or Ma. Really. You're family, so Mrs. Kelly just won't do."

Swanny had the same befuddled look on his face that most people did when encountering the storm that was Nathan's mother. He looked torn between bemusement and wanting to hug the woman.

It had taken a lot of persuading to get Swanny to agree to have dinner with the Kellys. He was self-conscious about his face, but then Marlene blithely ignored the scarring. She kissed, patted and otherwise made it a point to let Swanny know she didn't care. He'd instantly become another of her children.

"You boys want to retire to the living room and have a beer? There's a baseball game on," Frank Kelly said. "Leave the dishes, Marlene. I'll get them later."

Nathan grinned. His dad still treated them like they were . . . boys. His boys. No matter how old they got. They were still the children of Marlene and Frank Kelly no matter what.

Joe tossed down his napkin and rose. "Beer sounds good. Baseball sounds even better."

Rusty smiled impishly and darted a glance toward Frank. "Yeah, beer sounds great!"

Frank gave her a get-real look. "Very funny, young lady. You get lemonade."

"Hey, I'm eighteen now!"

"And?" Marlene asked.

Rusty rolled her eyes. "And it means I have three more years until I'm legally allowed to imbibe."

Marlene nodded approvingly. "Now you're getting it."

Nathan stood, as did Swanny, and they started to follow Frank and Joe into the living room. Rusty waited until Marlene had left to go get drinks then hurriedly rose and touched Nathan on the arm.

"Hey, can I talk to you for a minute?" she asked in a low voice.

Nathan frowned but hung back after motioning for Swanny to follow Nathan's dad and brother.

Rusty looked a little nervous and hesitant, neither of which were qualities usually attributed to her.

"What's up?" Nathan asked.

Things had come a long way in Rusty's relationship with the Kellys. His brothers to be specific. But Nathan had always been more . . . understanding . . . so she naturally gravitated toward him more than his siblings.

Another of Marlene's strays, Rusty had been taken in at the time when Rachel had been rescued and brought home after a year of being thought dead. The family situation had been volatile at best, and Rusty had added tension. She'd been defensive, bratty and sullen, but over time she'd earned her place and now she was as fiercely protective of the family as any natural-born Kelly.

"Look, I wasn't supposed to ask you this. I mean Marlene and Frank didn't want me to pressure you. I'm supposed to back off and let you breathe and stuff."

Nathan lifted an eyebrow. One would think he was a hair from barking at the moon in full werewolf gear.

She hurried on in a rush. "But I really want you there. I mean like more than everyone else. Not that I don't want everyone else there too, but it would be really great if you could make it as well."

He put his hand on her arm. "Rusty."

She quieted immediately, and her cheeks reddened.

"Just spit it out. Where do you want me to be?"

"Graduation," she mumbled. "It's this week. I would have said something earlier, I mean I didn't want to just spring it on you like this, but Marlene didn't want me to pressure you—"

"Of course I'll come."

"I know the crowd issue and that you don't like being around so many people since you got home and all—"

"Rusty, I'll come. I wouldn't miss it."

She looked up in surprise. Then a wide smile flashed on her face. "Really? I mean if you don't want to. Or if it's too much, I totally understand."

He smiled. "You only graduate once, kiddo. I'll suffer through it."

Her lips turned down and her expression grew worried.

"I was kidding. Of course I'll be there. The whole Kelly clan will be there. I'm sure Ma wants to frame that diploma. Has she already planned a party that includes the entire county?"

Rusty's eyes shone with relief. Her smile returned and she jiggled with excitement. Then to Nathan's surprise, she launched herself at him and wrapped her arms around him, squeezing tight.

"I wanted you there the most."

The words were muffled by the fact that her face was planted against his chest. He smiled and then hugged her back.

As she pulled away, she glanced back toward the kitchen. "Just don't tell Marlene I asked. Okay?"

"Lips are sealed."

As they started toward the living room, Rusty hesitated once more and turned serious blue eyes on him. "I'm so glad you're home, Nathan. I was—we were all—worried about you."

He ruffled her hair. "Thanks, kiddo."

It was nice to have family who worried about him. He was suddenly overcome with near-choking emotion. His eyelids stung and he cursed the onslaught of the aching relief of being home when he thought he'd never return here again.

Rusty slipped her hand into his and tugged him toward the

living room. It embarrassed him that she seemed to realize how unstable he'd suddenly become.

Swanny was sitting on the couch next to Joe, who'd slouched, tossed off his shoes and then kicked his feet up on the ottoman. He wouldn't admit it to anyone, but Nathan knew his leg still bothered him and he wasn't yet one hundred percent after taking a bullet. Nathan's own bullet wound had healed much faster. It had been a flesh wound and hadn't hit bone as Joe's had. Joe was training hard with a KGI team, but he still hadn't been cleared for missions. Physically, Nathan was probably more ready for active duty again than Joe was. And yet, Nathan had still not even considered joining his brothers.

Nathan's dad was in his recliner, remote in hand, and they all looked up when Rusty dragged Nathan into the living room.

"Your brothers are coming over," Frank said.

Nathan raised his brows. "All of them?"

"Yeah, they aren't happy you've been avoiding them—their words not mine."

Nathan bit back a curse. He glanced over at Swanny, who was engrossed in the game already and arguing with Joe over batting averages.

"We could sneak out the back," Rusty muttered.

Nathan chuckled and some of his anxiety lessened. The tension in his chest eased, and suddenly he could breathe again. He did want to see his brothers and his sisters-in-law and his sister-in-law-to-be, Sarah.

Sarah was quieter than even Rachel, and she still seemed ill at ease and overwhelmed by all the family members. It was obvious that Garrett was a total goner over the woman he was marrying. He never strayed far from her side, and now that Nathan was home, they were planning their wedding for later in the summer right before Rusty left for college at the University of Tennessee.

He looked at Rachel far differently now. Before he'd always been gentle with her, considered her fragile, as if she'd break at any moment. The whole family treated her like she was . . . weak.

Now he realized just what a disservice they did her. He couldn't even comprehend the strength it took to survive in hell for an entire year. He'd been ready to give up after two months.

He'd looked death in the face and accepted without blinking the inevitability of his own.

Rachel awed him and shamed him in equal parts. He had the sudden urge to see her again, even though it had only been a week since the last time he'd seen her. He wanted to hug her. To tell her how damn amazed he was by her. He didn't think his family told her that often enough. Maybe they'd never told her.

"Take a load off," Joe said.

Nathan blinked his way out of his thoughts and realized that everyone was staring at him. He wiped his palms down the legs of his jeans and settled onto the couch down from Swanny. Soon the room would be filled with his brothers and their wives. People would be sitting on the floor, spilled over the arms of chairs and the couch. And his mom would beam the entire time.

He glanced questioningly at Swanny, wanting to know if his friend was up for this. They'd spent the last two days alone at Nathan's building site until Nathan's mom had had enough and dragged them over for a real dinner, as she'd put it.

Swanny looked content—more content than Nathan—to be surrounded by so many warm people. But then Swanny didn't have family. He'd had no one to return to when he and Nathan had been rescued. In Swanny's position, Nathan would have given up hope a lot sooner. Only the drive to see his family again had kept him sane. What had given Swanny such determination?

If he could give Swanny a little peace by sharing his family, then Nathan would gladly do it. His mom would adopt him now anyway whether Swanny liked it or not. Nothing much stopped her when she set her mind to something, and collecting strays was a lifelong habit of hers.

"How is training going, Joe?" Frank asked.

Nathan traced one of the scars on his arm and didn't look over for his brother's response. His dad didn't mean anything by it. He worried about his youngest sons. The family was thrilled to have them both home, and their brothers were content to have them under the KGI umbrella.

Nathan hadn't made a commitment. He wasn't even talking the possibility. Not yet. Maybe never.

"Going good, Dad. I'm being assigned to Rio's team. Van is still working on a third team. That could be months in the works. He's a picky bastard."

"You'll be taking assignments already?" Marlene asked sharply.

Nathan turned his head to see his mom walk into the living room with that classic "mom" look on her face, which meant she was displeased. And worried. She put the tray holding the drinks down on the coffee table and motioned for them to get one.

Joe snorted. "If I had my way, yeah. But for now I'll just be training with Rio and his men."

Marlene frowned harder. "But they live away. Doesn't Rio live in some jungle somewhere?"

Joe grinned. "Belize, Mom. And yeah, he lives there. He doesn't train there. We'll train here at the new facility. It's why Sam busted ass to get everything up and running. Well, and we still have permission from Uncle Sam to train at Fort Campbell too."

"Well, that's something at least," Marlene muttered as she took a seat between Nathan and Swanny. "If it's all the same, I'd like for my boys not to take off the minute I get them home. Has your doctor even given you the go-ahead for this kind of activity?"

She put her hand on Nathan's leg and gave him a gentle squeeze, even though she didn't look his way or direct her statement toward him. While his brothers worried incessantly over Nathan, Marlene seemed content to give him time and space and not pressure him to do anything at all.

But that might be because she feared he was one short fuse away from exploding. Which would explain why she hadn't wanted Rusty to invite him to graduation. He sighed. He just wanted things to be normal, or as close to normal as possible. In the past she wouldn't have hesitated one iota to tell him where and when to be wherever she thought he should.

Joe laughed. "Ma, I'm fine. No, I'm not one hundred percent, but I'm almost there and I will be there the more I work at it. I'm not going to get better sitting on my ass and feeling sorry for myself."

Nathan didn't look at his brother, but he could feel the

weight of Joe's stare. He knew the statement was pointed. He knew Joe thought he should be able to move on, stay busy, forget the last year. Put it out of his mind.

That was Joe.

Joe wanted Nathan to start training. Joe wanted to pretend that nothing had ever happened to Nathan because it hurt *him* to think of what had happened to his twin.

Everyone had their own idea of how to fix Nathan. And maybe that was the reason Nathan had pulled back. Because the only person who was going to fix Nathan was Nathan and he didn't have that particular mystery solved yet.

The sound of the front door opening put an end to any conversation. A moment later, his brothers and their wives started pouring into the living room.

Baby Charlotte was immediately pounced on and passed from relative to relative and the smooches and cooing filled the room.

Nathan's palms grew slick again and his scars itched. He rubbed his hands down his pants but forced himself not to rub at his chest and belly or his arms.

His chest tightened painfully and suddenly he couldn't sit still any longer. He pushed himself upward, as if he were standing to greet the rest of his family. He forced himself to endure the backslaps from his brothers, but their voices sort of mingled together until it all sounded like a dull roar.

Murmuring an excuse that he had to go to the bathroom, he escaped to the kitchen and then stood over the sink, running water over his scarred arms while he tried to calm his rapid pulse rate.

After several deep breaths, he went to the fridge, fished out a beer and then retreated out the back door onto the deck. Inside they were no doubt openly discussing his continued distance and wondering how to break past the wall. Or maybe not since Swanny was there. But they were thinking it and exchanging helpless looks from some, determined looks from others. And probably drawing straws to see who came to find him.

If Swanny wasn't having such a good time and looking happier than he had since he'd arrived to see Nathan, Nathan would have already left.

He propped his beer on the porch railing and stared into

the darkness, listening to the soothing sounds of tree frogs and crickets. When the door opened, he sighed. When he turned around, though, he was surprised to see Rachel standing a few feet away.

He turned fully, leaning back against the wood railing. "Hey, doll. I didn't figure you would draw the short straw or that you'd even be in the running."

She tilted her head in confusion, the outside light shining over her dark hair. "Oh," she finally said. "You thought they sent me."

"They didn't?"

She took the few remaining steps that separated them and stood quietly next to him, her gaze directed to the woods behind his parents' house.

"No."

He turned back around so they were facing the same direction. "Sorry. I know I probably seem paranoid and touchy."

She smiled. "Understandable if you were."

"How are you? I mean really? You doing okay these days? I haven't seen much of you."

She glanced over at him. "Shouldn't I be asking how you're doing? And you haven't seen many of us."

He winced, although there was no accusation in her tone. His scars itched and he rubbed one hand up his arm before clasping it around his elbow.

"I understand how you feel," she said in a low voice. "Maybe no one has said that. Maybe because they *don't* understand. I know how overwhelmed you are and that sometimes you really just want everyone around you to pretend things are normal."

He sighed again. "Yeah, I know you do."

Because he'd been thinking earlier just how much he wanted to hug her, he pulled her into his arms and wrapped his arms around her much smaller frame. She laced her arms around his waist and hugged him back just as tightly.

"You amaze me."

She pulled away so she could look up at him. Her brows knitted together and a slight frown rested on her mouth.

"I don't know how you managed to survive for an entire year."

She pulled her arms back and then folded them across her chest, her fingers making little marks on her arms.

"Hey, I didn't mean to upset you. I understand. Believe me."

She shook her head. "No. It's okay. Really. People don't talk about it at all around me. It happened. I'm still dealing with it, but sometimes I wish that everyone would feel comfortable mentioning it."

"I guess I'm not to that point yet. I just want everyone to stop looking at me . . ."

"With pity in their eyes? With so much sorrow that you feel like you're going to drown in it? With a look that says they're hurting with you and for you, and you just want to make it all go away so they won't feel so bad and worry all the time?"

"Yeah, that."

"They're family. They love us. I actually understand them more now since you came back because I feel that way about you, and I stop myself at times and remind myself that the worry I feel is the same worry they felt for me."

Nathan looped an arm around her again and hugged her close. "Thank you for that. It means a lot. I know I don't act like it."

She shook her head. "You can't make yourself feel a certain way, Nathan. Believe me, I've tried. It takes . . . time."

"You're an amazing woman, Rachel Kelly. I just want you to know that. I was ready to give up and I was only gone for a few months. There were days when I thought it would just be easier to die. I wanted to die."

"Why didn't you then?" she asked softly.

His arm fell away and he turned to grip the railing with both hands. "Because someone saved me."

She didn't respond. Didn't ask him who. She just stood there and waited. He liked that about her. She wasn't pushy. She had such a quiet strength about her that wrapped around her. She calmed him like no one else in the family. Maybe that was why he was standing here waging a battle with himself over whether to confide in her. At least if she thought he was crazy, she wouldn't go sound the alarm to the rest of the family.

He raised one arm, dragged a hand over his face and let out a disgusted sigh. "You're going to think I'm nuts."

She put one small hand on his shoulder. A simple touch. Still no response. And she waited. He liked that about her too. She didn't lie and immediately deny that she wouldn't think he was off his rocker.

"I was there. I mean I was thinking about death and the inevitability of death and wondered why I was fighting it. I told myself that I was fooling myself that I would ever see my family again. Why continue to be strong and endure when it was pointless?"

She let out a small sound of distress and leaned in closer.

"And then she spoke to me."

Rachel tilted her head again. "Who did?"

"I don't know," he said. He wouldn't say her name. She'd begged him not to tell anyone about her. He was breaking that promise here with Rachel, but he would at least not give her name. Even if she wasn't real, it was important that he not betray her. "Maybe she was an angel. Maybe I imagined her. But she saved me."

"Even after my memory grew so hazy with the drugs they gave me, I held on to Ethan. His name. His image. As time went on, I convinced myself he wasn't real and that he was just my own personal warrior or angel. Take your pick. But he got me through my darkest days. I convinced myself that he would save me. Maybe it was all I had. It was either cling to that belief or just give up. I don't think you're crazy."

"That's not everything," Nathan muttered. "We talked. I mean really talked. And the thing is . . . Boy, does this get crazier by the minute. The thing is, I couldn't have imagined her because she emailed Van."

Rachel pulled sharply away. "You mean the email he got telling him you were in Korengal Valley? The one telling him to talk to Joe?"

"That's the one."

Rachel pursed her lips and blew out her breath. "Okay, so when you say you talked to this woman, you mean like she was in the next cell? Or she was part of the group of people who kept you prisoner?"

It would be so easy to say yes. He should say yes and just forget this whole conversation. He'd refused to even discuss the email with his brothers. They were frustrated as hell because they wanted answers, but if they even brought it up, Nathan shut down.

"Nathan?" she prompted when the silence grew longer.

"Look, just forget it. It's not important."

She reached forward with surprising strength and pulled his hands toward her. She clasped them and stared up at him, her expression fierce.

"It is important. Talk to me, Nathan."

He leaned forward and kissed her forehead. "Thank you for listening, Rachel. Really. But this is something I've got to work out on my own."

He saw the frustration in her eyes but also her understanding as he pulled away. Then she pushed forward and hugged him again.

"We love you, Nathan. We all do. Just remember that."

The door to the patio opened and Ethan stepped out but then hesitated when he saw Nathan and Rachel.

"Hey, man, get your own woman. I should have known you'd be off sweet-talking mine."

Nathan grinned and relaxed. This he could handle. Typical banter. He hadn't realized how much he just wanted to revert back to old times where his brothers gave him shit instead of looking at him like he was a quarter off a full dollar.

But then he hadn't helped in that area. If he wanted to be treated normally, he needed to stop putting up walls between him and his family.

"I can't help if a pretty woman prefers my company," Nathan drawled.

Ethan ambled forward and slid an arm around Rachel. "You two avoiding the family out here? I seem to remember Rachel slipping out here a time or two when things got overwhelming."

"I was just telling her how amazing I think she is."

Ethan smiled. "Well, I can't argue with that."

"Okay, you two, enough," Rachel grumbled.

She slipped out of Ethan's grasp, gave Nathan another quick hug and then headed inside, leaving Nathan alone with his brother.

"Everything okay, man?" Ethan asked when Rachel had shut the door.

"She's pretty damn special," Nathan said, ignoring the question.

"Yeah, I know. You two have a lot in common."

Nathan's lips quirked upward. "Oh? You think I look as good in a dress as she does?"

Relief flared in Ethan's eyes at the comeback, but then his expression grew more serious. "No, I meant you're both survivors."

CHAPTER 11

NATHAN'S eyes flew open and the splash of stars in the inky midnight sky instantly swam in his vision. They loomed close then backed away, and the world spun crazily around him.

He tried to sit up in the sleeping bag and promptly fell over, weak and disoriented. His mind was clouded, and random images flashed, none making sense.

Strange men, yawning faces and a sense of overwhelming fear.

What the hell was happening to him? He hadn't drunk that much beer. Certainly not enough to get a buzz, much less stupid drunk.

This wasn't like his other panic attacks. He hadn't been dreaming. It was one of the few nights that his mind had been blissfully free of the past.

There was such a sense of dread overwhelming him that his breaths puffed out and his stomach rebelled. His chest burned from the pressure. It was as if weight pressed down on him from every angle.

And then he felt her. Just one brief moment, as if she were desperately trying to reach out to him.

Shea.

Scared. Terrified.

It was *her* panic he felt. *Her* disorientation.

Shea!

He screamed her name in his mind. Then he yelled it hoarsely, the sound echoing through the night.

He tore away the sleeping bag that confined him, stumbling out onto the ground and to his knees. Beside him, Swanny shot upward.

"What the hell?"

Nathan shoved his hands into the grass, trying to push himself upward, but he was too weak, too disoriented to maintain his balance. He fell heavily to his side, cursing because he couldn't wade through the fog in his mind to reach out to Shea. She was there. He knew it. Was she trying to reach him? Did she need help?

He curled his fingers into the soil, trying again to right himself, to get up and battle the confusion. Swanny scrambled over, his face close to Nathan's.

"What's wrong, man? Do I need to get help? What's happening to you?"

Nathan snarled his frustration, grabbed on to Swanny and pulled. "Help me."

Swanny pushed to his knees and then stood, Nathan still gripping his hands as he pulled upward. He staggered to his feet, wobbling like he'd been on a bender from hell.

The world kept moving around him, dipping and swaying until nausea rose sharp in his belly and into his throat, clenching and squeezing until he couldn't breathe.

"What the fuck is wrong?" Swanny demanded. "Let me call a damn ambulance. Or at least drive you to the hospital."

"Just let me get my feet under me," he gritted out.

He put his hands to his head, sucked in breaths and then reached out again.

Shea, talk to me, damn it. Are you okay? What's going on? Please, just talk to me.

He caught just a hint of his name, and suddenly the disorientation faded. The shadows drifted away, leaving him sharply aware of his surroundings. The smell of a late Tennessee spring, verging to summer. The lake. The trees, the pine.

A breeze cooled the sweat that dampened his body, and he shivered in reaction.

She was gone. Like she'd never been there. Again.

"Son of a bitch!"

"Nathan, talk to me, man. What the hell is going on?"

He pushed away from Swanny and stalked toward the edge of the cliff overlooking the lake. Below, the water was inky, reflecting only a sliver of moonlight.

Was he losing his mind? Was he crazy? Was she real or not?

How could he explain the emails, the very real emails, if she wasn't real? He clung to that piece of evidence, the only thing he could point to with any assurance. If it weren't for those emails, he'd have already surrendered the last threads of his sanity.

"She's real, goddamn it."

"Who's real?" Swanny asked. "Who are you talking about?"

"She's real and she's in trouble and I have no idea how to help her."

Helplessness and frustration swamped him. Overwhelmed him. What could he do?

He cupped his hand over his face and dug his fingers into the corners of his eyes. He squeezed the bridge of his nose as he concentrated on the mess he'd awakened to.

None of it made sense. He hadn't seen anything. Only sensed it and had an experience so bizarre that he'd swear he'd taken some bad acid trip.

"Look, just calm down. We can talk about this."

Nathan shook his head. "Just let it go, Swanny."

There was a pronounced silence and then Swanny shoved in front of him, obscuring Nathan's view of the lake. All he could see was the determination gleaming in his friend's eyes.

"I won't let it go," Swanny said in a low voice. "I came here for answers. I haven't pushed. But something happened in Afghanistan. Something I can't explain. Now you're talking crazy and mentioning this woman's name, the same name you screamed when we were rescued. Whether you want to talk about it or not, you put your hands on me and something happened. I wasn't going to make it out of there. I knew it. You knew it. But then you did something. I'll never forget that feeling. Like sunshine warming me from the inside out. And the pain. Gone. I could breathe again. It was so damn peaceful that for a minute I thought it was the end."

Nathan looked up at the sky, closed his eyes and breathed out as his shoulders sagged.

"You played it off, man. And I let you. But you know you fed me a line of bullshit. Angels, God. Yeah, maybe, but you know more than you're letting on."

"I don't know! I wish to hell I did," Nathan bit out.

He balled his fist in frustration and pressed it to his forehead.

"Maybe I'm crazy. Maybe we both are."

"I'm perfectly okay with that explanation," Swanny said calmly. "But we aren't. Now stop holding out on me."

Nathan stumbled back toward the sleeping bag, sat down and pulled his knees to his chest. Beside him, Swanny crawled into his and stretched out on his side. For a long time, Nathan just sat there, staring into the distance. The silence was brooding, but Swanny waited. He just lay there and watched Nathan, waiting for him to speak.

"Her name is Shea," he said quietly. He wasn't betraying her because Swanny had already heard him calling her name on more than one occasion.

"Yeah, I gathered that much. The question is who is she and . . . well . . . who is she?"

"I don't know."

Swanny sighed and rolled to his back to stare up at the sky. "Has anyone ever told you what a frustrating son of a bitch you are, Nate?"

"I thought I imagined her. Right up until the time she emailed my brothers to let them know where to find us."

"How the hell did she do that? There weren't any women that I saw in that hellhole."

"That's just it. She wasn't . . . there. She was here," Nathan said, tapping the side of his head. "She talked to me in my head. I don't even know where she was."

Swanny turned back to his side and stared at Nathan, mouth agape. "You mean like psychic shit?"

"Well, she wasn't telling me my future," Nathan said dryly. "She's telepathic and she can . . ."

"She can what?"

"She took my pain away. Took it on herself. And when I was tortured, she took that too. She suffered. I hated it."

"Holy fuck," Swanny breathed. "You're serious?"

Nathan nodded even though he wasn't sure Swanny could see.

"That's some freaky-ass shit, man. You didn't imagine it? Like as a coping mechanism?"

Nathan made a dry sound of amusement. "I would have said absolutely yes except for the very real email that my brother received telling him exactly what I told Shea to tell him."

Swanny went silent. For a long while he lay there motionless as if grappling with whether or not to believe Nathan.

"Where is she now?" he finally asked.

"I don't know," Nathan muttered. "She was in trouble. She wouldn't say much. She was too determined to shield me from pain and get me the hell out of there. She was afraid, though. I could feel her fear. I felt it tonight."

"Damn."

"Yeah."

"What are you going to do?"

Nathan leaned back and pulled the sleeping bag around him as he settled down once more. "I don't know. What can I do? I know nothing about her. Just her name, and she begged me not to tell anyone about her. If I tell what I know, I could endanger her. I don't know enough to find her."

"That's fucked up."

"You don't think I'm batshit crazy?"

"Nah. In a weird way it makes total sense. I have no idea how it's possible. Maybe we're both crazy. But I know what I felt. I know that whatever she did, she saved us both. Instead of spending time worrying that I lost my marbles, I'm just going to be damned grateful she did what she did."

Nathan chuckled. "You certainly have a way with words, Swanny. The hell of it is you make complete sense."

"I do that every once in a while."

Nathan laughed again, and some of the tension seeped from his bones, leaving him exhausted and barely able to remain awake.

He relaxed and closed his eyes, but he was haunted by the music of her voice and memory of her warmth and gentle touch.

I'll find you, Shea. Somehow, someway, we're going to meet again. Even if it's just in my mind.

CHAPTER 12

THE tie was choking him and it already hung loose around his collar. He hadn't been inside the high school gymnasium more than five minutes when his skin started to itch and his airway was constricted.

Outside, a gentle rain fell, preventing the commencement ceremonies from being held in the stadium. So Nathan was trapped inside a stifling hot gym with several hundred other people.

His mom tugged him toward the seats that Sam and Sophie had saved for the family. It was actually an entire section where the Kellys had gathered along with "extended" family and friends.

Swanny was sitting this one out. That and the huge family celebration that would be held at Nathan's parents' house afterward. He still wasn't comfortable being around so many people. The scar on his face drew a lot of stares, some much bolder than others.

On the way up the bleachers, Nathan was treated to several hugs, exclamations, slaps on the back and welcoming smiles. Hometown hero and all that shit. He felt like a huge fraud.

Getting captured by the enemy didn't make him a god-damn hero.

He tugged at his tie some more until the knot rested well below the collar line and then he unbuttoned the top button. Feeling like he could breathe again, he took the seat next to his mom and smiled acknowledgments at the rest of the family. He didn't miss their looks of surprise at his presence, since none of them had invited him. Only Rusty had. They'd assumed he wouldn't come.

Joe was sitting toward the end, bouncing Charlotte on his knee. When he saw Nathan, he stood and handed the baby back to Sophie and maneuvered his way down to sit by Nathan.

"Hey, man. Didn't expect to see you here."

"Rusty wanted me to come," Nathan returned.

"We all did. I'm glad you came."

Nathan nodded, not knowing what more to say.

"You look like shit, man."

Nathan frowned and turned to look at his twin. Obviously Joe didn't suffer the same affliction of not knowing what to say.

"When was the last time you slept? You were looking good when Swanny first got here. You were smiling and joking again. Now you look like you haven't slept in a week and are about to freak out being closed in with all these people."

Nathan shrugged. He couldn't deny either assertion.

"What's going on with you, Nathan? I keep waiting for you to snap out of it. I get that what happened was bad. But you're not getting better. In fact, I swear you look worse now than you did three months ago."

Though Joe sounded frustrated, his words were tinged with worry. A worry that Nathan saw reflected in his family's eyes every time they looked his way.

"This isn't the place," Nathan said in a low voice.

"No, it's not. But where is? I can't talk to you. You're always working on that damn house, and if I come out and try to talk to you, you just hammer those goddamn nails and ignore me or you answer in one or two words. You've shut me out just like you've shut the rest of the family out. I'm not just one of your brothers, Nathan. I'm your twin."

Nathan's jaw ticked and he turned to stare at his brother. "What do you want from me?"

Joe's eyes narrowed and he leaned in closer. "I want you to start acting like a goddamn human being instead of a fucking corpse. You didn't die but you're determined to act like you did. I get that this fucked you up. I get it, okay? But it's frustrating as hell to watch you slip further and further away. At least talk to me—someone—and let us know how to help."

Nathan glanced down the bleachers to see the rest of his family discreetly and not so discreetly watching the interchange between him and Joe. Then he turned back to his brother.

"Look, man—"

He was interrupted by the request to rise for the Pledge of Allegiance and the National Anthem. As he rose, his mom slipped her hand in his and squeezed. Just a reminder that she loved him. God, he loved her too. He glanced at the rest of his family—his brothers—standing with their wives. Van next to Sophie, holding Charlotte, as the last words of "The Star-Spangled Banner" faded. Seth, the sheriff's deputy and honorary member of the Kelly family. Garrett next to his fiancée, Sarah, his expression content as she nestled against his side.

This was as ordinary as it got. Just another family gathering. The very thing he'd prayed so hard for when he'd been in captivity. Just another chance to see his family. Just be.

He smiled, and when the seniors made their entrance, his smile grew larger. He squeezed his mom's hand back and then pulled his hand from her grasp and wrapped his arm around her.

"I love you, Ma," he said close to her ear.

She turned and smiled. "I love you too, baby."

The joy and relief in her eyes were crushing. He wasn't the only one suffering. Logically he knew that. Had known it all along. But maybe he hadn't known just *how* much his family had suffered since his return—and before—when they had no idea if he was alive or dead.

He would be better. He absolutely would work not to close himself off from his family as much. But first . . . First he had to make peace with the issue of Shea.

FRANK Kelly had the huge barbeque pit out and the mouth-watering scent of hickory filtered through the air. In the sprawling backyard, shaded by oak trees, people laughed, talked and joked. The rain had long since stopped, and the sun had peeked from behind the clouds.

Rusty was enjoying being the center of attention—positively this time. It hadn't always been the case in her young life. Nathan knew she'd worked hard to overcome the circumstances of her childhood. She'd found a home with a family who loved and accepted her.

He watched as she carted Charlotte around, accepting congratulations and hugs from the family as well as the number of family friends Marlene had summoned for the occasion.

Everyone looked happy. Content. Enjoying the day and celebrating a rite of passage for a girl on the brink of adulthood. It should be a fucking perfect day, but here he was, on the outside, worrying about Shea. An invisible, probably imaginary manifestation of his tortured mind.

Except those goddamn emails.

He shook his head. He couldn't forget her. His life would be easier if he could. He could move on, work out his issues, enjoy being with his family, go to work with his brothers. Enjoy life and living.

But he couldn't forget her or all she'd done for him. He owed her a debt he could never repay.

"Nathan. How's it going?"

Nathan turned to see Donovan approaching, a beer in each hand. He held one out to Nathan as he came to a stop, and Nathan took it, but he didn't open it right away.

"Good," Nathan replied. "Nice day. Rusty's enjoying herself."

Donovan took a swallow of his drink and then glanced sideways at his brother. "So let's cut through the bullshit for a minute. I know everyone's dancing around you, afraid to say shit for hurting your feelings or whatever."

Nathan burst out laughing. "God, you sound so much like Garrett right now."

Donovan sent him a disgruntled look. "There's no need to get insulting."

Nathan chuckled again. "Just spit it out, Van. I'm not going to come apart at the seams."

"Well, thank God," Donovan muttered. "When are you going

to come to work with us? I'm recruiting a new team. I want you on it."

Blunt as ever. Donovan didn't much see the value in pussy-footing around a subject. He tended to have more tact than Garrett, who gave new meaning to the term *bull in a china closet*, but it didn't mean he was any less forceful in getting his opinion across.

"Why isn't Joe on the new team?" Nathan asked, avoiding the more direct question of when he'd agree to join KGI.

"He's training with Rio, but I don't have any intention of leaving him there. The last thing I want is to send my brother off to parts unknown with Rio and his cave dwellers the minute I finally get him home for good. Ma would have a kitten anyway, and I'd likely be ostracized from the family. Since I don't have a wife to cook for me yet, staying in Ma's good graces is kind of important."

Nathan grinned. "You pussy."

Donovan shrugged, took another drink and then turned his gaze back on Nathan. "So? What are your plans? I'll understand if you don't want to join KGI, but you can't just not do anything for the rest of your life. You and Joe could take this third team, but I have to know you're both ready for it."

Nathan sighed and finally opened his beer just to have something to do. It was tasteless on his tongue, but he swallowed eagerly, stalling. For what? More time? In some ways he hadn't had nearly enough. In other ways he'd had far too much.

"You know I planned to join KGI. We talked about it."

Donovan nodded. "Yeah, we did. When you and Joe got out. But that was before. I don't know much about what you're thinking these days at all."

"My plans haven't changed. Just delayed a little."

"Okay, that's fair enough. Got a time frame on your delay?"

Nathan's mouth quirked up. Right now Donovan sounded like a pushy, heartless son of a bitch. His brothers had probably argued over who got to come over for this little come-to-Jesus moment. Garrett would have wanted the task. Sam would have said hell no. For all Sam's anal hard-assedness, he wouldn't have wanted to push Nathan too hard. He took his responsibilities as the oldest Kelly brother way too seriously, and as a result, he tended to get a little carried away with the idea he had to take care of his younger siblings.

Donovan would have gotten disgusted with Sam's and Garrett's bickering and told them what morons they were right before coming over to do the dirty work himself.

"No time line. There's just something I have to do before I can commit," Nathan finally said.

Donovan's brow went up. "Like what?"

Nathan lifted one shoulder. "Just something I need to take care of."

"Anything I should know about?"

Code word for can I help.

"No. It's personal. Something I have to put to rest before I can give a hundred percent of myself to KGI."

"Fair enough. But don't take too long, Nathan. We worry about you. I'm only going to be able to keep Sam and Garrett off your ass for so long."

Nathan grinned. "I figured as much. You're so self-sacrificing, man. You hit me right here." He put his fist to his chest in a dramatic gesture.

Donovan flipped him off and then snatched the beer can out of Nathan's hand. "If you're going to be so goddamn rude, you can get your own beer."

Nathan lunged for Donovan's hand, but Donovan raised the beer over his head. Nathan laughed and reached up to grab Donovan's wrist.

"You're not tall enough to pull off that move, big brother."

"Fuck you," Donovan said rudely. "I may not be as tall as the rest of you Neanderthals but I can still take you down."

With a challenge laid down like that, there was no way Nathan could let it go. The two brothers went down, laughing and cursing as each wrestled for advantage over the other.

While such activity might ordinarily get them into trouble with Mama Kelly, she looked relieved to see her sons conducting business as usual. Frank grinned from his position at the grill, and Rusty let out a whoop that could be heard across the yard.

Their brothers gathered around, grinning like fools, while Nathan and Donovan rolled in the grass like two ten-year-olds.

Nathan flipped Donovan over his head and then rolled to his knees about the time Donovan caught him in a scissor lock. Nathan broke the hold and dove on top of Donovan, determined to pin him.

Donovan was smaller, but he was also a damn good fighter. Nathan didn't really expect to get the better of him, but it sure felt good to let off some steam.

One of Donovan's muscled arms snaked around Nathan's neck, and Donovan twisted so he was atop Nathan, holding the head lock while Nathan wheezed for breath.

Suddenly Nathan was disoriented. His surroundings blurred and spun, but not as bad as they had several nights earlier. There was a vague sense of mugginess, heaviness dragging at his limbs, but his mind was sharper this time.

Nathan.

He went completely still, his brother atop him, holding his arm around his neck.

Nathan, are you there? Please, be there. I need you.

Nathan started struggling, and when Donovan resisted, Nathan started throwing punches, kicking, pulling, anything to get loose of Donovan's hold.

He was dizzy, and fear and panic overwhelmed him. *Her* panic and fear.

I'm here, Shea! Don't go. I'm here. Talk to me. Don't leave.

"What the fuck is wrong with you?" Donovan burst out when Nathan almost connected with a right hook.

Ignoring his brother's bewildered demand, Nathan slung off the concerned touch of another of his brothers and broke away, his only thought to get as far away from everyone as he could.

When Sam stepped in front of him, Nathan curled his fingers into Sam's shirt and shoved him out of the way. Sam's eyes widened at the sheer strength it took for Nathan to toss him aside like he was a child.

"Leave him alone," Garrett barked when Ethan would have made a grab for Nathan. "Just back off."

Nathan took only enough time to shoot Garrett a grateful look before he all but ran to his truck. Quiet. He needed quiet. He needed a place he could concentrate. It would take everything he had, but this was important. Shea needed him. She was frightened, and now he realized it was her disorientation he felt. Her dizziness. Something was horribly wrong.

Hang on, Shea. Just hang on.

As he spun out of the driveway, his gaze briefly connected with his family, all standing and staring, their faces drawn in deep concern. And hopelessness.

CHAPTER 13

SHEA. *I'm here. Talk to me, baby.*

Shea nearly sobbed her relief but she had to focus. She didn't have much time, and telepathy took so much out of her. Energy she couldn't spare.

She had to keep running. They would be after her. And she was weak. So very weak.

Nathan.

Yes, baby, I'm here. Talk to me now. Tell me what's wrong.

His gentle words were infused with strength. But more than strength, confidence. His voice told her that he'd protect her. She'd be safe with him. She hadn't been wrong to reach out to him, to trust him.

I need your help.

You have to know I'd do anything at all for you. Tell me how and I'll come for you.

She splashed across a bubbling creek, her bare feet slipping on the muddy bank when she reached the other side. She put one hand down to break her fall but then pushed herself upright again and plunged deeper into the forest.

I escaped. They found me. Drugged me. They want Grace. Had to pretend to be weaker and more drugged than I was. When they moved me, I escaped, but oh God, they're coming after me. They won't rest until they get me back. I need your help, Nathan. Please.

She felt the strength of his will like a bolt of caffeine. His mind sharpened. Anger and then determination coursed through his consciousness.

Listen to me, Shea. Slow down and think. Get your breath and focus for me. Your instinct is to run, kill yourself getting out. You're probably making enough noise to wake the dead and you're leaving signs all over the place. Tracking you will be child's play. Even if you manage to elude them, they'll find you eventually.

She came to an abrupt halt, and then despair sagged her shoulders. Who was she kidding? He was right. Finding her would be easy. She didn't have a chance.

No! he reprimanded sharply. *That's bullshit, Shea. You're not a sitting duck. I'm going to tell you everything you need to know to make damn sure you escape.*

She swallowed and cocked her ear to the distance, straining to hear if they had drawn closer.

Tell me everything you can about where you are. Do you know? Is the terrain flat? Hilly? Are you in the mountains?

She inhaled sharply. The tang of salt danced through her nostrils. Mixed in was the scent of pine. A breeze ruffled her hair and she turned in the direction of the wind.

I'm facing the ocean. It's not far. There are lots of redwoods. Big ones. The forest is thick, but the floor isn't snarled and overgrown.

Okay, listen to me. Head toward the ocean. Where were you last? Where did they find you?

Shea began picking her way through the trees, following the direction of the wind blowing off the water. *I was in California. I was planning to head north, farther up the coast. But they found me. They kept me in my own hotel room for several days. Then when they moved me, I escaped. I'm . . . I'm not sure where I am now. They drugged me. So much is fuzzy.*

You're doing fine, he soothed. *Keep moving. From the description you gave, I'd say you're still in Northern California or maybe even Southern Oregon. I'm coming, Shea. As fast as I can get there. But I need you to keep yourself safe until I find you. You have to protect yourself until I get there, okay?*

She nodded grimly and then echoed her agreement through their link. Where would they expect her to go? She pushed ahead, hurrying, but taking greater care not to disturb the vegetation around her. Nathan's presence calmed her. His steady reassurance made some of the panic fade, and she was able to think more rationally.

And then fear skittered up her spine again and gripped her throat until she could barely draw a breath. *Nathan. I hear them. They're close!*

Find a place to hide. Get there and hunker down. Don't make a sound. No movement. Let them go by you.

She glanced frantically around, her gaze finally lighting on a huge redwood in the distance with a twisted, massive trunk that had a hollowed-out opening.

She lunged forward, going as quietly as she could, all but flying across the distance. *Oh please, oh please, let there be a place to hide.*

The tree towered over her. The base was broad and the roots extended in all directions, huge and steadying. She slid into the narrow opening, sucking in her breath, praying she would fit.

It was tight and only adrenaline gave her the strength to shove her way inside the opening in the tree. She sank back as far as she could, embracing the darkness. Things she couldn't bear thinking about flickered across her skin. Flies, insects, creepy-ass bugs. God only knew what else shared the interior of the trunk with her. It was all she could do not to shriek as something slid down her neck and back.

Through it all Nathan hadn't said a word, but she felt his presence, knew he was there, waiting patiently, not wanting to distract her from her goal. When she finally managed to calm herself down enough that she wouldn't risk giving herself away, she reached back out to Nathan.

I'm inside a tree. A really big tree full of really creepy things.

Better them than the men after you.

True. I don't hear them yet. I'm not sure what direction they went.

Just sit tight. Be very still. No sound. Do not panic. They might move right by you, but if you don't move, they won't find you. No matter what, you have to control your panic.

She leaned her head against the inside of the tree and flinched when she felt something crawl through her hair. It took every ounce of her discipline to remain so still when she wanted to bolt.

And then she froze. There was a sound not very far away. The creak of a stick breaking. Leaves rustling. And then even closer. Hurried footsteps.

She held her breath as sweat rolled down the sides of her neck. Her heart pounded so hard against her chest wall that she was sure it was an audible sound. She began to shake and cursed her lack of self-control.

Easy now. Be calm. I'm with you. Let them go by you. It won't be long now.

She closed her eyes as the noises got even closer. So close that they could only be a few feet away. Her pulse raced as she waited to hear the sounds retreat as they got farther away.

But they stopped.

She crammed herself as far back into that tree as she could go, pressing against the rough surface in an effort to stop the ridiculous shaking.

They were out there. Just a few feet away. Did they know she was here? Were they preparing to pull her out?

"She couldn't have gotten far. She was stoned on the drugs we gave her. She's probably wandering around in circles."

One of the other men made a sound of disagreement. "She played you, fool. She's probably already made it into town. We have to get there immediately before she can disappear again."

Shea held her breath again until black dots swam in her vision and her chest burned. As the sounds of them hurrying away reached her ears, she slowly let out her breath and then slumped against the tree in relief.

Wait it out. It could be a trap. Nathan's soft warning slipped into her mind. *Just stay there a few minutes. Listen for any sounds. When you crawl out, head the opposite direction they went. Then turn west to the ocean again. Be careful, Shea.*

She stayed there like he directed, because she was afraid to move. She was terrified that if she left the safety of her hiding place, they'd be waiting for her. She closed her eyes, wanting, needing the rest. Holding Nathan to her was exhausting.

Get moving, Shea.

She jumped, startled by the sudden intrusion into her mind. She hadn't realized she'd kept him so tightly bound to her. She'd thought he was slipping away, but he was there, as strong as ever, as if he were the one holding the connection and not her.

Come on, I need you moving. We need to get you someplace you're safe and well protected.

She pushed herself from the interior of the tree, desperately trying to ignore the exhaustion creeping through her veins. Holding her breath, she slipped from the confines of her hiding place and glanced frantically in all directions for her pursuers.

Not seeing or hearing them, she turned and hurried in the opposite direction.

Impressions from Nathan confused her. He was thinking about a jet and flight plans, how his family was going to worry and think he'd finally, truly gone over the edge. But the overriding thought that bombarded her on every level was his determination to get to her. To protect her.

That gave her the strength to forge ahead.

After thirty minutes of keeping up an exhausting pace, she came to an abrupt halt. She strained to hear. Faint but it was there. The sound of the ocean. And then a vehicle, louder and closer.

Nathan, I'm close to the highway or at least a roadway. And the ocean. I can hear it.

Okay, I don't want you on the highway. I don't want you visible. You can parallel it and follow it into a town. You need to be in a place where they wouldn't have such an easy time coming after you. But you also have to stay low.

She didn't offer that she had no money, no identification. Nothing. Everything she had was in her pursuers' hands. Anxiety ate at her. She worried for Grace. Worried that she would be unable to maintain the block that would prevent Grace from sensing the danger that Shea was in. If Grace knew, if she even suspected, she'd swoop in like an avenging angel and then they'd have her. Shea wouldn't allow it.

She topped a slight rise and there was the highway, curving around the edge of the ocean. She picked up her pace, careful to remain beyond the cover of the trees as she followed the highway north.

Traffic increased the farther north she walked. She was beyond exhaustion and had no recollection of the miles she'd already traveled. She concentrated on putting one foot in front of the other and remaining upright.

Then in the distance she saw a road sign and her breathing sped up. Finally she would be able to tell where she was. Something to tell Nathan. He could come for her.

Her pulse rocketed and she broke into a near run, her focus on being able to read that sign.

She nearly tripped over a fallen log and stumbled to regain her footing. Finally she was close enough to see the sign.

Crescent City city limits.

Crescent City, she said to Nathan. *I'm in Crescent City, California.*

Already on my way, baby. Find a place, lie low. I'll be there as fast as I can.

CHAPTER 14

"WE'VE got a serious problem," Sam said.

The Kelly family was gathered in the living room of Marlene and Frank's home. Marlene wrung her hands repeatedly despite Frank trying his best to calm her.

Ethan sat between Rachel and Sophie while Sarah stood across the room next to Garrett. Donovan and Joe were positioned by the fireplace, arms crossed over their chests, and Swanny stood alone, bewilderment and worry etched into his tired features.

Marlene had tried to foist baby Charlotte onto Rusty so the teenager would be removed from the conversation, but Rusty had flatly refused to leave the room. She was upset and thought that her inviting Nathan to her graduation had prompted his meltdown.

They all looked to Sam for information, but he wasn't sure they were prepared for this.

"Nathan took off in one of the Kelly jets an hour ago."

Not surprisingly, the entire room erupted in chaos. Donovan put two fingers to his mouth and emitted a shrill whistle then he held up his arms for quiet.

"What do you mean took off? As in had the pilot fly him somewhere?"

Sam shook his head, knowing Donovan already suspected what Sam was about to say. "No, he flew himself."

"Christ," Garrett muttered.

Joe swore. "What the fuck is he thinking?"

"Do we know where he went?" Ethan asked.

Sam ran a hand through his hair. Fuck, but he was tired. "He filed flight plans for Crescent City, California. Is that where he'll end up? Who knows? Who the hell knows what he's thinking right now? Anyone have any idea what's in Crescent City?"

"This is crazy," Joe said. "I thought . . . Hell, I don't know what I thought. One minute he and Van are laughing and horsing around. The next, he's on a plane to Crescent City? I think it's time the gloves come off. He obviously needs help beyond whatever self-healing bullshit he's attempting."

"Cut him some slack. He's fighting for what's left of his sanity," Swanny cut in.

Everyone turned to Swanny in surprise. He was a man of few words. Sam couldn't remember him ever willingly volunteering information. He was a "speak only when spoken to" person and sometimes not even then.

Donovan's arms dropped and he stepped forward, his focus solely on Swanny. "Do you know something, Swanny? One of the last things Nathan said to me was that before he could commit to KGI he had to do something. He wouldn't tell me what. Clammed up tight when I pressed. Next thing I know, he freaks out and hops a jet to California?"

Swanny lowered his head and grasped the back of his neck. He looked indecisive, as if he wasn't sure whether to betray his loyalty to Nathan. Sam understood that. He did. But fuck it. Nathan was his brother and he needed help whether the stubborn son of a bitch wanted it or not.

"Tell us, Swanny. Whatever you know. Now isn't the time to hold out. Nathan could be in trouble. We aren't going to let him go off half-cocked."

Swanny stared up at Sam. "You don't understand. How could you? We were in the worst sort of hell. We weren't living day to day or even hour to hour. We survived minute by excruciating minute. The next day was an eternity away and we didn't want it. Death wasn't the enemy. It was our salvation.

Our hope. Because only then would we be able to escape our reality."

Sam's gut clenched. His mom let out a soft cry of distress and turned her face into Frank's chest. Tears glimmered in Rusty's eyes and Rachel looked haunted by past demons. Demons Nathan had firsthand knowledge of now.

Garrett's and Ethan's expressions were grim. Every member of the family was pained by the heart-wrenching words that faltered from Swanny's lips.

Sam knew Nathan had suffered. Maybe he'd never know the extent or what Nathan had been chipped away to by the animals who held him. But he knew his brother suffered because he saw the pain and the isolation in Nathan's eyes every single day since his return.

"Is there more, Swanny?" Donovan asked in a quiet voice.

Swanny looked agonized. His jaw clenched and he glanced at all of Nathan's family, member by member, as if weighing whether or not to tell.

Sam took a step toward the man who meant so much to Nathan. Whom Nathan had protected, demanded that he be tended to before Nathan himself.

"Swanny, we want to help him, but we can't if we don't know everything. You aren't betraying him. You have to know that."

"I could be condemning him in your eyes," Swanny said gruffly.

"Never," Garrett ground out. "I don't care what you tell us. He's our brother. That doesn't change just because he's been changed."

To Sam's surprise, Rachel rose from the couch where she sat with Ethan. Her eyes were troubled and her hands shook as she stepped toward Swanny. Then she touched his arm, her expression understanding.

"It's about her, isn't it?"

Relief swamped over Swanny's face. He all but sagged. "He talked to you about her?"

There was hope in his voice that if Nathan had shared whatever it was with Rachel, then it wasn't solely Swanny's burden to keep his secrets.

Rachel nodded. "He said she talked to him. That she sent Donovan the email telling him where to find you and Nathan."

Donovan's head shot up, and he was about to explode with questions, but Sam flung his hand out to silence his brother, his expression fierce. Donovan's lips tightened but he settled back and didn't interrupt.

"Did he . . . Did he tell you everything?" Swanny hedged.

"I'm sure he didn't. He was very closed-mouthed about it all. But you aren't betraying him, Swanny. No more than I betray him by relating all he told me. We're his family and we love him. We only want to help. Not condemn. It doesn't matter to us what's happened, or whether he thinks he's crazy. We know he's not. But he needs our help."

Sweet, loving Rachel. It was like watching beauty tame a wild beast.

"Swanny, whatever it is you tell us, we're not going to condemn, judge or otherwise decide anything about Nathan other than we want to make damn sure he's safe and has the help he needs," Sam said. He eyeballed his brothers, making sure they understood the implied command.

"Her name is Shea," Swanny finally said. "I know nothing about her other than she talked to Nathan while we were held captive. According to Nathan, she took his pain for him. She even endured a torture session, shielding it and taking it for him. Don't ask me how. I don't know. It all sounds like bullshit, right? But Nathan took more torture than any of us. They worked harder on him. And when they finally decided they couldn't break him, they used him to try to break me. Only Nathan got us out of there. I was injured. I was bleeding internally. I couldn't breathe and I knew I was going to get us both killed. I asked him to leave me. He put his hands on me, and I swear to God, he did something to heal me."

The looks on his brothers' faces ranged from incredulity, to doubt, to "What is this dude smoking?" Sam shook his head in warning again. Hell yeah, it sounded crazy. He couldn't even wrap his head around it. But the important thing was that Nathan believed it. Swanny believed it. And now Nathan had gone off after his imaginary woman?

"He thinks she's in trouble. He's had episodes . . . Weird shit. Like maybe she was trying to talk to him again. I think it's what happened today, what pushed him over the edge. I don't know, but I'd bet everything I own that he's gone to Crescent City because he thinks that's where Shea is."

"Oh Jesus," Joe muttered. "This can't be good."

"What will you do, Sam?" Marlene asked.

He glanced at his mom and dad, saw the worry in their eyes, the helplessness that they couldn't seem to get through to Nathan.

He dragged in a breath because his first instinct was to take all the manpower KGI had behind it, haul ass to Crescent City and take care of business. As much as he wanted to do it, and knew it was what his brothers wanted to, he knew it wasn't what they should do. And it was killing him.

"What did Nathan say to you exactly, Van?" Sam asked. "Earlier when you talked to him about KGI."

"He said he had every intention of joining but that there was something he had to do—on his own—before he could commit. I tried to offer help. I tried to pry it out of him. He wasn't giving details."

Christ, but this was complicated. He wouldn't send Garrett. Garrett would want to go, would insist on going. But he should stay behind with Sarah. The two had already sacrificed much in deference to Nathan. Sam wasn't going to drag Garrett away now, especially when he had no idea what they were in for.

He glanced up at Rachel. Rachel, who seemed to know exactly what Sam grappled with. Her gaze was determined. Direct. It told him to send Ethan. It demanded that he send Ethan.

She would want the best for Nathan. She'd been very protective of him since he'd come back, and maybe it was good for Rachel to have someone to protect, since she still needed so much shielding herself.

"I think Ethan and Van should go," Sam finally said. It pissed him off to stand down from this one, but how could he convince Garrett to stay if he wasn't willing to do it himself?

"Wait just a goddamn minute," Joe exploded. "I'm not staying here. Fuck that."

"Joe!" Marlene reprimanded. Her scowl was fierce as she stared her younger son down.

"Sorry, Ma," he mumbled. "But it *is* bullshit and Sam knows it. I don't need his permission to go after my brother."

For once, Garrett was the voice of reason.

"I think Sam's right," Garrett said. "I think Ethan and Van should go and the rest of us should stay here. They'll call us in if it turns out to be something they need us for. Joe, right now Nathan doesn't need you on his back. I get what you're trying to do. I get that you're frustrated. I know you and Nathan are closer than the rest of us are. But that added pressure isn't going to help Nathan. It's just going to push him further away and isolate him all the more. Let Ethan and Van check it out and report back. Then we'll make a decision as to whether anything further should be done."

"He's not crazy!" Rusty burst out. "If he says he talked to this woman, I believe him. He wouldn't make up something like that."

Marlene pulled her into her arms. "No one thinks he's crazy, baby. We're all worried about him. That's all. And we want to help. Ethan and Donovan will handle it right."

Swanny looked up at Sam, determination gleaming in the shadowed depths. "I know I'm not part of your team, but I want to go. I need to do this for him. He refused to leave me. I'm not going to leave him."

Sam glanced at Donovan, and Donovan nodded.

"Okay, you're in, Swanny. Right now, you're the only one Nathan's talking to, so maybe you can figure out what the hell is going on."

CHAPTER 15

IT was pitch black when Nathan landed. The sky was overcast.
No stars. No moon. There was a murkiness to the air that left
him uneasy and stirred his panic.

He was impatient with the time it took to square away
paperwork and make sure the jet was adequately hangared.
His cell phone was buzzing his leg off. Missed calls, current
calls, texts and voice mails from his family.

He ignored them all but knew he had to tell them something. He picked up his phone as he jogged toward the parking
lot, where the rental was supposed to be waiting. He didn't
want to get involved in a conversation because there was no
way it could end well.

So he sent a text to Joe.

*I'm okay. Don't worry. Keep family off my back. I need to
do this. Be in touch soon.*

As soon as he hit Send, he shut off the phone and tossed his
pack into the jeep.

He'd tried to plan for any eventuality in the few minutes he
had to gather his wits and hit the road. But his one thought
was to get to Shea, however he had to do it.

He took a moment to reach into his pack, retrieve his pistol and make sure his clip was loaded. He pulled out the assault rifle, popped in the magazine and then laid it on the seat. He shoved the Glock into the shoulder harness and did a quick inventory of his supplies.

He had no idea what he was up against, but he was prepared for damn near anything.

Automatically he reached for Shea. They hadn't communicated much during the flight. She needed to rest and regain her strength, but he'd checked in periodically, always afraid that she'd simply be gone.

Shea. I'm here, baby. I'm not far. Where are you?

He felt her stir as though she'd been asleep. He felt her grogginess and then her sudden fear and self-condemnation that she'd allowed herself to drift off. He ached to hold her and to ease her fear, just as she'd once done for him.

I'm in a culvert. She struggled to clear her mind of the cobwebs. *There's a drainage ditch just past the sign saying two miles from the city limits. I hid there.*

Sit tight. Don't move a muscle until I get there.

Nathan roared down the highway, the headlights bouncing erratically off the landscape. He kept at the speed limit because he couldn't afford to be pulled over with a freaking arsenal in the jeep.

He was traveling in reverse of the way Shea had come in and as a result he passed over the culvert before he realized it. Swearing, he executed a sharp U-turn and spun back around. His headlights flashed over the sign Shea had referenced and he slowed to a crawl until he saw the deep drainage ditch cutting under the road.

His heart nearly stopped as he pulled onto the shoulder. His palms went slick on the steering wheel. His pulse raced so hard he was light-headed.

Just a few feet away was Shea. The woman—the angel—who'd invaded his mind. All his doubts surfaced, but all he had to do was open his door and get out. He would have his proof, and until now he'd had no idea how badly he wanted her to be real.

He needed her.

Needed to touch her. Needed to hold her. Needed to keep her safe.

He grabbed his flashlight, his gun, and scrambled out of the jeep. His feet skidded along the gravel and then he headed down the sharp incline.

"Shea?"

It felt weird to be speaking to her aloud. Her name came out hoarse and unsure. His grip tightened around his pistol when he heard a slight sound from within the culvert.

He shone the light inside as he raised the gun. He was met by wide, frightened eyes. His heart damn near exploded out of his chest. She was real. It was *her*.

"Shea, it's me, Nathan."

She raised her arm to shield her eyes from the light, and he yanked it down so the culvert would be illuminated but she wouldn't be blinded.

She tried to push herself upward, but she fell and bumped her head on the side of the culvert. He shoved the gun back into the holster then crawled inside, ducking low, and when he reached her, he did what he'd been dying to do from the moment she first slipped into his mind.

He grabbed her into his arms and molded her tight against his chest. She let out a small sigh and melted into his embrace, her body so soft and warm against him.

"You came," she whispered. "You came."

"I'd never leave you alone."

He stroked her hair and tried to calm his racing heart. She was real. She was here in his arms. He couldn't even take it all in.

Remembering where they were and that he needed to get her to a safer place, he carefully eased backward, putting enough distance between them that he could take her hand.

"Come on, baby. Let's get you out of here."

She gripped his hand, her fingers digging into his palm. She clung to him like he was her lifeline, but in fact she was his. He eased out of the culvert, one hand holding hers, the other cupped over her head to keep her from hitting it on the way out.

Once outside, she eased upward on unsteady feet. He quickly shone the flashlight beam over her to check for injuries. He frowned when he got to her feet. Her bare, scraped-up, bruised feet.

With a muttered curse, he pocketed the flashlight and then swung her into his arms to carry her up the incline to the jeep.

She didn't make a sound the entire way. She laid her head on his chest and burrowed into his hold. She clutched his shoulder like she was afraid he'd disappear.

He put her down long enough to throw his gear in the back and then he put her into the passenger seat, securing the seat belt around her. For a moment he stood staring down at her, awed by the fact that she was in front of him. Real. Tangible. Not in his head.

Her blond hair was bedraggled and lay limply against her head. Her blue eyes were dull with fatigue. She was dirty and disheveled, and he'd never seen a more beautiful woman in his life.

He reached out to softly caress her cheek, unable to resist the opportunity to touch her once more. She closed her eyes and slid her cheek over his palm as if she found as much pleasure in his touch as he did in touching her.

The sound of a distant car dragged him abruptly back to awareness. He slammed her door shut and bolted around to the driver's side. He pulled onto the highway seconds later and directed the jeep into the town of Crescent City.

He felt her gaze on him as he entered the city limits. He glanced sideways to see her staring at him. Did she know how affected he was by her? How gutted he was to finally be face-to-face with her?

"I can't believe you're here," she said softly, a thread of wonder in her voice. "I've imagined it so many times. I'm half afraid I'll wake up and this will all be a dream."

He lifted his hand and touched the side of her hair before running his finger over her cheekbone. "I was right. You are an angel."

She smiled faintly, but then her lips turned down into a troubled frown and the lights from passing streetlamps highlighted the shadows in her eyes.

"I'm afraid, Nathan."

"Shhh, baby. I'm going to take care of you. Just like you took care of me. First thing we're going to do is get the hell out of town. Go north. Put some miles between us and the assholes after you. We can't take the jet yet. It won't be ready, and

I want to stay away from the airport until we're ready to fly out of here. For now we'll get a place to stay so you can clean up and I can make sure you aren't hurt."

Her relief was palpable. Her entire body shook and she leaned back, resting her head against the seat. "Thank you. I was so scared. I knew I wouldn't make it alone and I don't know whom I can trust."

"You can trust *me*."

She nodded tiredly. "I know. I know."

"We have a long drive. I don't want to stop until we're well away from here. Tell me what I need to know while I drive. I'm sure we have a lot of . . . questions. About each other. About this . . . connection. But for now, let's put that aside so we can focus on the most important thing. Your safety."

She nodded again and then surprised him by reaching for his hand. She laced her fingers with his and let their hands rest on the seat beside her.

"I've been running from them for a year," she said quietly. "They killed my parents. They want me and my sister, Grace. But especially Grace."

"Okay, why do they want Grace so badly?"

Shea sucked in a breath. "She can heal people. Really heal people. I can take their pain but I can't fix them. Grace can. It was she who helped me help your friend when you were escaping."

He narrowed his eyes at her. "I'm not sure I get the difference. You take pain. You take on the wound. How is that not healing?"

She sighed and rubbed her head tiredly. "It's different. I know it all sounds crazy, but I can draw pain away from an individual. I even seemingly absorb the wound. But I don't really. It's temporary. Even the pain I take is temporary because after a while, it comes back. Because I don't heal them. I'm like a Band-Aid. A temporary fix. When it's all said and done, the affliction remains. You know like when you were . . . h-hurt . . ."

She drifted off momentarily, her face haunted by the memory of what he'd endured.

"When you were hurt, I took your pain but I didn't heal your injuries. You still bear the scars. You had the cuts, you bled. What I did for you was temporary. What Grace does isn't temporary. She actually heals the person. She takes the wound or illness, siphons it away like I do with pain and it's like they never had an injury or were sick. Like she did for Swanny. She did for him what I couldn't do for you," she said painfully.

If he hadn't already been exposed to all Shea could do, he would have said bullshit. But he'd experienced firsthand that healing ability. He'd thought Shea had done it. Swanny knew it too. He knew something had saved him.

"The problem is, healing comes at a great cost to Grace, which is why she has to be so careful. It's hard on her because she's so tenderhearted. She can't stand to see people suffer. She'd help them all if she could. But it would kill her. And so she tries to stay away from people as much as she can because she can't refuse anyone."

Nathan frowned. "Did helping Swanny hurt her? What happens exactly?"

"I wouldn't let her help him for long. Just enough that he could move again. But yes, it hurt her. Just like I take the wound or the pain of someone I'm connected to, she takes the actual illness or injury."

"But wait a minute, you take the injury too. I felt your pain, Shea. I could feel those cuts on you. I smelled your blood, goddamn it."

"It's different. I know it sounds far-fetched. Ridiculous even. In some ways I have it far better than Grace. The wounds do appear on me. I feel the pain. But it doesn't last long. They appear and then they fade. For the time they're present, they are very much real. I bleed, hurt, feel it as though it happened in real time, as if someone stood over me with a knife. But then they go away. With Grace, she takes on the injury or the illness, and her body processes it differently. At a much slower rate. She heals the wound itself, and so it takes her much longer to rid herself of the injury. She could die doing what she does. If she gets overloaded. If she does too much, her body could shut down and she wouldn't recover. We simply don't know and I'm afraid to risk her."

"Where is she now?"

Shea's mouth quivered and she picked up her other hand to wipe at her eyes. "I don't know. It's complicated. We can speak to each other. Like you and I did. But I don't because I can pick up things through the link. I can see things. The surroundings. It's possible I'd know where she is and I knew if I was ever caught that they'd try to get information from me in any way they could. So I closed myself off from her because I couldn't very well give them information I didn't have."

Nathan's blood ran cold. "What did they do to you, Shea?"

"It doesn't matter," she said wearily.

"The hell it doesn't!"

"It's over and done with. I escaped. Now you came. I'm safe."

"What did they do?" he ground out.

"They drugged me. They interrogated me. They wanted to know how to find Grace. I didn't know, so I couldn't tell them. Grace is safe. That's all that's important."

Nathan swore under his breath. She wasn't telling him the whole story. The idea of some bastard torturing her for information made him physically ill. She'd already endured far too much for him when he'd been in captivity.

"Do you know who they are?" Nathan asked. "Do you know anything about them at all?"

Her fingers tightened around his. "Grace was doing some investigating, but I begged her to stop. We can't take the chance. I suspect it's a government agency or group simply because they seem so well funded. They've dogged my steps for the last year. I move frequently. I never stay in the same place for long. Just long enough to earn enough money to keep running. The longest was two months in Kansas City, but they caught up to me there as well. I've tried to be methodical. I've tried to be unpredictable, but I swear I'm becoming predictable in my unpredictability. I'm so tired, Nathan. I don't know what to do anymore. I don't know how much longer I can keep evading them."

The hopelessness in her voice made Nathan's gut tighten. "You're not alone anymore, Shea. You have me now. I'm not going to let those bastards hurt you. We'll figure this out. Together."

She squeezed his hand again. Tears shone in her eyes, reflected in the glow of the dashboard. "Thank you."

He squeezed back. "No. Thank *you*, baby. I got to see my family again because of you."

CHAPTER 16

NATHAN pulled into the lot of a small motel just as the sky was starting to lighten to the east. They had driven through the night, stopping only long enough to get food and water for Shea. He'd wanted to examine her for injuries, but she'd insisted they keep going. She had just dozed off a half hour before, and he hated to wake her, but he didn't want to leave her unprotected for the time he needed to arrange the room. Neither did he want her to be seen by anyone who could identify her to her pursuers. Which meant she needed to be awake and prepared for anything.

He gently shook her. Her eyes popped open and she stared around in a near panic before her gaze settled on him. Then she sagged into the seat in relief.

He palmed his Glock and then extended it to her, stock first.

"Know how to use this?"

She took it without hesitation, chambered a bullet and then thumbed the safety. Guess that answered his question.

"I'll be right back. Watch out. Only shoot if you have to."

She nodded, but her attention was already focused away from him and on the area surrounding the parking lot.

Nathan hurried in, paid for a room and then went back out for Shea. He'd purposely scoped a motel with rooms that opened on the outside so that Shea would never have to travel through the lobby.

Before he allowed her out of the jeep, he draped one of his fleece jackets around her and pulled the hood over her hair.

"Can you walk?" he murmured. Carrying her would gain too much notice.

She swung around, and it was then he remembered her bare feet. With a curse, he rummaged in his bag and pulled out a pair of his socks.

He slipped them on and then helped her down. He handed her the key and said, "Go on ahead. I'll get the bags."

She glanced at the number on the tag and then walked in the direction of the door sporting the same number. Nathan watched her walk away in his socks, absurdly captivated by the image.

He grabbed his bags, locked up the jeep and then headed for the room. The door was left slightly ajar, and he pushed it open with his foot. As he shouldered his way in, he saw Shea sitting on the edge of the bed.

She looked up and their gazes locked. He dropped the bags to the floor, kicked the door shut with his foot and then strode over to where she sat.

She stood at the same moment he reached her, and he crushed her into his arms. She wrapped her arms around his waist and held on just as tightly as he held her.

He inhaled her scent, uncaring of the blood and dirt and grime that permeated her hair and clothing. He was holding her. Finally holding her.

"You're real. You're real."

She pulled away, looked up at him, the same answering emotion shining in her blue eyes. With a groan, he lowered his mouth to hers. He couldn't hold back. Nothing in the world would have kept him from kissing her in that moment.

He was overcome.

Her mouth, sweet and warm, melted against his. He'd never felt something so completely right in his life. As if everything had worked up to this moment.

She felt small and delicate in his arms. She quivered even

as she kissed him back, her lips moving in a slow, sensual slide across his.

He was wrecked. Completely and utterly wrecked.

He gripped her shoulders and pulled away, his legs weak and shaky. He should be caring for her. Seeing to her needs. But he couldn't keep his hands from her. The need to touch her, to reassure himself that she was finally . . . his.

Yes, his. And not finally. She'd been his from the moment she'd touched his mind. Perhaps it was why he'd gone crazy when she left him. It was like having a part of his soul ripped out. The months since had been a torture of a different kind. But now she was here. In the flesh. Not just in his mind. And he'd be damned if he'd let her go again.

"We need to get you cleaned up, baby. Let me go turn on the shower so it'll warm up then we'll get you out of these clothes. I want to see how bad it is."

She stirred, a protest forming on her lips. "I'm okay, Nathan. Really."

"I want to see that for myself."

His tone brooked no argument and finally she nodded, her shoulders slumping in defeat. He left her long enough to turn on the shower and then he came back where she still stood by the bed.

"Do you need my help?"

Slowly she shook her head. "Let me get cleaned up first, Nathan. It looks worse than it is right now. There's no sense you getting worked up. After I shower, you can see."

He frowned. It was likely the opposite was true. It was worse than he thought, and she wanted time to clean up to try to make it look better.

"I'll be waiting when you get out," he murmured. "I have a first aid kit in the jeep. I'll get it while you're in the bathroom."

SHEA stood under the spray, eyes closed, her brow creased in pain. She'd scrubbed the blood and dirt from her body, but there was nothing she could do about the bruises.

Her legs shook uncontrollably. She'd barely been able to soap her hair because her hands quaked so violently. Reaction had set in and she was a hot mess.

Falling apart.

The horror of the last days hit her like a ton of bricks. She should be jubilant. She should be relieved. She was free. She was safe. Nathan was with her. He'd protect her.

Instead, tears rolled down her cheeks and her knees threatened to give out. She covered her face and tried to control the sobs that bubbled from her chest.

Strong arms came around her. The water turned off, and she stood dripping wet and hiccupping as sob after sob escaped.

Nathan pulled away long enough to wrap a towel around her shaking body and then he lifted her into his arms.

"It's okay, baby," he murmured against her forehead. "You're safe now. I've got you."

He set her on the bed then pulled the blanket around her. He kissed her temple. The top of her head. He rained kisses down on her face. Her eyes. Her cheeks.

She turned her face into his neck and burrowed into his warmth. And his strength.

For the longest time he merely held her as silent sobs spilled from her chest. He caressed her hair, ran his hand down her blanket-covered body and simply sat in silence while he waited for her to collect herself.

She loved that he didn't seem to fall apart at her distress. Or that he didn't demand to know what was wrong so he could fix it. He acted like he understood.

When her sobs diminished to soft puffs of air and the shaking ceased, he pulled her carefully away from his body and stared down into her eyes.

Without a word, without asking permission, he slid the covers down her arms, baring her flesh to his sharp gaze.

Though there was nothing sexual in his assessment, she was achingly aware that his gaze tracked over her naked body.

He pulled at the towel, his hands gentle and nonthreatening. He touched every bruise, his expression fierce. His fingers brushed over the cuts and scrapes she'd collected in her flight through the forest.

The more he discovered, the blacker his expression became. Then he turned her and sucked in his breath at the jagged cut on her thigh.

He grasped her arms and turned her back to meet the fury in his eyes.

"What the hell did they do to you, Shea? And don't tell me nothing."

She closed her eyes against the sudden burn of tears. Damn it, she'd only just managed to stop crying and now she was weepy again. A mess. An emotional mess.

"They wanted me to tell them about Grace," she choked out. "I refused. You can guess the rest."

He cupped her jaw and feathered his thumb across her cheek and then her lips. "Tell me."

"They beat me, okay? They held me down and they meted out a very calculated, unemotional beating meant to break me. When that didn't work, they refused to give me water or food and then they beat me again."

Tears streaked down her cheeks. Nathan's face had whitened. His eyes looked tortured, dark and frightfully cold. His hand shook on her face and he looked very much like she felt.

"And the cut on your leg? How did you get it?"

She glanced down and her stomach revolted as the memory of what she'd done came back with startling clarity. Pain snaked down her leg, phantom pain, as if she were enduring the knife slicing her skin all over again.

"They implanted a tracking device. When I escaped, I knew I had to cut it out so they couldn't find me so easily."

"Son of a bitch!" he cried hoarsely. "My God, Shea."

To her shock, his eyes glittered with tears and grief. For her. She swallowed painfully, overcome at the emotion that shone on his face.

"My God, baby, what you went through. It makes me sick. You've already been through so much for me. Why didn't you call for me before now? I could have helped you. There was no need for you to have gone through any of this. I would have helped you. You have to know that."

She turned her face so that her lips brushed over his palm. She cupped her hand over his and kissed the rough skin. Then she trailed her hand up his arm, crossing over the scars that marred the once smooth flesh.

She touched every one and glanced up at him to see his reaction. He looked sick, like he wanted to pull away from her. She could tell he didn't want her touching him, drawing attention to the scars that crisscrossed his body. How many more were there that she hadn't yet seen?

"You had already endured more than any human should ever endure," she said softly. "You needed time to heal. To go home and be with your family again. You needed to learn to live again, to want to live. I couldn't ask you to help me when you needed so much more than I did."

He flinched when she put her fingers to the scar on the side of his neck. He tried to turn away, but she levered herself up and cupped her hand over the puckered flesh.

"Don't hide from me, Nathan. Don't hide your scars from me. I more than anyone know how you received them. They aren't ugly. They're beautiful. Honorable. Signs of courage and of unflagging determination."

He caught her hand and slid it down his neck to his shoulder before holding it there firmly in place. Then he leaned until his forehead touched hers and their lips were tantalizingly close.

"How is it possible that you're more beautiful in person than you were as an angel in my mind when I was in that hell. I didn't think it was possible and yet here you are, so fucking exquisite that I can't even talk around the damn knot in my throat."

He pulled the towel all the way from her body and then laid her gently back on the bed. He touched every bruise and then, to her shock, he put his mouth to one. Then another. He pressed gentle kisses to every hurt, to every ache.

Chill bumps raced across her skin, puckering her nipples into tight points. Her heart constricted as he moved meticulously down her body, lavishing sweet loving attention on her wounds.

It was a delicious mixture of arousal and emotional fulfillment. It wasn't overtly sexual, but it didn't mean she wasn't achingly aware of his every touch.

She'd never felt so cared for in her life.

"Beautiful. So beautiful," he whispered. "Mine."

She shivered at the quiet vow. His. Yes, she was his. He was hers. That decision had been made the moment she'd first heard his call.

When he got to the cut on her thigh, he pulled back and hauled the first aid kit from the floor onto the bed. With a touch so light she barely felt it, he cleaned and dressed the wound. After he finished taping the bandage, he lifted her just enough to lay her on the pillows and then he pulled the blankets to cover her naked body.

He bent down and kissed her forehead. "Get some sleep, Shea. You're exhausted and you're going to need your strength."

"Where are you going?" she asked fearfully.

He kissed her again. "I'm not leaving you. I'll be back. I just need to take care of a few things. We'll both get some rest and we'll travel tonight when the chances of you being spotted are fewer."

CHAPTER 17

NATHAN paced the confines of the motel room, occasionally glancing at the bed where Shea slept. He was about to crawl out of his skin. She lay still, curled into a ball as if she were trying to protect herself even in sleep.

That was his job now. She was no longer going to go it alone. It pissed him off that she'd been alone for as long as she had.

He had to think. Shea feared discovery above all else, and she'd absolutely be against him calling in his family. But how could he not? He had no idea what he was facing, and his priority was keeping her safe no matter how he had to do it.

The logical thing to do would be to call his brothers for help. They couldn't very well think him crazy now if he produced a real live woman.

The irrational part of him didn't want to share Shea with anyone. He wanted her with him. He needed her. He didn't want to have to deal with intrusions, and his brothers would most certainly be intrusive.

But he couldn't do this alone. If it were just him in danger, he'd face it head on and kick some ass. But he didn't want Shea exposed or hurt in any way. She'd suffered enough, and it was high time someone took care of her like she seemed to take care of the world around her.

He checked all his weapons, laid a knife on the nightstand beside his Glock. Then he propped a chair underneath the doorknob. Afterward he dragged the small table over to the window so that no one would have clear entry into the room.

Shea was probably starving. She hadn't eaten much before when he'd grabbed a sandwich from a convenience store deli. She'd picked at it while they drove. When she woke, he'd make sure she ate better. Then they'd talk about their next move and his desire to call in his brothers. Hell, he'd just put her on the jet and fly back home. How better to protect her than to have her right in the middle of all the Kellys?

He rubbed his face. But he couldn't do that to his family. He couldn't just open them up to an unknown enemy. Nor could he expose Shea and her abilities to so many others, even if he trusted them more than anyone else.

He'd call Sam. He'd know what to do. Just as soon as he talked it over with Shea. They needed help. She couldn't dispute that.

He glanced toward her again, his vision fuzzing with fatigue. There was nothing else for him to do until she woke up, and if he didn't get any sleep, he wasn't going to be any good to her.

He dug into his bag for a clean pair of boxers and a T-shirt. Then after another look in her direction to make sure she was still sleeping, he turned his back to undress.

He quickly shed his clothing and pulled on the clean boxers. He picked up the new T-shirt to pull it on, when he heard a sound from the bed.

He jerked around, still holding the shirt to his chest to see Shea staring at him with stricken eyes. Her gaze was riveted to the scars that covered his body.

Shame crowded in that she'd see him, his ugliness, his marks of weakness.

"I'm sorry," he said in a low voice. "I didn't think you were awake."

She shook her head. When he started to retreat to the bathroom, she held up her hand. "No. Don't go."

He stood a moment, the shirt clenched tight in his fists. "I don't want you to see."

She sat up, holding the sheet to her breasts. "See what,

Nathan? I've seen you at your worst. There's nothing you can show me that will shock me."

Her expression was so fierce, almost angry. He was rooted to the spot, unsure of what to do. Hit the bathroom? Hurry up and finish dressing? He felt exposed and he didn't like it one bit.

"Come here, Nathan," she said softly.

His brow furrowed.

"Please."

He hesitated but then walked toward the bed. He still held the shirt to his chest when he eased onto the edge beside her.

She leaned forward and the sheet slipped down enough that he caught a glimpse of the plump swells of her breasts. The dark imprint of her nipple tantalized him from underneath the thin sheet.

She tugged gently at his T-shirt until he reluctantly allowed her to pull it away. Then to his surprise, she let the sheet fall from her chest as she got to her knees and edged toward him.

Heat flushed through his body, tightening his groin. He couldn't quite breathe right. Nothing he did seemed to pull enough air into his lungs. Even bruised and fragile, she was the most beautiful thing he'd seen in his life. It took all his restraint not to pull her into his arms and make love to her.

It didn't matter that, until a few hours ago, he'd never actually seen her before. She went deeper than physical attraction. He wasn't even sure what he felt was physical. It was emotional. She belonged inside him. Deep. The kind of emotion you didn't ever get rid of.

He shivered when she placed her palms on his chest, right over two gnarled ridges of skin. To his further shock, she pushed until he was forced to recline on the bed. She hovered over him, her eyes glowing. Then she lowered her head and pressed her lips to a scar over his shoulder.

He sucked in his breath, shocked when she slid her mouth lower to the next scar, beside his collarbone. And then just as he'd kissed every bruise, every scrape and every hurt on her body, she kissed each of his scars.

He stared in wonder as she kissed the line next to his navel. Then she dropped lower, sliding off the bed to kneel so she could reach the scars on his legs.

When she reached his feet, she kissed the top of his foot, carefully tracing the puckered scar that curved to his toes.

Her touch was light and so tender that he ached. He had no idea how to respond to such unselfishness. There were no words that could have convinced him that she wasn't repulsed by his body. But her sweet, loving kisses convinced him when nothing else could.

"You don't repulse me, Nathan."

For a moment he'd forgotten that she could slide into and out of his mind. She would have sensed his doubt. His fear.

She crawled back onto the bed and knelt at his side, staring down at him as she slid her fingers over the scars on his belly and chest.

"How could you? Every scar is a testament to your strength and your will to live. They're beautiful. Like you."

Placing both hands on his chest, she leaned down. Their gazes locked, and he realized she meant to kiss him. Every part of his body and soul reached for her, strained for her, wanting her touch with a need that verged on obsession.

She licked her lips just before she pressed them to his. It was a little nervous gesture that melted his heart.

He reached up to frame her shoulders and he kissed her back, no longer bothering to hide the fact that he wanted her more than he wanted to breathe. He'd already pretty much given up breathing for her.

Their lips fused hotly. They fit. So goddamn perfect. Her body molded softly to his. Such a contradiction. Softness to his hardness. Smooth to his rough. Perfection against imperfection.

He wrapped his arms around her and slid his hands up her body. He massaged the plump globe of her behind while his other hand stroked up her spine and into the silk of her hair.

"If you had any idea how many nights I lay dreaming of this. Of you," he whispered hoarsely.

Her breasts pushed into his chest. Her nipples rubbed erotically through the smattering of hair and they puckered into hard points.

"I've dreamed of you too, Nathan. Of us. Like this. I feel like I've known you for so long. Like I've been waiting for this moment."

He wrapped one arm tightly around her and rolled until she was underneath him, his knee wedged between her thighs. Then he kissed her. Like he'd been wanting to from the moment he heard her voice again.

He devoured her mouth. Hungry. So damn hungry. She was a missing piece of himself and now he had her back. After he'd felt so damn empty for such a long time, the sudden sense of completion threatened to unhinge him.

"I have to make love to you, Shea."

It was a demand, a request and a plea all wrapped up in one simple statement.

She cupped his face in her hands and stared up at him, her eyes as hungry as his. "Yes, Nathan. Yes."

He claimed her mouth again as he settled between her thighs, his cock bursting through the material of his boxers. As badly as he wanted to bury himself as deep and as hard inside her as he could get, he forced himself to hold back. The last thing he wanted was to hurt her. This had to be perfect. As perfect as she was.

He kissed her neck, inhaling her scent, wanting it imprinted on his brain. He never wanted to forget how she smelled, how she felt in his arms, her body covered by his.

Then he slid his mouth down over her collarbone and lower to the satiny plumpness of her breasts. She sighed and arched into him when he claimed one of her nipples.

So velvety. Plush. He loved the feel of her in his mouth. Loved her taste and how she went so soft every time he sucked at the taut nub.

He ached to touch her but he hated to put his hands on the softest, most sensitive places of her body. She was fragile. His hands were rough. Fingers calloused. Scars on the back sides. The contrast of such ugliness to such beauty turned his stomach.

Her gaze softened and she reached down for his hands, bringing them to her breasts. She cupped his hands over the mounds and then rubbed her fingers up his arms to his shoulders.

"Touch me, Nathan. Make me yours. I want your hands on me. Your mouth. You're so perfect."

He shook his head. "Perfect? Hell, Shea, you're the perfect

one. So goddamn beautiful. Look at me. Really look at me. I look like some damn jigsaw puzzle. I look like fucking Frankenstein's monster and here I am acting like I have the right to touch you."

She rose up, curled her arms around his neck and pulled until their faces were just inches from each other. "I gave you the right. You're not a monster. I wouldn't care if you were. I think you're perfect. Just so perfect. You came for me. You saved me. You kissed me like I was the most precious thing in the world."

"You are," he whispered. "You're the most precious thing in *my* world."

"Then make love to me. I've waited so long."

He reached down to push his boxers away. He kicked impatiently at the material until it fell to the floor. She parted her thighs farther and slid her legs along his before wrapping her slender limbs around his.

His dick was so rigid that he groaned. It slid between her thighs, rubbing along her tender folds. He reached between them and gently parted her flesh. His thumb found her sweet heat as he positioned himself at her opening.

Ah hell, he didn't want to hurt her but he didn't know how much more he could take. He was dangerously close to his climax and he hadn't even gotten inside her yet. He felt clumsy and inept as a lover, and yet when he lifted his gaze, he found her looking at him as though he were the most desirable man in the world.

To see himself the way she saw him? He couldn't even wrap his brain around why she looked at him with her heart in her eyes, like he was . . . special. Like he belonged to her and she'd take on anyone who said differently.

"You won't hurt me, Nathan. You'd never hurt me."

He closed his eyes and slid deep into her. She gasped and quivered around him. For a moment he thought he had indeed hurt her, but when he opened his eyes, all he saw was pleasure and joy reflected in her beautiful eyes.

She grasped the sides of his face, her fingers lacing around to his nape. She rubbed her thumbs over his cheekbones and then pulled him down. Her lips fused with his. Hot and sweet.

He withdrew and then surged forward again, a groan escaping as her satiny heat closed around him, gripping him like a fist. She was unbelievably tight. So tight he couldn't imagine how she could accommodate him without it hurting.

Again he tried to control the raging instinct to power into her, to dominate, claim. His breath tore raggedly from his chest, burning as he clenched his jaw.

"Nathan."

His name, so sweetly said. She smiled up at him and caressed his face with gentle hands. He kissed her palm and closed his eyes as she clenched around his cock. Warm, wet and so damn exquisite that his eyes rolled back in his head.

She lifted her hips, taking the choice from him. Her movement sent him deeper, and she let out a moan that sent shivers of delight down his spine.

"Please, Nathan. I need you."

He could no more deny her than he could deny the overwhelming urge to claim her. He fastened his hands over her hips and began to thrust. With each push into her body, the more he lost of himself. The more he became hers.

She went slick around him, liquid silk. Her fingers dug into his shoulders as she lifted her hips to meet his every thrust. His fingers slid around to cup her buttocks and he helped her, lifting as he pushed and rode harder, deeper.

"Tell me you're close. Can't last much longer," he gasped.

Instead of answering him, she kissed him. Hot and breathless, her tongue licking over his. He was lost. So very lost.

He was spilling into her before he could even think to make sure she was with him. Mindlessly he thrust, each glide releasing more of himself into her. And through it all she touched him, caressed him, made soft sounds of acceptance and pleasure.

He slipped his fingers between them once more and found her heat. He thrust again as he stroked the taut nub of flesh. He wouldn't leave her until she'd gained as much pleasure as he had.

She cried out as he thrust again. And then again, all the while gently stroking her clitoris. She went hot and liquid around him in a rush. She strained upward, every muscle in her body rigid.

"That's it, baby. Come for me."

She writhed uncontrollably, her behind lifting from the

mattress. She cried out again and then touched his hand to stop his gentle manipulation. He withdrew and then lowered his body to hers and rolled to the side so he could hold her close.

She lay against him, naked, her limbs twined with his. Her chest rose and fell rapidly and her breath huffed out over his neck. And he thought that, in this moment, he'd never experienced something so perfect. So fucking beautiful that it made his teeth ache.

This wasn't sex. This was something so deeply emotional that he couldn't even find words to describe it. He'd missed her with every cell and now she was finally here. A part of him. Linked so intimately with him that nothing could come between them.

He stroked her back, enjoying the feel of her skin against his palms. Then he kissed and nuzzled her neck, just wanting to inhale her sweetness all over again.

"Did I hurt you?" God, don't let him have hurt her. He never should have pushed her into this, but he'd been helpless to stop it.

She kissed his shoulder and snuggled deeper into his embrace. "You were perfect, Nathan. So very perfect."

CHAPTER 18

PAIN splintered through Nathan, and he came awake with a gasp. For a moment he thought he was having another dream, reliving his captivity. But he felt it again, a thin blunt object smacking his flesh.

He made a grab for his arm and breathed away the sensation and in the process bumped into Shea's sleeping form. She lay beside him, curled into a protective ball, the sheets in a tangle at her feet.

She flinched and made a low sound of distress and it was then he realized it was she who was dreaming. She who was reliving her captivity, and he was still so closely linked to her that he felt everything she was experiencing.

His gut tightened in rage and his throat knotted at what she'd endured. His hands shook as he turned and pulled her into his arms.

"Shea. Baby, wake up."

When he got no response, he called to her with his mind.

Shea. I've got you. No one can hurt you now. Wake up and look at me. Feel me. I'm right here. I have you.

She came instantly awake. No gradual climb to consciousness. Her eyes flew open and her breath exploded from her lips in harsh puffs.

"Grace," she croaked.

Nathan frowned. "Grace?"

She scrambled to sit up in bed. Her hands shook. Her entire body shook. She raised her hands to wipe away her hair but then buried her face against her palms and rocked back and forth.

Distress radiated from her like a beacon. Her shoulders started to twitch and he realized with alarm that she was crying.

Her mind was a chaotic mess. He frowned at the images of her captors and then he saw a beautiful, dark-haired woman. Taller than Shea. Toned and tanned. Just as quickly as he caught the image, his mind went completely blank. Shea had slammed the link shut and closed herself off from him.

It stunned him how empty he suddenly felt. A surge of hurt followed by anger built before he could call it back. It felt like a betrayal. Like she didn't trust him.

The thoughts were irrational. But he couldn't turn them off no matter how much he thought she was justified in her caution.

He wasn't sure what he was supposed to do now. She shut him out so maybe she didn't want him prying. So he sat there, feeling like an idiot as she wept into her hands.

Then the decision was made for him. She turned and flung herself into his arms, holding him so tight that for a moment he couldn't breathe.

"I'm sorry," she choked out. "I didn't do it to hurt you."

He eased his arms around her and stroked her back, trying to comfort her.

"What the hell is going on?" he asked softly.

"I just didn't want you to see. It was so overwhelming and I couldn't shut it off, so I shut you off instead."

His hold tightened around her. "That's bullshit." He took another breath and tried a more tactful, sensitive approach. "You and I are quite a pair, aren't we, Shea?"

She pushed up to face him, her eyes drenched with sadness and shame. "What do you mean?"

He touched her cheek, his heart growing soft at the sight of her tears. "We both try to hide from the other and yet we have a more intimate connection than any two other people on the planet. You can't hide this from me any more than I can hide my scars from you. Why would you demand to see my shame and then hide yours from me?"

She sighed and then her lips turned up into a rueful half smile. "I knew it would upset you and I didn't want to be the cause of that."

He leaned forward and kissed her nose. "How about you let me decide what I want to be upset about? Damn right it upsets me. The idea of you in those bastards' hands makes me crazy. But it doesn't mean you're going to hide it from me to protect my fragile little psyche. Anything that involves you, I want to know about. Are we clear on that?"

She smiled. "Crystal clear."

"Good. Now come here."

He pulled her against him and kissed her hungrily. They'd just made love a few hours earlier and yet he still ached. His need for her defied logic. He couldn't explain it any more than he could fight it.

Already he was as hard as a rock, his dick straining upward, tenting the sheet that covered his thighs. He pushed impatiently at the covers, not wanting any barrier between them.

He settled her astride his thighs so that his erection rested against the blond curls that covered her tiny mound. She looked so damn sexy sitting atop him, her blond hair disheveled and falling over her shoulders. Her eyes were sweet and sleepy looking, but when he cupped her breasts, her pupils flared and her eyes went more black than blue.

He loved the feel of her plump breasts against his fingers. Small against his much larger hands. He rubbed his thumbs over her nipples, fascinated by the hardening nubs.

Unable to resist, he stroked over her shoulders, down her back then around the curve of her waist and then over her hips and underneath to her buttocks. He couldn't get enough of simply touching her.

She was the softest, most beautiful thing he'd ever touched. There was a reverence to his caresses. He didn't feel worthy to touch her but he wanted it more than anything.

She let out a sweet sigh as his hands coaxed back up her body to her breasts. She swayed atop him, her eyes closing as a dreamy smile glowed on her lips.

"Like that?" he murmured.

"Oh yes. I love to be touched."

"And I love touching you. I wonder if you even realize how much I've dreamed about this. Having you right here in front of me. Me holding you. Tasting you. So deep inside you that you realize we won't be apart again."

Chill bumps raced across her chest and shoulders. Her fingers tightened on his arms and her breathing sped up. Her pulse jumped in her neck, and as he pulled her closer, he could feel the rapid fire of her heartbeat against his chest.

"Inside you," he whispered. "Deep. Hard. Over and over."

Her breathing became shallower and her eyes glazed. She licked her lips, which were already swollen from being ravaged by his. The image of her mouth around his cock exploded into his mind. Sweat broke out on his forehead, and he had to work to keep from ejaculating all over her belly.

Smooth. Real damn smooth.

She smiled then. A wicked little smile that should have been a warning but he was too dumbstruck over having her naked and in his arms, her luscious breasts pressed tightly to his chest.

Carefully she pushed away, leaning down to kiss a scar across his chest. She swiped her tongue over the puckered flesh, and he groaned both in protest and sheer pleasure. She wasn't the only one who liked to be touched. He could sit here for hours if only she'd put her hands on him and caress him, pet him, touch him. Just touch him.

She placed both palms at his shoulders and then glided downward, stroking and petting, not missing an inch of his flesh as she wandered down his body.

When she got to his groin, his cock got even harder, and he hadn't thought it was possible. He was about to split apart at the seams. Moisture beaded at the tip of his erection, and if he so much as moved, he was going to come.

And then she stuck her tongue to the base and licked all the way from bottom to top.

He bolted upward, his ass coming off the bed and tightening so hard that his muscles screamed in protest.

"Oh shit. Shit. Shea, baby, stop. Just for a minute. Oh God, I'm going to come."

She smiled and carefully wrapped her fingers around his

cock before licking just the tip. His fluid gleamed on her tongue and then she closed her lips over the head and carefully lowered, taking him entirely into her mouth.

Ah hell, she'd been in his mind. Of course that was it. She saw what he'd fantasized about. Guilt crowded in. She was only giving him what she knew he wanted. He felt selfish and about two inches tall.

Stop thinking so much, Nathan. Just relax and enjoy it. I love pleasing you. I love that you want me so much.

So beautiful. So damn beautiful and sweet. Your mouth, Shea. My God, your mouth. I've never felt anything so good.

She smiled around his erection and continued her sensual assault on his senses. He threw back his head as his orgasm roared through him like a freight train.

He raised his hips, wanting deeper, desperate for her silken heat. Harder and deeper. He slid over her tongue, butting against the softness of her throat. And she took him all, never complaining, never pulling back.

Desperation clutched at him. Pleasure, razor sharp, almost pain. Faster. Harder.

His mind went completely and utterly blank. And then it was filled with her. Only her. Her face. Her smile. Her angel's voice. Her scent. She rushed through him like she'd been injected into his veins. It was heady. He was drunk. Drunk on her.

He gasped aloud when the first jet of semen hit the back of her throat. He worried that he'd appalled her, that he'd gone too far. He should have had more restraint. He never should have taken it this far or allowed it to happen.

He felt the warm squeeze of her mouth around him, felt her drink of him and swallow as she continued to suck him deep.

He had no defense against her. None. He didn't want any. He was hers. Absolutely hers.

She laid her head against his thigh and let him slide from her mouth. Her hair spread out over his lap and her sleepy blue eyes were trained on him, watching him as he gathered his shattered senses about him.

He was gut shot.

She trailed one fingertip over his lessening erection, captured a drop of semen and then tucked her finger into her mouth, licking the tip.

His body roared to life. His cock jumped and hardened. Lust powered through his veins, shocking him with its ferocity. How the hell could he want her again so quickly?

Need grabbed him by the balls and had a choke hold on his dick. He hauled her up and then rolled her beneath him, his body already straining toward her, wanting to bury himself inside her sweetness.

Dear God, what she did to him. He felt like some kind of superhuman. Not bound by normal limits. All he knew was that he had to have her. Had to brand her, possess her, make her his.

He slid into her welcoming body, felt her gasp of pleasure and of acceptance. He stared down into her eyes, willing her to see what he saw, that she was his. That no one would ever take her away from him again.

This time would be for her. He wanted to give her back the pleasure she'd so selflessly given to him.

Touch me, Nathan. Let me feel you. Love you touching me.

The words floated erotically through his mind. Oh yes, he'd give her what she wanted.

He began a gentle exploration of every inch of her body. No part of her was left untouched as he caressed, petted, kissed and licked his way up and down her skin.

He eased out of her when he went lower, and then when he worked his way back up, he thrust into her again, keeping himself a part of her as much as he could while he lavished affection on her.

The sensual haze in her mind was seductive and alluring, like the most potent aphrodisiac. He could sense what he did to her and it made him feel ten feet tall. This gorgeous, delicate woman enjoyed his touch. Craved his touch. Beauty and the beast. It was so appropriate.

He was scarred and ugly. She was perfect and beautiful. And yet she looked at him with wonder. Thought of him as her hero. Wanted him to love her. And he did. God, he did.

His body arched over hers, covering her protectively even as he pumped in and out of her body. He tried to hold back his strength, afraid of hurting her, but she was having none of that.

She urged him on, whispering in his mind to take her, own her. Until he stroked in and out, mindlessly, pleasure consuming him and her.

He felt her orgasm as soon as it crept over her. Her entire body tightened around him, gripping him and holding him as he thrust deeper.

Only when she relaxed and melted into his arms, her breathing hard and ragged, did he allow himself to fall over the edge once more.

She held him, murmuring against his ear, stroking his back and just hugging him close as he emptied himself deep inside her body. And afterward, she held him there, refusing to let him move, though he feared he was too heavy for her.

But she held him tight, so he settled down over her, molding to her flesh and pressing her into the mattress. She let out a contented sigh and nuzzled her face against his chest.

Finally he moved to the side, pulling out of her warm clasp. He arranged her just so because he couldn't bear to be separated from her yet. Then he kissed the top of her head and squeezed her tight.

Shea lay in Nathan's arms and let calm blanket her. She felt protected. She felt safe.

It hadn't even crossed her mind that the whole situation was bizarre. That she'd for all practical purposes just met this man a few hours before and she'd had sex with him the same day.

She'd known him so much longer. She'd lived in his mind. He'd lived in hers. They'd experienced more together than any other couple ever would.

She turned into the crook of his neck and kissed the pulse point. He responded by pulling her tighter into his arms and caressing her bottom with one large hand.

She sighed. She loved his touch. Loved *how* he touched her and the way he looked at her.

"I didn't use anything. Either time. I'm sorry, Shea. It was stupid and irresponsible of me."

There was clear aggravation in his voice. And regret.

She smiled against his chest. "I don't care."

"But I should have protected you better. Are you on anything? Is the timing right for you to get pregnant? I don't have any diseases, I swear. I haven't had sex in a damn long time."

She squeezed him and kissed his collarbone. "I know. We're fine, Nathan. I'm on birth control and I'm safe too."

"I'll buy condoms," he said gruffly.

She smiled again. He wasn't even attempting to say that they wouldn't have sex again. No remorse. No regret for what they'd shared.

It was clear in his tone that he had every intention of making love to her at every opportunity. An assumption she didn't mind at all.

"If you do, fine. But if you don't, I'm perfectly okay with not using them. I'd actually prefer not to. With anyone else, I'd insist. But you aren't just anyone. I hope you know that, Nathan. I've never felt this . . . this connection to anyone else."

He went quiet for several long moments. She could feel the thud of his heart as his mind worked through a tangle of thoughts.

"Then why did you leave me after my brothers came for me in Afghanistan?"

The quietly voiced question made her heart squeeze. How he must have felt abandoned. It had killed her to go so silent, but she hadn't any more to give.

She wrapped her arms tighter around him, wanting to ease the gruff hurt in his tone. "I had to. I was too weak. Maintaining the connection for as long as I did had rendered me helpless."

"Was I the reason they caught you? Were you too weak to escape because of all you did for me?"

She heard the snarl in his voice. He was angry that he could be at fault. She shook her head. "No, Nathan. They didn't catch me until much later. I moved frequently. I changed my hair color often. Blond to red, back to blond. Brunette, dark and light brown, back to blond. I even wore colored contacts. I tried to change vehicles as often as I could, but I was running out of money and I was scared to hold a job for too long in the same location, which meant keeping the same car. It was how they found me. They tracked me to California. They ran my car off the road, knocked me out, and when I regained consciousness, I was in the hotel room I'd rented."

He stiffened and then kissed the top of her head as he continued to stroke her body. "How long was it before you escaped?"

"I don't know," she said honestly. "What day is it today?"

"June first."

She couldn't conceal her sound of dismay.

"What?" Nathan demanded.

"I was with them over a week," she whispered.

He cursed and buried his face in her hair. "You should have called for me immediately."

"I tried. I did. They drugged me. They kept me drugged. They would allow me to become lucid only for short intervals so they could question me."

"I want to kill those sons of bitches."

"So do I," she murmured. "Grace isn't safe. They'll step up their efforts to find us both now that I've escaped."

"I don't want you to worry, baby. We'll work this out, okay? Right now I need for you to know you're safe and that I'm going to protect you."

She nodded again. He leaned away and kissed her forehead. "It's getting close to dark. I'll need to go out and get us something to eat. I'm not leaving you alone, so that means you ride with me. I wanted to wait until dark so the chances of you being spotted were fewer."

"And then? What do we do then?" she asked anxiously.

He settled her against the pillows and then swung his legs over the side of the bed, reaching for the boxers and T-shirt he'd discarded hours earlier.

"We need to talk about our options."

It was the way he said it that made her go tense. Almost as if he knew she may not agree with his plan.

"Okay, what *are* our options?"

He hesitated a moment and then turned his head to her. "Let's get you something to eat and then we'll talk."

She sat up and pushed her hair from her face. She didn't have a thing to wear and she wasn't putting on the same pair of ripped-up, stinky, dirty clothes she'd run all over California and Oregon in.

When she put her plight to Nathan, he frowned as if he hadn't considered the issue of clothing. He rummaged in his bag for a moment and then pulled out a pair of sweatpants that looked at least a foot too long for her and a pullover white T-shirt that looked like it hit the bottom of her knees.

She wouldn't win any beauty contests, but they would work until she get could get something else to wear.

As she pulled on the clothing, Nathan stashed his gear into his bag and removed the chair from the door. He did a quick check of the room to make sure they weren't leaving anything and then he stood by the bed waiting for her to finish.

"Aren't we coming back?" she asked, wondering why he'd left nothing in the room.

He nodded. "We'll come back so you can eat and we can make plans, but if someone comes in here while we're gone, I don't want anything to point them to you, and I damn sure don't want to clue them in that I'm in the mix. It works to our advantage for them to still think you're alone and helpless."

She scowled. "I wasn't helpless."

He grinned. "No, baby, you aren't helpless. That wasn't what I meant."

He watched her pull on the pair of socks he'd given her and frowned. "I'll get you some clothes and shoes as soon as I'm able."

She nodded her agreement and then stood, wincing when she put her weight on her soles.

"Wait here," he ordered.

He took the bags, walked out the door and shut it behind him. A moment later he returned empty-handed and motioned her over. He turned around and gestured for her to climb onto his back.

Touched that he'd noticed how sore her feet were, she hopped up on his back. He hooked his arms underneath her knees and hoisted her higher. He kicked open the door and carried her out to the jeep.

When he got to her side, he turned around so she could climb in without her feet ever touching the ground. Then he hurried around to the driver's side to get in.

"What do you feel like eating?" he asked as he drove out of the parking lot.

She shrugged. "I don't care. Whatever's quick and convenient. I'm so hungry, I could eat just about anything."

On the edge of town, he found a sub shop with a drive-in so he pulled in to order. Since Shea wasn't picky, she just let him order whatever. It didn't matter what it tasted like. She just wanted something in her stomach.

He got several bottles of water, for which she was grateful. She downed the first before they ever got out of the parking lot. The sandwich she'd wait for until they were back at the motel.

"I got you two," he said. "You can eat one now if you want."

Well, since he put it that way. She dove into the sandwich like a rabid predator eating a kill. She didn't look in Nathan's direction, sure he was probably appalled. By the time they got back to the motel, she'd already devoured the entire sandwich and was eyeing the next.

This time, she slid out of the jeep before Nathan could come around. Yeah, her feet hurt like hell, but he wasn't going to be able to carry her everywhere, so she had to suck it up and deal. The quicker she worked out any pain and was able to move on her own, the better off they'd both be.

He frowned but didn't protest. However, when she started toward the door of the motel room, he lifted her off her feet and turned, putting her behind him.

"Stay here until I check it out."

"Yeah, good idea. Sorry."

Again, he thrust his Glock into her hand, but not before pushing her back toward the jeep so she'd be hidden from sight. Then she waited patiently while he went into the motel room. After a moment he came back out, took the gun and led her inside.

She settled on the bed and opened the second sandwich. He sat closer to the headboard and began eating his food. Halfway through her sandwich, her stomach rebelled at the overstuffed sensation, and she reluctantly wrapped the rest back up. She still felt desperately hungry even being overbearingly full.

Shea, are you there?

She dropped her sandwich and came instantly to attention.

Grace! Where are you? Are you all right?

I've been doing some searching.

The shaky edge in Grace's voice unnerved Shea. Fear scuttled up her spine and whispered around her ears. Shea shut her eyes and concentrated fiercely on keeping any thoughts as to what she endured from her sister. She'd warn her, most definitely, but the last thing she wanted was for Grace to relive the horrors Shea had gone through. When she opened them again, she breathed through her nose and focused solely on the link between her and Grace.

Nathan had put down his sandwich at the first sign of Shea's change in demeanor. He leaned forward, his expression fierce. "What is it, Shea? What's going on?"

She held up her hand to silence him even as she reached more fully out to Grace. For the first time she actively fixed her attention on Grace's surroundings, looking for anything to tell her where her sister might be.

Tell me where you are, Grace. Things have changed. I'll come for you. Just tell me where you are.

Grace was too distracted by something else. She didn't even act like she heard Shea.

Shit, someone's here.

Who's there? Grace, talk to me, damn it. Are you in danger? You have to be careful. They found me. They'll find you. You can't stay out in the open. I can help you now. Just tell me where you are.

There was no response from her sister. It was as if she hadn't heard Shea's frantic warning. But Shea could feel the awful fear radiating from Grace. It slammed into her, pushing all the air from her lungs.

They weren't our parents, Shea. I've got to get out of here. I'll reach you later.

And then Grace was gone. The link went black and so silent that it was suffocating.

Grace! Where are you? Damn it, Grace, talk to me! What did you mean they weren't our parents? Who's there? Are you in danger?

Shea dropped her face into her hands and rocked back and forth as nothing but the awful silence filled her mind.

CHAPTER 19

NATHAN pried Shea's hands from her face and forced her to look up at him. "What's wrong, Shea? Talk to me. What the hell is going on?"

"Grace," she croaked out. "Oh God, Nathan. I think Grace is in trouble. No, she *is* in trouble. She's scared out of her mind."

"Did she talk to you? What did she tell you?"

Her eyes were wide with panic and her lips trembled.

"Calm down, baby," he said in a low voice. "Breathe. Just take a few deep breaths and steady yourself."

Her brow furrowed and she frowned. "She said they weren't our parents. What could that possibly mean?"

"Is that all? Think, Shea. What else did she say?"

"She said she was doing some searching. Then she said that someone was there. Then the part about them not being our parents and she had to go."

"Okay, let's back up. Where is there? Where was she?"

She made a sharp sound of frustration. "I don't know! She didn't say!"

Nathan smoothed his hands up her arms and squeezed her shoulders. "You said that you wouldn't communicate with her in the past because you were afraid you'd see her surroundings. Did you see anything this time? Think about it. Go back over it in your mind."

Shea closed her eyes, her brow drawn in concentration. He could feel the tension radiating from her in waves. Then her eyes flew open, her lips parting in a gasp.

"Nathan, she was at our house! In our living room! Oh my God, she went back."

"Did you sense anything else? Did you see who was there? Did you pick up any impressions from her?"

Shea shook her head, her lips twisted into a grimace. "She was afraid. Startled. Nathan, we have to go there. She could be in serious trouble. What if they have her?"

"Whoa, wait a minute. I'm not putting you into the open. And I'm damn sure not letting you go back to a place you've already been hunted. They killed your parents, Shea."

"We have to get there," she argued. "It's not too far. Up the coast north of Lincoln City."

Nathan pinched the bridge of his nose between his fingers. "You're telling me that the place you lived, the place where some assholes murdered your parents and you fled for your life, is only a few hours from here? Mind telling me what the hell you're doing so close to the area they almost got you in the first place?"

Shea shot him a quelling look. "I've been all over the damn country in the last year. I've tried to be unpredictable. I'd hoped that this was the last place they'd think to look for me. When I first made connection with you, I was in the Midwest."

"That's damn well where you should have stayed," he growled. "Or at least as far away from here as you could."

She huffed impatiently, pushed him aside and rose from the bed. She picked up the Glock from the nightstand, checked the clip and then tucked it into the waistband of her sweats. As if the too-large pants were going to hold the damn gun.

"Just where the hell do you think you're going?"

She eyed him steadily. "I'm going back to my parents' house to find Grace. She's there and so was someone else. Maybe it was nobody but I'm not going to wait around to hear from her."

"Christ, Shea. You're not going alone."

"Then get your ass up so we can get the hell out of here. I'm going with or without you, so make up your mind."

Nathan stared at her, at the challenge and determination in her eyes. But he also saw that she was scared out of her mind. Her hands were curled into the legs of her sweats. She was terrified.

She fidgeted under his scrutiny and then some of her bravado slipped and her eyes turned pleading.

"I'm not being stupid here, Nathan. I have you with me. I just have to make sure she's okay."

"And what about you?"

Impatience flashed across her face. "I don't matter! Grace does!"

He bolted to his feet, anger flashing hot. He got into her face and gripped her shoulders. "You matter to *me*, goddamn it."

She went silent, their gazes colliding and holding. Then she dropped her head and sighed as all the fight seemed to go out of her.

"We have to go, Nathan," she said quietly. "Who else is going to help her? She's all the family I have left."

He ran his hand through his hair and let out a ragged sigh to match hers. "I can call in my brothers. They'd help."

She clutched at his arms and returned her gaze to his, pleading and fierce. "We don't have time! Yeah, sure, call them in, but we can't sit around waiting for them to show up or come up with some plans. There'll be questions. Questions I can't even answer. And while we're sitting around figuring out the best way to do things, my sister is out there alone and frightened."

Fuck it all but she had a point. And if she were the one out there, he wouldn't wait around for his brothers to come charging in. He hadn't done that. As soon as he'd known Shea was in danger, he'd done what was necessary to get to her as fast as possible. How could he ask her to sit back and do what he himself had been unwilling to do?

"Yeah, okay, we'll go. But you're going to do precisely what I tell you. No questions. No arguments. You listen to everything I have to say."

She bit her lip as if to stifle immediate argument and she nodded her agreement.

"And then, Shea? I'm calling in my brothers. If I call them now, they're going to want me to stand down until they get here. For now, we do it your way. But then, it's my way."

She nodded vigorously again and then threw her arms around his neck, pulling him down into a toe-curling kiss. "Thank you. I have no right to ask this of you, but thank you. I don't have anyone else to turn to."

So maybe they weren't at a point in their relationship where she felt it was her right, but Nathan was going to make damn sure she knew she had every goddamn right to ask it of him. He sure as hell wasn't going to trust anyone else with her well-being. She was his. The sooner she realized it, the better the understanding would be between them.

"Let's get our stuff and get the hell out of here," he muttered. "We still have to get you clothes, shoes, and I'll need to pick up other supplies on our way."

ATTIRED in jeans, a T-shirt and a windbreaker, Shea had to admit she felt human again. She flexed her toes, happy with the fact that the thick socks prevented discomfort in the new tennis shoes.

Nathan had stopped at an all-purpose store two hours out of Crescent City and they'd set a land speed record for buying the things they needed. He'd hustled her back into the jeep, his gaze constantly sweeping their surroundings.

Even as they drove farther north, his eyes constantly rotated between the rearview and the sideview mirrors to make sure they weren't being followed.

She took the opportunity to study him unobserved. She hadn't hesitated to ask him for help after she'd been able to escape her captors. It hadn't even been a question. Who else could she have turned to?

But even then, she hadn't been sure if that deep bond between them would survive once they met face-to-face. And yet, it was instantaneous. Renewed. Stronger even than before.

She'd looked at a man who'd been molded by the events of the last year and she saw strength. Endurance. He was, in reality, everything that she'd come to know during the time of his captivity.

Honorable. Determined. Beautiful.

Yes, beautiful. He'd hate that description. Her seeming obliviousness to his physical scars baffled and discomfited him.

He was the kind of man who existed only in fiction. Confident and yet vulnerable. Determined to protect her at all costs.

She was fascinated by him and drawn by an inexplicable force. But their relationship had been forged in the fires of hell. Already they'd endured more than most other couples would ever endure in a lifetime. They'd been tested, together and individually, and yet here they were, clinging to each other, each the salvation of the other.

Yes, she was his. She didn't refute it. And he was hers.

It sounded so easy. So pat. And yet, their path still lay difficult and winding in front of them. She didn't have the luxury of a relationship, a normal courtship, dreams of a life filled with love and children and family.

How could she ever hope to achieve such a thing when she was doomed to always looking over her shoulder? She had to protect Grace. She had to protect herself and she couldn't ask someone else to bear those same burdens.

Nathan had already given more than any man should ever be asked to give. For his country. His family. Himself even. He needed the comfort and support of his family. And while she desperately needed his help now—she had no choice but to ask it of him—she could never hope to have any sort of a future with him when such a thing would place him in constant danger.

She was a realist. Yes, the idea saddened her. She mourned for what might have been, but she wasn't going to allow herself to dwell on it because it brought her nothing but sadness.

Nathan would always be a part of her—the *best* part aside from Grace. But some things just weren't possible or even plausible. For her, a normal relationship was one of those things.

A year ago, she wouldn't have imagined such a pragmatic attitude. She was a romantic. What woman wasn't at her very heart? She wanted the same things other women wanted. Love. A husband. Children eventually. Things to fill her life and complete her.

She'd spent years in denial over her gift. Never once had she imagined that it could interfere with having a normal existence. It was naïve of her. She could admit that. But who ever considered that violence would suddenly be thrust into their life, forever changing the course of it?

Maybe it was irresponsible of her, never considering the repercussions of having telepathic abilities. But in her scope, her gift wasn't world changing. It wasn't even some great power with the ability to change the world. Yeah, she could talk to people in their mind. So what?

Now she was facing the consequences of such denial. Her parents had paid the cost and so had Grace.

She couldn't be stupid any longer. And she absolutely had to find a way to take control of her life. She refused to spend the rest of her life running from some faceless, nameless enemy.

She hadn't wanted Grace to risk investigating, but she also realized that her sister was the smart one. She was being proactive because she wanted her life back. Shea had spent the last year running, hiding, just trying to survive and keep her sister safe. It was time to change all that.

Shea raised her gaze to Nathan's profile again. She had help now. She wasn't alone. Nathan had resources she couldn't even begin to imagine. No, she didn't know whom she could trust—or if she *should* trust anyone. But she did trust Nathan, and by proxy, she'd trust whomever he chose to place *his* trust in.

What other choice did she have?

CHAPTER 20

"TELL me more about your childhood. How did you and Grace hide your abilities from your friends? People at school?"

Shea started in surprise. She'd long since directed her stare out the window at the passing scenery. Her excitement and dread had grown as they drew closer to the house she hadn't been back to since she and Grace had fled a year ago.

"We just didn't use them," she said simply. "Our parents drummed into us from as early as I have memory that we had to keep our secrets. No one outside our family was to ever know."

Nathan frowned. "That shows remarkable restraint. Kids talk to their friends. Let things slip. Let's face it, children aren't very secretive."

Shea shrugged. "We didn't have friends. We were home-schooled. Our parents were super careful about who we were exposed to. We were never allowed to have other kids over. At the time, it all seemed so normal. It was our existence. It wasn't until later that I looked back and realized it was like living in a survivalist family. Deep paranoia. Suspicious of everyone. No social life. One of the biggest fights I had with my parents was when I wanted to go away to college. I thought my father was going to lock me in the basement."

Nathan's frown deepened and Shea held her hand up. "I know what you're thinking. My parents weren't assholes. To someone else they absolutely would sound like the worst parents ever. They were loving. We had a good childhood. Was it a normal childhood? Well, no, but they did the best they could."

She looked down at her hands as sadness crept through her chest. "Grace and I never understood. We thought they were too overprotective until the day they were killed. Then we understood that everything they'd done over the years had been absolutely necessary. They died protecting us."

He reached over to catch her hand and gave it a gentle squeeze. He waited a moment as though to allow her to gather her emotions and then he pressed on.

"Were your parents ever approached before? Did anyone show up at your house? Anything strange happen or do you ever remember them being afraid, more than usual, I mean?"

"We moved frequently. There was one time in particular, we'd only just moved into a new house in a new state. We'd been there maybe six months? My parents got a phone call and they were so agitated. They tried to hide it from me and Grace, but we could hear them arguing in their bedroom. My mom especially was a mess. She ordered me and Grace not to leave the house, even to go into the yard, and by that weekend, we'd packed and left."

"You didn't hear why?"

Shea shook her head. "The official story was that Dad got a better job somewhere else, but we knew that wasn't true because they didn't even act like they knew where we were going. Always before when we'd moved, Dad had gone ahead, found us a place and we moved from house to house. This time, we checked into hotels and we just ended up on the Oregon coast. I don't think it was planned. I think they'd reached the end of their resources or maybe they thought they'd outrun whatever it was that spooked them."

"How old were you then?"

"I was sixteen. Grace was seventeen. They told us that we had to change our names, at least on paper. They wanted us so used to using those new identities that they wouldn't allow us to use our real names even in the house with each other."

"And you didn't question this?"

His incredulous tone annoyed her.

"Of course we did. We were teenagers. We weren't stupid little girls anymore who did without questioning. They couldn't very well feed us a line of bullshit anymore. So they told us the truth. They said that there were people who wanted to exploit my and Grace's abilities, but Grace's in particular. My dad told me it was important to protect Grace because she was more fragile. Her ability could kill her.

"We moved into a bigger house on the coast. A fortress really. It had a panic room with an underground escape route that led away from the house. My father made us practice. He timed our escapes. He drilled us over and over on what we were supposed to do if the worst happened. He just never went into what the 'worst' was, but we found that out the day they were killed."

"Where the hell did your parents get the money for a setup like that?" Nathan asked.

"That part I don't know," Shea replied. "Before we'd always been on our own. I mean they'd have to work odd jobs, whatever they could find. My mother sewed, did crafts, had a vegetable garden. Money was always tight. When we moved here, suddenly we had this big, secure house. Money wasn't an issue because neither of them worked. It came from somewhere but Grace and I never knew where. Maybe a part of me didn't want to know because then I could keep on pretending I had a normal life and we weren't in any sort of danger.

"I wanted to move out and go to college and I thought my mom was going to have a heart attack over it. She completely freaked. She got so upset that I dropped the subject and continued to live with them. Grace and I took online courses. Eventually we started to get out more in the community, which gave my parents no end to grief, but maybe they realized they had to grant us some freedoms or we'd just move out, and they feared that more than anything.

"Dating was an experience. My dad ran background checks on everyone Grace and I even talked to. He didn't like us to go anywhere by ourselves. He always taught me and Grace to stick together no matter what. So you can imagine that made having a sex life difficult."

Nathan scowled. "I'd rather not hear about your sex life."

Shea laughed. "There wasn't much of one. Certainly no grand romances. I don't even think Grace gave it much effort. Certainly not as much as I did. I wanted . . . I wanted normalcy. I wanted to feel like I was just like any other woman out there."

"I'll be more than happy to provide you with your sex life," Nathan muttered. "And you're not just like every other woman out there. You're special. And I don't mean because of your goddamn abilities."

This time her smile went soul deep as she looked at how disgruntled—and uncomfortable—he was saying those words.

"Maybe normal is overrated," she said softly.

"Bet your ass it is. The two of us will never be 'normal,' and I'm okay with that."

She leaned over to kiss his cheek and then laid her head on his shoulder. "What are we going to do, Nathan?"

She said nothing more, because to voice her doubts, all the thoughts she'd already battled, was to make them all the more real, and for just a moment she didn't want to think of a future—an impossible future—she couldn't have.

"We fight. We do whatever we have to do to keep you—and Grace—safe."

It comforted her that he was so resolute and that he now included Grace in his vow to protect. But he was just one man. A man already damaged by fighting. And this was not his fight. She'd drawn him into it when she'd called for him. No, even before, when she'd first reached out to a man whose need was greater than her own.

Many would say—he would say—that he owed her. But Shea hadn't helped him expecting anything in return. She'd helped him because she couldn't do anything else. And yet she needed him. He was the only person she would allow herself to trust.

She must have dozed because she awoke when he gently nudged her with his shoulder.

"We're approaching Lincoln City. How much farther north is it?"

She sat up, wiping the fuzz from her eyes, and then studied the roadway in front of them.

"Not far. Just a few miles."

"Okay, I don't want to just drive in, especially since we have no way of knowing what we're dealing with. Do you remember where the tunnel from the panic room comes out?"

Her chest tightened, constricting her airway. Her throat seemed to close off and she willed herself not to freak out.

Deep breaths, Shea. Don't lose it now.

She sucked in another breath and tried to keep her response calm and focused so Nathan wouldn't know she was about to come apart.

"Yes, I remember it. It should still be accessible, but who knows what's been done to the house and the panic room? The house has solar panels and the security system is powered that way. My father was determined that something as simple as a power outage would never put us in danger or trap us."

"If Grace was just there, then at least part of the house is still intact," Nathan said quietly.

After giving him directions, she closed her eyes and tried to reach out to her sister just like she'd done ever since they'd last lost contact.

Grace. Please answer me. Talk to me. We're here. Where are you? You have to tell me. We can help you.

The result was the same as it had been over the last several hours. Dead silence.

She bit the inside of her cheek to control the tears because the very last thing Nathan needed was an overwrought, distraught female to contend with.

Nathan touched her cheek. Just a warm, gentle brush, his fingers idly caressing down to the line of her jaw.

"We'll find her, baby. You wouldn't talk to her because you wanted to keep her safe. Have you ever considered she's doing the same thing for you?"

She glanced over and gave him a watery smile. "Probably. It doesn't mean I'm not pissed at her for refusing to talk to me."

He shook his head. "You do so much to protect others and then are so vehement that they not do the same for you. Get used to it. Your days of sacrificing everything are over."

She jerked her gaze back to the road. "There, just ahead. Take the turnoff to the right, away from the coastline."

They pulled onto a narrow dirt road that quickly tapered to what looked like an old ATV trail.

"Pull up so we aren't seen. We'll have to walk the rest of the way."

Nathan maneuvered off the trail but then turned the jeep around and backed farther into the woods so they'd have a fast exit if they needed it.

He turned off the engine but put his hand over Shea's leg when she would have opened her door.

"Not so fast. We need to be clear on a few things first."

He shoved a clip into a Glock and handed it to Shea. Then he reached into the back for another handgun and an assault rifle. He rummaged in his bag for a moment and then produced several extra clips for the guns. He handed two to Shea and she shoved them into her pocket.

Then he turned to face her. "This is going to be a quick in and out. We go in, see what there is to see and then we're getting out. Stay behind me at all times unless I tell you differently. If I tell you to shoot, start shooting. If I tell you to run, you get your ass out no matter what I'm doing. Understand?"

She nodded, swallowing back her nervousness.

"If for any reason we get separated, you get back to the jeep and haul ass."

He pulled his cell phone out of his pocket and handed it to her.

"My brothers' numbers are in there. Labeled Sam, Garrett, Donovan and Joe. You'll be able to reach at least one of them. If things go bad, do *not* wait around for me. You run and you keep running and you call my brothers and tell them what's gone down."

"I got it."

Nathan nodded and then opened his door. "Okay, let's do this."

CHAPTER 21

SHEA led Nathan through the trees and into a particularly dense section of vegetation. She kicked aside a piece of camouflage netting to reveal the cap that sealed the tunnel entrance. Nathan handed her his rifle before squatting down to pry open the lid. He stared into the darkness for a moment before returning his gaze to Shea.

"I'm going first and then I'll call up for you."

He hopped over the side, his feet finding the rungs of the ladder and then he rapidly descended, his head disappearing from view.

A moment later he called softly up to her and she lowered his rifle. She tucked the pistol into her waistband and then went down into the tunnel after him.

When she reached the bottom rung, he wrapped his hands around her waist and lowered her to the concrete floor.

"Stay close," he murmured.

The pathway was illuminated by dim running lights on the left and right. The air was stale and musty as if the tunnel hadn't been used for some time. Her gaze was riveted to Nathan's back and her foot collided with an object on the floor, pitching her forward.

She bumped into his back and he came up short, reaching a hand back to steady her.

"You okay?"

She frowned and looked down at the offending object to see it was a small, leather-bound book. She squatted to pick it up and leaned it toward the light.

Her pulse ratcheted up when she opened it to the first page. It was her mother's handwriting. The shock of seeing the familiar script wrenched her heart. She rapidly flipped through the other pages and realized it was her mother's journal. Shea hadn't known she'd kept one.

Nathan bent down to look over her shoulder. "What is it?"

"My mother's journal," Shea replied. "I'm unsure of how it got here. I didn't even know she kept one."

How *had* it gotten here? Unease prickled up Shea's spine. It seemed likely now that this was the way Grace had come just recently. Had she dropped it? Had she been pursued and caught? Had she left it for Shea to find?

She rose and shoved the small volume in the front waistband of her jeans so that it was crammed against her belly. Then she adjusted her grip on the pistol and nodded at Nathan. "Let's go. I'll look at it later."

They continued down the long corridor until they reached the door leading into the panic room.

Nathan examined the key pad and then turned back to Shea. "Do you have the code?"

She stepped forward and punched in a series of numbers. "It's 3272*4824. Just in case you need it and I'm not here to do it."

He frowned at that statement, but it would be pretty damn stupid not to plan for the worst.

The lock snicked and Shea started to push the door open, but Nathan stuck his arm out and shoved her behind him. He entered the room, rifle up, his gaze rapidly scanning the interior.

He motioned for her in a quick, impatient gesture. Feeling like a complete fraud and not at all sure of this stealth mumbo jumbo, she raised her gun and followed Nathan in. She just hoped to hell no one jumped out at them, because she couldn't be entirely sure what would happen.

She was a good shot. At the range. Which was entirely different from shooting at an actual person when under enormous stress. A paper target posed no threat. You could take all bloody day to aim. You could breathe normally. No stress. Just point and shoot.

Not so much here.

Everything was still online and working. There were video monitors mounted along one wall with a view of each room in the house as well as the front, back and side views of the exterior. What Shea saw made her gasp.

She walked forward, her gaze riveted to the sheer destruction evident on the monitors.

"My God," she whispered.

Nathan studied the monitors with her, his gaze moving over each one as if searching for any threat.

The living room—all of the rooms—were a mess. Nothing had been left untouched or undamaged. The furniture was destroyed. Picture frames lay broken on the floor. Vases, artwork, dead plants, her mother's beloved wildlife figurines and the glass curio cabinet where they'd been housed were all in pieces, scattered through the room.

The entire house had been ransacked. Not just ransacked, but completely and utterly destroyed as if the person responsible had been in a rage. Or they hadn't found what they were looking for.

Was this what had happened after her parents had been murdered and Shea and Grace had fled? Or had this been done more recently? Had her parents been left to rot in the house or were their bodies disposed of to conceal the evidence of the crime committed?

"Jesus," Nathan muttered. "Looks like a damn war zone."

Shea froze when her gaze skittered across the monitor that had a view of the dining room. The carpet that had borne the bloodstains of her parents was gone. Someone had removed it. Why? But she still saw the pool of blood in her mind. Tears filled her eyes and she looked hastily away.

In her mind, an endless loop played and she saw her father valiantly trying to protect her mother. Heard the intruders demand to know where the girls were. She saw him gunned down when he refused to give them any information on his daughters' whereabouts and then her mother throwing her body over her husband as she sobbed and pleaded for their lives.

She shut her eyes and viciously shoved the images from her head. She'd looked away then too, no longer able to bear to see what happened. Grace had called her a heartless bitch when Shea had dragged her toward the door and shoved her into the tunnel.

But she'd known there was nothing she and Grace could do and she'd made a vow that her parents wouldn't sacrifice themselves for nothing. She'd keep Grace—and herself— safe. Her mom and dad wouldn't die in vain.

Who had done this? They'd gone to great lengths to conceal the deaths, disposing of the bodies, removing the blood-soaked carpet. Yet they'd trashed the house and left it in shambles? It didn't make sense, which was why she suspected that the house had been ransacked much more recently. Like when Grace had been here and had been frightened away by intruders.

When Nathan spoke, she jumped. She'd been so lost in her thoughts that she hadn't heard him move toward the door leading out of the panic room into the rest of the house.

"Same code?"

She nodded. Her heart jumped into overdrive and her hands shook so much that she wrapped both around the stock of the gun in an effort not to drop it.

The stock was slick and she took one hand away from it to wipe it down the leg of her jeans. Then she switched hands so she could rub the other one.

There had been no sign that anyone was in the house. No sign of Grace. Had the house been that way when Grace had arrived? Or had this been done by whoever had startled Grace?

Fear gripped her by the throat and threatened to choke her.

Where was Grace now? And was she okay? Why the hell wouldn't she communicate with Shea? Or was she unable to?

That was what scared Shea the most. The thought of Grace hurt and unable to call for Shea was paralyzing.

"Let's move. I don't want to spend any more time here than necessary," Nathan said when the lock released on the door.

She collected herself and moved into the hallway behind Nathan. Her gaze scanned each room, but what was she looking for? Everything was a complete and total mess. How would she even know if there was something missing?

Then she remembered the journal tucked into her jeans. She looked down and fingered the edge. She was convinced now that Grace must have dropped it. What Shea didn't know was if it had been an accident or if Grace had intended for Shea to find it.

She forced her attention back to her surroundings. Nathan kept his head up as he crept from room to room. He toed through a few of the fallen items but quickly moved through the house.

When they reached the kitchen, Nathan glanced into the garage and then turned back to Shea. "Try to contact Grace again. Everything is quiet here. I don't see any fresh blood, and it's hard to tell if there was a struggle. Too big of a mess."

Shea's stomach dropped and she poured all of her energy into the effort to reach out to her sister.

Grace. Please, talk to me. I'm here at the house. Things are a mess here. I need to know you're okay. Tell me where you are. I'll come get you. I'm safe now. You can be too.

Only empty silence greeted her plea.

"She's not there, damn it!"

Nathan touched her arm. "Don't get worked up, Shea. You don't know that anything has happened to her. I need you to stay calm and focused."

She blew out her breath and battled tears of rage and frustration. How was she supposed to be calm and focused? She was standing in the place where her parents had been murdered. A place that her sister had come back to and from which she had now disappeared.

Glass exploded around them, sending slivers slicing over Shea's neck and shoulders. Then she hit the floor as Nathan threw her down and covered her with his body.

"Cover your ears and close your eyes!" he yelled hoarsely.

She barely had time to close her eyes before a loud explosion registered and then splashes of color appeared in her vision even though her eyes were tightly shut. Her hands over her ears did little to buffer her from the concussion of sound.

Before she could collect herself, Nathan was dragging her toward the panic room. She stumbled as she got to her feet but promptly staggered. Her balance was off and her ears were ringing. Those damn patches of black still obscured her vision and no amount of blinking made them go away.

Behind her, more breaking glass and then the shattering of wood urged her forward.

The world spun so crazily around her that nausea rose sharply. Her head hurt. Her ears throbbed and she felt sick as a dog.

Finally Nathan hoisted her over his shoulder and ran the rest of the way toward the panic room. As soon as they were inside, he tossed her down, slammed the door and set the locks.

The gun. She'd dropped the damn gun.

She held her hands to her head and staggered upward, willing the room to stop spinning.

"What the hell was that?"

"Flash grenade. Can you see? I need your help here. Do you know anything about the surveillance system?"

She shook her head to rid herself of the residual effects. Nathan sounded like he was a mile away but at least her vision was slowly ridding itself of the spots. Her head hurt like a son of a bitch.

"What do you want to do? I know a little. Just what my dad showed me and Grace when he set everything up."

Nathan pointed to the monitor that showed two men stealthily moving into the kitchen from the garage door. She gasped, her mind becoming sharper as she stared at the guns they held.

"I need to get this surveillance to my brothers. Do you have the passwords to the computer system? We have to be quick. I want to upload the footage of these jokers so we find out what we can about them."

For a moment she blanked.

"Come on, Shea. Think. We have to get out of here. These aren't your average baddies here. Your high-tech security system won't withstand a grenade. They'll just blow a hole in the damn wall."

"It's—it's DLGSP."

"That's it?"

"No. No, just give me a second."

"We don't have a second, Shea. Give me the rest of it, damn it."

She closed her eyes and replayed inputting the password. The first letter of each family member's name in order of age. Then the number of members.

"It's 4. The number 4 and then Peterson spelled backward. All uppercase. NOSRETEP. The entire password is DLGSP4NOSRETEP."

Nathan typed in the letters and then entered a series of commands. He watched one of the monitors and zoomed in one of the men, who moved slowly down the hallway toward the panic room. He took a series of still shots and then captured a thirty-second video.

Shea surged forward. "Oh my God, Nathan. The cameras would have caught Grace when she was here! We'd know what happened to her!"

Nathan cursed and muttered under his breath as his fingers flew across the keyboard. "I'll have to start the upload of that entire day and just hope it doesn't get interrupted if they blow this place. We don't have time to babysit it."

"They're coming down the hall," she said urgently. She frowned and leaned forward as one of the men began attaching something to the wall. "What are they doing?"

"They're preparing to blow their way in here."

She glanced frantically around, cursing again that she'd dropped the gun when the flash grenade had gone off. She reached for the pistol tucked into Nathan's back waistband, pulled it out and pointed it toward the wall.

"Come on, come on," Nathan murmured as he hunched over the keyboard. He pounded a key and then reached for Shea. "Let's go."

He pushed her ahead of him and into the tunnel. After they'd gone just a few steps, another explosion rocked the pathway. The walls shuddered and she stumbled.

"Run!" Nathan urged.

They fled down the passageway. She hit the bottom rung of the ladder and started to scramble up, but Nathan grabbed her ankle.

"Get your gun up. I'll cover you from behind. Don't hesitate to shoot. I'll be right behind you."

She gripped the pistol tighter and then hauled herself up the rungs. At the top she only hesitated a moment before she leaped through the opening and rolled rapidly away, her gun up.

Seeing no one, she called down to Nathan, "All clear!" But he was already pulling himself over the edge.

"Get to the jeep. They won't be far behind."

She got up and ran.

When they got to where Nathan had parked the jeep, to her surprise, he directed her toward the driver's seat. "How are you behind the wheel?"

"I can drive."

"You'll know the area better than I do. Get us the hell out of here and I'll try to keep any heat off us."

She jumped into the driver's seat, still holding the pistol in her left hand. She keyed the ignition and roared onto the bumpy path leading back to the highway.

"Any particular destination?" she yelled.

"Just keep off the main roads and get us as far from here as possible. We'll figure out the rest later."

She spun gravel and dirt in a wide arc when she turned onto the highway. She pressed the accelerator to the floor and checked her rearview mirror for any sign they were being followed.

As they approached the driveway to her parents' house, a black SUV shot forward to block the road. She slammed on the brakes and jerked the wheel to the left to avoid a collision.

She hit the ditch on the opposite side and nearly flipped. The jeep went up on two wheels and she wrestled for control. The jeep came down with enough force to jar her teeth and she rammed her foot to the floor once more.

Nathan jerked around in his seat, leaned out the window and fired off several rounds. Glass shattered in one of the SUV's windows and a tire blew as the vehicle attempted to execute a turn around to pursue them.

"Nice shot," Shea yelled.

"Keep driving. I'm sure they have more than one vehicle."

She glanced in the rearview mirror to see yet another SUV barreling up on them. "Yeah. I'd say you're right about that."

She rounded a sharp corner and did a double take when a Suburban crossed the center lane, then veered into her lane before easing back over just enough to straddle the dotted line.

"I've always sucked at chicken."

"Huh?" Nathan said without turning around. He squeezed off another set of rounds.

Shea gripped the pistol in one hand, leaned as far to the left as she could while still maintaining control of the jeep and began firing at the oncoming SUV.

That got Nathan's attention. He jerked around just as the windshield exploded on the SUV and it veered wildly to the right after one of the front tires came apart, tossing pieces of rubber in all directions.

Shea passed on the left after yelling at Nathan to duck. Surprisingly, he didn't offer a single argument. Once they were past, he rose cautiously back up and glanced over at her, a glimmer of a smile curving his lips.

"You're such a badass. I like that about you."

"They off our tail?"

"Yes, ma'am. All clear, at least for now. Let's get the hell out of here."

She glanced sideways at him. "You got a plan?"

"Yeah. It's time to call in reinforcements."

CHAPTER 22

SHEA drove steadily east, keeping to smaller roads as Nathan had directed. It had been hard for her not to hit the interstate at the first opportunity. Wouldn't their pursuers expect them to stick to rural roads? Wouldn't it be safer on the interstate where there were more cars?

Trying to psychoanalyze a faceless enemy had left her exhausted and on edge. She kept constant look out the rearview mirror until her neck ached from all the back and forth.

"Pull over," Nathan said.

Startled, she glanced over at him.

He pointed to the sign for an upcoming gas station. "Pull in there so we can get gas, but first, we'll switch so that I'm driving. I want you to stay in the passenger seat and pretend to be asleep. There's a blanket and a cap. Pull it low over your face and cover up with the blanket. You've got cuts from the glass. I don't want to raise any suspicions, nor do I want anyone to get a good look at you."

She pulled to the side of the road and they hurriedly rotated. He handed her the blanket and arranged the cap over her hair, pulling it low so her eyes weren't visible. After he was satisfied that she was sufficiently covered, he pulled back on the highway.

A few moments later, the jeep slowed.

"We're pulling in. Keep still and pretend you're asleep. I'll pay the guy in cash so I don't have to get out."

Though she remained still as he'd directed, she kept watch from half-lidded eyes as an attendant walked over to pump their gas. Nathan rolled the window down, put a finger to his lips and then handed the man some money.

Nathan rolled the window back up and settled back in his seat. To anyone else, he looked relaxed, but Shea knew better. His eyes were in constant motion, looking left, right, ahead, and then checking all the mirrors.

His hands gripped the lower portion of the steering wheel and even his feet were in position in case he needed to drive away fast.

A few minutes later, the attendant appeared at the window holding the receipt. Nathan waved him off and eased away from the pump.

Still, Shea waited until they were on the road and Nathan reached over to touch her arm.

"You can sit up now."

"Where will we go?" she asked as she pushed the blanket down her legs.

"I want to turn south and head back toward Crescent City. The jet is hangared at the airport there and is the most expedient method of travel, not to mention the safest if we can manage to get there in one piece."

"We can't leave yet! We don't know if Grace is here. Or where she is. We need to be able to watch that surveillance footage."

"I said I want us there so we have that option," he said calmly. "I'm going to call my brothers in. I sent the footage to Donovan. I just hope to hell it was all uploaded before they blew the shit out of that room."

"Who were they, Nathan? I don't understand. I don't understand any of it. No normal people come into a house and blow a hole in the wall. They looked . . . military."

His expression tightened. His face darkened into a cloud and his eyes took on a brooding heat. "They certainly looked professional."

"I'm scared. If these people are military, what chance do we have against them?"

Nathan dropped one hand from the wheel and reached for Shea's hand. Her fingers trembled against his palm and he squeezed, unsure of what to say to reassure her.

Hell yes, they'd looked military. Black ops. Off the books. Just like KGI. Who knew who was running the show, but they damn sure meant business.

Shea stiffened as if just remembering something and then pulled out the small leather journal that she'd found in the tunnel. She ran her finger over the surface, a mixture of grief and uncertainly in her eyes.

"You can turn the light on. It won't bother me," he said softly. It was getting dark enough that he doubted she'd be able to read for long in the fading light.

She let out a sigh that was tinged with sadness. "I don't want to draw that much notice. I'll read it when we get to wherever we're going." Then she glanced up. "Are we getting a room? What are we doing exactly?"

"I'll get us a room. Not the same place as before. Then I'm going to call my brothers. After we talk, you and I will decide—together—what our next step will be."

She stared at him in a way that made him want to pull the jeep over, forget the danger they were in and haul her into his arms.

It was like he hung the damn moon, and all he could think was that he'd damn near gotten her killed because he hadn't listened to his first instinct, which was to get her as far away as possible and lock her in the deepest, most secure vault he could find.

"Thank you," she said in a sweet, husky voice. "It means a lot when you say *we*. It makes me feel like I'm not quite so alone. It makes me not quite so afraid."

A possessive snarl rose to his lips. He had to swallow it back. This caveman reaction he had around her was baffling. It took over his senses and rendered him incapable of rational thought where she was concerned.

Getting so crazy over a woman simply wasn't him. He liked—no, he loved—women. He mostly understood them or at least he knew the right things to say and when to keep his mouth shut.

He never had a shortage of women friends or even sexual partners. At least before his captivity. But none ever commanded this overwhelming insanity that seemed to grip him when he was with her. Hell, not even with her. All he had to do was think about her.

"It's going to be *we* from now on," he bit out. "There is no *you*. No *me*. Only *us*."

Her eyes widened. Her mouth opened but then shut as if she had no idea how to respond to his directive. Good. Some things she just needed to accept. This was one of them.

Their lives—their souls—had been inexorably entwined from the moment she slid into his mind. There was no easy way to separate her from him, and he had no desire to try.

He wasn't some helpless captive. It wasn't like he had no choice and was stuck with this connection to Shea. He wanted her with every part of his heart, mind and body. The connection that had been forged in hell was only growing stronger the more time they spent together physically and mentally.

"We have a few hours yet. I know you're pretty keyed up, but is there any chance you can rest? Are those cuts bothering you?"

In response, she frowned and lifted her fingers to touch the nicks and cuts on her neck. The blood had long since dried and her obvious puzzlement told him that she hadn't even realized she'd been injured.

There was one particularly long gash where a larger piece of glass had caught her. The blood was still wet there. It didn't look too serious but it needed cleaning and possibly a stitch or two.

"I'm fine," she murmured. "Not sure I can sleep, but I'll try."

"We'll figure this out, Shea. My brothers are the best there is at what they do. We'll find Grace. We'll find out who's behind this."

"I want to believe you, Nathan. I want it more than anything. I'm trying. I trust you more than I trust anyone."

"I know, baby. Soon this will all be over and we can focus on more important things."

She raised one eyebrow but he left the statement dangling. She knew damn well he referred to him and her, but now wasn't the time to press further. He'd let her know she belonged to him. For now it was enough.

CHAPTER 23

NATHAN pulled off at a rustic lodge situated on Lake Talawa. He left Shea in the jeep and went inside to inquire about vacancies. There were several empty cabins situated along the shoreline and one deeper into the woods, away from the others. The clerk jokingly referred to it as the honeymooners' lodge.

Nathan played along, grinning his delight over being afforded privacy. He made the appropriate jokes about getting away for a few days, took the keys and then hurried back out to Shea.

The road leading back to the cabins was narrow and dusty. The moon shimmered over the water, reminding him of home. In other circumstances, he'd be thrilled to be on the lake. Throw back a few beers with his brothers. Do a little fishing. Be lazy and talk about old times.

In truth he wasn't looking forward to a reunion with his brothers. They were going to be understandably pissed that he'd taken off. Not just taken off on his own, but appropriated a KGI jet in the process. Yeah, Sam was going to have a kitten over that one.

But if they could help him keep Shea safe, he'd take whatever ass kicking they wanted to dole out.

He parked behind the cabin so the jeep was out of sight. Then he gathered his gear, motioned for Shea to get out, and they headed toward the dark cabin.

Soon they were inside. It was a little musty but otherwise clean. It had all the basics, but Nathan didn't plan to be here long enough to worry over whether the kitchen was stocked.

His first priority was to see to Shea. She looked shell-shocked. Her eyes were glazed, whether in pain or confusion, he wasn't sure.

"You need to hit the shower," he told her. "I need to take a look at those cuts. One of them looks pretty bad."

She lifted the backpack that contained the new clothes they'd purchased and shuffled toward the bathroom. Exhaustion and adrenaline letdown radiated from her. Imminent crash. He saw it coming a mile away.

He followed her inside the bathroom and found her sitting on the closed toilet seat, her shoulders sagging. She looked so damn vulnerable, but he knew her to be anything but. Okay, so maybe she was vulnerable, but she definitely wasn't a shrinking violet. She was a big surprise in a little package. Fierce and unafraid to get the job done.

His admiration for her grew with every passing minute he spent with her.

He tossed his bag onto the counter and then knelt in front of her, gathering her hands in his. "You okay?"

She nodded. "I will be. I promise. I'm not freaking out on you, Nathan."

He smiled. "I never thought you were. Can you take that shirt off? I need to get a look at those cuts. You caught several shards to the back as well. Cut ribbons into your shirt."

She glanced up in surprise and then tried to turn to look over her shoulder. It didn't surprise him that she didn't realize the extent of the cuts. She likely hadn't felt a thing at the time. But now that she was coming down, she would start feeling the discomfort.

Carefully he peeled away her shirt. She wasn't wearing a bra and her breasts bobbed free of constraint, soft and so plush. He stood and glanced down her back, relieved to see only knicks and shallow cuts along her shoulder blades.

There was one cut in the curve of her neck, running over the ridge of her neck. That was the one he suspected needed stitches. The rest could be cleaned, medicated and allowed to heal without dressing.

"You'll be okay taking a shower on your own?"

She gave him a disgruntled look and then waved him away.

"When you get out, stay undressed long enough for me to take care of those cuts."

She nodded and rose to turn on the shower. Taking his cue, he left the bathroom and went into the living room to call his brothers.

He turned on his cell phone, ignoring the cacophony of notifications of voice mails, missed calls and text messages. Still, the most recent message, from Joe, caught his eye and he clicked to read the full text.

You're pissing me off, bro. We've never worked like this. You're holding out on me. Since when did we ever keep shit from each other?

Joe was right, and it didn't make Nathan feel any better to know he'd hurt his twin. Joe might sound all pissed off, but deep down he was hurt over Nathan's avoidance and, worse, his refusal to tell Joe what was going on.

He sighed. It would end now, but it might not be enough to make up for the last months in his brother's eyes. It had taken him the entire drive to work up the nerve and figure out exactly what he wanted to say and in the end, he still didn't know how to explain it all. He had to just believe his brothers would take his word on faith.

He punched in Sam's number, irritated with how nervous it made him to make that call.

"It's about goddamn time," Sam snapped as he answered the phone. "What's going on, Nathan? Are you all right? And where's my goddamn plane?"

Nathan grinned at the pissiness in Sam's voice, because despite the anger, there was a deep thread of worry and relief coming through loud and clear. He thought of all the things he'd decided to say, but the only thing that came to his lips was the simple truth.

"I . . . I need your help, Sam."

"Was that so goddamn hard?"

Nathan's brow wrinkled. "What the hell are you talking about?"

Sam sighed. "Was it so goddamn hard to ask your family for help?"

"Look, I know I've been difficult. I'm sorry."

"I don't give a shit about that. Tell me what you need. Are you okay?"

"I'm fine. Really. But Shea's not. She—we—need help."

There was a long silence. "And Shea is . . . ?"

"She saved me, Sam. She's the one who sent Van the emails. I can't even go into all she did for me. You'd never believe me anyway. But she's in trouble and we need help."

"Tell me where you are," Sam said sharply.

"In a cabin on Lake Talawa. About eleven miles south of the Oregon border. Last cabin on the path past the sign for the campsites. Place is called Wilderness Camping 'with all the modern conveniences,' or something like that."

"Sit tight. And don't move."

The line went dead and Nathan ruefully put the phone down. Just like Sam. Few words. To the point. And always with the orders.

He fiddled with the phone for a moment, contemplating the urge to call Joe. Guilt weighed heavily on him. The one person he should have called first was the one person who'd have to receive the news from Sam.

He tossed aside the phone again because what the hell was he supposed to say? Joe would have to understand. Maybe he would, maybe he wouldn't, but right now Nathan's focus was on Shea. It had to be. Shea didn't have the support network that Nathan had. She had no one. Just him and, by proxy, his family.

The bathroom door opened and Shea padded out, a towel wrapped around her slender body. In that moment he felt like the biggest asshole on earth because he wasn't thinking about tending her cuts. All he could think about was pulling the towel away and wrapping himself around her as tightly as he could.

His dick agreed because, as she neared him, it swelled painfully against his jeans.

She stopped in front of him and then moved into his space, positioning herself between his splayed knees. She was so close, he could smell the scent of her soap. Light and floral. He leaned in closer, inhaling as his mouth hovered just above where the towel covered her breasts.

He touched her legs and then ran his hands up her thighs underneath the towel until he cupped her rounded bottom. Only when he glanced higher to see the ragged edge of the more serious cut on her shoulder did he let his hands fall.

"You make me forget what I'm supposed to be doing."

She leaned toward him, allowing the towel to slip the barest amount. If anything, it made her look even more alluring and vulnerable, standing before him, her eyes soft, her curves barely hidden by the scrap of damp material barely clinging to her body.

Her lips hovered just above his as she stared down at him. And then she pressed her mouth to his. Warm. A shock to his senses.

She framed his face in her hands, and it took him a moment to realize that the towel had slipped down her body and pooled at her feet.

Oh hell. A warm, lush, naked woman coming on to him? Nothing in the military had prepared him for an onslaught like this. The never-surrender thing went right out the window, and he started waving the white flag like a dog wagging his tail.

Her back bowed inward as she pressed her breasts forward until his chin was buried in the valley. Her fingers trailed through his hair and then she pulled him upward to meet her lips once more.

Damn it, he was trying to do the right thing here.

He reached up to catch her hands. "Shea, baby, I need to bandage those cuts. Put some antibiotic ointment on them or something."

She pulled away from him and stared down with eyes drenched in emotion. Need. Pulling at him until it was impossible to deny her anything at all.

"I need *you*," she whispered. "I was so scared today, Nathan. I'm still scared. I'm sick with worry. Right now I need you to love me. I need you to touch me so I'll feel safe again. Being with you eases me in a way I can't explain."

He was at a loss to describe how affected he was by her words. She needed him. Yes, she needed protection. Someone to help her, to care about her. But it was more than that. She looked at him like he was the only man she saw, as if there was no one else who could do for her what she wanted and needed.

Scarred, worn, his sanity questionable, and she wanted him still.

He pulled her against him, enjoying the sensation of her bare flesh against him. He loved her smell. How silky her skin felt against his fingers. How she was plump in all the right places. He loved every curve and swell. How delicate she appeared and yet she was a force to be reckoned with.

The perfect package. Far too perfect for someone as damaged as he was. Even as he recognized the disparity between them, he wanted her. He had to have her. She completed him in a way no one ever had or would, and so he held on to her, because the thought of being without her was another kind of hell. Worse than being held captive and tortured.

He rubbed his cheek along the top of her breast, before nuzzling down to her nipple. He tugged it between his teeth and gently sucked until it formed a turgid point on his tongue.

He *loved* the way she melted into his body. Loved the way she fit him. She made the most beautiful, erotic sounds. Every little gasp and moan had him so hard that he could barely breathe. Hell, he'd give up breathing if she would keep making those sweet sounds of contentment.

She ran her hands over his shoulders and then gently pulled away. Her nipple slipped from his mouth, wet and glistening, puckered and straining forward, a temptation for him to latch back on.

"Undress for me," she said, her voice as silky as her skin. "I want to see you. You have such a beautiful body."

He shook as he stood. He'd never felt so unsteady on his feet. Her words soaked into the darkest parts of his soul, bringing light that chased the shadows away.

He'd come home feeling ugly. Tarnished. Not the same man who'd left. He felt . . . dirty. Unworthy. Not just on the surface. The scars were the tangible results of his shame. But deeper, below those scars, lay the self-loathing and doubt. But with Shea, he felt . . . whole. He didn't feel the shame that so frequently pulled at him. Or the frustration over the anxiety and panic that still plagued him at the most unexpected times.

With her, he felt like he was on top of the fucking world. Like he was her damn hero. Like he mattered.

He loved her for that. God, yes, he loved her, and if that didn't fuck everything up, he didn't know what did.

"What are you thinking?" she asked quietly.

He caught her gaze, saw that she was staring up at him intently. It puzzled him because she always seemed so in tune with his thoughts. She resided in his mind as well as his heart, and yet she stared at him as if she truly didn't know the direction of his thoughts. Hell, maybe they were too scattered for even her to sort out.

"I . . ." No, he couldn't tell her that yet. He'd sound as crazy as everyone thought he was.

He could think it. He could act on it. But saying it aloud made him feel so goddamn vulnerable. Shaken. And scared. Hell yes, scared. Not things he wanted to experience again.

Instead he began to undress, his gaze holding hers. He may not be able to say the words, but he could tell her with his eyes. His hands. His mouth and his body. He wasn't worth a damn with words anyway. He much preferred action.

He pulled his shirt off first and tossed it across the room. He fumbled with his fly next, his fingers clumsily glancing off the button. He bent as he rolled the denim down and picked up one leg and then the other to kick out of the jeans.

When he straightened, the hunger in her gaze gave him a jolt. She boldly stared, caressing as though she were physically touching him. No inch of his body was spared her scrutiny, but this time he didn't shy away. He didn't try to hide from her.

There was no revulsion in her eyes, only lust. Desire. And something deeper that he didn't dare speculate on.

She stepped closer so their bodies touched. Then she placed her palms over his chest and rubbed lightly up to his shoulders and then down his arms, her fingers glancing over the ridges of his muscles.

She took another step, forcing him to back up until he bumped the edge of the bed. She put her hand in the center of his chest and pushed him just hard enough that he fell back on the bed, his hands going behind him to brace himself so that he sat half reclined, his legs hanging off the mattress.

Her lips quirked up into a tiny smile that sent shivers racing down his spine. And then she crawled onto the bed like a feline on the prowl, straddling his hips in all her naked glory.

"I had in mind for you to touch me. For you to comfort me. To make me feel safe. I was going to make you do all the work. But I've changed my mind."

His eyebrows went up at that.

She crawled up over his body until her weight forced his hands away and he fell back onto the bed so that he lay flat on his back.

"I've decided that I'm going to do the touching. And the comforting. I'm going to make love to *you*, Nathan. Any objections?"

"Oh, hell no," he breathed.

She leaned down and kissed the hollow of his chest. Her tongue swept out and then traced a path up to his neck. She nibbled and nipped, her teeth grazing where his pulse was about to pop right out of his neck. Then she moved up to suck gently at his ear.

He was already leaking. He could feel the sticky dampness on his cock. This woman just did it for him. All she had to do was look at him and he was a goner. And now she was seducing him with words and that wicked mouth of hers. How the hell was he supposed to withstand such delicious, delicious torture?

Her mouth found his. Hot. Wanton. Swollen. Their tongues tangled. Breathless. Her taste on his tongue. And then she was gone again, sliding down his body with tantalizing slowness as she licked her way over his chest, to the sensitive flesh of his belly and lower.

The little vixen sank her teeth into the inside of his thigh and he damn near came on the spot. He was breathing so hard that he was starting to see spots dance in his vision and his lungs felt like someone was squeezing them with both fists.

His balls ached. His dick was screaming for mercy and twitching uncontrollably. He'd never been so hard in his life.

And then she pressed the tip of her tongue to the base of his cock, just above his sac, where the thick vein began its upward trek up the tender, supersensitive back of his erection.

Slowly she slid her tongue upward, taking her time as she teased and nibbled ever so lightly. By the time she made it to the tip, he'd lost any vestige of control he thought he had.

The first spurt of semen shot onto her cheek, and he groaned partly in dismay, partly in pleasure. He was too far gone. He couldn't stop the inevitable.

Undaunted, she closed her mouth over him and sucked him deep as he continued to come in hard, rapid, seemingly never-ending streams.

He dragged his fingers through her hair, stroking, holding her, pulling at her. His movements were frantic and un-schooled. It shamed him that he had so little control and no finesse where she was concerned. And yet nothing in her de-meanor suggested that she was in any way disappointed.

She stroked him lovingly with her mouth and her hands. She touched him with gentleness that he felt in the deepest parts of his heart.

After a moment, she laid her cheek over the top of his thigh and continued to work him down from his orgasm with her hand.

"Shea, I'm so damn sorry," he said when he finally got control of his tongue.

She raised her head, her brows furrowed in confusion. "What are you apologizing for?"

His cheeks heated and he prayed she couldn't see him actually blushing. "I think that might give new meaning to the word *premature*."

She smiled then, dazzling him, warming him like a ray of sunshine. She crawled up his body and snuggled into the crook of his arm. She laid her head on his chest and rubbed her hand up and down his side.

"Tonight was all for you, Nathan. I love that you want me so much. That I can drive you crazy. I wanted it to last but only because I wanted to give you more pleasure. You didn't disappoint me and you have no reason to be embarrassed."

He pulled her up and rolled until they faced each other.

"You did give me pleasure. So much that I can't even feel my feet. 'Thank you' sounds so lame. I don't even have the words to tell you what you mean to me."

She smiled again, this time a shy, adorable smile as she ducked her head self-consciously. It delighted him that she could be so bold and wanton one minute and adorably shy the next.

He leaned in to kiss her because he couldn't stand not to. Just as their lips met, a knock sounded at the door.

CHAPTER 24

SHEA stiffened, her eyes growing wide with apprehension. Nathan scrambled out of bed and motioned her toward the bathroom as he yanked his clothing on.

"Get the pistol. Then go into the bathroom and get dressed. Hurry. Don't come out until I tell you. Understand? And if anyone but me comes through that door, you shoot."

She nodded and quickly did as he directed.

He grabbed one of the rifles, made sure the other was within easy reach, and then he eased over to the door. There was no way to know who was out there. It might just be the manager. But Nathan wasn't taking any chances.

Jamming the rifle to his shoulder, he threw open the door and to his shock came face-to-face with Donovan. And he didn't look pleased to be greeted with the barrel of a rifle.

Nathan eased the rifle down, even more surprised as he saw Ethan and Swanny standing on either side of Donovan.

Donovan looked pointedly at the gun. "Planning to shoot us?"

Nathan gestured for them to hurry in and he shut the door behind them. "How the fuck did you get here so fast? I just spoke to Sam an hour or so ago."

"We might have already been in the neighborhood," Ethan said.

"You didn't exactly cover your tracks that well," Donovan pointed out. "We trailed you to Crescent City. We were there when Sam called us and told us you were here. We grabbed a faster gear and hauled ass up here."

Swanny hung back, his silent gaze taking in his surroundings. While Ethan and Donovan were focused on Nathan, Swanny was checking out the rest of the room. Almost as though he were looking for someone. Shea?

What was Swanny doing here anyway?

When Nathan asked just that question, Swanny finally turned his stare to him.

"You didn't expect me to just leave you in whatever mess you've gotten yourself into. If you did, fuck you."

Nathan let out a sharp chuckle. "No, I guess I didn't. I should have expected this. The real question is how you got these hard-asses to agree to let you come."

Ethan and Donovan exchanged raised eyebrow glances.

"Hard-asses? He's calling us hard-asses?" Donovan asked in mock incredulity.

"So where's Shea?" Ethan demanded.

"In the bathroom," Nathan said in a tight voice. "I'll go get her."

The moment Shea was mentioned, Swanny looked uneasy. He turned his face away so that the side that wasn't scarred was facing the rest of them.

Nathan went to the bathroom door and knocked softly. "Shea? You can come out. My brothers are here."

The door opened and she stood there, clutching the Glock, looking nervous as hell and so uncertain that he softened from head to toe. He reached in to take her hand and then pulled her to him, uncaring of whether his brothers could see or not.

"You have nothing to worry about," he murmured.

"But they know about me," she whispered back. "They'll think I'm crazy."

He pulled her back so he could look down at her. "Then I'm as crazy as you are. Swanny's here too."

"Swanny?"

She pushed Nathan aside and strode into the room, staring at the three men assembled.

Ethan and Donovan stared at her with open curiosity while Swanny kept his face averted. Donovan's eyes widened when he caught sight of the Glock that Shea was holding.

"Swanny," she whispered. She thrust the gun at Nathan and then hurried over to Swanny.

He wore a look of panic as she turned him to face her. She grasped his hands and stared up at him with soft wonder.

"Swanny, it's really you."

The poor guy looked terrified by the tiny woman standing in front of him. He acted like he didn't know whether to shit or go blind.

Then she threw her arms around him and hugged him fiercely. Swanny's dismay turned to bafflement and finally wonder. Shea pulled away and then put her hand to the scars on Swanny's face. Shame crowded into his eyes but she was having none of that. She leaned up on tiptoe and kissed his scarred cheek.

"I'm so glad you're okay. I worried so much about you and Nathan over the last several months."

He stared at her with an open mouth. He closed it and reopened it multiple times but nothing seemed to come out. Then his entire expression softened and he reached tentatively to touch her hair, almost as if he wasn't quite sure he wasn't having a hallucination.

"Thank you," he said hoarsely. "I'll never forget what you did for Nathan and for me."

She squeezed him again and gave him another kiss on the cheek. Then she seemed to realize that Donovan and Ethan were staring at her. She flushed and all but ran back to Nathan. He caught her hand, squeezed and pulled her into his side.

"Shea, I want you to meet my brothers, Ethan and Donovan. Guys, this is Shea."

He wasn't entirely certain how his brothers were going to handle a potentially awkward situation. To his surprise, Donovan stepped forward and took Shea's hand from Nathan and held it in his own.

"I owe you a great debt," Donovan said gravely. "You returned my brother to his family. For that you have my thanks."

She flushed with pleasure and gifted Donovan with a beautiful smile.

"I'm Ethan," Ethan said as he pushed forward. "I'm happy to meet you, Shea."

She included Ethan in her smile, but she clung shyly to Nathan's side.

"Not to cut short the pleasantries, but maybe you better fill us in on what's going on," Donovan said. "The abbreviated version if you don't mind. We need to get the hell on the road. We can talk more at length on the plane."

Shea frowned and looked like she'd argue, but Nathan squeezed her hand, silently asking her to hear them out. Her mouth relaxed, and he eased her to the bed so she could sit.

He sat next to her while Swanny slid down the wall by the window to sit on the floor. Ethan leaned against the door and Donovan slouched in the rickety chair by the desk.

Nathan glanced down at Shea. *I have to tell them everything. You know that.*

She didn't react to his form of communication but nodded her acceptance.

Carefully he explained Shea's abilities. There was a lot of doubt reflected in Ethan's and Donovan's faces. Not Swanny's, though. Swanny just nodded and his expression remained impassive.

When he got to the part where Shea left him after his brothers rescued him in Afghanistan, he urged Shea to take over and relate her part.

In a halting voice, she recounted the time she spent on the run. She was candid about Grace, their parents' murder, and was equally blunt about her treatment at her captors' hands.

The other men's expressions turned black, and Donovan scowled so hard that Shea looked warily at him.

"I'd like to get my hands on those assholes," Donovan muttered.

It didn't surprise Nathan that Van had such a fierce reaction to Shea's story. He was a born sucker for women and children, and he got violent when either were abused.

"Tell us about Grace," Ethan said. "Where is she now?"

Shea's mouth turned down into a sad frown. "I don't know. She went to our parents' house. The last time I talked to her, I saw enough to know she was there. It's why Nathan and I went there today."

Donovan turned his sharp stare to Nathan. "You did what?"

Again Nathan recounted the events for his brothers. "I uploaded video surveillance footage to your email. I was hoping you'd be able to take a look. If Grace was there, we should be able to see what happened. I also got shots of the guys who were there today before they blew a hole in the wall. Van, they looked military. They weren't amateurs, that's for damn sure."

Ethan's expression blackened. "You should have damn well waited for us before going into an unknown situation like that. You pull a stunt like that again and I'll kick your ass."

"It was my fault," Shea quietly interjected. "I had to go. I didn't know if Grace was still there. Or if she was hurt or if she'd been captured. I had to know. I had to see what I could find out. Nathan wanted to call you in but I worried it would take too much time and that we'd be too late if we waited."

Donovan stared hard at Shea, his eyes going soft. "It would seem to me that you've spent a hell of a lot of time looking out for everyone but yourself."

Shea shook her head in denial.

"You've got us to do that now," Donovan continued. "We're not going to let these assholes—whoever they are—so much as get near you again."

Ethan nodded his agreement.

"What do you want to do, Van?" Nathan asked. "I don't think we should bring this kind of trouble home."

"We could take her to one of the safe houses," Ethan suggested. "There's the cabin Sam took Sophie to in Virginia."

Donovan frowned for a long moment. "I'll call Sam, give him an update on the situation and we'll figure out our best course of action. Either way we're getting the hell out of here."

"But what about Grace?" Shea demanded. "I can't just leave here. I won't leave her."

Donovan acknowledged her with a nod. "I need some time to go over the footage Nathan was able to upload. We have to put the pieces together and come up with as much of the puzzle as we can. We can't do that here. We need to be in a safe place where I also have access to all of KGI's resources."

Shea slapped her hand on her forehead. "The journal. God, Nathan, the journal. I just forgot all about it. Maybe there's something in there."

She started to scramble off the bed, but Nathan snagged her hand. "There'll be plenty of time to read it when we're in the air. Right now our priority is getting you the hell out of here and to a safe place."

When she would have protested again, he pressed his mouth to hers. When he drew away, he ran his hand over her hair. "We aren't going to leave Grace, baby. I promise. I need to get you away from here. Once we're out of here, I swear to you we'll do everything in our power to locate her."

Slowly she nodded.

"I'll get Resnick to put some feelers out to find out what government agency might be interested in Shea's and Grace's abilities," Donovan said.

Shea raised her head in alarm. "No! You can't tell anyone else about us!"

Donovan held up his hand. "We aren't going to tell the world. Just Resnick. He's someone we trust. He has no incentive to fuck us over. We do too much of his dirty work for him. If the government is looking for you, he'll find out. A faceless enemy does us no good. We need to know exactly whom we're dealing with. The only way to do that is to go on the offensive and not wait around for them to find us. We hunt them. Not the other way around."

"Hell yeah," Swanny said, speaking up for the first time. "Count me in."

Nathan almost laughed at the enthusiasm in Swanny's voice. It was the first time Nathan had seen him worked up about anything since they got back from Afghanistan. Hell, it was the first time that Nathan had felt a purpose. It felt pretty damn good.

CHAPTER 25

THEY took off the next morning after sending the other jet ahead to a different location as a decoy. After a few derogatory remarks from Donovan about Nathan stealing a Kelly jet, Nathan endured a lecture about leaving KGI in a lurch if they'd been called up for a mission and been left with limited transportation means.

Shea had separated herself from the men. And Nathan. He wasn't entirely sure he liked it. But she was curled up in the corner of the wraparound couch, a reading light on as she flipped through the journal she'd found at her parents' house.

His brothers were talking, but Nathan had tuned them out. His focus was on Shea. It was obvious whatever she was reading distressed her. She was pale. Her fingers gripped the edges of the book and she turned each page with a seeming sense of dread. Almost like she was afraid of what she'd find.

He wanted to go over to her. He wanted to pull her into his arms, but she had a tangible barrier constructed, both physically and mentally. He'd briefly tried touching her mind, more to reassure himself than to reassure her, but she was blocked off. She'd shut the door on him, and it frustrated him even as he knew she needed this time alone to process whatever it was she was reading.

It took him a moment to realize that Donovan was talking to him. Only when Ethan nudged him did he turn and stare at his brothers, his mind blank to whatever they'd been saying.

"Don't you think it's time you told us what the fuck is going on with you? Has been going on with you? Is it Shea? Is she why you've closed yourself off from the rest of us? Why you refused to come to us for help until now?"

Donovan spoke in low tones so that Shea wouldn't overhear, but Nathan still glanced back to see that she was still firmly involved in her reading.

Then he turned back to his brothers and Swanny. At least Swanny would understand.

"What was I supposed to do, Van? There were times I thought I was crazy. Certifiable. She was with me when I went through unimaginable hell. She suffered it with me. She took my pain, my torture, and made it her own. And why? She didn't know me. She put herself at risk. Huge risk."

"You should have told us," Ethan said. "We would have understood. What we didn't understand is why you put this wall between you and your family. Hell, it wouldn't have mattered to us if you were crazy as a loon. At least we could have helped."

"How could you understand when I didn't understand myself?" Nathan asked in a tired voice. "She left me when you came for me, that last time, when I knew I was finally going to get out alive. I went crazy because, for so long, she was all I had. She was the only hope I had. She was like this talisman for me and then she was gone. And then I began to wonder if she was real. Maybe I'd imagined her. But it always came back to those emails. The ones she sent Van. But then I had no idea how to find her, how to reach her, much less how to explain her to you. Everyone was already tiptoeing around me like they were afraid I'd lose my shit and start barking at the moon. And maybe I was. I just knew that I had to come to terms with what happened on my own. And then . . ."

He broke off, chanced another look in Shea's direction.

"She's a fucking miracle. My miracle. The day of Rusty's graduation party, she spoke to me and she was so afraid. I knew those bastards had taken her then. Several nights before that, she'd tried to reach out to me, but she was drugged and all I felt was her confusion and disorientation, but I knew it was her, and I knew something was terribly wrong. But again, what could I do? I didn't know where she was. I didn't even know who she was. Just her name. I've never felt so goddamn helpless in my life. But then she called for me. She'd escaped and was running for her life. Those bastards tortured her. They drugged her and tortured her and there wasn't a goddamn thing I could do about it. But I could get to her as fast as I could. I could do that much. And I could do everything in my power to protect her. So I did.

"Could I have asked for your help? Yeah, but then I would have had to explain everything. I would have had to combat your disbelief. We would have wasted time that Shea didn't have while you decided whether to believe me or lock my ass up in some mental facility. By the time we came up with some damn plan and coordinated KGI and figured out who was going to do what, it would have been too late for Shea, and I wasn't going to let that happen."

Ethan's lips tightened into a fine line. He understood. He understood all too well and Nathan knew it. He'd once been faced with the situation of having to go in and rescue his wife, and he of all people knew Nathan's frustration and why he'd made the choices he did.

Swanny merely nodded. Didn't offer words, just nodded his agreement.

Donovan sighed and ran a hand through his hair. "I get it, man. I do. I just wish you'd come to us from the start. It's been killing us to see you this way and not know what if anything we could do to help. You're my brother and you have to know there isn't a damn thing I wouldn't do for you. Whether you're crazy or not."

Nathan smiled. "I know. I do know that, Van. I know I could have done things differently, but at the time it was what I thought I needed to do. I hate that I hurt you and the rest of the family. But when I came back . . . I wasn't the same man. I wasn't sure I could ever be that man again."

Donovan put a hand on Nathan's shoulder and squeezed. "You haven't changed. No matter what you might think, you haven't changed. Not to your family. We love you and support you unconditionally."

Then Donovan glanced over at Shea. "We've got a shitload of stuff to process. I've been in touch with Sam. Our first priority is safety. Our second priority is figuring out who we're dealing with. I'm going to analyze the footage you uploaded and hope to hell it gives us something to work off of. Sam is also ringing Resnick's bell to see what info he'll cough up."

Nathan nodded. "She goes nowhere without me. Just so you know. It's not an option."

Ethan snorted. "Hell, like we can't figure that out? I'm tempted to call Ma and rat you out, but no one wants her on our asses right now. I'm more afraid of her than I am of a whole terrorist cell."

Donovan didn't look as convinced. "I get that you want to protect her, Nathan, but it's entirely possible the safest option for her won't be tagging along with you."

Nathan was already shaking his head. "She's tough, Van. She's saved my ass more than once. Her looks are deceiving. She's got more steel in her spine than a lot of men I know. She won't accept us sticking her in some hole, and furthermore I don't want that. I want her with me. All the time."

Donovan blew out his breath. It went against his grain to ever put a woman in danger. His instinct was always to bury them as far underground as possible and then go kick whoever's ass threatened them.

But Nathan knew that Shea was different. She'd been on her own for a year, and she wasn't going to fall apart at the first sign of danger. They were . . . partners . . . for lack of a better term. He needed her every bit as much as she needed him. She kept him centered. Grounded. And the only way he'd ever be convinced of her safety was if he could see her at all times.

Donovan opened his mouth to speak but then fell silent, his gaze riveted to Shea. Nathan turned to see her get up from her seat. She wobbled a little as she started toward where the men were gathered. Her face was pale and her entire demeanor told him she was in shock.

She gripped the closed journal and took another step. This time he hurriedly rose and crossed the distance to take her other hand. He led her to where the others sat and then simply put her on his lap so she could be near him.

He wrapped his arms around her and whispered close to her ear. "It's okay, baby. Whatever it is, we'll face it together."

"You need to know this," she said, her voice scratchy.

Realization hit him in the gut. She'd been crying, even though the signs were gone from her face. He pressed his lips to her shoulder, not knowing what else he could do to comfort her. Not until they knew what she'd learned from the journal.

She raised haunted eyes to his brothers before turning her gaze on Nathan, hurt and confusion brimming in her liquid gaze.

"Grace was right. They weren't our real parents."

CHAPTER 26

SHEA'S chest hurt so badly that she could barely squeeze air into and out of her lungs. She was more afraid than ever. Terrified.

And everything she'd thought she'd ever know about herself—her life—was all a lie.

Nathan kissed her shoulder again, and his hand slipped up and down her other arm in a soothing pattern. His brothers and Swanny looked curiously at her, their gazes going from her face to the journal she held so tightly in her grasp.

"I don't even know how to explain it." Numbness was rapidly spreading through her veins until she felt disembodied.

"Start from the beginning," Donovan said gently. "What did you mean by they weren't your real parents?"

Her breath hiccupped out of her mouth and her shoulders drooped with fatigue and disillusionment. "Apparently my parents . . . the people who raised me . . . were scientists. They were heading a top-secret, government-funded project. No one but a few high-ranking government officials even knew of its existence, and they were all military officials. My mother remarked in her journal that it was doubtful the president or members of Congress ever knew about the project."

"What the hell were they researching?" Ethan asked.

"They weren't researching," Shea said softly. "They were creating. Me and my sister, Grace. Though now I wonder if she's even my sister."

Nathan stiffened against her. "Wait a minute. Back up."

She stood, suddenly no longer able to sit still against him. She paced away and then turned to face the assembled group again.

"According to my mother . . ." She shook her head and swallowed back the knot in her throat. "According to Andrea Peterson, Grace and I were lab-created experiments. Who knows who my real parents were. I doubt they even knew each other. They chose 'samples' from a selection of people who were particularly gifted and possessed 'unusual talents,' though none of the so-called abilities are outlined in her journal. And then these samples were basically mixed, implanted in a volunteer uterus, and they took the baby when it was born."

The looks of horror on the men's faces were a mirror of her own disgust. Nathan's face was drawn tight, his eyes dark, nearly black.

"What was their objective?" Ethan asked.

Shea sighed. "I don't know. I'm not even sure Andrea knew. She was told they were going to study psychic anomaly occurring in the human population and how or if it could be reproduced through controlled experiments. But she grew increasingly more concerned with the way Grace and I were used. She expressed guilt and remorse for being part of a 'devil's creation.'"

Tears burned the edges of her eyes. Devil's creation. That was what her own mother considered her and Grace. Some abomination, not from God. She and Grace had been created in some sterile laboratory to be poked and prodded, their abilities used for God only knew what.

Nathan stood, as if he couldn't remain seated a moment longer. His fingers were curled into tight fists and his agitation was broadcasting so strongly that it filled her mind, swamping her with his rage and his horror.

She turned away, no longer able to stand the terrible look in his eyes.

His hands slid over her shoulders, and he turned her, almost roughly, to face him. He gripped her, holding her there so she had no choice but to comply with his silent demand.

"I don't know what the hell you're thinking right now," he said in a low voice. "I don't know because you've shut yourself off from me. I can only guess as to why, but it's bullshit. You have to know I don't give a damn. You're not some lab experiment. Not some accident of science. You're a fucking miracle. *My* miracle. I don't give a shit how you came into existence but I thank God every day that you did. Has it ever occurred to you that you were born with a much higher purpose? One that transcended whatever fuck of a reason those bastards played around in their goddamn lab for?"

She stared up at him in awe, so shocked by his vehemence that she couldn't even begin to know how to respond. What could she say to that?

A tear slid down her cheek and he thumbed it away, his expression so fierce that it should have scared her. And then he simply pulled her into his arms, cupping her head to his chest as he held her tight enough to crush her ribs.

She didn't care. She only cared that he held her, that she absorbed his strength, his warmth and, oh God, the aching awareness that she mattered so much to him.

He tangled his hand in her hair and then pressed his mouth to the top of her head. He trembled against her, part in anger, but she could feel the emotion pouring into her mind.

"What else, Shea?" he asked quietly. "We need to know everything. But I need you to know that I'm here. I'm not going anywhere. You aren't alone. And I don't give a flying fuck how you came into existence."

She pulled away and smiled shakily up at him. Then she laced her fingers with his and squeezed. She glanced sideways at Swanny and Nathan's brothers, embarrassed that they'd witnessed her upset.

She tugged one hand away from Nathan and wiped hastily at her face, pushing aside her hair. When she would have pulled away from Nathan entirely, he tightened his hold on her hand and guided her back to where they'd been sitting.

This time he settled her between him and Swanny. He

made sure they were touching, his leg against hers, his hand covering her knee.

She sucked in a deep breath, determined to make it through the rest of the telling without breaking down again.

"Andrea and Brandon were appalled at the treatment Grace and I received. It wasn't that we were being tortured or beaten or abused, but we were treated as test subjects, not babies. It was all very cold. We were fed and our basic needs seen to, but little else. We endured endless testing and experimentation. In one entry, Andrea recounted that Grace was purposely cut with a knife to gauge my reaction. Conversely, I was also injured to test Grace's ability to heal me. And they logged the results, analyzed them, brainstormed ways of utilizing our abilities in a military setting."

"What the hell did they expect you to be able to accomplish?" Ethan demanded.

Shea glanced at Nathan's brother. He was bigger than both Donovan and Nathan. Taller, broader shouldered. Black hair and startling blue eyes. Nathan was slightly taller than Donovan, but he had a similar build. Lean and muscular. Donovan was a bit heavier, but Shea guessed that under normal circumstances Nathan would have been bulkier. His body was still carved by the time he'd spent imprisoned and nearly starved.

Nathan's hair was lighter than Donovan's and his eyes were dark brown. Donovan's were green, mesmerizing for the odd shade. Not lighter, but not emerald either.

Alone, one of them was enough to intimidate the most fearsome person. Together? They were formidable.

Her gaze drifted to Swanny, her thoughts momentarily interrupted by her analysis of the men she'd now place her trust in. Her heart wrenched. He was tall and lean. Almost haggard in appearance. His cheeks were hollow and his skin was stretched tight over his bones. And the scars on his face were still puckered and raw looking, even months after his rescue. They would take time to heal. They'd never disappear, but with time some of the redness would fade and they wouldn't look quite so vivid or angry.

She very nearly reached for his hand, but curled her fingers into a fist instead. He wouldn't appreciate her pity, and how did you pity a man who'd survived hell? You didn't pity him. You admired him.

"Shea," Nathan prompted softly.

She flinched, embarrassed at how she'd drifted. She tried to focus her thoughts again. She seemed to be drifting in a sea of confusion, anger and heart sickness.

She glanced back up at Ethan and bit at her bottom lip. Her stomach clenched and she couldn't explain the sudden nerves or the panic creeping up her spine.

Baby, take deep breaths. I'm here. I know this is a lot to deal with. We'll do it together.

The loving, soothing voice in her head sent waves of comfort through her veins. She visibly relaxed and sent Nathan a look of gratitude. His brothers glanced sharply at Nathan as if they were aware that something had transpired between him and Shea, but they didn't know what.

Again she refocused on Ethan. "I'm sorry," she said in a quiet, even voice. She was proud of the fact that her voice no longer sounded choked or full of tears. She was determined to get through this.

Ethan's expression softened. He looked like he wanted to reach out and take her hand or offer a gesture of comfort. It seemed odd, because he appeared so aloof. All business.

"Take your time, Shea. I know this has to be difficult for you."

She nodded. "To answer your question, again, according to Andrea's journal, there were several possibilities the organization that funded the research wanted to explore. Remote healing for one. Having someone far removed from the dangers of war or battle with the ability to heal through a psychic link."

"Holy hell, is that even possible?" Donovan asked.

Swanny nodded, injecting himself into the conversation for the first time. Then he glanced sideways at Shea. "Was it you or your sister inside me, when I was so injured?"

"It was Grace," Shea whispered. "I didn't have a connection to you. Only Nathan. Nathan and I were the conduits to you."

"That's incredible," Donovan muttered. "Jesus, I can see why they're so hot to track you and your sister down. Can you imagine what this would mean? You'd basically have an inde-structible fighting force. They'd go down and then get right back up."

Shea shook her head. "It's faulty. All of it. It takes a terri-ble toll on Grace. I doubt she'd be able to heal more than one person at a time, and if the wounds were mortal, they could kill her. Even if they didn't, she'd be too weak, too devastated, to continue on. And I can't even heal, which makes Grace the more valuable commodity. I have no doubt they're after us both, but it only makes sense they'd want what Grace has to offer more."

Ethan ran a hand through his hair. "This sounds like some freaky sci-fi movie. No offense, Shea."

She nodded sadly. "It does, doesn't it? Imagine finding out your entire life is one of those freaky sci-fi movies."

"So you can't heal?" Donovan asked.

"No. I can't even control my telepathy. I heard Nathan. But why not Swanny? Why not everyone else? It's frustrating. I'll hear someone out of the blue. They may not even be in danger. It could be perfectly normal. Someone summarizing a gro-cery list. Or someone in need. Someone sad. Happy."

"It sounds pretty damn awful," Ethan said grimly. "How the hell do you deal with that? It would make me crazy."

"But you did heal," Donovan said, his brow creasing in concentration. "You were a conduit for Grace. I'd say that makes you every bit as valuable as Grace."

Shea shrugged. "Who knows if that's what they think? I haven't stuck around long enough to ask questions. I just know I don't want my sister anywhere near them."

"I think it's naïve to think they wouldn't want to harness your abilities as well," Donovan persisted.

"Their only concern when they held me down and beat me was to extract information about Grace," she said flatly.

Donovan held up a hand. "Bear with me here. I'm not try-ing to be an asshole. They beat you, but you told Nathan it was a methodically executed beating. They hurt you, no doubt, but they didn't damage you. They were careful not to risk hurting you seriously, and by that I mean broken bones, internal inju-ries. They were trying to manipulate you with pain and fear but they had no intention of killing you."

"Well, of course not. I hadn't told them anything about Grace."

Donovan shook his head. "They want you both, Shea. You need to realize that. You're as valuable to them as your sister. How would they even know what the full extent of your abilities are? They haven't had access to you since you were a child."

"He's right," Nathan interjected. He smoothed his hand over her leg as he spoke.

"What happened?" Ethan asked. "How did you end up with the Petersons? You were raised as their children and they never told you the truth. You have no memory of the laboratory?"

Shea shook her head. "In her journal, Andrea wrote that she and Brandon grew increasingly upset over our treatment. They'd been with us, studied us since our births, and they felt a bond to us. They considered us theirs because no one else acted as our parents. They planned their escape meticulously. For months. And then one night, they took us and ran."

"Amazing that they were able to keep you hidden from them for all those years," Donovan murmured.

"We moved a lot." She turned to Nathan, a frown twisting her lips. "We talked about this before and it makes even less sense to me now. We never had a lot of money. Mom and Dad always scraped by doing jobs where they could be paid cash. But then we moved to that house in Oregon. You saw it. It's huge. It's on the ocean. It has state-of-the-art security and surveillance. We never seemed to worry about money after we moved there. So what happened? Why did we suddenly stop running? Where was the money coming from? They didn't work. They spent their time homeschooling us, making sure we never went out in public. We didn't have friends. I'm sure the townspeople thought we were crazy recluses."

The men traded frowns. Swanny sat forward, his fingers forming a point. He glanced at Nathan and then at Ethan and Donovan. "That's a damn good question. It certainly would appear that the Petersons got help from someone. Was there anything in the journal to explain it, Shea?"

"No. That's what's frustrating. She chronicled the events of our early years and she did so after the fact. It was like a written account almost as if she wanted us to know the truth one day. But her entries stopped when we moved to Oregon. Her last entry only says, 'God willing, we won't have to run any longer.' "

"Pretty damn cryptic," Nathan muttered.

"It certainly adds another dimension to this whole mess," Donovan said in a grim voice. "The Petersons got help from someone, but who? And what was their motive?"

Shea rubbed her forehead in an attempt to ease the strain and the thudding ache that pounded at her temples. Nathan pulled her to him and kissed her brow and then replaced her hand with his own, gently kneading.

"I don't know. I swear I don't know. I feel so stupid. I knew my life wasn't normal. I didn't always know that, but when I got older, I knew it was downright strange. Still, I never imagined this. How could I have? I thought my parents were just protective of Grace and me. They feared our abilities being discovered and what our lives would be like if that happened. I misunderstood their fear obviously, but I chalked up all of their eccentricities to concern for their daughters."

"Shea, look at me," Donovan said.

She lifted her gaze to see Donovan and Ethan both looking at her and Nathan with determination in their eyes. Gone was the skepticism, the doubt. All that remained was burning sincerity.

"KGI has a lot of resources. There isn't a lot we can't find out once we set our minds to it. But beyond that, you're important to Nathan so that makes you important to us. KGI is an organization, yes, but we're a family first. And we go to the wall for family. Every time. No questions asked. No conditions."

Her chin quivered as she fought the tide of emotion his heartfelt words wrought.

"I don't make promises lightly. I don't bullshit people. We're going to do everything we can to get to the bottom of this. I can't guarantee that we'll ever know who was the mastermind of the experiments on you and Grace. But what I can guarantee is that we're going to do everything in our power to keep you safe."

"And Grace?" she asked anxiously.

"And Grace. I need time to look at the surveillance and to

gather as much intel as I can, and then I promise you that we will find your sister and we'll give her the same protection we give you."

She leaned forward and gripped his hand in both of hers. She included Ethan in her gaze. "Thank you. I've been so worried. I don't know what to do anymore. I didn't want to involve Nathan, but I couldn't turn to anyone else."

Donovan smiled and glanced beyond her to Nathan. "I'd say you chose well. I pity the fool that tries to get between you and him."

"Damn straight," Nathan muttered.

NATHAN hovered over Donovan while he tied off the last stitch he'd set in Shea's shoulder. Her face was tight. She was pale, but she hadn't done much more than flinch as the suture pierced her skin.

When Nathan had learned that Donovan had only a skeleton med kit with him and the only anesthetic he had was topical, he'd flat out refused to let him stitch Shea up. They could wait until they reached the safe house. He wasn't about to let her endure unnecessary pain.

It had been Shea who insisted that it be done and over with. Donovan had assured Nathan that the cut was shallow enough that the stitches wouldn't have to be set deep and that he could do the job with minimal pain to Shea.

Nathan was convinced that Shea bore it so stoically because she wanted to avoid him losing his shit if she cried out.

"You done?" Nathan asked.

Donovan sighed, tore off his gloves and gave Nathan a disgusted look. "Yeah, I'm done."

Shea battled a smile.

"What?" Nathan demanded.

"You," she said. "You asked him that at least a dozen times. He'd have been done earlier if he hadn't had to stop so many times to tell you no."

"Sorry," he mumbled. "You okay? Does it hurt? Van should have something for pain. He's a walking medical unit. Well, usually anyway. Maybe not so much this time."

Shea looked up to where Donovan was putting away his supplies. "Is there anything you don't do?"

Donovan donned a thoughtful expression and then shook his head. "Nope."

Ethan laughed from his seat several feet away. "You walked into that one, Shea."

Shea seemed baffled by the teasing that already included her. It was something that Nathan missed all too much. He hadn't realized how much he'd missed just being a part of the Kelly family. Endless teasing. Joking. Fierce loyalty.

And now Shea was experiencing it firsthand.

Exhilaration hurtled through his veins. He couldn't have imagined the immense satisfaction he'd experience seeing Shea accepted into his family. Although Ethan and Donovan didn't constitute the entire Kelly clan, he couldn't imagine the rest doing any differently. They'd love her just as he loved her. How could they not?

He had no idea how the hell he was going to work this out, but the one thing he knew was that he absolutely could not imagine a life—his life—without Shea. She'd become as essential as breathing to him.

He didn't question it. Didn't argue. Some things just were. And this was one of them. The biggest thing of his entire life.

"I know that look," Ethan murmured.

Nathan swiveled around to see that Ethan had come up behind him while Donovan had taken Shea to the side to finish cleaning the suture area.

"It's the way Sam looks at Sophie. The way Garrett looks at Sarah. The way I'm sure I look at Rachel every time she walks into the room. You have the look of a man who is only sure of one thing. That the woman he's looking at is his, that she's the most essential part of himself."

Nathan eyed Ethan warily. "Since when have you gotten so in touch with your feelings?"

Hell, it was one thing to think this kind of shit, but who stood around discussing it with his brother? Nathan's discomfort level had just skyrocketed. Yeah, he was done for when it came to Shea, but he didn't want to discuss her with anyone else. Not yet. It was still too new. He wanted to keep every part of her to himself. He didn't want to share her and damn sure not his feelings about her with anyone.

Ethan smiled faintly. "It's amazing how losing the one person who matters most in the world will change your perspective in a lot of ways. Getting Rachel back—getting that miracle second chance with her—makes me aware of a lot of things I would have ignored in the past or considered myself too manly to talk about. I'll give you shit with the best of them, but I also see the way you look at her. I like her, Nathan. She's tough. But more than that, she gave you back to us. I'll always love her for that no matter what."

"Fuck you for trying to make me cry," Nathan muttered.

Ethan chuckled but then his expression turned serious again. "You know what? You're starting to sound like the old Nathan. I guess I have her to thank for that too. Goddamn it, you're my brother and I didn't think I'd ever see you again, and then when I did, I wondered if we'd really ever have you back even though you were here and alive. You were a damn shell and I'm so fucking relieved to see those glimpses of you."

Nathan eyed his brother warily. "For God's sake, don't hug me."

"How about I take you out behind the cabin when we get there and kick the ever-loving shit out of you instead?"

Nathan grinned, the ache in his chest easing just a bit. "How about you try?"

Ethan stared at him a long moment. "Welcome home, man. Just . . . welcome home."

Home. Yeah. It did feel more like home now that he'd found peace. Shea. She was his peace. She'd been what was missing and why there had been such a yawning hole in his soul ever since his return.

Now it was up to him to return the favor and give her that same peace. He didn't have a hell of a lot else to offer her. He was damaged. He wasn't even sure what he was going to do with the rest of his life. But no other man would ever love her as much as he did. He knew that much. And no one else would be willing to give his life to protect her. Because he would if that was what it took.

He'd give her the goddamn moon if she wanted it.

He wasn't the best man for her. She could do a hell of a lot better. But he wasn't going to look a gift horse in the mouth. He'd savor every single moment with her and hope like hell that, when everything was over with, she'd want to stay. With him. Because there wasn't a thing on this earth he wouldn't do to make her happy and feel secure.

CHAPTER 27

"WELL, well, looks like the entire welcome wagon is here," Donovan said as he stepped off the plane, dragging his gear with him.

Shea squinted against the sunlight as she stared onto the tarmac to see what looked like an entire military outfit. It was an imposing sight. Men . . . wait, there was a woman in the middle of them. Smaller but she had a look of all business. Her hair was pulled into a ponytail and she wore a baseball cap so that the brim shielded her eyes.

On further inspection, the men looked to be sectioned off into groups. Not so much that they'd been partitioned intentionally, but it was like certain individuals gravitated toward each other and the result was three sections of badass-looking men—and woman—and they were all staring at her and Nathan.

Nathan bumped into her from behind, grabbed her hand and all but hauled her down the few steps. Ethan and Swanny came up behind them, flanking Nathan and Shea. She appreciated that show of support. It was silly, really, but maybe they'd realized how terrified she was of exposure. Regardless, she was extremely grateful that she didn't have to face these people alone.

It took her a moment to realize that Nathan was every bit as nervous and agitated as she was. He stared forward, silent and tense. His mind was a chaotic whirl of regret and worry.

Her heart softened and her anxiety slid away. What did she care what these people thought of her? Nathan was behind her and so were Ethan, Donovan and Swanny. Right now Nathan needed her not to be a whiny twit. He needed her strong.

She slipped her hand into his and squeezed just as they'd done for each other time and time again. The action seemed to startle him, and then he looked down at her, warmth building in his eyes, replacing the worry.

You're not crazy, Nathan. No more than I am. If they think it of you, they aren't worthy of your respect or your regard. But they don't. They love you. Look at them. They're as worried as you are. They're afraid to approach you. They don't want to do anything wrong. So they're waiting for you to make the first move.

As if reinforcing the very thing that Shea had spoken in Nathan's mind, Donovan put his hand on Nathan's shoulder and urged him forward.

You're amazing. Thank you. I didn't realize how . . . unsure . . . I was about all of this. Not about you, baby. I need you to know that. Things have been off between me and my family—my brothers—ever since I came back from Afghanistan. This is the first time I've really faced them openly. I'd never admit this to anyone else, but I'm terrified.

The frankness in Nathan's thoughts staggered Shea. He didn't try to shield anything from her. He was an open book. That kind of trust was unimaginable.

Three men broke from the group and approached. The others remained behind, bags at their feet, calmly surveying the scene in front of them.

At least one of them had to be one of Nathan's brothers. Maybe all three. But there was one who looked an awful lot like Ethan. Black hair, startling blue eyes. But bigger. Not by much, but he seemed to dwarf the others with his presence. It wasn't just his build, though he was certainly a big guy. It was his expression. His demeanor. He wasn't someone you'd ever want to cross. At least not without a gun and at least a hundred yards between you.

The one standing to the right had lighter hair but the same blue eyes. Definitely another Kelly. There was concern but also relief as he stared at Nathan. No condemnation just a healthy dose of relief.

When her gaze swept to the left, she felt a jolt all the way to her toes. Her mind was suddenly crowded with a surge of emotions. Anger. Relief. Confusion. Impatience. The man was broadcasting loudly in her mind. He briefly glanced over her. Dismissed her with brief irritation. He was irritated by Nathan's seeming preoccupation with her. He didn't understand why Nathan would drop everything to go to her. Why he wouldn't ask his twin for help.

He felt threatened by her.

"Joe," she whispered. This was Joe, Nathan's twin brother, and she could slip into his mind just like she could slip into Nathan's.

In a twisted way it made sense that she'd be able to connect to Nathan's twin. But then little about her telepathy made sense. So much of it was random that it actually did surprise her that this could actually be called predictable. It made sense that her psychic link could be forged with the person Nathan was closest to in the world. And nothing about her gift had ever made sense before.

Joe glanced up at her sharply, his eyes narrowing. He couldn't have heard her faint whisper but perhaps he'd heard it in his mind. She would have to carefully guard her thoughts around him and focus her connection so it would only extend to Nathan.

She didn't want to know what his brother thought nor did she have any desire to communicate with him in such an intimate manner.

She took in several steadying breaths. She would not allow herself to be afraid or intimidated. Nathan needed her. This was difficult for him, made more so by the fact that he was thrusting her into his world and expecting his family to risk their lives to protect her.

"I'm Shea," she said in an even voice before anyone else spoke. "Shea Peterson, though there is some doubt as to whether that is my real last name. I am, however, very real. I'm telepathic. I'm sure you have doubts where I'm concerned.

I don't blame you. Nathan risked a lot to help me. I'm sure you question why he would do it. And why he would expect you to help me as well."

To her complete astonishment, the man in the middle, the one she thought looked so similar to Ethan, took a step forward, pulled her into his arms and hugged her so tightly that she worried she'd suffer broken ribs.

He lifted her off her feet, squeezed a little harder and then kissed her right on the forehead.

"I'd be pissed if he didn't expect us to help. I'm Garrett, by the way. Nathan's older brother. This is Sam on my right and Joe to the left. We've heard a lot about you, Shea. But you'll understand if we're more interested in hearing about you straight from the source."

"Put her down, moron," Sam said in a dry tone. "We need to be on our way. We can save the pleasantries for later."

Garrett put Shea down but then he faced Nathan, staring at his younger brother, his expression giving nothing away. Then, as he'd done with Shea, Garrett pulled Nathan into a tight hug and pounded him on the back.

"You've got a hell of a lot of explaining to do, little man."

Nathan punched Garrett in the gut. "Watch who you call little man."

Garrett grinned and rubbed his abdomen. "Nice to see you haven't wussed out on me in the last months. Was afraid you'd turn into a girl or something."

Shea frowned, sure that there'd been an insult in there somewhere.

Joe still hadn't said anything. He stared at Nathan like he was waiting. Sam glanced back at the twins and then tucked an arm around Shea's shoulders. "Come on. We should get you into the SUV. Beavis and Butthead there will come along after they've had their come-to-Jesus moment."

Shea looked back in concern, but Garrett nudged her away. "They've got a lot to work out between them. Joe needs to vent his spleen. This has been brewing between them for months now. The sooner they get it out in the open, the sooner things will get back to normal. As normal as things ever get in this family."

Still she hesitated. She didn't know these men. Didn't

know the group of men still standing in the background. She didn't want to intrude on Nathan's conversation with Joe, but neither was she going to get into a vehicle full of strangers without him.

"I'll wait for Nathan here," she said firmly, stopping several feet away from the line of SUVs.

Garrett looked surprised, and then grudging respect flashed in his eyes. He glanced over at the men standing to the side and motioned them over.

"Shea, I'd like you to meet the other members of KGI. I don't know how much Nathan has told you about us, but we're a private organization that does jobs no one else can or wants to do."

"Could you be a little more vague?" she muttered.

He grinned but didn't respond.

He pointed to a darker-skinned man with longish, unruly black hair and dark eyes. "This is Rio, one of our team leaders."

Rio flashed her a smile. "Nice to meet you, ma'am."

Behind him, his team lurked, silent and tense as if ready for anything. Garrett didn't single them out, which was just as well. She'd never remember all their names and her head was already spinning. Did it matter if she knew who they were? It sounded bitchy and ungrateful, but she was only concerned with Nathan.

Garrett then pointed to a tall man with blond hair and piercing blue eyes. Cold eyes that made her shiver as he stared at her.

"That's Steele, our other team leader, and that's his team just behind him."

Steele didn't offer a greeting. He just nodded and then took a step back. Which was fine with her, because he unnerved her.

Swanny stepped in next to her. Relieved, she took his hand and clung to it. All these people made her nervous, and she was grateful for Swanny's comforting presence. Which she supposed didn't make a whole lot of sense given that she'd only just met him too, but they had a bond through Nathan and she felt at ease around him.

He glanced down in surprise and she thought she had offended him or unnerved him with her gesture, but when she started to pull away, his grip tightened around her hand, and to her further amazement, he offered a smile. A genuine smile. It was the first time she'd seen any emotion, good or bad, on his solemn features.

"They're a little hard to take all at once," he whispered down to her.

She smiled and nodded because that was exactly what she'd been thinking.

"But Garrett is right. You should be in the SUV and not in the open. I'll go with you until Nathan makes it over."

It was then she realized Garrett hadn't called his men over for a meet and greet. They'd positioned themselves strategically around her. A protective shield, since she'd balked about getting into the SUV without Nathan.

Feeling like a moron, she nodded and allowed Swanny to guide her toward one of the waiting vehicles. He climbed into the back with her and shut the door. Garrett got into the front passenger seat while some of the others separated to go to the other vehicles. Donovan, Ethan and Sam remained outside at a discreet distance from where Nathan and Joe stood, and Shea realized they were looking out for their brothers.

"Did I cause this?" she asked softly in Garrett's direction. "This problem between them?"

Garrett turned so he could look at her. His gaze softened and he didn't look as formidable as he had before.

"No, you didn't. This is something that has to be worked out between them. They're very close. They've always worked and served together. A lot has changed for both of them, and when Nathan came home to us, Joe just wanted things to be the way they were before. They'll be fine. You have plenty enough to worry about without being concerned that you're the cause of a brotherly rift. In this family someone's always pissed off at someone else, but we get over it real quick," he added with a grin.

Shea nodded but her gaze remained fixed on the two brothers facing each other a short distance away. It was all she could do not to slip into Nathan's mind. To offer him support. To know what was being said, but she wouldn't intrude on his privacy.

She knew all too well how much he loved his family. They'd been all he'd focused on when he was in captivity. Whatever it was keeping the two brothers apart would be resolved. It had to be.

NATHAN stared at his twin in silence. This was a new situation for him, being so unsure of where he stood with the sibling he was closest to. Joe was tense and a little unsure himself. He seemed poised to say many things, but he held back. Maybe he was afraid of making Nathan angry.

Finally Joe broke the silence. "Why, man?"

Nathan didn't pretend to misunderstand the question. He drew in a breath, unsure of what to say to his brother. He didn't fully understand things himself. He was only now starting to feel like he was piecing himself back together and he had Shea to thank for that. He had a hell of a lot to thank her for. She gave him purpose. Purpose he hadn't had in months.

"Why didn't you ask me for help?" Joe asked quietly when Nathan continued to be silent. "You had to know I'd understand. You had to know that I wouldn't have judged you. Hell, even if I thought you were off your fucking rocker, I would have done anything to help you. I hated seeing you like that. I've never felt so goddamn helpless in my life, and it pissed me off that you locked me out. You closed yourself off from the rest of the family. Okay, I get that, but not me. I'm not just another member of your family. I'm your twin. We have a bond that goes much deeper than just family."

Nathan blew out his breath. The raw edge in Joe's voice cut as deep as any knife wound he'd received. "You're right. I'm an asshole. I'm sorry. I know it's not enough but I'm sorry. I was coping the best I could. It's a sorry excuse but I wasn't ready to share Shea with anyone. There were days I convinced myself she wasn't real and that I was an idiot for clinging to the belief that she was. And when she asked for my help and I knew she was in serious trouble, I just couldn't wait. I had to go. I *had* to. She risked everything to save me. I couldn't stand by and allow anything to happen to her."

Joe studied him in silence for a long moment. "She means that much to you."

Nathan slowly nodded. "Yeah, she does. I don't expect you

to understand, but she and I have something that I can't even explain. I need her. And now she needs me."

Joe jammed his thumbs into the pockets of his jeans. "Don't pull this shit again, man. Swear to God, I'll kick your fucking ass, and I don't give a shit what kind of shape you're in. You need my help, you goddamn ask for it."

Nathan pressed his lips together to keep from smiling. "I'm asking now."

Joe punched him in the shoulder. "Okay then. That's better. Now let's get the fuck on the road so you can fill me in on everything. And I mean everything."

"Not going to hug me?" Nathan mocked.

Joe gave him a look of disgust. "Garrett's turned into an emotional wuss since he hooked up with Sarah. I'll let him do all the mamby-pamby shit. Besides, what you need is a swift kick in the ass. If you want a hug, go see Ma."

Nathan laughed and started toward the SUVs, where Shea waited with the others. Relief was so stark that his knees shook. He was back. God, he was back. Home. With his brothers.

There was no sweeter feeling in the world. It had been a hell of a long journey, most of it of his own doing, but he was back, and with each passing day, he was beginning to feel whole again.

CHAPTER 28

NATHAN slid into the SUV beside Shea and instantly pulled her close to his body. Not resisting, she turned just enough that she could curl into his side and rest her cheek on his shoulder.

He softly kissed her brow. "Tired?"

She nodded.

"How's your shoulder feeling?"

"It was just a little cut. It doesn't hurt at all. Barely enough to worry over putting a Band-Aid on."

The driver's door opened and Sam got in, glancing in the rearview mirror as he keyed the ignition.

"How far to the safe house?" Nathan asked.

Sam leveled a stare at him. "We're taking you home."

Shea raised her head in confusion. Nathan stiffened beside her and shook his head in denial.

Sam held up his hand. "Before you start arguing, this isn't negotiable. Van and I discussed this before you left Crescent City. We flew you here so that anyone monitoring flights out wouldn't be led to our back door. It's not the most expedient route home, but we're more concerned with no one dogging our steps. I know you didn't want to bring this to our doorstep, but we built that compound for a reason. We need to avail ourselves of the resources there, not be holed up in some damn safe house with our balls flapping in the wind."

"Nice of him to let me know," Nathan muttered.

Sam raised an eyebrow. "And you've been so cooperative so far? I told Van to do whatever the hell he had to do to get your asses on that plane. If you want to be pissed at someone, be pissed at me."

Shea stared anxiously at Nathan. She hadn't even realized she was squeezing his hand with bloodless fingers until he gently pried them away and then kissed each tip.

I don't want you to worry, baby. Trust me. If you trust no one else, trust me and believe that I'll keep you safe. What Sam says makes sense. I trust them with my life. With yours.

She leaned forward, touching her forehead to his shoulder.

It's not just me I worry about. Or Grace even. I believe that you'll protect me. That your family, your organization, will try to help Grace—and me. But what of your family? You didn't want to bring me to them. You're worried for them. Nothing has changed. If anything, things are more dangerous now. I never wanted to drag others into this mess that Grace and I are in. We just want to be . . . normal. Free. Free to live a normal life where we can see each other. Laugh and visit together. Be sisters.

How can I feel relief that I'll be safe when others are risking danger to themselves to ensure that Grace and I are protected?

"That must be one long-ass conversation," Garrett said.

Shea jerked around guiltily and caught Garrett staring at her and Nathan in avid interest. He'd known that they were communicating telepathically. She watched closely for his reaction but all she saw was curiosity.

"Are you two finished and can we get on the road now?" Sam drawled.

"Yes," Nathan said.

"No," Shea said at the exact same time.

"We'll go with yes," Garrett muttered and motioned for Sam to drive.

Shea's lips tightened in irritation, but Nathan put a finger to her jaw and gently turned her back so she faced him.

"Listen to me," he said in a low voice.

No, please, she begged. *Not out loud. I don't want them to overhear.*

His expression softened and he trailed one finger down the side of her cheek. *I want you with me. I want you to meet my family. You have to know that's got to happen at some point. You're important to me, Shea. Not just some job. I trust my brothers and I know damn well they'd never do anything that would place our family in danger. And Sam's right. We need the KGI resources. Offense, not defense, remember?*

I remember.

Is there some other reason you're reluctant to go to Tennessee with me?

She hesitated, her chest tightening with an uncomfortable burn.

Shea?

I'm just confused. About us. What are we, Nathan? This whole situation has such a surreal quality. When it was just us, it was easy . . .

His brow furrowed. *What was easy?*

To pretend, she offered softly.

His gaze narrowed and a frown marred the line of his mouth. *Exactly what are we pretending here?*

She tried to ease away and sit back against the seat, but he hauled her over his lap so that her legs dangled in the seat between him and Swanny.

There was nowhere to go. No way to escape his burning gaze. He looked almost angry.

She sighed. *It's easy to pretend that we're normal. That we have a chance at a normal . . . relationship. You know, go out on an actual date. You take me out to dinner. We make cutesy conversation. I try not to think about whether you'll kiss me at the end of the night. I subtly check out your butt when you get up. Those are what normal people do. We don't have a chance of any of those things. We don't have a chance at a relationship.*

She shook her head and rubbed her palm over her eyes. *This whole conversation is ridiculous. I can't even believe I'm saying this stuff. We don't even know each other. It's arrogant of me to even be telling you we don't have a chance of anything. Who's to say I'm anything more than an obligation to you?*

As soon as she said it, she knew she'd made a huge mistake because suddenly she was being stared down by one big, pissed-off mass of seething male. His fury enveloped her. Oh yeah, he was angry.

He grasped her shoulders and hauled her toward him until there was no space between them and their breaths mingled hotly on her lips. His nostrils flared, and to her shock, he crushed his mouth to hers.

At first she was mortified that he was kissing her in front of Swanny and his brothers, but after only a moment she forgot everything but the feel of his lips against hers. The waves of emotion flooding her mind. He was angry, yes, but he was also frustrated. And worried.

He kissed her like he wanted to remove every bit of doubt crowding her mind. Like he was proving her wrong.

Then he gentled the forceful bruising of his mouth and stroked his tongue over hers, velvety rough and warm. His kiss turned from frustration and punishment to shivery seduction.

He slid his hands up her neck to delve into her hair even as he pulled her closer, impossibly close, until their tongues were tangled, mouths sealed, and her nostrils flared with the effort to take in air.

He stroked again with his tongue and then withdrew only to nip at her bottom lip, sucking it strongly into his mouth. He nibbled and toyed and then slid his tongue sensuously over the area where he'd bitten as if to soothe. When he finally drew away, his breaths were harsh explosions in the confines of the backseat, and his eyes were dark, nearly black, as he stared back at her.

You look at me and tell me you think you're some goddamn obligation to me. You look at me and tell me that we're pretending when the connection between us is the most tangible, overpowering thing I've ever felt in my life. If this is pretending, then I damn sure don't want to know what reality is. Do you honest to God think I swooped in for a quick lay and to repay some debt to you and that I'll go on my merry way once you and your sister are safe again?

She dropped her gaze as heat flooded her cheeks. The fury in his voice, the *hurt* evident in his tone, shamed her.

Goddamn it, Shea, you mean everything *to me. You mean more to me than I have the words to explain. Is it normal? Who gives a damn if it's normal? Fuck normal. You and I will never be normal people. If normal means I'm not with you, then I* never *want to be that man.*

He nudged her chin upward as he said the last. Tears filled her eyes and then she threw her arms around his neck, holding him so tight as her body shook against his.

Oh God, his words scared her and filled her with such hope and longing all at the same time. She wanted to believe him. She wanted to let herself believe in the fantasy she'd built in her mind.

He tugged her gently away from his neck and kissed her softly on the cheek where it was damp with her tears. He stroked through her hair, all the while staring at her with so much . . . love . . . oh God, love.

We may not have the most conventional path that a couple has ever traveled to get together, but you're here and I'm damn well not letting you go. And I don't give a damn who knows it.

She leaned her forehead against his again and touched his cheeks with her fingertips. *I want that too, Nathan. I swear to you I want it. I'm just so afraid that we'll never have it. I'm afraid of what I've done by dragging you into this mess. I'm afraid of what it's done for any chance that you and I have of being together.*

He lifted the hair from her neck and let the strands run through his fingers as they stared at each other, so close that she could feel the light brush of air when he blinked.

Trust me, Shea. We'll find a way. I need you to believe that. We aren't alone. I have my family behind me and I'm in front of you. Always. I'll protect you with my life because you are my life. If that sounds dramatic, fuck it. You've been mine since the day you answered me in my darkest hour. You heard me when no one else did or could. You reached out to me. You saved me. We have an unbreakable bond forged in the fires of hell. I won't allow anything or anyone to come between us.

I trust you, Nathan.

But do you believe me? Do you really believe everything I've just said to you? Damn it, Shea, I've just gutted myself in front of you. I've made myself as vulnerable as a man can make himself to a woman. It's the same as if I just handed you a knife and offered you my balls, for God's sake. And I don't even give a fuck. Because I have no pride when it comes to you. There is nothing I wouldn't do or say to make you understand that I love you. I fucking love you. *There, I said it. Do you believe me now?*

He sounded so pissed off and angry that the admission had been torn from him that she had to battle the smile forming on her lips.

They'd held the link between them for so long now that fatigue and weakness crept over her shoulders until they sagged. She still wasn't back to full strength and she was tired and worried. Holding the link even for this long was taking a toll, but she battled fiercely, because this was more important than anything else.

Her lips trembled. Her fingers splayed out over his face, and she kissed him gently on the mouth. Panic scuttled around her chest and down into her stomach, but how could she not lay bare her soul? Just as Nathan had just done for her.

I believe you. The words whispered from her mind into his, and she could feel her energy fading as she fought to control the pathway. She took a deep breath and took the plunge. How could she not when he'd done the same? *I love you too, Nathan. So much. It scares the hell out of me. I can't lose you. I don't want to lose you.*

She felt his relief so stark, so powerful that it flooded her on all levels, overwhelming her with the sheer intensity of his emotions.

"Thank God," he muttered aloud.

She let her head slide down to his shoulder, and she pressed her face into his neck, so weary and exhausted. Weak from maintaining the intense flow of communication between them.

He gathered her in his arms and cursed softly under his breath.

"I forget what it does to you," he murmured. "I'm sorry."

"I'm not," she said drowsily. "I wouldn't trade those words for anything."

He pulled a hand through the strands of her hair, gently stroking her as he pulled her even closer into his body. "No," he said quietly. "Neither would I."

CHAPTER 29

THEY drove straight through, stopping only for gas. Nathan held Shea close to him, reluctant to even let her sit next to him in the seat. She slept off and on, sometimes stirring and raising her head, her sleepy gaze staring out the window, her brow wrinkled in consternation. He'd soothe her, kiss her and then lower her back to his chest with a soft admonishment to rest.

He loved the way she melted into his arms. He could feel his brothers and Swanny watching him at intervals, but he tuned them out and focused on Shea.

She was tucked trustingly in his arms, her head nestled just below his chin. It was a testament to just how worn out she was that, apart from the few times she woke to ask where they were, she slept.

As they drove through Paris and neared Kentucky Lake, Nathan's gut knotted. The convoy of SUVs crossed over the bridge in the early hours of the morning. The water below was inky black, reflecting nothing of the starless sky above.

Shea stirred and raised her head, this time not looking anywhere but into his eyes. She touched his mind, a brush of warmth and comfort. His unease had disturbed her sleep and now she sought to soothe it.

"We're almost there."

She tensed and this time it was *her* unease that bit at him and not his own. She glanced over at Swanny, who sat staring straight ahead as if she and Nathan weren't even present.

"Stop worrying," Nathan murmured.

She eased to the side and made an awkward attempt at stretching. She'd only gotten out of the SUV once in the last twelve hours when she'd gone to the bathroom during a refuel. He rubbed her back and slid his hand up to massage her neck when she arched again.

They turned off the highway paralleling the lake, and Sam punched the button to open the security gate leading into the Kelly compound. It was cloaked in darkness, but Shea still edged forward, her gaze trying to take in their surroundings.

Sam parked in front of the imposing building that housed the war room. On either side, more SUVs pulled in and the team members began piling out.

Nathan opened the door but motioned for Shea to stay put. He stood, framed behind the open door, and stared over the top at Sam.

"What's the plan? Where do you want Shea?"

"How is she?" Sam asked in a low voice.

"More rested than she was. I think she's doing fine."

Sam glanced at the others as Donovan keyed the code to open the doors and then back at Nathan. "For now, bring her in. Van wants to go over the surveillance you sent him. We could use her eyes. Afterward you can bring her to my house. You and she can stay with me and Sophie. Or if you prefer, one of the others. Whatever you're most comfortable with."

Joe came to stand beside the SUV where Nathan and Sam were conversing. "They can stay with me and Donovan for now."

The statement was more of a command than anything else. Nathan had split his time between his own homesite and the house he shared with Joe and Donovan. Referred to as the bachelor pad by the rest of the family, since they were the only brothers still single.

Sam, Garrett and Ethan had constructed their homes—or rather Sam's was the only one completely finished. Ethan's was close to completion, but he and Rachel still lived in their original house outside the compound until the new house was move-in ready.

Garrett and Sarah had only just moved into their home before Rusty's graduation and Nathan's sudden departure. The couple would marry soon, provided Nathan could stop interfering in their plans. The thought made him grimace. He liked Sarah a lot. She was tough. A lot like his other sisters-in-law, Sophie and Rachel. He wanted her to be happy and settled.

But now he wanted the same for himself and Shea.

Sam shrugged. "Whatever Nathan feels is best."

Joe glanced questioningly at his brother and slowly Nathan nodded.

"Let's get Shea inside," Sam said.

Nathan, who'd been shielding Shea from the outside, turned and ducked so he could see into the SUV. He held out his hand and her palm slid over his as their fingers twined. He helped her out and wrapped his arm around her shoulders until she found her footing.

They followed Sam inside the KGI headquarters, where the others were waiting. Donovan was busy on the computer while the others were seated in front of the large LCD screen mounted on the wall. He looked up as Nathan and Shea entered and motioned them over.

"I'm downloading the footage now. I want you to watch carefully, Shea. Let me know if you need me to freeze-frame. Or if you want to go over something again. Don't worry about absorbing it all at once. I understand this will be upsetting for you. Take your time. And mention anything, no matter how small or seemingly insignificant. We'll talk it out, okay?"

Shea flashed Donovan a grateful smile, and Nathan nodded his own thanks in his brother's direction for handling Shea so gently and showing her so much understanding.

She left his side to take a seat not far from where Donovan stood by the computer. Nathan followed behind and then simply plucked her up and settled her onto his lap. She glanced quickly to the others, but he leaned her back against his chest, a clear message to her that he didn't give a fuck who saw what.

She was his. He didn't give a damn who knew it, what they thought, and he wanted her to know that.

She jumped suddenly when the screen blinked and a curvy brunette with long hair flashed into view. She wore cargo trousers and a formfitting tank shirt that highlighted her lean, well-toned body. She was fit and it was obvious she kept herself that way with a strict regimen.

"Grace," Shea whispered.

"That's your sister?" Donovan queried.

She nodded and leaned forward as Donovan resumed the footage.

Grace crept stealthily through the house, her eyes wary and alert. Clutched in her hand was the journal that Shea had found in the escape tunnel. As she entered the living room, she paused and tears filled Shea's eyes. This was where she and Grace had talked. She was watching her sister communicate with her. A smile softened the tense expression that Grace had worn and then she glanced down at the journal she held and Shea knew this was where she'd told Shea that they weren't their real parents.

The furnishings were still intact, which meant the ransack had occurred after Grace's arrival. Everything looked exactly as it had been before her parents were killed. That was what stuck out to her. There was no evidence that murder had been committed. Who'd cleaned it up?

Shea focused back in on the footage to see Grace's head jerk upward and then she flew toward one of the windows. The sound of breaking glass and heavy footsteps filled the silent room.

Grace looked left and right, clear indecision and panic racing across her face. Then her eyes hardened and she bolted into the hallway. There were four frames on the screen, and Donovan followed her progress from room to room as he enlarged each of the ones she ran through.

She raced into the panic room, and slammed it shut.

Donovan turned to Shea. "Are there no cameras inside the panic room?"

She shook her head. "Only on the outside. The idea was to be able to see out, not in. My father set it up so that it was the ultimate safe room."

"He did a pretty damn good job," Garrett muttered.

"Look," Ethan said, directing everyone's attention back to the monitor.

A soldier moved through the living room, and behind him, another appeared.

Everyone leaned forward, coming to attention as they studied the men going through the house, methodically searching. They completely destroyed the house. They were responsible for the damage Shea and Nathan had encountered.

"She spoke to me. I mean just before she ran. She said that someone was there," Shea said.

Nathan hugged her a little tighter.

The room went silent as they watched the men sweep through her parents' house. Nathan's eyes narrowed. They didn't move like they were chasing Grace. Maybe they hadn't even known she was there. But they were looking for something and they weren't a run-of-the-mill civilian operation.

They wore black military head nets, so only their eyes were visible. Nathan took in every detail of their appearance, looking for anything that could identify them, but they were covered from head to toe. Boots and fatigues and they carried military-issue rifles.

Unless some survivalist underground cult was after Shea and Grace, the U.S. military certainly was. This looked special ops. Probably some damn group that didn't even exist, and that made Nathan damn nervous.

Once the footage of Grace abruptly ended, Donovan keyed the more recent surveillance from Nathan and Shea's visit. Nathan watched grimly as he and Shea stole through the house and entered the kitchen. His brothers frowned when the sound of breaking glass occurred and he and Shea hit the floor just before the flashbang grenade detonated.

Nathan leaned forward, his gaze narrowing as he studied the intruders making their way into the house after he and Shea had disappeared into the panic room. Like the men who'd been after Grace, these looked military. They seemed more careful, however. They didn't touch or disturb anything. It was apparent they weren't looking for something but rather somebody. They didn't even hesitate before honing in on the panic room.

He didn't like it. Didn't like it one damn bit.

"Now ain't that some shit?" Garrett muttered. "Anyone want to take a stab at this one?"

"What have you heard from Resnick?" Nathan demanded.

Sam's mouth twisted and he glanced toward Donovan. "Not a damn thing. We explained the sitch, asked him to do some digging, but he went radio silent shortly after."

"I don't like it," Nathan muttered.

"Neither do we," Donovan said.

Shea bolted to her feet, leaving the confines of Nathan's arms. She paced back and forth, her gaze still riveted to the screen while the scene played out over and over as Donovan kept going back.

"What are we going to do to help Grace?" she blurted out. "She's out there alone. I'm here with all of you. Nothing's going to happen to me but the same can't be said for her. She's not talking to me. I've tried to reach her. I'm terrified for her."

Sam rose and put his hand on Shea's shoulder. "We'll send a team. I promised you we'd protect her. I made you that promise and I'm going to keep it. We have to find her first, but we'll do it."

He turned in Steele's direction, but before he could open his mouth, Rio stepped forward.

"I'm going."

Sam's eyebrows went up. Garrett turned to his team leader in surprise. Rio's gaze was riveted to the screen where Donovan had paused the replay of Grace standing in the living room.

"I'll find her. I'll protect her," Rio said shortly. "These assholes won't get their hands on her."

To Nathan's further surprise, Shea hurried over to where Rio stood and she stared up at him, her expression pleading.

"She's special. She's never done anything to hurt anyone. Just the opposite. Don't let them take her and use her. They'll kill her."

Rio's gaze softened as he stared down at Shea. Then he took her hands in his and offered a gentle squeeze. The rest of the room seemed locked on to the strange vibe emanating from Rio and now the rest of his team as they stepped forward.

"I'll find your sister, Shea. I'll bring her home to you."

She leaned up on tiptoe and kissed the big man on the cheek, and then as if getting over whatever fear she had of him before, she threw her arms around him and hugged him tightly.

"Thank you," she said fiercely. "I'll never be able to repay you for this. She means everything to me."

Rio looked a little befuddled as he stepped away and extricated himself from Shea's hold. Then he smiled down at her. "I can see why Nathan is so enchanted by you."

But as he glanced back up at the monitor, where Grace was frozen on the screen, a look of fear in her eyes, his gaze hardened all over again.

He looked over at Sam and Garrett. "Any problem?"

Sam slowly shook his head. "No. No problem at all."

"Then get me all the intel you have on Grace. My team will move out immediately."

CHAPTER 30

BY the time Rio was satisfied that Shea had given him every pertinent detail about Grace she could possibly think of, Shea was exhausted. But at the same time, hope bubbled inside her chest. These men were confident that they'd locate Grace and that they'd bring her back.

Shea was surrounded by warriors. Men who put their lives at risk to protect and help others. They'd made her a promise, and she knew they didn't make them lightly.

Rio and his team fascinated her. Quiet, determined. They seemed to stand back and study what went on around them. The giant of a man who seemed to serve as Rio's right hand was named Terrence, and as big and as terrifying as he should have seemed, to Shea he resembled a big teddy bear. Not that she'd ever breathe those words where he could hear her. He might snap her like a twig.

But he'd been kind and understanding with her as they'd questioned her about her sister, and he, like Rio, had made a solemn promise to bring Grace back to Shea.

All too quickly, they were gone. Shea had no idea what they were using as their starting point or even what they'd been able to glean from talking to her. But they packed up their gear and said they were bugging out. And then they were simply gone, leaving her slightly baffled. How was she to know what they were doing? But then she doubted they'd be reporting to her. She just hoped they reported to someone, because the prolonged silence between her and Grace was making Shea sick with worry.

She closed her eyes and reached out to her sister as she'd done so many times over the past days. *Don't worry, Grace. Someone is coming for you. We have help now. I wish you'd talk to me so I could explain. These men will help you. Like they've helped me.*

The void was nearly her undoing. It was like not having the gift of telepathy at all. Like she was talking to herself.

She tried to shake off the melancholy direction of her thoughts. She focused back in on the happenings in the war room.

It seemed everyone was doing something. The entire room was abuzz with activity. It made her anxious and on edge. She stood, no longer able to bear sitting so still when everyone was moving around her.

Her legs were wobbly, but then she felt completely off balance by everything. She hated how out of control her life had become. She valued order and quiet. Growing up the way she had, always moving at a moment's notice, had made her appreciate the sudden peace that she and her family had enjoyed when they'd moved to Oregon. She'd craved it. Normalcy. And above all, she liked to feel in control at all times.

In the last year she'd become a paranoid, panicky mess of a woman and she hated every minute of it. She wanted her life back. No, not back. She just wanted a life. A new one. Devoid of all the fears of the past.

She may have been some damn lab experiment, but she was a human being with feelings. If the bastards who'd created her thought she was expendable, that she was only destined to be some lab rat they poked and prodded on a regular basis, they could all fuck themselves and go straight to hell. She would never go back to that.

"Shea."

Donovan's soft address broke through her dark thoughts. Some of the rage abated and she blinked to bring him into focus. He was standing in front of her, a look of concern on his face.

"I want you to meet the team that will be responsible for your safety."

Her brows drew together and the panic was suddenly back, knotting her throat until she had difficulty breathing.

"What do you mean?" she croaked. "What about . . ."

She glanced over to where Nathan stood with his brothers and bit her lip, determined not to blurt out what she'd been about to ask.

She returned her gaze to Donovan and the group assembled closely around him. The team leader stood closest to Donovan and stared coolly at her, his eyes like blue ice. His hair was blond—muddy blond with lighter streaks through the short-cropped strands. It was easy to tell he was the authority figure. He commanded respect and it was obvious he got it from every member of his team.

"This is Steele."

"Miss Peterson," Steele said in acknowledgment.

"Behind him are Cole, P.J., Dolphin. To his left are Baker and Renshaw."

Shea tried to smile but she couldn't contain her dismay.

Across the room, Nathan turned to look at her and he frowned. Their gazes connected and then she felt him explode into her mind, so different than when she connected with him.

His presence was forceful. Indomitable. Overwhelming her and yet filling her with his very essence.

What's wrong? It was a quick, impatient demand. She felt his resolve to fix whatever it was upsetting her.

For a moment she couldn't even formulate her thoughts. It was ridiculous. She was being ridiculous. She should be on her knees giving thanks, but she didn't want this team to protect her. She wanted Nathan. She didn't want to be separated from him. Not even for her safety.

"Jesus."

She heard Nathan across the room. He stalked over, looking angrily at Donovan even as he pulled her into his arms. For a long moment he simply hugged her to him and then he pulled her away, grasped her shoulders and stared hard into her eyes as if willing her to not only hear him but to *feel* him as well.

"I'm not turning you over to Steele and his team. I'm going

to be with you every minute of every day. Do you understand that? Yes, Steele's team is assigned to your protection. We need them. But it doesn't mean they're going to take you away somewhere and that I won't be with you. Where you go, I go."

Relief made her weak, and worse, her eyelids burned with tears.

"Well, Christ," Donovan muttered. "That wasn't what I meant for you to think, Shea. I'm sorry."

She shook her head and forced herself to get it together. "I was being stupid. I'm the one who's sorry. I should be grateful. I just panicked for a moment."

Nathan pulled her to him and silenced her with a long, deep kiss. It amazed her that he gave so little thought to where they were or who observed. He never seemed to care.

She shivered as his tongue swept over hers, rough and yet so gentle and caring. He was a fascinating mix of intensity and patience. He was fierce and demanding and yet he always demonstrated such loving tenderness with her.

He loved her.

She reminded herself of that fact. He'd given her the words. Very pissed off words but all the more meaningful for the frustrated way he'd expressed the emotions he felt toward her. It seemed to make him crazy that he couldn't make everything perfect, that there were so many obstacles confronting them, and yet he refused to let anything deter him.

"This is better than a romance novel," P.J. said with a wistful sigh.

"You read that stuff?" Cole demanded.

Shea pulled away from Nathan but he still held her close, tucked into his side as they faced Steele's team.

"Why the hell do you ask the question like that?" P.J. said, annoyance evident in her tone and expression.

"You just didn't seem the type," Cole mumbled.

She flipped him the bird, and Shea had to bite her lip to keep from laughing. P.J. was easily half Cole's size but she also looked like she had the confidence to take on the much larger man. She might even kick his ass. The idea intrigued Shea greatly.

"I'm tempted to shove one of my romance novels up your

ass," P.J. said sharply. "But I love my books too much to desecrate them like that. I'll settle for my boot."

Cole held up his hands in surrender. "I won't say another word. Romance novels are great. I love romance novels. I think everyone should read them."

Dolphin snickered behind Cole, and Cole whirled to glare at him. P.J. smirked and sauntered back to the couch, where she flopped down.

"So what do we do now?" Shea asked anxiously. "Are we leaving? Do we know anything more than we did before?"

"For today we're going to stay put," Donovan said. "I'm going to ring Resnick's bell again. Sam's trying to reach him now. I know that bastard probably knows more than he's letting on. There isn't much that goes on that he doesn't at least have the resources to find out about. He's got his fingers in so many dark holes and crannies that half the world is probably afraid of ever pissing him off. He could probably bury any number of world leaders and military brass."

"You think he can help us?" Shea asked.

"Do I think he can? Yeah, I do. The question isn't can he. The question is will he. We were polite before. Now we aren't going to be so nice. We've done Resnick plenty of favors. It's time for him to pay up."

"Can we trust him?"

Donovan looked surprised by her question, but then his lips turned up into a half smile. "As much as we can anyone who has dirt on everyone who has ever worked for Uncle Sam either officially or unofficially."

She nodded. "If you trust him, then so will I."

Nathan kissed the side of her head. "I know you're worried, baby. But you don't have to be anymore. Rio will find Grace. Resnick will give us information on who or what headed the experiments on you and your sister and then we'll go after them."

"You make it sound so simple," she said wistfully. "I want it to be that easy, but God, nothing in my life has ever been easy. I'm afraid to believe it could be now. I feel like I'm waiting for the other shoe to drop and something horrible is going to happen."

"We want you to feel safe, Shea," Donovan said softly. "And not just because you're someone who needs help. You're family now. We look out for our own."

She blinked in surprise and then turned her gaze up to Nathan in bewilderment. He merely smiled down at her and then kissed the tip of her nose.

"Everyone has accepted the inevitable except you. You're it for me. They know it. I know it. It's time you start believing it too. I'm not going to let anyone or anything change that. You're mine. I'm yours. It's as simple or as hard as we make it."

Her knees wobbled as a ridiculous giddy sensation stole over her. The room was closing in on her and she desperately wanted to be in the sun for a few moments. Breathe in fresh air. Process everything that had been said over the last few hours. It all seemed so unreal and yet it was real. Very, very real.

"Let's get you to the house," Nathan said. "It's been a long night and an even longer morning. You have to be on overload by now."

"Let me holler at Sam, and Swanny, Joe and I will go with you," Donovan said.

NATHAN and Shea followed slowly behind Joe and Donovan as they walked into the lakefront cabin where Donovan still lived. Swanny came in behind, and he and Joe tossed their bags down on the couch.

Donovan turned to Nathan. "You guys can take the back bedroom. Swanny can bunk with either me or Joe."

Nathan gently squeezed Shea's neck and massaged. "If you want to grab a shower and change, I'll show you the bathroom."

A shower sounded next to heaven. As did clean clothes. Her stomach growled, and she realized it had been hours since they'd eaten.

Joe glanced sharply at Shea and frowned. Then he looked over at Donovan. "What have we got to eat around here? Shea's starving."

Her stomach tightened and she stared open-mouthed at Nathan's brother. She snapped her lips closed and looked away. Damn it. He'd heard her thoughts.

How are you doing that in my head?

Her gaze snapped up and she took a wary step back.

I'm not going to hurt you, damn it. Is this how you talk to Nathan?

Slowly she nodded and then caught herself.

Yes. Nathan and I can communicate this way.

Can you talk to just anyone?

No. It's . . . I have no control over it. It just happens.

Joe frowned again. *Then why me?*

I don't know. Maybe because you and Nathan are twins and so closely linked. I didn't mean to. I'm sorry if it made you angry. I wasn't trying to pry.

With a sigh, Joe walked over and took Shea's elbow. Nathan's eyebrows shot up and then came together as he stared in confusion at his brother.

"Can I have a word with Shea?"

Nathan's frown deepened. "What the hell is going on?"

"I just need a minute. We'll step outside."

Nathan was going to protest, but Shea put her hand on his arm.

It's okay, Nathan.

She let her hand slide off his arm as he nodded. His gaze followed as Joe led her out the back door and onto the wooden deck that overlooked the lake. She closed her eyes as sunshine washed over her and she inhaled deeply. A breeze lifted her hair and tickled her nose. It was so very beautiful here.

He stopped at the railing, where they stood sideways to the lake. For a moment he simply stared off in the distance and then he leaned against the wood with his hip and glanced down at her.

"Look, it's apparent we got off on the wrong foot, or maybe no foot at all."

"We only just met," she murmured.

"And yet you look at me like I'm an ax murderer and you apologize like you think I'm going to take your head off."

"I'm not sure what you want here," she said slowly, drawing out the words.

He blew out his breath. "This connection between us, I mean it's special, right? You said you couldn't speak to just anyone like that. But you could with Nathan and now with me."

She nodded.

"My brother came back from Afghanistan a different man than he left. But you know what? The important thing is that he came home at all. The odds were against him. Swanny's told me more about what happened than Nathan has, and if you hadn't been there, with him I mean, they both would have died."

"He wouldn't have died," she said quietly. "He wouldn't have given up. I don't care what he said."

"Maybe I agree with you there, but knowing the hell he went through and the fact that you took it for him . . . I don't have the words to express my gratitude. I know everyone's thanked you. They're grateful. But Shea, he's not just my brother. He's my twin. He's my best friend. You didn't just give him back his life or give him back to his family. You gave *me* back a part of myself. And now there's this connection between us like what you share with Nathan. In a weird way it feels right. Maybe . . . Maybe one day I'll be able to repay the favor you did the Kelly family. I don't profess to know a whole lot about this telepathy thing, but if you ever need me or need help, I hope you'll call for me as you did with Nathan."

She smiled at the sincerity in his tense expression. His dark eyes, so much like Nathan's, were fastened intently on her.

"I'm glad it doesn't freak you out. Not everyone takes it well, this stranger popping into their head."

He shrugged. "It's actually kind of cool. I think it's neat that you and Nathan can communicate while you're apart."

"Thank you. For saying all of that."

He leaned down and kissed her lightly on the cheek. "No, Shea, thank you. I feel like I'm getting my brother back and I owe that to you."

As he pulled away, he glanced back toward the house. "Now let's get back inside before Nathan paces a hole in the floor. I'll talk Van into pulling out the grill, and we can do burgers and hot dogs."

She blinked as she tried to wrap her head around doing something so normal. Granted they weren't moving out until the next day while Nathan's brothers took the time to do more investigating, but somehow she'd imagined being huddled in some closed-off room, hiding under a bed or something.

An afternoon of freedom sounded next to heaven.

She followed Joe back inside to find Nathan waiting, his brow furrowed as he observed them walking up. Shea slid her arms around Nathan's waist and laid her head against his chest.

He instantly relaxed and rubbed his hand up and down her spine.

"How about doing some burgers, Van?" Joe called. "We're starving."

Donovan came out of the kitchen and gave Joe a look of exasperation. "Is there anything wrong with your arms?"

"I cook a mean burger," Swanny spoke up.

Everyone turned to the other man in surprise. He so rarely spoke that he tended to blend in.

"My grill is your grill," Donovan said with a grin. "I never turn down a meal I don't have to cook."

"I can help you make the patties," Shea offered.

Swanny smiled. "I'd like that. Thanks."

She was positively gleeful over the simple idea of an afternoon barbeque. It was just so normal and mundane. She actually loved to cook, loved spending time in the kitchen, but she hadn't done so in a long time. She ate on the go mostly, just like she lived her life. Always on the run.

"I'll take some burger out and do a quick thaw on it," Donovan said. "I should have everything else, but if not, we'll send Joe up to the grocery store."

"Love how I got volunteered for that," Joe said dryly.

Donovan's cell rang and he instantly picked it up. "Hey, Ma," he said in greeting. He grinned. "Yeah, he's here. Back safe and sound. Did you doubt us? I told you we were going to drag him home one way or another."

Shea glanced at Nathan to get his reaction and found him smiling, his eyes soft with love. Her heart squeezed a little.

Donovan listened a moment and then glanced quickly in Nathan's direction. "Uh, yeah, that's true, but I'm not going to speculate on anything, Ma. You need to hear that from Nathan."

"Uh-oh," Joe said in a low voice. "Busted."

"Lunch? Well, we're doing burgers or about to. Um, hang on, okay? Let me ask."

He put the phone over his chest and whispered in Nathan's direction. "Ma wants to come over. To eat with us." He glanced apologetically at Shea. "But you know she just wants to meet Shea, whom she's already heard about. Are you up for this? I can always tell her no."

Shea glanced up at Nathan, suddenly nervous and unsure.

Baby, stop.

Nathan's gentle words spilled through her mind, filling her with warmth and love.

We don't have to do this now.

No, it's okay. I mean I don't mind as long as you don't. It's kind of a big step to introduce a girl to your mom, you know.

Then he smiled at her, and the depth of emotion in his eyes blew her away. If there was any doubt before, it was gone in an instant. His gaze was so tender, so full of love, that she felt near to bursting.

She's going to love you. Just like I do.

She hugged him tighter and buried her face in his chest.

Donovan cleared his throat. "Um, if you two are finished, Ma is still on the phone."

Heat stained her cheeks as Shea looked up, but she saw teasing in Donovan's eyes. She relaxed and leaned into Nathan again.

"Of course she can come," Nathan said. "Maybe she won't worry so much now."

Then to Shea, he turned and tipped up her chin. *You've got to relax, baby. Stop worrying every time my brothers know we're communicating. They aren't going to think any differently of you because you're different.*

I'll try. This is all just so . . . baffling.

He smiled and leaned forward to kiss her. *Wait until you experience the entire family together.*

She sighed wistfully. *I think I'd love it.*

She'd been so wrapped up in her conversation with Nathan that she hadn't realized Donovan was already off the phone.

"Okay, so Swanny, all we'll need are the burgers. Ma is sort of taking care of the rest. You know her. She always comes bearing enough food to feed an army."

"She *does* feed an army, doesn't she?" Shea asked.

Donovan looked at her in mock horror. "Bite your tongue,

woman. She feeds Marines. Well, and she feeds these army rejects too." He gestured toward Swanny, Joe and Nathan.

"Watch it, Bo Peep," Joe drawled. "Not only is your Marine ass outnumbered, but we're bigger than your scrawny ass. You don't have Garrett to back you up this time."

"So all of you served in different branches of the military?" Shea asked.

"Unfortunately, Donovan and Garrett joined the Marines," Nathan said, sniffing in disdain. "Ethan really went against the grain and joined the navy. He was a SEAL before he resigned his commission. Sam, Joe and I all served in the army. Obviously we're the more intelligent of the Kelly gene pool."

"And the rest of KGI? They all seem very military."

"Not all, actually," Donovan said. "P.J. is a former S.W.A.T. team member."

"P.J. is the woman, right?" Shea asked.

"Yeah. She's a crack sniper. Best we have," Donovan replied.

"She's impressive," Swanny broke in. "Hell of a shot, from what I hear."

Donovan nodded. "The rest of Steele's team is all ex-military. Rio's team, on the other hand . . . Rio is a bit of an unknown. And by that I mean his past is highly classified. He came recommended from some very highly decorated military officers. So yeah, I'd say military, but I'd say he was definitely off the books."

Shea sent him a puzzled look.

"He means not official. Not recognized," Nathan explained. "Meaning he didn't really exist in whatever organization he served under."

Her lips turned down into a frown. "That sucks."

"Terrence, his right hand, likely served with him. The two are close. I'd swear *they* were telepathic because they do some freaky silent communication," Donovan continued.

"And Rio is the one who went after Grace," she said softly. "How do you know . . . I mean if he was so shadowy and no one really knows who he works for, how do we know he can be trusted?"

She could tell they didn't entirely like her question, but they controlled their responses.

"Rio is solid," Donovan said quietly. "He's as solid as they come. If he said he'll bring Grace home to you, then he'll do it or die trying."

Shea could sense just how resolute Donovan was about Rio, and it eased some of her worries. Just hearing about the accomplished men and woman of KGI made her feel safer and more at peace than she'd been in so very long.

We'll keep you safe, Shea.

It wasn't Nathan who spoke to her, but Joe. He'd sensed her worry and sought to ease it. She looked over and smiled and marveled at how good it was to feel joy again.

CHAPTER 31

AN hour later, after showering and changing into clean clothes, Shea was elbow deep in hamburger meat. Nathan, Joe and Donovan were several feet away in the living room, talking about Resnick and a lot of other things she didn't understand. But Swanny was quiet, and she found she enjoyed the silence as they worked.

It amused her that this big, scarred, badass-looking military guy was evidently shy or self-conscious. Probably a mixture of both. It also amused her that he was very exacting in his measurements. Apparently he loved to cook and he was a perfectionist in the kitchen.

He directed her every movement, told her just how much spice to put in the meat. Even how to form the patties.

"Are you joining KGI?" she blurted out when the silence had stretched a little too long.

He swiveled and stared at her in surprise, the scar stretching slightly on his cheek as his expression grew thoughtful.

"No. Maybe. I don't really know," he finally amended. "I went with Donovan and Ethan because Nathan needed me. No other reason. I knew something was going on with you and him, and I felt like I owed it to both of you to be there, to do whatever I could. But even without that obligation, I would have done it. Nathan is my friend."

He went quiet again, and Shea warred with herself over whether to press the conversation. She was curious about him but didn't want to make him uncomfortable either.

"Do you have family?"

A shadow crossed over his face. "No."

He didn't offer more. It was frustrating, because if she pursued this line of questioning now, it would be awkward and obvious.

"Well, I suppose if you join KGI, they'll be your family."

He paused a moment and then the corners of his mouth lifted ever so slightly. "I hadn't thought about it that way, but I suppose you're right."

She shaped another patty and laid it on the piece of wax paper where the others were neatly aligned. A knock at the front door sent a jolt up her spine and she froze, hands still dug into the burger.

A moment later, an older couple came through the living room, and Shea watched as the woman immediately wrapped Nathan up in a fierce hug.

This had to be his mom and dad.

For several moments, they hugged Nathan and talked in rapid tones. Joe glanced her way several times as if to offer silent support. Or maybe he just sensed how freaking shot her nerves were.

And then they turned her way and Nathan's mom stared directly at her as if trying to make a judgment from across the room. Just as suddenly, her expression softened and she smiled a warm, gentle smile. She hurried across the room, and as she reached Shea, she opened her arms, pulling Shea into a hug every bit as fierce as the one she'd given Nathan.

Shea had no idea what she was supposed to do, so she stood there while Mrs. Kelly patted and hugged her. When she finally drew away, she kissed Shea on the cheek and grasped her shoulders to get a better look at her.

"I'm getting hamburger all over you," Shea said with a grimace as she held her hands up.

"Oh, honey, I've had far worse. It'll wash up just fine. I'm

Marlene Kelly, by the way." Then she pointed over her shoulder. "That's my husband, Frank."

Frank moved forward and pulled her into a hug that was gentler than Marlene's had been but no less warm or sincere.

"It's very nice to meet you, young lady," he said gruffly. "You'll pardon an old man getting emotional, but you made it possible for my boy to come home. I'll never forget that."

Shea's cheeks tightened uncomfortably at the love and acceptance already in their eyes. And yet she welcomed it like sunshine after a snowstorm.

"We're so very glad you're here," Marlene said in a soft voice. "I know my boys won't let anything happen to you."

Shea smiled at the confidence in her voice. "Thank you. I'm very glad to meet the people who mean so much to Nathan."

Marlene turned again to Frank. "Bring in the stuff from the van if you don't mind. I'll set the picnic table on the deck. It's a perfect day to eat outside."

NATHAN stood outside with his dad and brothers as Donovan readied the grill. His mom had arranged the picnic table so that there were plenty of snacks and drinks, not to mention the fixings for the hamburgers.

Cold beer in the cooler. A breeze off the lake. Blue skies unmarred by a single drifting cloud.

It was all the more sweeter now than ever before. He savored every single day back in Tennessee, surrounded by his family. And now Shea.

He looked up as Swanny walked onto the deck holding a cookie sheet piled high with the burgers. Swanny handed the tray off to Donovan just as Shea and Nathan's mom walked out behind Swanny.

Nathan held out his hand, wanting Shea close to him. She walked to him and slipped her hand in his automatically, as if she hadn't given it any other thought. He liked that.

He wrapped his arm around her, anchoring her against his waist while his mom stood to the side and beamed. In her mind she already had them married, settled in Nathan's finished house, and she was no doubt plotting grandchildren too.

And while that might terrify some men, Nathan didn't mind it at all. He already knew what he wanted. He'd known from the very start. It had never been a question of him wanting Shea permanently in his life. He needed her. She was his other half, and he didn't mean that in a cutesy soul mate kind of way. She literally was the other half of his soul. Their connection—their bond—was one that not many people shared, he didn't care how much in love they were.

He just hoped to hell she felt the same and that, when this was all over, she'd want to stay with him. Here. Somewhere else. It didn't matter to him. Yeah, he loved his family. Loved his life here. But he'd be happy anywhere Shea was, and if that required living elsewhere, he wouldn't think twice about it.

They were careful not to discuss Shea's situation in front of his parents. Instead today was a day to simply enjoy and to forget the shadow that hung over them. For a few hours, Nathan would pretend that this was his life. His life with Shea.

Marlene fussed endlessly over Swanny. She bullied him when the burgers were served and he only took one. Nathan smiled because his friend didn't have a chance in hell. Nathan's mom was a force of nature and she'd already decided that Swanny was going to be her next adopted chick. She even made him sit by her when they all took their places at the table.

Then Frank simply reached out and took his wife's hand on one side and Donovan's on the other. Donovan in turn reached for Nathan's. Nathan slipped his hand over Shea's at the same time Joe, on her other side, took her other hand and then reached next to him for Swanny's hand, and Marlene completed the chain when she gripped his other hand.

In his gruff voice, Frank said a prayer, thanking God for bringing Nathan back to his family. For introducing Swanny into the Kelly fold and finally for Shea. He asked for His hand of safety to surround Shea and then he asked Him to bless the food before them.

After issuing a solemn Amen, which was echoed by everyone at the table, Frank looked up, still holding tightly to his wife's and son's hands.

"Never forget that family is the most important thing. No matter how far your life takes you away, your family is always here. And if you're nothing else in this world, you're a Kelly, and that makes you loved."

Nathan's throat tightened. He raised his gaze to stare at his dad. Yeah, he understood the message. Don't push your family away. They loved you no matter what.

Frank nodded in Nathan's direction and then released his hold on Marlene's and Donovan's hands.

"Let's eat before the meat gets cold," he said.

Shea dug in and guilt tugged at Nathan. Joe had been right. She was starving. Though how he'd known that, Nathan wasn't sure. Or maybe he just guessed.

"They're wonderful, Swanny," Shea said as she licked one of her fingers. "Best burger I've ever had."

Swanny smiled when the others added their praises.

"Seems to me that I could step down from the barbeque pit now that we have an expert," Frank said.

Swanny held up his hands. "Oh no, sir. You see, a team is required for these matters. Preparation is only one part of the whole. It can be prepared masterfully, but if it's not grilled to perfection, then preparation doesn't matter one bit. I respectfully suggest that you continue manning the Kelly grill."

Marlene reached over and patted Swanny's hand. "Then you'll just have to make sure you're here to do the preparing."

Shea grinned in Swanny's direction, and Nathan caught the words she mouthed. *I told you so.*

Unsure of what that was all about, he began fixing Shea another burger. When he offered it to her, she looked like she was going to say no, but he plopped it onto her plate with a one-word directive. "Eat."

She ate half of it before finally pushing the plate away with a groan. "That was so good, but I'm stuffed now."

Swanny started to get up to collect some of the plates, but Shea got to her feet, maneuvering from the picnic table, and then leaned over to put her hand on Swanny's arm.

"You stay out here, Swanny. I'll clear the table. You were in the kitchen all afternoon."

"So were you," Swanny said in amusement.

Marlene stood and, at the same time, pushed Swanny back

down, her hand firm on his shoulder. "I'll help Shea. You stay here and visit with the boys."

Nathan watched as Shea and his mom disappeared into the house bearing armfuls of dishes. Without a word, Donovan and Joe stood and Nathan followed right behind. Frank chuckled as he, too, rose.

"Glad to see my boys haven't forgotten all I taught them."

Donovan grinned. "More like I don't want my ass in a sling."

They began collecting dishes and clearing the table while Swanny sat and watched them in confusion. "Now wait a minute. I was forbidden to help and was ordered to maintain my station, but you guys are all helping."

"I don't much believe there's such a thing as woman's work," Frank said. "I've always brought my boys up to help out whether it's with the cooking or cleaning. Now, their mother will give orders and usually I'm not one to teach my children to disobey their mother, but there are times, and this is one of them, when you just don't listen to her."

Amusement flared in Swanny's eyes. "Ah, okay. I think I get it now. I should get my ass up and help no matter what she told me."

Frank nodded and handed him a stack of dishes. "Exactly."

CHAPTER 32

DUSK lay over the lake like a blanket. The sky was painted in lavender shades of pink and purple, and the water reflected the incandescent glow of twilight.

Donovan had lighted citronella torches around the deck to keep the mosquitoes at bay. Everyone was sprawled in deck chairs, enjoying the evening after a day filled with food, laughter and the comfort of just being home.

Marlene eased the sliding glass doors open and slipped outside, closing them quietly behind her. "We should go, Frank. I'm sure they're all tired."

Nathan sat forward, wondering why his mom was practically tiptoeing outside. "Where's Shea?"

His mom smiled as Frank stood beside her. "She's inside asleep on the couch, so everyone needs to be quiet on the way back through."

Nathan pushed upward and out of his seat. He went to the door and quietly opened it, stepping in, his gaze scanning the living room. As his mom had said, Shea was curled up on the couch, her head resting against the arm.

She looked incredibly small, her legs drawn up to her body. Her arms were wrapped tightly around her, as if she protected herself even in sleep.

The others came in behind him, glanced Shea's way and smiled. His mom and dad came over to give Nathan a hug and then motioned that they were leaving.

"I'll take her to bed so you guys don't have to worry about waking her up," he said to the others after his parents had left.

It was only half the truth. He wanted to be alone with her, hold her, touch her. He wanted her with a gut-clenching need that defied explanation.

He slid his arms underneath her and lifted her from the couch. Her eyelids fluttered and then opened, revealing sleepy blue eyes.

"Sorry," she murmured. "I didn't mean to fall asleep."

He smiled and kissed her forehead as he carried her down the hall to the bedroom. He shouldered his way through the door and then eased her down on the bed so she sat up, her legs over the edge. Then he knelt beside the bed and began unlacing her tennis shoes.

"I wonder if you have any idea how much today meant to me."

She cocked her head and sent him a curious stare.

He tossed her shoes and then leaned in close and got up on his knees so that he was between her legs and nearly at eye level with her.

"Seeing you there, surrounded by my family. It was like coming home in a whole new way. Maybe it's why I had such a difficult time when I came home from Afghanistan. I was home but you weren't here, so for me there was something missing. But now?"

He couldn't even finish the thought because emotion was tugging at his throat, closing it in.

"I love you, Shea," he whispered.

She leaned forward, framing his face with her hands, and she kissed him. Long and sweet. Warmth traveled through his body and to his heart. He wrapped his arms around her and pulled her as tight against his body as he could fit her.

And he kissed her back. Hard, soft, all stages in between. He was rough and then tender.

"Make love to me, Nathan," she whispered softly against his ear.

"I am, baby. Absolutely I am."

She sighed and melted against him, going soft in his arms. God, he loved the way she felt.

He nibbled the sensitive skin just below her ear and then kissed his way down the curve of her neck to her shoulder. Her breathing ratcheted up and she arched into his mouth.

Her taste. Her scent. The feel of her. They all drove him wild. Made him insatiable, a man always teetering on the edge of control. In many ways she settled him, but when it came to wanting her, there was no help for the desperate, edgy need that lived inside him.

Shea kissed his neck, inhaling his smell and taste as he traced a similar path down hers. It felt as though it had been an eternity since they'd last made love when in reality it was such a short time ago.

Anxious to see him, to be able to touch him, she pushed gently at him and then rose to stand in front of him.

"I'll undress for you if you'll undress for me," she murmured.

"Deal."

Their gazes locked, never once breaking away, they began to undress, keeping that connection between them all the while. Shirts, jeans, even socks went sailing across the room until finally they stood naked before each other.

Drawn to the lean hardness of his body, she placed her palms at his sides and then smoothed them upward, trailing over the crisscross pattern of scars that marred the smoothness of his skin.

She knew it discomfited him when she acknowledged them in any way, but it was important to her that he know she accepted him and every single one of those scars. They were beautiful reminders of his endurance. They weren't ugly. Far from it. They were a testament to his courage. To his unflagging resolve.

"You're so beautiful," she breathed.

He cocked one eyebrow. "And you're nuts."

She laughed but then sobered again. "You are, Nathan. I'm so in awe of you. You have so much courage and so much character. I can see it in your family. It's reflected in each and every one of them. The Kellys are special, but you . . . You're extra special."

"You make it so there's nothing I can say," he said hoarsely.

"Good," she said, smiling up at him. She leaned up on tip-toe to brush her mouth across his lips. "All you need to do is listen and accept. You call me your miracle, but Nathan, you're mine as well, and you need to know that."

He lifted his hands, pressed them to her arms and then slowly slid them upward to her shoulders. He spread his fingers and brushed his thumbs across her collarbone before going lower to graze across the tips of her breasts.

Then he cupped the mounds in each palm, lifting slightly before bending down to take one nipple in his mouth. He sucked lightly until the soft peak became a rigid point. He moved to the other, ran his tongue over the sensitive, puckered flesh before sucking it between his teeth.

"You are so fucking beautiful inside and out, Shea Peterson. I've never known anyone more beautiful."

Her heart tugged at the sincerity in his voice, the raspy edge that told her how hard it was to voice his feelings aloud.

She moved in close, until their bodies pressed against each other, heated, bringing her to instant awareness.

His erection was cupped against her belly and she slid her hand between them to gently encircle it. With her other hand, she reached down to cup his sac, caressing him intimately as she stroked over his length.

"Take me hard, Nathan. Hard and fast. We could spend all night touching and kissing, but what I need tonight is you. Just you. Nothing else."

"Ah hell, baby," he groaned.

He swept her up into his arms, his eyes so dark that it sent a shiver down her spine. It was as if she'd unleashed the beast or at the very least given him permission to lose control.

He crawled onto the bed and put her down in the middle. He loomed over her, his features tight and strained. Even though she'd told him what she wanted, she knew he held back. He didn't want to hurt her. Didn't he know he couldn't?

She reached for him, wanting, needing him so much. Only he could fix the empty ache in her heart. Only he could erase the fear that seemed such a permanent fixture in her life.

Only he could keep her safe.

"Please," she whispered.

His palms hit the bed on either side of her. His knee nudged impatiently at her thighs and then he was over her, inside her in one breath. Deep. Hot. Hard.

Her back arched upward to meet his thrust. Her hands flew to his shoulders, her fingers digging deep as pleasure exploded through her body.

Not that endless foreplay wasn't very nice, and Nathan certainly had talent in that area, but this instant, explosive coming together was electrifying.

It felt primal. It *was* primal. Claiming and taking. Possession. He covered her, thrusting, hovering protectively over her even as he demanded his due.

Oh God, she was never going to last and she wanted it to go on forever.

His eyes bore into hers, dark and fiery. His jaw tightened with each thrust and he watched her closely even as he drove deeper into her body.

She started to close her eyes, but he stopped, embedded tightly.

"Look at me."

She refocused her gaze on him, saw the love and also the edgy need burning so bright in those velvet brown eyes.

"Look at me. Stay with me. Always."

He slowly withdrew and then thrust powerfully back into her.

"Is this what you wanted?" he strained out. "Is this what you need?"

She wrapped her legs around him, lifting her hips to meet each and every forceful lunge. "Yes," she whispered. "I need you, Nathan. Just you. I need this. I need your strength."

"You have it, baby. You have it and me. Always. I swear."

Their gazes locked, she writhed beneath him, the edgy rise already upon her. Sharp and yet delicate. Hard and yet so utterly gentle. She was lost in him. Lost in the power of his possession.

This *was* what she needed. To feel that she belonged to him. That she was his and that he'd never let her go. She wanted to feel owned, protected, unbelievably cherished. And he made her feel all of those things and so much more.

"Use your hand, baby," he whispered. "I want you to go first. Touch yourself. Tell me how deep you want it."

His words danced erotically over her ears and sent her that much closer to the edge. She moved her hand down her belly, tight between them, and lower until her fingers slipped down to where they were joined.

For a moment, she caressed the part of him that still remained outside her opening and then she moved back up, through damp, sensitive folds, to her clit.

"That's it. Damn," he groaned. "You just tightened all around me."

"Harder," she gasped out. "Please don't stop, Nathan. I'm so close."

He pulled back and plunged again. Harder and deeper. Then again, with so much power that it drove her farther into the mattress.

She couldn't catch up. Couldn't breathe. So she held it, straining higher and higher. He pushed into her, so tight. She was so full. He overpowered her senses. All she could process was him. Inside her body. Owning her. Staking his claim. Giving her the most unimaginable pleasure she'd ever experienced.

He lowered his head to ravage her mouth. Hot, possessive kisses. Their tongues clashed and rolled over each other. He tasted her from the inside out and then ran his mouth down her face to her neck.

He sank his teeth into the ultrasensitive area over her pulse point and, at the same time, swiped his tongue erotically over the area where he nipped.

He seemed determined to give her everything she'd asked for and so much more. More than she could even take.

She moaned softly and then louder as her orgasm came roaring over her like a runaway train. He drove hard and held himself there.

"Oh God, Nathan. Don't stop. Please don't stop," she begged.

She forgot all about his order for her to look at him. She closed her eyes and cried out as he pushed deeper still. She was unraveling at a speed that left her breathless.

And then she hit her peak in one shattering, mind-numbing explosion.

He was pushing into her faster, harder. His hips slapped

the backs of her thighs and then her legs fell away as he forced them wider apart.

He shifted so his weight was squarely over her and then he leaned his head down until his forehead rested against hers.

"I love you," he whispered.

He thrust again and then closed his eyes as he shuddered with his release.

"Open your eyes. I want to see you."

His eyes flew open again and he smiled at her teasing reminder of what he'd told her just earlier.

He thrust slower and more gently now but he kept their bodies joined as he settled himself carefully so that their bodies were flush.

She wrapped her arms around him and hugged him close, loving the warmth and strength that emanated from his flesh to hers. She kissed his shoulder.

I love you too, Nathan.

CHAPTER 33

SHEA awakened to a long, hard body shifting over her and sliding up her body. Nathan parted her thighs and slid another long, hard part of himself deep inside her.

She let out a contented sigh and lazily opened her eyes to see him staring intently down at her.

"I love morning sex," he murmured. "I love seeing your hair all spread out over my pillow, your body wrapped around mine. I love watching you sleep. So beautiful."

She arched an eyebrow. "So would that be you love morning sex in general or you love morning sex with *me*?"

He chuckled. "You, baby. Definitely you. Only you."

"That's better."

"There shouldn't be any doubt," he whispered as he eased forward again.

He kissed her lazily, drawing out the pleasure for both of them with slow, gentle strokes. It was markedly different from the night before. She'd wanted his urgency then. The borderline desperation, the loss of control. She'd wanted it raw and rough. Just as now she needed his reverence and gentleness.

He rocked over her, kissing and caressing until her orgasm

whispered softly through her veins. Then he found his own release and gently lowered himself to her body.

"I forgot the damn condoms last night and this morning," he said in disgust.

She smiled. "The ship has already kind of sailed on that issue, hasn't it? What's that old saying about closing the barn door after the horse is already out?"

He sighed. "I know. I just should have protected you better."

She snuggled into his arms and pushed her head under his chin. "You protect me just fine."

A knock sounded at the door, sending Shea scrambling for the covers. Nathan chuckled. "No one's coming in, baby."

"Nathan?" Joe called through the door.

"Yeah, what is it?"

"We're heading out. Thought you and Shea would want to come with."

"Give us ten, okay?"

"No problem."

"Ten minutes?" she squeaked.

Nathan grinned at her. "Better get a move on. We run a tight ship around here."

She sent him a disgruntled look but threw the covers off and hurried for the bathroom.

SHEA leaned into Nathan during the short drive back to the KGI compound. They parked outside the headquarters and Nathan ushered her inside with the others.

Sam and Garrett were already there. She wasn't sure what Sam was doing, but Garrett was watching the surveillance footage again, a frown of concentration etched deep into his features.

The very last thing she wanted was to rehash that footage and see Grace all over again.

"Ethan will be over soon," Sam said when he looked up and saw everyone enter.

"Any word from Resnick?" Donovan asked. "The bastard hasn't answered any of my calls."

Sam shook his head. "Nothing. He's pissing me off."

Shea paced restlessly, focusing away from the huge LCD screen that seemed to dominate the room. At one point, Nathan cornered her, trapping her by placing both arms on the wall on either side of her.

"What's wrong?" he asked softly.

"Can we just get some fresh air? Just you and me?" Her gaze inadvertently caught on the screen again and she frowned.

He looked over his shoulder, following the direction of her gaze, and then his eyes flashed in understanding. He pushed away from the wall and tangled his fingers with hers.

"Come on. We'll go out the back."

After explaining to the others where they were going, Nathan directed Shea down a long hallway leading to another door with a data entry keyboard. He punched in the code and the door slid open.

She was nearly blinded by the sudden wash of sunlight, but it danced over her skin, leaving warmth in its wake. When her sight adjusted to the brightness, she stared over the landscape to the drop-off where the lake spread out over the horizon.

There was an odd beauty to the compound. Much of it was still wooded, natural, forested. Green. But then in the middle of such an outdoor paradise was a helipad, the imposing building that housed the war room, and there were cleared areas that looked like something out of a basic training scenario.

One half looked very much like a military base, but then the other side was a complete contrast. There were three beautiful homes nestled among trees that backed up to the drop-off to the lake. They all looked new and . . . cozy. Not a word she'd use to describe the rest of the facility.

"Who lives there?" she asked, nodding in the direction of the houses.

Nathan turned, his hands shoved into his pockets. "The one on the far right is Sam's. He lives there with his wife, Sophie, and their daughter, Charlotte. Next to him is Garrett and Sarah's house. They've only just moved in and they plan to marry soon. They met just before I went MIA. They wanted to wait to get married until they knew one way or another about me. I met her for the first time when she and Garrett came to see me in the hospital where I was recovering."

Shea grimaced. "I'm surprised you don't hate me for leaving you."

"I wasn't happy about it," he confessed. "I did some serious battling with my sanity for a long while. But I understand why. You gave up so much for me."

"What about the last house?" she asked, looking away from him and toward the house in question.

"Ethan and Rachel will live there. It's not quite done yet. They have a house a few miles away. They'll put it on the market when they move here."

She thought for a moment, running the names and faces of all his brothers through her mind. "And what about Donovan and Joe? And . . . you?"

Nathan pointed to a spot away from the other houses. It was thick with trees and overlooked the lake, unlike the others.

"That's Van's spot. He's in no hurry to build, though. Maybe he'll wait until he gets married. I'm not sure what he's planned."

"And you?"

He held out his hand. "Come on. I want to show you something."

Intrigued, she slipped her hand into his and let him lead her toward a grove of trees that rested down the cliff's edge from Sam's home. There was a worn path that wove through the mature trees and the mounds of honeysuckle that seemed to take over the entire area.

She inhaled, enjoying the sweetness, and then closed her eyes as the breeze blew in off the lake, filling the air with even more of the perfume.

When she reopened her eyes, they'd burst into a clearing where the frame of a house stood. It faced the lake and they'd come in to the back of the house. He walked her around to the front, where she could see a wooden porch already constructed.

It would be the perfect place to sit out and enjoy the view of the lake. She could imagine evenings in a porch swing, watching the sun go down, waiting for the stars to pop out and enjoying the scattering of fireflies over the landscape.

The image was so poignant that it brought a lump to her throat.

"Whose is it?"

"Mine," he said quietly. "Or it will be. It's small. I mean nothing huge. But very open. After . . . After I came back, the idea of living in a house with small rooms and closed-in spaces freaked me out. So I designed the house to be basically one big open space. The living room leads into the kitchen and there's an eat-in area. And then the master bedroom, but it's pretty open too. There aren't many rooms, but they're all large and open."

He suddenly snapped his lips shut as if he knew he was babbling. Her heart squeezed a little and she wrapped her arms around his waist, hugging him to her as she stared at the creation he'd begun.

"Are you building it yourself?"

"Yeah. That's why there isn't much done. It was something to do. Something to occupy my time and give me some time to think about what I was going to do. It sounds like an excuse, but I felt like I was waiting."

"For what?" she asked softly.

He turned in her arms to stare down at her. "You. I was waiting for you."

He touched her hair and trailed his fingers through the strands, gathering them and then letting go. Then he glanced back up at the house and she could literally feel his nervousness grow with every breath.

"Can you picture yourself here, Shea? Could you live here with me?"

Her lips parted in surprise. Not so much that he'd imagine them being together. She had a pretty good idea of how committed he was to the idea of them having a future together. But it still seemed so . . . nebulous. Not real. No matter how much they talked about it or he scowled and grew angry at her reservations.

But now it seemed so final. And it was hard to picture herself living a fairy tale existence in a beautiful home with a man who loved her when her sister was out there somewhere and Shea couldn't be sure she'd ever see her again.

She felt guilty for even thinking of being so damn happy when she couldn't guarantee the same for Grace.

The longer she went without responding, the more nervous

he grew, and she realized that her hesitancy was giving him all the wrong ideas. Her heart throbbed just a bit as she picked up the threads from his mind. He worried the house wasn't good enough for her. That *he* wasn't good enough for her. That he was too damaged. That he couldn't make her happy.

She slipped back into his arms and wrapped herself around him until he was surrounded by her. Then she leaned up on tiptoe so she could reach his mouth. She touched his cheek, directing him downward, and kissed him softly.

"The house is perfect. I can't imagine a more beautiful place."

"But can you see yourself here? With me?" he asked gruffly.

She smiled. "I can see myself anywhere you are, Nathan."

His relief was palpable. Then he smiled. "Wait here just a second. There's something I want to show you."

GARRETT stared at the screen and rewound the footage to start just after the flashbang grenade exploded and the intruders entered the house behind Nathan and Shea's flight to the panic room.

Ethan came in, and Garrett held up a hand in absent greeting before returning his attention back to the screen.

It had bugged him the entire night before. He hadn't been able to sleep for replaying the images in his head. Something was wrong, something he couldn't quite put his finger on. So he watched it again, studying each frame, looking for what was making his internal alarm beep like a mo-fo.

Donovan and Ethan came to stand beside Garrett and stared up at the screen.

"What's up, G?" Donovan asked. "You've been watching the same few seconds of tape for the last fifteen minutes."

Garrett frowned and then hit the keyboard to pause on the front man. "There. Look at that, Van. See his hand? Can you zoom in on that?"

Donovan shoved him over and then typed a rapid succession of commands. The screen capture zoomed on the screen and then the resolution sharpened.

"Holy fuck," Garrett whispered. His gut knotted and his pulse started pounding like a jackhammer. He wasn't wrong about this. He wasn't goddamn wrong about this. And if he wasn't wrong, then they were in some deep shit without hip waders.

Sam stalked over, Steele on his heels. "What's going on?"

Swanny sauntered up behind Steele and looked on with interest.

Garrett gestured toward the image on the monitor. "Take a look at his hand. You recognize that? I remember it from when we were down in Del Rio, when things went to shit with Sophie. Kyle Phillips led a black ops team that Resnick provided. That signal. It's different. I remember thinking it was like they had their own language and fuck the Marines, even though, hey, they're Marines, right?"

Sam stared hard at the screen, his features frozen. Then his eyes narrowed in fury. "Zoom in, Van. On his left hand. Ring finger."

Garrett glanced at Sam in confusion and then back at Donovan, who was already furiously tapping the keyboard.

The man wore black gloves, but when Van zoomed all the way in and cleaned up the image, it looked very much like the tip of his ring finger was missing. The glove tip was flatter there and not defined like the other fingers.

"Son of a bitch. Son of a bitch!" Donovan swore.

"What the hell is going on?" Ethan demanded. "Will someone tell me what the fuck I'm missing out on here?"

"It's Kyle Phillips," Steele bit out. "He led the team that assisted us in Del Rio. One of Resnick's pets if I'm not mistaken. He's missing the tip of his left ring finger."

Sam's lips curled into a snarl, his eyes blazed with rage. "What the *fuck* is Resnick's man doing in Shea Peterson's home?"

Garrett and Donovan looked at each other at the same time. "Get Nathan and Shea back in here now," Garrett barked.

SHEA smiled as Nathan disappeared from view and she turned to stare out over the lake while she waited for him to return. It truly was a beautiful spot and secluded from the others. It afforded Nathan privacy while still being close to his family.

She took another step toward the lake, inhaling the scent of pine, honeysuckle and the slight damp in the air from the mist blowing in.

What if she and Nathan really could have a life here? Together? Now that one of KGI's team had gone in search of Grace—well, if they found her, brought her to Shea and offered them their protection—what was to say that they couldn't live here? Under the protection and umbrella of KGI?

It was pretty fanciful and she was way jumping the gun, but how else were she and Nathan ever going to have a life together if Shea didn't factor in everything into the equation?

Sometimes things just weren't simple, and this was just such a case. Maybe she and Grace would forever be running. Maybe they'd never be truly safe. Did Shea dare throw caution to the wind and settle here with Nathan and trust that KGI could handle any problems that arose?

She sighed and started to turn back toward the house. It did no good to dwell on the future when the present was still so up in the air. One day at a time. What mattered now was that Grace was found and that both of them stayed out of sight until Nathan and his brothers could determine who wanted them and why.

She hadn't fully rotated when she was knocked off balance by a hard body from behind. A strong arm snaked around her, preventing her fall, while a hand was clamped tight over her mouth.

Fear and panic exploded through her. She kicked, struggled and tried to scream, but the grip only tightened.

Nathan!

"Easy with her," a second man barked from behind her. "Resnick's orders were that under no circumstances was she to be harmed."

Oh God. Resnick. He was the man Donovan wanted to talk to—had *already* talked to about her and Grace. Son of a bitch. She'd known it was a mistake. A huge mistake to trust anyone!

She tried to focus her mind, to make that connection to Nathan, when a sharp prick in her arm had her making a muffled sound of pain from behind her captor's hand.

"Sorry, Miss Peterson. It had to be done. I can't have you using your telepathy to alert anyone to our presence."

The world did this crazy swinging thing, and black spots floated in and out of her vision.

The hell of it was, the man actually did sound regretful. The grip eased around her body, and then she was simply swung over the second man's shoulder and he ran toward the drop-off as if her weight was negligible.

She was too drugged to scream when a helicopter suddenly appeared, hovering at the very edge, so close that it would only take a small jump to clear the space between the cliff's edge and the inside of the chopper.

Oh God, no, surely he wasn't going to . . .

He never hesitated. He ran and then they were airborne for the briefest of moments before they hit the floor of the helicopter with enough force to knock the breath from her.

He tore off his mask and stared down at her, his eyes clouded with worry. He was young. And handsome. And there were at least three of him.

"Are you all right?" he shouted as the helicopter swooped away.

She wanted to kick him right back out of the helicopter. Of course she wasn't okay. But she couldn't speak. It was all she could do to even keep her eyes open. Her tongue was dry and stuck to the roof of her mouth. She was so damned scared that she wanted to curl into a ball and cry.

But that wasn't going to help her now.

Her eyes rolled back into her head and still she fought to remain conscious.

Nathan.

It was weak. A mere whisper. A plea for him to hear her.

But all that awaited her was suffocating darkness that closed in from every direction.

CHAPTER 34

FEAR and panic blew over Nathan like a tornado. And then it was gone just as quickly, leaving him unsettled and dizzy. His mouth went dry. He dropped the plank of wood he'd gotten to show Shea and ran back to the front of the house, clawing at the plastic, ripping an entire sheet from the frame as he stumbled to where he'd left Shea.

She wasn't there. He turned in a rapid circle. She wasn't anywhere.

"Shea! Shea!" he yelled. *Shea, where are you, damn it? Talk to me. Tell me where you are, baby. Help me help you. I feel your fear. What's happened?*

Nothing.

The sound of a helicopter sent him sprinting down the path toward the edge of the cliff. He topped the slight rise in front of the house and then stared down just in time to see the unbelievable.

Some motherfucker with Shea tossed over his shoulder leaped from the edge of the cliff toward a helicopter hovering a few feet away.

Time stopped. He couldn't breathe. Oh God, what if he didn't make it?

When both landed inside the helicopter, Nathan nearly

went to his knees in relief. But then he bolted into action and ran along the path paralleling the lake, keeping his eye on the rapidly fading helicopter.

Fuck it all, the goddamn thing had already become a blip on the horizon. It wasn't a helicopter he recognized and he'd flown plenty. He knew every helicopter flown by the military whether it was the army or another branch of the service. This was none of those.

He'd never seen an aircraft like this one. He hadn't heard it until it was literally on top of them. Which meant some goddamn top-secret prototype had just snatched Shea literally out of the air.

"Nathan! Nathan!"

He pulled up, nearly gutted by the cramp in his side, and turned to see Garrett hauling ass over the uneven terrain in his SUV. He braked hard when he reached Nathan, sending dust flying in all directions.

Donovan leaped out, Sam right on his heels.

"What the hell happened?" Donovan demanded.

"Shea," Nathan gasped. "The bastards took her. I was in the house for only a minute and they had a helicopter waiting. Crazy bastard threw her over his shoulder and jumped from the edge of the drop-off into the chopper."

Garrett's expression was fierce. "We didn't hear a fucking chopper."

Nathan shook his head. "This wasn't a typical military helicopter. I've never seen anything like it. I only heard it when it got damn close. I've heard . . . I mean I've heard shit about prototypes for super stealth choppers that can't be heard over a couple hundred yards away. Just didn't think they existed yet."

"Talk to her, man," Van urged. "Find out what's going on with her. Get her to give you any information she can."

"Don't you think I've tried?" Nathan yelled. "I've got nothing but this yawning black hole in my mind. She's not there!"

Garrett put his hand on Nathan's arm. "We know where to find her."

Nathan looked at his brother in confusion, sure that he hadn't heard correctly. "What the fuck are you talking about?"

"Resnick's boys were behind the break-in at Shea's house," Donovan said grimly. "The bastard has been tightlipped with us because he's behind it or at least he has a big hand in it. He must have loved me coming to him for information. Fuck me. I all but gave him a detailed map of how to find her. I'm going to kill him."

Nathan tried to clear the haze of rage and confusion that was clouding his mind. "Wait a minute. *Resnick* has her?"

"Yeah, or at least he knows who does," Sam said. "Come on. We've got a house call to make. That little son of a bitch is going to regret this."

"If he so much as touches a hair on her head, I'm going to gut him and leave him for the vultures," Nathan hissed.

"And we won't do a goddamn thing to stop you," Garrett promised. "Now let's go. We left Ethan and Swanny with Steele and his team, and they're likely having a kitten for wanting to blow something up. Looks like they're going to get their chance."

SHEA came to awareness but was careful not to convey that she'd regained consciousness. She was no longer in a helicopter. She knew that much at least. Nor was she moving. She was lying on a couch. A couch? As tempted as she was to open her eyes, she forced herself to have discipline and carefully determine what she could without any noticeable change in her breathing.

It was silent. She strained to listen for any sign that she wasn't alone. But all she heard was the light hum of a central air-conditioning system.

She allowed one slit in her left eye, and when she didn't immediately see anyone else in the room, she opened both eyes and quickly examined her surroundings.

Seeing no one, she shot to her feet and then nearly went down and face-planted on the floor. Holy hell, but whatever they'd given her must work for elephants too. She sank back onto the edge of the couch and shook her head, trying to clear the muzziness that surrounded her like fog.

There were two ways out of the room. A door and a large window. She had no idea where the door led, but she was going to check out the window first. It was already dark, which meant she'd been out for hours.

Shea, goddamn it. Where are you? Talk to me. Just talk to me. Let me know you're okay. Let me know where to find you. We're coming for you, baby.

She dropped to her knees, holding her head in agony. Each word sent splinters into her brain until she moaned and closed her eyes. She rocked back and forth, so shaken and in so much pain that her stomach was a tight ball of nausea.

Nathan.

As soon as she tried to reach out to him, pain speared through her skull and down her spine. Overwhelmed, she leaned forward and vomited. It took her several long moments to regain her composure and for her to stop the violent heaving of her stomach.

A gentle hand touched her shoulder, and she reacted on instinct. She turned and lashed out, first with her hand, landing the heel of her palm on the bridge of her captor's nose. She was on her feet in an instant and followed up with a vicious kick to his balls.

He doubled over with a grunt and she nailed him with a right hook to the jaw. Not leaving anything to chance, she snapped her foot into the side of his head and sent him reeling to the floor.

The dull gleam of a pistol secured in his shoulder harness sent her scrambling to yank it free. First she hit him on the back of the head with the butt and then she quickly frisked him for extra clips.

She felt like doing a double fist pump when she found not only two extra clips, but a smaller Sig Sauer secured to an ankle holster. She pocketed it and the knife from his pocket and then ran for the door.

She wasn't sure what she'd been expecting. Maybe some underground compound. A top-secret government facility in some cave. Or maybe even a basement in some underground Washington D.C. test facility. Whatever she'd been expecting, this wasn't it.

She was in a freaking house. A normal-looking house that from all appearances someone lived in. Damn it. She hadn't thought to frisk the dude for keys to a vehicle. They had to have gotten her here someway.

She crouched down in the hallway when she heard voices

in the next room. The stock of the pistol was slick in her hand and her pulse raced. She didn't want to have to kill anyone. She wasn't saying she wouldn't do it. But it didn't mean she was ready to start pumping people full of lead.

On the other hand, these assholes had scared her to death, they'd drugged her and they'd jumped off a cliff into a helicopter. And whatever they'd given her had affected her ability to use her telepathy.

Yeah, she was just pissed off enough to shoot and get the hell out of this place. Wherever this place was.

She ducked into one of the other rooms, realizing it was a guest bedroom. For God's sake. Were they in suburbia? This was getting more bizarre by the moment.

Footsteps passed in the hallway and she knew she only had moments before it was discovered she'd escaped. She ran to the window and forwent trying to be stealthy.

She kicked out the glass, making a big enough hole that she could get out without being cut to shreds. Then she ducked through and stepped into empty space.

She barely had time to utter a foul curse before she hit the ground with a painful thump. All the air left her and she couldn't draw in a single breath. It hurt too much.

Hell, she'd never even considered that she was in a two-story house. It was dark. She was still disoriented from the drugs. She just wanted to get the hell out of that creepy place.

Gasping painfully, she rolled and pushed herself to her knees.

"Damn it, Shea, what the hell are you trying to do, kill yourself?"

She grabbed the pistol and shot to her feet, backing away from the man who stood a short distance away.

He held his hands up and took a step forward. "I'm not going to hurt you. Put the gun down so we can talk."

She shook her head. "Too late, asshole. This whole ordeal has been anything but a cakewalk. If it's all the same to you, I'm getting the hell out of here."

He frowned and then lunged toward her. She squeezed the trigger, and a moment later, he dropped to his knees holding his arm and wearing a bewildered expression.

"You shot me."

"Well, duh." *Moron*.

She turned and fled, making damn sure she kept a tight hold on the gun.

"Shea, wait! Don't go!"

The man was insane. She was tempted to shoot him again, but the rest of his goons would be after her. She turned and sprinted down the street wondering where she was and how the hell she was going to get back to Nathan.

CHAPTER 35

THEY surrounded the house in the darkness. Nathan was on edge, his unease growing with every minute he was separated from Shea. He worried that his continued efforts to reach her would only weaken her, so he'd controlled the urge to continually call out to her.

Donovan had gone on a rampage and called in every favor ever owed to him in an effort to track Resnick down.

Steele and his team were in position. P.J. and Cole were in two of the oak trees on the edge of the property with their sniper rifles. Swanny, Nathan and his brothers were taking the front. Steele and the remainder of his team were taking the back.

It took all of Nathan's restraint and military training to sit back and wait for the command to go in. Everything inside screamed at him that his woman was in danger. That these assholes had her. That he should go in and take down everything in his path until he had her back.

Joe put a hand on his shoulder, a silent gesture of support. Nathan stood there in the dark, seething, readying himself to kill.

His nostrils flared and his grip tightened on his rifle when Sam held up his hand in silent readiness. Sam gave the silent countdown and then gave the order to go in.

Much like the onslaught Nathan and Shea had suffered when they'd gone to her parents' house, KGI went in with the sole intention of overpowering the occupants. Several flash grenades went off. It looked like a staccato of strobe lighting going off throughout the house.

There were three men in the kitchen surrounding another man sitting in a chair. Resnick. Nathan stared at the blood smeared down Resnick's arm and felt his stomach bottom out.

Swanny, Ethan and Joe broke away to clear the rest of the house, while the others blew into the kitchen like a hurricane.

"Down! Down! Down! Get down!" Garrett yelled.

The three men hit the floor while Resnick merely raised his arms toward the ceiling. A sound from behind Garrett alerted Sam and he leveled his rifle over Garrett's shoulder. Garrett and Donovan kept their rifles trained on the men on the floor.

"Don't even think about it, Phillips," Sam growled. "Stand down. This isn't worth getting your ass shot over."

The young Marine's lips thinned but he lowered his weapon and Sam went to collect it.

"What the fuck, Phillips? Who the hell are you taking orders from these days?"

"From me," Resnick said wearily. "Goddamn it, I need a cigarette."

Donovan motioned for the three men on the floor to stay down while Sam went around behind Phillips and patted him down. He then directed him to put his hands behind his head and leave them up where they could be seen.

Swanny, Joe and Ethan burst into the kitchen just then.

"Rest of the house is clear," Ethan said.

Sam directed him over to cover Phillips and then Sam stalked toward Resnick.

But Nathan was there first, fury boiling in his veins. Sam stepped in between him and Resnick and shot Nathan a meaningful glance. Yeah, it meant calm his ass down, but it was easy for Sam to think that. If it was Sophie in danger, Sam would be batshit insane.

"What the fuck, Resnick?" Sam thundered when he turned back to the other man. "Nathan wants your ass on his wall and I'm tempted to let him have at you. I'd be very careful what you do and say over the next little while because he wants to kill you. I want to let him."

"Where's Shea?" Nathan demanded. "Tell me where she is, and if you've hurt her in any way, so help me God, you're a dead man."

"She's not here," Phillips said from behind them.

Nathan whirled around, his gaze finding the younger man. "Where the hell is she then? It was you who tossed her over your shoulder and made that dumb-ass jump into the helicopter. You could have killed her!"

"If my orders were to kill her, she'd be dead," Phillips said evenly. "My orders were to deliver her safely. I did that. There was never a question of her safety."

"Fucking Marines always think they're such bad-asses," Ethan muttered.

Garrett raised his eyebrows at his younger brother but let the insult pass.

"Where is she?" Nathan bit out again. "I don't give a shit what your orders were. I only care about where she is now."

To Nathan's surprise, Phillip's cheeks colored and he fidgeted. Suddenly he didn't look like the supercomposed, always-follow-orders badass. He looked . . . embarrassed.

"She escaped."

Seven mouths fell open. Joe stepped forward and stared at Phillips. Then he smirked. "She kicked your ass, didn't she?"

"Fuck you," Phillips muttered.

"Look, she freaked out when she came around," Resnick interjected. "I thought we had more time. She came to, Phillips was supposed to see to her, and she escaped."

Sam quirked up his eyebrow as sudden understanding flashed across his face. "Is she what happened to your arm?"

Resnick nodded, his expression still tight with pain. "She shot me when I tried to prevent her escape. Hell, she jumped out of a second-story window. I was worried she was hurt. She basically told me to fuck off and then shot me before she ran like a damn jackrabbit."

"Fierce!" Garrett crowed. "I knew I loved that girl. You deserved everything you got, Resnick."

"Did you send someone after her?" Nathan asked in a deadly quiet voice.

Resnick shook his head. "Look, it just happened. I was just sending the men out to find her."

Nathan moved in close and stroked the barrel of his rifle down the column of Resnick's neck until Resnick broke into a sweat. "Your next move is to back the fuck off. Then you're going to tell us what the fuck you were doing in Shea's parents' house. You're also going to tell us why you're so goddamn interested in Shea and Grace Peterson. And then you're going to forget you ever knew anything about either of them."

Resnick shook his head, his eyes determined. "I can't do that."

"Why the fuck not?" Nathan snarled.

Resnick's head dropped and he let out a weary sigh. "Look, Donovan, can you patch me up here? This arm's hurting like a son of a bitch and I need to be able to use it. I'll tell you everything I know while you work."

Nathan shook his head. "Hell no. You don't get shit from us until you tell us what the fuck is going on. I don't give a fuck if your arm rots off. Shea is out there scared to death and unable to communicate with me. I'm not leaving her a minute longer than necessary. I'm going after her and you're going to arm me with everything I need to know about what I'm walking into."

"Christ. At least give me a goddamn cigarette."

Garrett reached for the crumpled pack on the kitchen counter and tossed it along with a lighter in Resnick's direction. Resnick tore half the packing off as he dug out a cigarette. Using his good arm, he shoved the end of the cigarette into his mouth and then raised his hand to light it.

A moment later, he inhaled deeply and then exhaled a long plume of smoke.

"So Shea can communicate with you?" Resnick asked Nathan. There was intense interest in his usually inscrutable gaze. "Can you talk to her or does she have to open the channel?"

His curiosity only served to piss Nathan off more. And Resnick knew it.

"Fuck you," Nathan said in a deadly voice. "She isn't some goddamn lab rat for you to poke and prod on."

Something dark flickered in Resnick's eyes, giving him a haunted look. "Shea was never in any danger from me. Not me."

"Really?" Nathan asked coolly. "You could have fooled me."

"Why weren't you straight with us?" Donovan demanded. "You clammed up the minute I asked about Shea. And you knew, goddamn it. You knew about her and you used the info I gave you to move in and snatch her. That's bullshit and you know it. Is this how it's going to work from now on? We can't trust anything that comes from you?"

"It's a goddamn different situation!" Resnick seethed. "This is personal. I was protecting her, okay? I knew you guys had no idea what you were dealing with. How could you? I was doing what was best for Shea. There are people after her who don't give a damn who lives or dies as long as they get what they want, and they want her and Grace. Suddenly she surfaces on your radar? What the hell? You have no idea what we're dealing with here."

"And you damn sure didn't do anything to change that fact," Sam growled.

"What people and why are you so involved?" Garrett barked at Resnick. "What's your stake in this? It's not like you to get personal about anything. You'd hang your own mother out to dry if it furthered your purpose."

Resnick's lip curled back into a snarl and he glared Garrett down. "You don't know anything about me, so back the fuck off. Just because we work together or I throw you a job here and there doesn't mean you know shit about me or what matters to me."

"So explain it to us," Donovan said impatiently. "We're wasting time here, Resnick. Spill it or I'll goddamn shoot you in the other arm, and you know I'm just pissed off enough to do it. What you did was bullshit and you know it."

"Fuck him," Nathan spit out. "Let's go. I don't have time for this shit." Then he turned to Resnick and got into his face until they were nose to nose. "Don't you ever come near Shea again. You don't even say her name. You forget she ever existed."

"Fuck *you*," Resnick snarled back. "There's a goddamn possibility that she's my sister. I'm not leaving her safety to chance and definitely not to KGI. You guys are good. I get that. I wouldn't have you do work for me if I didn't think you were the best. But you don't know what you're dealing with here, and I didn't have time to debrief you. I had to move and move fast because Shea and Grace were running out of time. As it is, Grace has dropped off the map. But I could save Shea and I did what I had to do."

"She's your what?" Nathan demanded. What the fuck? This just got more twisted by the minute. "Wait a goddamn minute. Shea told me how she was born. Or rather how she was created. You're full of shit, Resnick."

Resnick's eyes grew shadowed and suddenly he looked so much older than he was. "I'm not full of shit. I was born in that same goddamn lab. Shea and Grace could both be my sisters. And even if they aren't my blood, I feel a kinship to them that can't be removed just because of genetics. I have to make this right for them once and for all. I don't give a damn what it takes."

CHAPTER 36

EVERYONE stared at Resnick like he'd just admitted to being a terrorist. Maybe that wasn't far off the mark. Nathan glanced sideways at his brothers to gauge their reactions. They didn't have time for this shit. Evidently Resnick agreed.

"Look, we don't have time for this right now, but I swear to you, I'll explain everything. I won't leave out anything. But you have to go after Shea. Bring her back."

"Oh, so now you trust us to track her down after she kicked your guy's balls in," Sam drawled. "How ironic."

"What the fuck did you do to her?" Nathan demanded. "Why can't she communicate with me? Why would you take that away from her? I'd know where she is right now if you hadn't fucked with her."

"It's only temporary," Resnick said warily. "I did it so she wouldn't have you on our asses."

Ethan cleared his throat. "And how's that working out for you?"

"You better hope it's temporary," Nathan seethed. "And you better hope I find her quick and that she's okay. I'll hunt you down, Resnick. There isn't a place you can hide from me."

Joe put his hand on Nathan's shoulder. "Come on, bro. I'm with you. Let's go find Shea. We can take Steele and company, leave everyone else here to sit on the trash so we can take it out later."

Nathan turned to stare into his twin's eyes, saw answering resolve there. Always looking out for each other. It was as it should be. Nathan hadn't been the best at guarding Joe's back over the last months, but Joe had never stopped standing at Nathan's. Not even when Nathan was doing everything he could to push his twin away.

Nathan held up his hand and Joe grasped it. Then they started for the door.

"Now wait just a goddamn minute," Sam said in exasperation. "I don't know who you two knuckleheads think you are or what you're doing, but you don't run this operation. And Steele damn sure won't take orders from either one of you infants."

Donovan lowered his rifle and then glanced toward Ethan, Garrett and Sam. "You stay here. Swanny and I will go with them."

Garrett didn't look happy, but then he never was happy about anything that kept him out of the know.

"Steele, fall back. Have P.J. and Cole stand down. We're out of here," Donovan said into the radio. "Shea escaped and is on her own. It's imperative we find her before things get any worse."

HER head hurt. Not just headache hurt. It felt like someone had hit her with a sledgehammer and half her skull was caved in. She was so overwhelmed with nausea that even breathing was a chore.

And she was pissed.

She was tired of all the crazies in her life. The dude whose house she had been taken to gave her the creeps. Like in a stalkerish "I'm not going to hurt you but I'll confine you to my dungeon for the next ten years and never let you come out" kind of way.

She shivered and trudged down another alleyway that reeked of garbage and God only knew what else. She had a good imagination. She didn't really need to know.

At least she knew where she was now, thanks to her flight

through the streets. The problem? It was several states away from Tennessee. Charleston, South Carolina, was a beautiful city. It really was. Just not so much right now when she had no money, no ID, no idea how to communicate with Nathan—it wasn't as if she had his phone number.

Lord, but she was getting loopy, and if she didn't get rid of the headache soon, she was going to vomit everywhere.

She was afraid even to think about reaching out to Nathan. The pain was already so overwhelming that anything else she did to intensify her agony would send her straight over the edge.

Still, she had to try. What other options did she have?

She stepped from the alleyway and then hurriedly crossed the street. She'd been in this situation before. Nothing had changed. She'd been running for a year. She could do this without freaking out. Or at least that's what she kept telling herself.

Focus, Shea. Just focus, damn it.

The problem was that before she only had to run. It didn't matter where she went as long as she was able to melt in a crowd somewhere, disappear, lie low. Now? It wasn't that easy. She didn't want to go off alone again. She wanted to be back with Nathan and his horde of overprotective brothers and all their hulking team members.

She slowed in her walk. She'd felt safe with them, but she hadn't been. Maybe that was her reality. Maybe she'd never be safe with anyone. She'd allowed herself to be reeled in by the fantasy of being able to rely on someone else. To have someone to protect her. Hope had been fierce within her after dealing with cold, hard reality for so long.

And the minute she'd let her guard down and allowed herself to depend on someone else? She'd been thrown over some psycho G.I. Joe wannabe's shoulder and nearly tossed off a cliff.

Say it with me. Safety is an illusion.

Nothing like a good shot of optimism to boost her spirits.

Seeing an empty bench by a bus stop, she sank down onto it, watching warily around her for anyone who looked remotely threatening. She needed to clear her damn mind. She needed to figure out what to do.

She had no money, no ID. If she got stopped by a cop for any reason, she was so screwed. She had stuff stashed in a few places, but that didn't do her any good when she had no way to get to it.

Damn it. Grace wasn't talking. Shea's head splintered when she even tried to call out for Nathan. She wanted to bury her face in her hands and cry like a damn baby, but she was too disgusted with herself to give in to that particular drama-fest.

She sat for several moments and purposely blanked her mind. She rubbed soothingly at her temples and tried to shake off the aftereffects of the drugs they'd given her. It was the only explanation for why she couldn't use her telepathy.

And then she panicked. What if it was permanent? Who knew what kind of crazy crap they'd given her? She quickly realized the absurdity of thinking such a thing. They wanted her abilities. They didn't want to destroy them.

She sucked in air through her nose and then held her breath as she whispered Nathan's name in her mind.

The stabbing pain nearly flattened her. She pitched forward, gulping desperately in an effort not to cry out. There was so much pressure in her skull, it felt like it would burst at any moment. Like a volcano. It literally felt like something was about to break apart in her head.

But then she heard him. A faint whisper, so light she wondered if it was wishful thinking.

Shea, where are you, baby?

Oh God, she couldn't answer, could she? What if something did burst in her head? What if she had some freak aneurysm? What the hell was going on with her?

She rocked back and forth, trying not to let any sound escape.

"Miss, are you all right?"

Shea jerked her head around to see an elderly man sit down on the bench next to her. She nodded jerkily. "I'm f-fine."

He gave her a doubtful look and she shot to her feet. She hurried away, knowing she probably drew more attention than if she'd just sat there, but she didn't trust herself not to completely lose it and that would definitely gain her far more attention than if she simply walked away.

She hugged herself close and hunched down as she passed block after block. The streetlights blurred in her vision and she winced every time she inadvertently made contact with passing headlights.

It was like having a headache on steroids. The mother of all migraines. Every sound, every touch, every shard of light was so overwhelming that she couldn't even process her thoughts. She couldn't put together the simplest of plans and so she wandered through the city like some zombie.

She nearly stepped off the curb in front of a car when she was yanked backward. The hand on her arm was crushing, and she winced as she tried to pull away.

"Th-Thank you," she tried to murmur but it came out as unintelligible garble. And then she looked up and her stomach bottomed out.

It was a face she'd seen many times in her nightmares in the last weeks. He'd beaten and brutalized her and been ruthless in his determination to extract the information he wanted from her.

Nathan had told her that it wasn't just Grace these assholes wanted. He was resolute in his opinion that they wanted her just as much. They'd taken too much care not to seriously injure her.

So if they didn't want her dead, and had no intention of killing her, she had absolutely nothing to lose by making the mother of all scenes.

As if reading her mind—who the hell knows, maybe he had—his grip tightened around her wrist until she let out a cry of pain.

"If you try anything, I'll break your arm," he hissed. "I will make you suffer unimaginably. If you cooperate, you'll get to see your sister again."

Her eyes widened in fear and her stomach clenched. Was this what had happened to Grace? Did these bastards already have her?

"Where is she?" Shea demanded, ignoring the roaring in her head.

"Get in the car," he directed as a dark sedan pulled to the curb and stopped. "Do it or I'll make you regret the day you were born."

"Don't you mean created?" she said in disgust.

He shoved her forward into the open backseat and then climbed in beside her. "Drive," he directed.

Oh God, Nathan, I hope you can hear me. The drugs they gave me, it makes using my telepathy unbearable. The pain is horrific. I can't do this for long. They found me. They have me again. Not the same as who took me from you. Different. The ones who had me first, the ones who tortured me. Help me, please. I was in downtown Charleston, but I have no idea where they're taking me. I'll try to establish a link when the pain is gone.

It was too much. She grabbed her head as tears streamed down her cheeks. She rocked back and forth moaning and sobbing. Her abductor looked at her like she'd lost her mind, and then as if realizing what she'd been doing, he yanked her head up by her hair.

She saw his fist coming and didn't even try to dodge it. At the moment she welcomed oblivion with open arms.

CHAPTER 37

AS soon as Nathan, Joe, Swanny and Donovan hit the front, where Steele was already waiting with his team, a wave of agony hit Nathan so hard that his knees buckled and he went down.

"What the fuck?" Joe demanded. He dropped down next to his brother and grasped his arm, trying to steady Nathan's descent.

Donovan grabbed Nathan's other arm and then bent over as he and Joe eased him to the ground,

"What's wrong?" Donovan asked sharply. "Talk to me, Nathan. Is it Shea? You're scaring the shit out of me here."

"It's Shea," Swanny said sharply. "Something's going on and it ain't good."

But Nathan wasn't focused on his brothers. He was caught in a myriad of pain, like needles were poking into his head. The inside of his skull felt scraped and turned inside out. Dear God, was this what Shea was experiencing?

And then he heard her. So desperate, her voice cracking under the onslaught of agony.

Oh God, Nathan, I hope you can hear me. The drugs they gave me, it makes using my telepathy unbearable. The pain is horrific. I can't do this for long. They found me. They have me

again. Not the same as who took me from you. Different. The ones who had me first, the ones who tortured me. Help me, please. I was in downtown Charleston, but I have no idea where they're taking me. I'll try to establish a link when the pain is gone.

He roared his frustration and tried to scramble to his feet, but the lingering waves of pain—her pain—had crippled him. He couldn't seem to be able to get anything to work right. Dear God, the horrific agony she was enduring and he was helpless. Goddamn helpless while those bastards had their hands on her again.

"Nathan, goddamn it, talk to me!" Van shouted.

"Get off me! Just get away from me. Give me a minute."

Donovan backed off but Joe remained down, his hand locked around Nathan's shoulder.

"Let me help you up," Joe said in a low voice. "Then tell us what happened. We're wasting time, man. Push through it. She needs your help. It was her, wasn't it? Do you want me to try to get through to her?"

Joe's words cut through the lingering pain and confusion and already Shea had faded away, gone from him, the blank void he'd grown to hate so much replacing the overwhelming torment.

His mind went quiet. So damn quiet. He preferred the agony over this blanket of silence because at least then he'd had a connection with her. He'd heard her. And now there was nothing.

He grasped Joe's hand and hauled himself upward. For a moment he staggered and leaned into his brother. Joe wrapped his arm around Nathan's shoulders and simply held on.

As soon as he got his bearings, he turned and stalked back into the house, leaving Joe and Donovan to call after him. He barged into the kitchen, where Resnick still sat there smoking that damn cigarette while Shea was in the hands of people who had brutalized her.

"You son of a bitch!" Nathan roared.

He knocked the cigarette from Resnick's mouth in one punch. Resnick went sprawling to the floor and Nathan went down after him. The kitchen erupted in chaos as Resnick's men attempted to intervene.

Sam and Garrett pulled their guns while Donovan and Joe attempted to pry Nathan from Resnick.

It took the combined efforts of Donovan, Joe and Swanny to finally get Nathan off Resnick. No one made a move to help the man from the floor. He slowly picked himself up, wincing at the injury to his arm that was still unattended. He wiped at the blood that streamed from his nose and mouth and he backed up until he leaned against the counter.

"What the fuck is wrong with you?" Resnick demanded. "You're supposed to be out looking for Shea."

Nathan lunged for him again and Sam placed his body between his brother and Resnick, his gaze boring into Nathan.

"He went crazy outside," Donovan explained. "Something happened to Shea, and he went nuts and stomped in here to kick the shit out of Resnick. Not that I have a problem with that, but I'd like to know what the fuck is going on."

"That makes two of us," Garrett spoke up.

"You did this to her," Nathan choked out. "You stupid son of a bitch. You took away her only means of self-defense. Those goddamn drugs you gave her make using her telepathy impossible. She's in unimaginable pain every time she tries to communicate. You can't *imagine* the agony she's enduring."

Resnick went white and he looked like he was going to be ill. "No, that's not what should have happened. It's experimental, yes, but there haven't been any side effects. It just prevents a person from focusing enough to maintain a telepathic connection."

"I felt what she's feeling," Nathan yelled. "She felt like her head was going to explode, like something was breaking inside her skull, but she bore it to reach out to me because those assholes have her again. Do you have any idea what they did to her the last time they had her?"

Resnick slowly shook his head, his face going paler by the second.

"They beat her. They tortured her. For days she endured hell because she wouldn't give them information about Grace. After she escaped, she asked me for help. She'd tried to do so before, but they kept her too drugged to maintain a pathway. And now because you're a stupid fuck, she's back in their hands and she can't give me any goddamn information because you shot her full of drugs that prevent her from using her gift."

Resnick's hand shook as he dragged it through his hair. "You have to know I didn't intend for this to happen."

"I don't know anything," Nathan snapped. "You claim to care about her. You think she might be your sister. Where the fuck do you get your idea of family from? What is *wrong* with you?"

"Save the insults, okay? I fucked up. I just wanted to protect her. I had no idea that you and she were involved. I didn't even know how the hell she ended up with KGI. I thought I could remove her without having to explain anything. I wanted to protect her and Grace without anyone finding out about their abilities. I still don't know how she got involved with you or how she knew to ask you for help."

"Because she saved me," Nathan said in a fierce voice. "She heard me out of all the other voices in the world and she answered. We formed a bond long before we ever met face-to-face, and I'll be damned if I let you or anyone else break it."

Joe slid his hand over Nathan's shoulder again. "No one's going to do anything. We'll get Shea back."

Just hearing the conviction in his brother's voice settled Nathan. As he glanced around the room at his other brothers and Steele and his team members, he saw the same conviction in every one of their faces.

Garrett turned to Resnick, his eyes so cold they'd freeze a polar bear. "It's time for you to start talking. We need every piece of information you have on this lab where you and Shea were conceived or created or whatever the fuck you want to call it. We need names, organizations, and we need to know who'd have an interest in them now. Or who would even know about them."

"Do you have their abilities?" Sam asked as he took a step closer to Resnick.

Resnick shook his head. His nostrils flared and his lips flattened into a thin line. "I was a . . . failure. A dropped experiment. Disappointing results. They went back to the drawing board after I was born. It wasn't until many years later that Grace and then Shea were born."

"So what, you just hung around the lab? I'm having a hard time wrapping my mind around this," Ethan said. "It doesn't add up and it damn sure doesn't make sense."

Resnick lit another cigarette and blew out a cloud of smoke. "There wasn't anything else to do with me. I was the first. They didn't have a plan for what happened if I didn't yield the results they were looking for. After me, they adopted out babies that didn't work out. But they kept me."

"Who is they?" Nathan asked impatiently. "We're wasting time here. I'm not interested in your life story."

"The project was started during the Cold War. At first the U.S. was primarily interested in psychic and telepathic powers. They wanted a way into the heads of people in positions of power. They wanted their secrets. It sounds far-fetched, yes, but then a whole lot of secret research is pretty damn unbelievable.

"There wasn't any solid success until after the Cold War ended. That's when Grace and Shea were born. At first there was a lot of excitement that the two girls could communicate telepathically with each other. But then when their ability to heal and take on pain was discovered, it marked a complete one-hundred-and-eighty-degree turn in the possibilities."

"Okay, so who do we like for this?" Nathan demanded. "The government? Some unheard-of, nonexistent shadow group of the CIA who want to keep experimenting on Shea and Grace?"

"*Where* did they get the donors?" Donovan cut in. "Shea said that according to her mother's journal they paired egg and sperm from donors who had remarkable abilities. That doesn't explain how they laid hands on these people. Hardly something you can advertise for."

"I don't know the answer to your question, Nathan," Resnick said in a low voice. "But we'll use whatever resources I have to find out. I swear it." He turned to Donovan. "That's exactly what they did. They studied each and every case of special abilities. Some turned out to be hoaxes, but there were others who clearly displayed unique talents. Years went into cataloging and searching out men and women with psychic or paranormal gifts. They were tested extensively and then semen samples were taken from the men and the females had eggs removed. Then began an experimentation on mixing and matching certain profiles to see what the result would be."

"It all sounds fucking unreal," Ethan muttered.

"I was a failure. As were many of the offspring that were created in the lab," Resnick continued. "In fact, Grace and Shea were the only two who displayed marked abilities. You can imagine the excitement they caused when it was discovered what they could do. There were others with questionable abilities but nothing that was tangible, that was there in black and white, that could be proven, and most important, controlled and reproduced at will. That is what they were looking for, and that's why Grace and Shea aren't safe. They want them not only for what they can do, but for the possibilities their offspring would provide."

A chill went up Nathan's spine, and fury gripped him all over again. There was no fucking way Shea was going to spend her life being tortured and have her eggs taken to produce mass offspring in hopes of having one or two who shared her remarkable ability. The mere thought made him sick to his stomach.

A sudden thought occurred to Nathan and he met Resnick's gaze. "You were the one who helped the Petersons, weren't you? When they moved to Oregon. It's how you knew about the house there and why you sent Phillips there to find Shea."

Resnick gave a resigned sigh. "Yes. I didn't locate the Petersons or the girls until they were nearly adults. The Petersons took the girls and ran when they were very young. Just toddlers. I was glad. I hated seeing what was done to them. I was just a teenager who was helpless to do anything but watch while they were treated like objects.

"They were why I pursued a job in the CIA and why I worked my way into the upper echelons of the intelligence community. I not only wanted to find and protect them but I wanted to keep my ear to the ground so I'd know if there was an effort to regroup or if anyone began digging around for information on the girls.

"The project folded after the Petersons escaped with Shea and Grace. There was a fear of discovery. No one knew when or if the Petersons would go public. One day the project was alive and well. The next day it was a ghost town."

"And you?" Sam asked. "Where do you fit into all this, Resnick? What did you do after the project folded? Or did you keep your hand in it all this time?"

Resnick's lip curled at the distrust in Sam's voice. "Since I was conceived in a lab, I didn't officially exist. I didn't even have a name, though the Petersons called me Adam. For the first created man. But I had no official identification. No birth certificate. To the world I didn't exist. It was pretty easy to disappear, start over, create my own past. It didn't take long to get a birth certificate and a social security number. Things were much easier back then. Not as much red tape. And once you're in the system, you're there. And so I became Adam Resnick. More importantly, my connection to the research project has never been known."

Resnick stopped for a moment and then he tiredly ran a hand over his jaw. His injured arm hung loosely at his side and he had a gray cast to his skin. He looked beaten. Regret radiated from him in waves.

"For what it's worth, I'm sorry, Nathan. I didn't know. I couldn't have known. I only wanted to protect Shea. I still want to protect her."

"Then let's find out who the fuck has her," Nathan ground out. "Last time they caught up to her in California and they held her in the vicinity for a week. She escaped and I found her in Crescent City, hiding in a culvert. They kept her drugged the entire time. She remembers little except the torture, so she couldn't tell me anything about who they were."

Resnick sighed. "I've looked for her and Grace ever since the Petersons turned up dead and the girls disappeared. I knew they were in serious trouble. I made sure the Petersons' bodies were removed and nothing got out about their deaths. The house belonged to me under an assumed name, and on paper the Petersons were renters. They kept to themselves and never involved themselves in the community, so it's doubtful anyone ever knew they were gone. I made sure the house was kept up in case . . . in case one of the girls ever came back."

"You mean you intended to nab them as soon as they showed up," Nathan said darkly.

"I would have taken them in, yes," Resnick said calmly. "I would have done anything to protect them. Unfortunately, I wasn't the only one watching the house, and Phillips and his team got there too late to help Grace. I was determined to at least bring Shea in. When we failed to intercept her at the house, I knew that eventually you'd take her home, so we waited for our opportunity and took it."

"Who else is watching?" Sam demanded. "Who else wants them?"

"I don't know. But I plan to find out."

"So what now?" Garrett demanded with his trademark impatience. He was positively fidgeting with all the talking going on, an impatience that Nathan shared.

Resnick pushed off the edge of the counter. "Now we find the fucks who have Shea and we go blow some shit up."

Ethan grinned. "Now we're talking!"

CHAPTER 38

TORTURE was preferable to this hell. Her sanity was slowly being eaten away.

She was in a clear plastic tube, the sides pressed to her arms so she couldn't move. Bands circled her ankles, her wrists and even her neck. That one was the worst of all because she fought the sensation of choking every second she was conscious.

They'd already taken blood samples. It had all been sterile and very methodical. No one spoke to her. They treated her like she was a nameless, faceless object. Soulless. No one. Just another research project. Was this what it had been like for her and Grace in the beginning?

What did they want from her? Tears pricked her eyelids and her vision blurred. She was a human being regardless of the circumstances of her birth.

This wasn't right. None of it was right. She and Grace deserved to be left alone. Running from a faceless enemy was no way to live.

She glanced fearfully over at the monitor positioned to her left. She had to calm her thoughts. Make everything blank.

The electrodes attached to her head monitored brain waves and activity. She'd already learned the hard way that the consequence of her trying to communicate telepathically was horrific pain, not only from the lingering effects of the drugs but from the electrical shock that speared through her body every time her brain activity increased.

But telepathy wasn't the only thing that would raise the level of her brain activity. She had to be careful to temper her emotions.

She felt like the negative reinforcement rat. Eat, zap. Do the wrong thing, zap. Zap, zap, zap.

Yeah, she was starting to lose her mind. It wouldn't take much at all to sever her fragile grasp of reality. She was clinging by a thread, and right now it seemed a lot easier to just let go and check out.

She hadn't tried to contact Nathan for hours now. She could still feel the lingering pain from her last effort. The empty void in her mind was hell. The claustrophobic capsule they'd crammed her in was hell. She knew in that moment that she didn't *want* to connect with Nathan. She never wanted him to know how this felt. He'd already endured so much torture, and knowing what was happening to her would send him right over the edge.

RESNICK paced back and forth in the basement of his home that served as his office away from his headquarters in D.C. "She should have been able to communicate with you by now. Have you tried reaching out to her recently?"

"I won't do it again," Nathan said fiercely. "Every time I do, I can feel her pain. It's horrific. I won't put her through that. I can feel her confusion, her emptiness. She's so goddamn alone and she's hanging on by the thinnest of threads and the pain is unimaginable. We have to give her more time."

"I could try," Joe said in a low voice. "You're too worked up, man. We need to keep her calm. If she feels what you feel, I can't imagine what that does to her. I'm more objective. At least let me try. Maybe I'll cause her less pain."

Nathan sighed, knowing his brother was probably right at least about him being too worked up. "I appreciate you trying to help, man, but this thing with Shea, it's random. She told me she has no control over whom she can connect to."

Joe slowly shook his head in disagreement. "She can speak to me. I've heard her in my mind. Back when we first met. I felt her and then I heard her. I thought at first that I was imagining it, but yeah, it was her."

Nathan stared at his brother in confusion. "What?"

"She didn't tell you?"

"No, she didn't tell me. I had no idea. Why didn't *you* tell me?"

Joe held his hands up. "Whoa. It's not like she was cheating on you with me or anything. She was afraid I'd be pissed because she could hear me and vice versa. It was the reason I asked to talk to her alone back at the house. So we could iron out a few things."

Nathan gripped the back of his neck and glanced at his other brothers, who were attempting not to seem interested in the current conversation. Unsuccessfully, since everyone's eyes were glued to the twins. "I had no idea. I mean how?"

Joe shrugged. "She thought maybe because you and I were twins and were so close. Who knows why? You said yourself it was random. She said as much too. But I told her if she ever needed anything to call for me. Maybe I can reach out to her instead. It's worth a shot, right?"

Indecision rolled through Nathan. The last thing he wanted to do was make her suffer more, but he also needed to find out where the hell she was. Resnick was working on it. He had every available resource allocated to finding Shea. But damn it, things were moving way too slow for Nathan's liking.

"Let him try, man," Swanny said in a low voice. "We have to find her before it's too late. We have no idea what those bastards are doing to her, and if it's like you already said and she's hanging on by just a thread, how much more can she take?"

Nathan glanced again at his brothers. Then at Steele and his team. Even Resnick and his team headed by the young Marine, Phillips. Everyone was tense. Ready to move at a moment's notice. They were just waiting. Waiting for word, information, Shea's location, so they could go in and kick ass.

It had been hours. While Resnick had gone to work pulling out every stop in his search for information, Nathan, Swanny, Joe and Steele's team had scoured the streets of Charleston. They'd questioned people endlessly, until finally they'd hit pay dirt when an elderly man getting off a bus had mentioned seeing a young woman in extreme distress. He'd pointed them in the direction she'd gone, and from there, they canvassed a four-block radius until they'd found one witness who'd seen her getting into a black Toyota Avalon.

Resnick had pulled metro surveillance for that location, and sure enough, hours before, they saw a man forcing Shea into a vehicle. They'd even gotten a license plate number, which so far had yielded them exactly nothing.

"I don't know, Joe. It's . . . hard. You'll feel what she feels. I don't know how to prepare you for that."

"Maybe not," Joe argued. "You love her, man. You're emotionally involved. What you feel for her and *through* her is magnified ten times. I like her, yeah, but I'm not in love with her. I don't have the emotional connection to her that you have. Let me try at least. If I sense I'm causing her too much pain, I'll break away immediately. That's even assuming I can reach her. I don't know how to do this shit."

Nathan closed his eyes and breathed deep. Joe was right about one thing. They had to at least try. Whatever pain she endured leading them to her would be worth if it they could bring her safely home.

He'd failed to do the one thing he'd promised her. Keep her safe. It was an easy thing to promise. Something to make her feel safe. But they were just words, and he hadn't been able to make that happen, even with the backing of KGI and his family.

Resnick was partially right. He, and his brothers, had no idea what they were dealing with. They were only just starting to understand, and they still didn't have the entire picture.

Nathan put his hand on Joe's shoulder and looked him in the eye. "Just focus on her. Think about her and remember what that pathway felt like. Then open your mind and call for her."

Joe took a deep breath. "Okay then. I'm going to do it."

Resnick stopped his pacing and moved in close to where Joe and Nathan stood with Swanny. Nathan's lip curled in distaste, but Resnick was focused on Joe, watching as Joe drew in a deep breath and closed his eyes.

Around them, the others leaned forward, some taking steps

to get closer to Joe. There was intense curiosity but also determination on everyone's faces. Quiet descended until the only
sound that could be heard was breathing.

Joe sucked in his breath and then exhaled long and slow.
He purposely blanked his mind in preparation. He didn't want
any distractions. This was important. Nathan was suffering.
Shea was suffering. If he could somehow get through to Shea,
then he could help them both.

He closed his eyes, and the rest of the room fell away. His
awareness of the others became dim as he focused solely on
that pathway to Shea. When he was completely relaxed and
felt the sensation of familiarity, he sent out a cautious inquiry.

Shea? Can you hear me? It's Joe.

He kept it short, fearful of causing her unbearable pain. He
waited, his breath held, his fingers curled into tight fists.

At first there was quiet and then he felt a slight stirring in
his mind. It was unlike anything he'd ever felt before. A burst
of warmth, but with that warmth came a flood of terror, panic
and clawing pain.

He flinched but held on to that pathway with every part of
himself. Immediately he could see her surroundings. Felt what
she felt. Experienced all she was experiencing.

She was being held in a long, plastic tube that opened from
the top. Steel bands clamped around her wrists, ankles and
neck. He could feel the horrible panic over the belief that she
would choke.

Dear God. He didn't even know what to do to try to make her
feel better, to take away the awful fear that ate at her sanity.

She closed her eyes and everything went black. He could
feel her battle to remain calm.

*Open your eyes, Shea. Open them for me, sweetheart. Let
me see what you see.*

There were electrodes attached to her head. When she opened
her eyes, he saw through them to the machines monitoring her
brain activity. She was trying valiantly to keep her mind quiet,
but one of the lines spiked too high and suddenly he was
assaulted with an electrical shock that sent him to his knees.

He folded over, holding his stomach with his arms, and
then he had to put one down to the floor to prevent himself
from pitching forward.

"Oh my God," he rasped out, each word laced with pain.

"What is it?" Nathan demanded. "Goddamn it, Joe, talk to me. What's going on?"

Joe held up his hand to silence his brother. He couldn't lose concentration now. Not now. He had to fix this. He had to find a way. He was so fucking furious that she was being treated like some kind of an animal that he wanted to kill someone.

He tried to soothe her, sending her waves of comfort and love, but it was hard when his mind screamed revenge and retribution. He forced the blackness away and brought to mind all the things that made him happy.

Summer rains. A good book in a hammock. A day of fishing on the lake. Hanging out with his brothers. Seeing his mom and dad again. Knowing that Nathan was alive and coming home.

Then he forced that comfort to Shea and once again spoke to her.

Nathan is with me. Try to remain calm. Don't speak back to me yet. Just listen. Gather your strength. Focus on the one thing that will help us the most in finding you.

Focus, Shea. Will the pain to go away. You're strong. You can do this. Nathan and I are coming for you. Do you understand me? We're going to get you back and then we're going to take apart those sons of bitches who hurt you.

Breathe, baby girl. Breathe and calm yourself. And then I want you to think about the one thing you can tell me. Don't even say it through your mind. Just picture it. Close your eyes and imagine what it looks like. I'll see what you see.

She closed her eyes, shutting off his vision of her surroundings. She relaxed and some of the pain faded away, leaving her weak and shaky. Her nerve endings twitched and her fingers jumped spasmodically. Those fucking bastards. He'd take great pleasure in making them suffer for what they had done to her.

Slowly, the blackness drifted away and he got the sense of being outside. He bobbed up and down. It felt like someone was carrying him and then he realized he was reliving Shea's memory. What she wanted to show him.

The surroundings came into view. Mountains. Crisp, clean air. The scent of pine. Cool temperatures. He shivered as the chill crept over his skin. Gravel crunched underneath the feet of the man carrying her. A doorway. Slowly her gaze drifted higher, above the door.

UFV5591

Then everything went black again.

"Uniform, Foxtrot, Victor, five, five, niner, one," he said urgently. Then he repeated it again until he heard Swanny say from seemingly a mile away that he'd gotten it down.

I've got it, Shea, he said gently. *Rest now. Save your strength. We'll find you. Cooperate with them. Don't do anything to anger them. Stay alive. We'll come for you.*

He wiped his face and took several deep breaths in an effort to clear his mind. He felt so goddamn weak. He didn't know how Nathan managed to maintain any lengthy communication with her.

Swanny and Nathan hauled him to his feet, and he sank into the chair that Donovan had shoved forward. He put his face forward into his hands and leaned over, still trying to put it all together.

Nathan took the chair next to him and pushed it so he sat face-to-face with his brother. Joe was pale and shaking. He finally raised his head so that his gaze met Nathan's, and Nathan saw something there he didn't like. Worry.

"Tell me," Nathan bit out.

The others gathered silently, all waiting for Joe to relate what he'd discovered.

Joe looked pissed. Angrier than Nathan had seen him in a long time. But he also looked raw and worried. Nathan's gut knotted because he was scared to death to know what Joe had found out.

Joe lifted his gaze to Nathan, pain still reflected in his eyes. "They have her in some goddamn cage. It's like some futuristic cryotube or something. It's narrow and long, plastic or glass. See-through and it opens from the top.

"She can't move. She has clamps around her wrists and ankles and also at her neck. That's the one that causes her panic because she feels like she's constantly choking."

Rage exploded in Nathan's mind until he shook worse than Joe did. Swanny put his hand on Nathan's shoulder in an effort to calm him.

"It's worse, man," Joe said in a low voice. "They have electrodes attached to her head that monitor her brain wave activity. That's why when you try to talk to her, she suffers so
horribly. She gets an electrical shock every time her brain
activity spikes above a certain level. They've tried to disable
her ability to speak to anyone. To ask for help."

Nathan upended his chair and he shot upward. "Son of a
bitch!" Tears burned his eyelids. He was so furious and so
damn scared for her that he didn't even know what to do. He
was unraveling at the seams as fear choked the breath out
of him.

Oh God, the thought of her in such pain, and the awful fear
she experienced every waking moment, was more than he
could bear. He had to get to her. Whatever it took.

He turned back to Joe, his fingers balled, seething with
rage and sorrow. "What are those numbers? What do they
mean?"

Joe didn't look any better. Now that he'd had that connection with Shea, he'd experienced everything she was going
through, and you only had to look at Joe to know it was hell.

"I told her to close her eyes and try to remember anything
that would help us locate her. I didn't want her to try and say
anything telepathically. I just wanted her to remember something, *anything*, and hopefully I would be able to pick up on it
through my link to her.

"She remembered being carried. She was dimly aware of her
surroundings. Mountains. Scent of pine. Cooler temperatures.
And then she looked at the door leading into the building and
those letters and numbers I recited were above the door."

"That's it?" Nathan asked in frustration.

"It might be enough," Resnick said slowly.

Nathan jerked his head in Resnick's direction. "What do
you mean?"

Resnick walked over to his computer and rapidly typed in
a series of commands. In a moment, he brought up a picture of
what looked to be a compound carved into the side of a
mountain.

"That's it!" Joe said excitedly. He lunged toward the monitor and pointed as he looked back at Nathan. "That's it. See
the numbers above the door?"

"Okay, so what the fuck is it?" Sam asked, for the first time pushing into the conversation.

Resnick clutched the back of his neck and rested the curled length of his arm against the side of his head.

"It's where this all began."

CHAPTER 39

"I guess what they say is true. Anything the government wants to hide, they stick in New Mexico," Garrett muttered.

Nathan didn't say anything. He was staring out the window of the SUV as they sped the remaining distance from where they'd landed toward the Sangre de Cristo Mountain Range. Wheeler Peak was the highest mountain in the range and the highest peak in New Mexico, but it was one of the lesser mountains that housed the top-secret research facility.

While hikers flocked to the more popular areas, the research facility was in a nondescript, hard-to-find valley, and access was only available from the south.

According to Resnick, the facility had been closed for years and the project had been shelved after the Petersons escaped with Grace and Shea. But now Nathan doubted just how much Resnick really knew.

"I think we're idiots for trusting him," Ethan said, not even bothering to disguise his hostility as he stared Resnick down.

Resnick fiddled with a cigarette but didn't light it, probably because Sam was giving him an "I dare you" look.

"I'm probably going to lose my job over this," Resnick snapped. "I don't give a goddamn if you trust me or not. I'll be lucky if I don't do jail time for this shit. Depending on how far up the line this goes, I might have already signed my death warrant. Now if you think that's dramatic, fuck you. People have been silenced for far less. You'll need to watch *your* asses after this."

A sick knot formed in Nathan's stomach. He didn't want this for his family. He didn't want them to have to worry that in a week or a month or even a year they or the people they loved could be taken out all because they got involved in this thing with him and Shea.

Nathan looked up to see Sam's gaze boring a hole through him. There was reprimand in that stare, almost as if he knew exactly what Nathan was thinking.

"I don't give a goddamn if it means we have to move to some remote island that's not even on the map. There is no fucking way I'm going to lie down while someone in my family needs my help. I'd do it for Sophie, Rachel and Sarah. I'd sure as hell do it for the woman you're going to marry."

"You are going to marry her, aren't you?" Donovan asked dryly. "Tell me I'm not busting my ass here and you end up not having the balls to propose."

"Swear to God, you two need to shut the fuck up," Nathan said around the knot in his throat.

He was overwhelmed by the unwavering support of his family. Even when he'd done his best to push them away. Even when he didn't deserve the sacrifices they made for him. They were still there. Always there. No conditions. No questions asked.

"I expect a goddamn invitation," Resnick cut in. "I'll be out of a job. I'll want the free booze."

"Holy shit, did he just make a joke?" Donovan asked. "Mr. Uptight, makes Garrett look like a poster child for serenity, made a joke?"

"Fuck you," Resnick said in disgust. "I've put up with your shit for years. The upside of unemployment is that I won't have to see any of your sorry asses again."

"Make that a double fuck you," Garrett said darkly. "I'm sure there was an insult aimed at me somewhere in all that."

"Resnick's missing us already," Ethan said solemnly. "I think I might have a tear or two."

The vehicles pulled to a stop and silence fell. Expressions

went completely serious. Tension vibrated through the SUV holding Nathan, Resnick and his brothers.

SUVs pulled up on either side of them. One carrying Kyle Phillips and his team. The other carried Steele and his team along with Swanny.

They got out and, after conducting a weapons check, gathered at the front of the vehicles. Resnick stood with Sam in front of the three groups.

Resnick held up a topo map and pointed to a low-lying area that led north into an area surrounded by three higher peaks on all sides. "We're here. We could drive in. This road goes on for another mile before you turn off onto a dirt road leading to the compound. It used to be heavily monitored. Video surveillance. Iron gate. Lots of no trespassing, dire warnings, property of the U.S. government, et cetera, et cetera, all the usual 'keep the fuck away from here or we'll shoot your ass' type of stuff.

"If it's being used again, I can't imagine they aren't employing the same security measures and I'd imagine they've beefed them up."

"I still don't get it," Garrett said. "It seems awfully stupid to go back to the same facility they used before. Risky at best."

Resnick shook his head. "Who would know? The Petersons are dead. Grace and Shea were too young to remember this place much less get anyone back to it. They have Shea. They may even have Grace. We don't know. Two of the scientists are dead. Two others went back to Russia. I know because I immediately did a search of everyone who was involved in this whole thing.

"All that's left is me. And the few members within the government who okayed funding and got reports on the research findings, and believe me, none of those people are going to be lining up to do anything that would bring attention to this project or their involvement in it.

"If they're getting this program up and running again and are using Grace and Shea as the basis of their research, they don't want their dirty laundry aired, which is why they took out the Petersons and went after Grace and Shea. If they've made the connection between me and the Petersons, I'll be next," Resnick said quietly.

Donovan grimaced. "Well, fuck it all. I was going to take great joy out of letting Nathan nail your sorry ass to the wall and now we're going to have to protect you too? You sure know how to ruin a man's day."

Sam stepped forward and Resnick and Donovan went silent. It always awed Nathan how much respect Sam commanded.

"Here's what we're going to do. Resnick said there are two entrances into the facility. The front door and the not so obvious back door. We can find the front door. We'll need Resnick's help to find the back entrance. So he's going to go with Steele and his team. Except P.J. I want her positioned at the front entrance and Cole at the back entrance. If things go to shit, I want the two of you to take out anyone who isn't us or Shea Peterson and provide cover for us.

"The rest of us will go in, take out any threats, locate Shea and get the hell out as quickly as possible. I've already given you all the GPS points of our rendezvous point. We're on a tight time line. I want this to be a quick in and out. Clean and smooth. Just another day at the office. The chopper will be waiting to get us the fuck out of here. Don't be late."

"With all due respect, sir, where exactly do we fit into this extrication plan of yours?" Kyle Phillips asked as he stepped forward.

The Marine didn't look at all happy not to have received orders and for all practical purposes had been ignored from the start.

Sam's eyes narrowed. "The very *last* thing we need is for you to be the one who finds Shea. In her mind you're responsible for where she is right now. What I need for you and your team to do is back P.J. and Cole up. Make sure no one comes in or goes out of this place except my team and Steele's. And be our backup if things go bad inside."

Phillips's lips tightened, but Nathan had to hand it to the man. He obeyed orders. Without question. Without hesitation. Phillips gave a quick nod, took a step back and then signaled his men to fall back. In a moment's time, they'd melted into the trees surrounding the facility buried in the mountain.

Sam gave the signal for Steele and his team to take position. P.J. remained with the Kellys while the rest of her team disappeared over a rise with Resnick to circle around back.

"Let's go," Sam said.

They paralleled the dirt road for the mile in, and when they reached the turnoff, they kept farther into the trees and picked up their pace for the last half mile.

Even though they knew where to look for the entrance, it was still difficult to find. It was very well disguised and surrounded by aspens and pine.

"Are you in position, Steele?" Sam asked into the radio.

After Steele responded in the affirmative, Sam ordered everyone to check in and confirm their positions. P.J. slung her rifle over her shoulder and climbed up a steep, rocky rise that overlooked the front.

Then Sam turned to his brothers. "Okay, you know what to do. Let's get in, get out and get the fuck back home."

Donovan hurried forward, ducking low to remain below the surveillance cameras aimed at the front. The others quickly followed suit until they were all hunkered down, plastered to the wall, waiting for Donovan to gain access.

He took out his handheld unit that hooked to a key card and swiped it through the security keypad. Within seconds, the door slid open and they rushed in, guns up.

As Resnick had warned, there were three hallways, one to the left, one to the right and one down the middle.

Sam pointed at Donovan and Joe and motioned for them to take the right hall. He directed Garrett and Nathan to take the middle and then jerked his thumb at Ethan to come with him to the left.

Garrett glanced at Nathan as they started down the hallway. "We'll find her, man. We'll get her out of here."

CHAPTER 40

A tear slid down Shea's temple and disappeared into her hair. It worried her that she seemed to slip away with each passing hour. She was beyond the pain. She didn't really feel it any longer. But she had a hard time conjuring up the simplest of things.

Her mind was a vast landscape of nothingness. Every once in a while she would try hard to remember what her purpose was. There was something she had to do. But when she did so, she was immediately assaulted with more pain and so she let herself slide farther into the abyss because there the pain wasn't present. Her fear and anxiety faded to nothing. And she floated. Free.

Even as she knew this was all wrong, she was helpless to change it because she no longer had the strength to fight. She'd been brought to this place to be poked and prodded. Studied and observed. A nameless, faceless test subject with no feelings or rights. Her humanity had been wiped away as if it had never existed. Here, she mattered to no one.

She heard whispers in her mind. They called her name, but she desperately shoved them away and closed herself off, wanting to avoid the inevitable crush of pain if she allowed them to grow louder or, God forbid, she responded.

What did these people ultimately want? Did they already have Grace? Was it why they weren't questioning her about her sister? It was Shea's worst fear, that everything she'd done in the last year was for nothing.

A distant explosion rocked the tube she was imprisoned in. It shook one of the electrodes free, but there were still three attached, and fire sizzled through her body as fear spiked her brain waves. Above her one of the fluorescent lights crashed to the floor, just missing her makeshift prison.

The lab went into chaos. Screams, yells, equipment falling and being turned over as they all scrambled like rats to flee the room.

Shea strained at her bonds but there was no budging the bands. Panic set in and she started hyperventilating as the tube seemed to close in on her. Oh God, she couldn't breathe. What was happening? Was it an earthquake?

Her mouth opened in a silent scream and then she yelled hoarsely as another electric current bolted through her body. She closed her eyes and retreated back into the void where insanity was the preferable alternative. To a place where there was no pain and no fear while everything around her went to hell.

JOE slammed back against the wall just as Donovan flattened himself against the other. Bullets zinged from the opposing hallway and into the wall a short distance away.

"Motherfuckers," Donovan swore. "On my count, you go high and I'll go low. One, two . . . three!"

Joe turned the corner as Donovan went to the floor, guns up. Joe took out the two armed guys on the left while Donovan downed the remaining one on the right.

"Let's go," Donovan barked.

An explosion rocked the building and Joe reached back for the wall to steady himself. "Sounds like Garrett's already having his fun."

"It's going to get interesting now. Keep your eyes peeled. Shoot first and don't get *your* ass shot."

"You have such a knack for stating the obvious," Joe muttered as he broke into a run down the hall.

They passed the downed men, and Donovan stopped long enough to snag a security badge from one of them.

"Oh, come on," Joe said. "You're telling me the king nerd can't get anywhere without a security clearance card?"

"Eat me," Donovan growled. "This'll take less time. Provided it works. If it doesn't, we'll just blow our way in."

Joe grinned. "I like the way you think when you don't have your head stuck in a computer."

"I'm so kicking your ass when this is over."

They ran down the corridor until they came to an open door. Donovan held up one hand then kicked in the door and went in, gun up as he swept the room.

"Clear here," Donovan said.

They continued their path down the hall, finding evidence of hasty exits. There were overturned equipment, papers scattered everywhere, even a running faucet.

When they came out of the current room, a shot sounded and Donovan went down. Joe turned, laying down a heavy spray of bullets as he hit the ground to cover his brother.

Joe nailed one in the chest and he fell heavily. The other, Joe got in the leg and he disappeared around the corner before Joe could get off another shot. He turned his attention to his brother.

"Van, goddamn it, talk to me. Are you hit?"

"Get the fuck off me. I can't breathe," Donovan growled. "Fucker just winged me. I'm all right. Let's clear the rest of the hall."

Joe carefully pushed himself off his brother but kept careful watch as Donovan picked himself up from the floor. When Joe glanced down, he saw blood smeared on the white tiles.

"You're bleeding, goddamn it. Where did you take the hit?"

Donovan put a hand to the tear in his sleeve. "It's just a graze. Few inches over he'd have hit the Kevlar and then we wouldn't be having this stupid conversation about blood."

They moved more slowly down the hall, each facing a different direction. Donovan walked forward and Joe backed his way after his brother. At each open doorway, they stopped to clear the room but left frustrated each time.

"This is bullshit," Donovan said into his receiver. "We're coming up empty. What about the rest of you?"

"Steele and company are engaged. Phillips is helping round up everyone running from the building. They haven't been able to clear their section. We're making our way back as fast as we can," Sam said.

"Us too," Nathan relayed.

Joe could hear the frustration in his twin's voice and the ache. He was afraid for Shea. Afraid he wouldn't find her but also afraid of what he'd find if they came across her.

"We have to find her," Joe said in a low voice to Donovan.

Donovan nodded and continued their path through the maze of rooms.

They burst into a room and quickly scanned the interior. Joe frowned, and for a moment it felt like someone had punched him in the stomach. He lurched forward, ignoring Donovan's order to be cautious.

He turned in a circle, staring, remembering what he'd seen during his brief connection to Shea. "This is it, Van. This is where they had her!"

Donovan hopped over a chair on its side and turned the corner of the L-shaped room. Joe came up beside him and froze as he stared at the cylindrical cage. And it was a cage. There were no bars but it was no less a prison.

"Dear God," Donovan whispered.

Joe bolted forward, his hand running along the top of the enclosure where Shea lay, her eyes glassy and fixed on the ceiling. Electrodes were attached to her head, though one had fallen off and lay by her ear. The monitor that he'd seen was to her left.

"Son of a bitch! We have to get her out of here, Van."

Joe dropped his rifle and clawed frantically at the lid, trying to figure out how it opened. "Damn it, Van, how do I get her out?"

Donovan hurried around to the work station where the computers were and began tapping furiously at the keys. Joe stalked around to the other side and cut the lines that fed from the electrodes to the machine monitoring her brain activity. Then he leaned over the enclosure, pressed his hands to the plastic and put his face over hers.

Shea, can you hear me. Talk to me, sweetheart. They can't hurt you now.

She didn't move. Didn't acknowledge him in any way. He felt nothing through their pathway. Just silence and nothingness. Calm. Eerie calm.

"Goddamn it, hurry, Van! She's not doing good. Not at all. We have to get her out of here."

"I'm doing the best I can. I'm flying blind here. It's a complicated system. I'll get it. I'll get it."

Joe continued to stare down at Shea, his fingers splayed out, pressed to the cool surface. He only thanked God that it wasn't Nathan who'd found her. He'd have gone ballistic and there would have been no controlling him.

Suddenly the top lifted and started to open toward him. He backed off and ran around to the other side. The locks around her neck, wrists and ankles popped open, but she didn't react.

Gently, Joe reached in and lifted her from the enclosure. She was limp against him and her head lolled onto his shoulder. Shit, this was scaring him.

"We have Shea," Donovan said tersely. "I repeat, we have Shea. Give us your status."

"Go out the front," Sam barked. "We're engaged in heavy fire. Back is not secure. P.J. will be covering your exit. Take one of the SUVs and meet us at the rendezvous point. Once we're clear, we'll meet you as scheduled."

It fried Joe's ass to even think about leaving his brothers behind, but they couldn't carry Shea into the line of fire. And he couldn't send Donovan because he was Joe's only cover, since Joe was carrying Shea out.

"You heard the man. Let's go," Donovan bit out.

AS Nathan listened to the exchange between Donovan and Sam, he nearly went to his knees in relief. They hadn't said anything about Shea's condition, but they had her and that was all that was important. She was safe. His brothers wouldn't let any harm come to her.

"Throw a fucking grenade and let's be done with this shit," Garrett snarled from across the wide-open area that was at the heart of the facility. All hallways led from the huge epicenter, and it was at the center where the security forces for the lab had taken a stand.

What the fuck they had to fight for was beyond Nathan, but maybe they feared certain death if they simply surrendered. While Nathan would love to accommodate them, Resnick wanted to do it by the book. Maybe he was still angling to keep his job.

Steele and his team, along with Resnick, were closing the gap and they'd soon have the holdouts between them. Sam, Garrett, Nathan and Ethan had taken position while bullets zinged by them and kicked up plaster from the walls.

"I'm coming in behind you."

Swanny's voice came over the radio, and Sam frowned. "What the fuck are you doing out of position? You were supposed to be with Steele."

"I got a little sidelined with an issue," Swanny drawled. "It's all better now."

Nathan grinned.

"Fall back then," Sam directed. "Rendezvous with Joe and Donovan. They're going out the front with Shea. They'll need cover. P.J. is manning the front. We have it here."

"Roger that." There was a long pause, and then Swanny said, "Don't worry, Nate. I'll take good care of your girl."

"I know you will," Nathan murmured.

"Coming your way, Sam," Steele barked. "Waded through the riffraff. Phillips is rounding them up. Let's finish this one and head to the house."

"That gets a hooyah from me," Ethan piped in.

"Hooyah, baby," Cole echoed. "This is like ducks in a row at the fair. Too easy, drill sergeant. Too easy."

"Move in," Sam ordered.

Garrett lobbed a flash grenade and then they swarmed.

"Stay low! Stay low!" Sam yelled.

Some of the combatants had already given up and lay flat on the floor, hands over their heads. Others stumbled unsteadily and attempted to raise their guns to shoot.

Nathan dropped to one knee and laid down a round of fire, taking down two targets as they took aim at Garrett. He did a quick scan of the room as his brothers pushed through.

"Hold your fire! Hold your fire!" Sam ordered. "Targets are down. I repeat, targets are down."

Nathan could see that Steele and his team had pushed

through and now stood across the center of the complex. As he started to rise, pain seared through his side, knocking him sideways.

He stared down in disbelief to see that one of the fallen security forces had plunged a knife into his side. It was reflex to yank the knife back out. It hadn't gone to the hilt.

He let out a guttural cry but threw aside the knife before leaping forward onto the man who'd downed him. He grasped the man's head and wrenched sideways, until he heard the snap of the other man's neck.

He threw the man down and then put his hand to his side, feeling sticky warmth spread over his palm.

Shit.

He glanced up in time to see his brothers rushing forward, uncharacteristic fear on their faces. He tried to push himself upward but started to tilt forward instead.

Garrett got to him first and caught him before he could pitch forward.

Nathan pulled his hand away and stared down at the dark red that coated his entire palm.

"That son of a bitch stabbed me!"

CHAPTER 41

JOE and Donovan were just about to the front entrance when Swanny caught up to them from behind.

"Want me to take her?" Swanny asked.

"No, you go ahead with Donovan. Cover me and make damn sure P.J. knows we're coming out," Joe said tersely.

He hadn't said a word about Shea's condition, but the truth was, he was scared shitless. It was obvious she'd checked out. Her eyes were still open, but they were vacant and lifeless. Her vitals seemed normal. The lights were on but nobody was at home. Who the hell knew what all she'd endured this time?

"Get your asses into the trees," P.J. said in an impatient voice. "My orders are to get you to the truck so you can haul ass out of here."

They broke into a run, and Joe held Shea tighter against him so she didn't flop like a rag doll. When they burst through the trees, P.J. rolled from her perch atop the rise where she'd taken position and fell in behind Joe to cover the rear.

"What's her condition?" P.J. asked as they hurried back the way they'd come in.

"I don't know," Joe said shortly. "It's not . . . good."

"I'll take a look when we get back to the SUV," Donovan called back. "The important thing is she's alive."

Yeah, she was alive, but Joe wasn't at all sure what that meant anymore. The longer she lay in his arms unmoving and unresponsive, the more dread gathered in his stomach. He didn't want to think of what this would do to Nathan.

Nathan was finally coming around. He had fire in his gut again. He had purpose. The Nathan who'd come home from the hospital after recovering for weeks had been a stranger to Joe, and he hadn't like it one bit.

He wanted his best friend back, and this could change everything.

Please, Shea. Come back to us. Nathan needs you. Show me you're still in there somewhere. You're safe now. They can't hurt you anymore. I understand why you've gone away. But you can come back now. Come back for Nathan. He's lost without you.

They broke into the small clearing where the SUVs were parked and still Shea hadn't stirred in his arms. Donovan jerked open the back and motioned for Joe to lay her down. Joe was about to do just that when she went completely stiff in his arms.

She let out a cry of pain and seemed to ball in even tighter. Her breathing changed from the shallow, light respirations to fast, jerky bursts that seemed to tear out of her throat.

Joe sat her on the edge of the SUV, careful not to bump her head on the upright door.

"Oh Jesus," Donovan breathed.

Joe followed Donovan's gaze to see blood spreading rapidly over her side. "What the fuck? Van, she wasn't hurt! I examined her myself. She wasn't bleeding. I would have damn sure noticed that amount of blood."

Shea's eyes lost their glassy dullness. Her pupils dilated and sweat formed on her brow. Her fingers curled into tight little balls, and she bent over as if in unimaginable pain.

Joe caught her and then laid her gently on her uninjured side. He crawled over her, into the truck, and pushed at her shirt, looking for the source of the bleeding.

"Holy shit. She's got a wound in her side, but I swear to you, Donovan, this wasn't here before!"

Donovan pushed in beside him and then swore. "I can't even move in here. Get her down. Lay her on the ground so I can see what I'm doing."

Joe pulled her out. P.J. hurried in and helped him ease her down onto the ground. Swanny knelt beside Shea and gently pushed aside her hair in a gentle gesture that Joe found irritating. What the fuck was the man doing? She was going to bleed to death and he was worried about her hair?

"What's happened to Nathan?" Swanny asked. "Talk to me, Shea. And listen. He wouldn't want you to do this. He has people to help him. You can't take this for him this time. Do you understand me? You'll hurt him far more by doing this. You're too weak to take this from him. Let him bear his own pain this time. I swear to you we'll get him out. Do you hear me? Snap the fuck out of it and look at me, damn it!"

"Swanny, what the fuck?" P.J. demanded. "Get the hell away from her before I do it for you."

Swanny ignored her and turned to Donovan. "Ask Sam what the hell just happened to Nathan. Do it. She's taking his pain. She's absorbing it just like she did before when he was being tortured. Only this time she doesn't have the strength to do it."

Fear grabbed Joe by the throat. Donovan went pale and he cupped his hand over the mouthpiece so the wind wouldn't interfere.

"Sam, what the hell is happening in there? I need to know what's going on with Nathan and I need to know yesterday. Our situation is critical."

"Nathan's down," came Sam's grim reply. "Took a knife to the side. Garrett's trying to stop the bleeding now. We're on our way with him now. What the fuck is going on with you?"

"Oh Christ," Joe whispered. "How bad, Van? We need to know how bad." He glanced at Shea as fear took a firmer hold. She'd give her life for Nathan. He knew it like he knew his own name. But Nathan's life wouldn't be worth shit without her, and her sacrifice wouldn't mean a damn thing in the end. He couldn't let this happen.

Instead of waiting for Donovan, Joe broke in. "You be honest with me, Sam. Tell me how bad it is. Shea's in a bad way because she's taking his pain and she's bleeding heavily. It's his injury that's causing her bleeding. She'll die because they're connected and she thinks she has to save him. So you tell him to find his way to her and you make him tell her that he's going to be goddamn fine. I don't care if he's lying or not. If we lose her, he's lost to us anyway."

"He's not going to die," Sam snarled. "You tell her that. You connect with her. Don't you dare let her die. I'll make sure Nathan knows what's going on, but don't you let her go in the meantime. You do whatever you have to do to keep her alive. Lie to her. I don't care. Just get the job done."

Joe dropped to his knees beside Shea and shoved Swanny aside. He lifted her head, holding her close, while P.J. put both hands over Shea's side in an attempt to stop the bleeding. Donovan moved in with a med kit, and he and P.J. began to work on a pressure bandage while Joe focused his entire being on forging a connection with Shea.

NATHAN could tell whatever was being relayed to Sam wasn't good and he cursed the fact that he'd lost his earpiece when Garrett converged on him to stop the bleeding. He knew he was right when his brothers and even the members of Steele's team and Resnick regarded him with a mixture of fear and dread.

But what worried him more was that his pain was easing. The warmth he'd long ago associated with Shea spread through his veins, replacing the burn with soothing comfort.

And yet he couldn't feel her. Not in the way he'd always been able to in the past. He could feel what she was doing for him and it made him furious. But it was as if there was some giant roadblock to Shea.

His stomach churned and his hands began to shake.

"Tell me, goddamn it," he bit out. He wanted answers and he wanted them now.

He threw off Garrett's hand and tried to get up, but Garrett hauled him back down and forcibly kept pressure on his wound. Dread mounted in Nathan's chest until he could barely draw a breath.

"You go, Sam," Resnick said hurriedly. "My men and I will stay behind to do cleanup. I'm going to have to call this in and let the chips fall where they may. I may be out of a job, but until they tell me otherwise, this is hugely classified and I can't just leave things here for anyone to stumble over. But

I promise you this. I'll get answers before I call it in. We'll make these fuckers talk so we know what the hell we're dealing with."

"And if they decide to silence you?" Sam asked.

Resnick's face hardened. "My team is loyal to me. They take orders from me. I won't go down without a fight, and if that's the way this is going to play out, then I won't remain silent. I'll go public in a big way. I won't let this happen to Shea again. Grace is still out there. I won't let this happen to her."

"I don't like leaving you," Sam said.

"You're wasting time," Resnick said impatiently. "You heard what Joe had to say. Your priority needs to be her and Nathan. Now get the hell out of here."

"Someone tell me what the fuck is going on," Nathan snarled. "Where's Shea? What happened?"

"She's taking your pain," Garrett said quietly.

"Yeah, I know that much. Where is she? Why are you all looking at me like that? Why can't I reach her?"

Sam knelt by Nathan's side. "You have to talk to her, Nathan. And we have to get you to her as soon as possible. She's bleeding heavily. She's sensed that you were hurt but she's out of it. She's been out of it ever since Joe found her. He hasn't been able to break through. You have to or we're going to lose her. Do you understand me? She was in no condition to take this on, but she's afraid you're going to die. You have to convince her otherwise and break the connection before it kills her."

All the blood left Nathan's face. Fear knotted his gut and panic rolled over him like a tidal wave. No. Oh dear God, no. Not again. Never again. She'd taken more for him than she ever should have taken.

"Take me to her," he demanded. This time when he pushed upward, Garrett didn't stop him. Instead he and Ethan each got an arm and hauled him to his feet.

"You're not going to like this, but we can move a hell of a lot faster if we just carry your ass," Garrett said.

Without waiting for Nathan's response, Ethan and Garrett hoisted him up and took off double time for the back exit, Steel and his team leading the way.

Shea. Baby, where are you? You have to talk to me. I'm okay. I'm not dying. It's just a flesh wound. The knife didn't go deep. Do you hear me? Shea, you have to listen to me. You have to break off. Somehow you're connected to me even though you aren't aware of what's going on around you. It's our bond. It's unbreakable. No one can take that from us. But baby, I need you to break away. Please, you have to do this. For me. I can't lose you, and you're too weak to endure this. For once let me be strong for you. This wound is nothing. I wouldn't lie to you about that. I'll need a few stitches and I'll be good as new.

He sucked in his breath. His heart felt near to bursting out of his chest. He had so much fear and he hated that he couldn't find that pathway to her, couldn't break through the wall of silence that seemed to shield her on all sides.

She was protecting herself. She'd erected the wall to keep the pain away and now he couldn't break through.

Don't do this. Please don't do this, Shea. Let go of me. Let me take this for you. You've protected me for so long, baby. For once let someone else take care of you.

I love you. I love you so damn much. Come back to me.

CHAPTER 42

"**WE** can get Nathan patched up in Taos," Ethan said. "But what about Shea? How the fuck do we explain identical stab wounds? I thought when she took pain and shit that the phantom wound disappeared quickly?"

They were still two klicks from the rendezvous point, but they were hustling over the terrain, like Nathan weighed nothing. Ethan and Garrett were easily keeping pace with Sam and the others.

"Want me and Dolphin to take over?" Cole called back to Garrett.

Garrett shook his head and kept moving. Nathan dragged himself from his concentration on Shea to answer Ethan's question.

"She'll heal. Or usually she would. It's temporary. But now? I don't know. Joe and Van said she was out of it. Unresponsive. I can't reach her. Joe can't reach her. It's like she's checked out but yet she sensed what happened to me, and her automatic reaction was to take the pain because she didn't want me to suffer. She's not strong enough to do that, and if I can't get her to snap out of it, she'll bleed to death."

"We're nearly there," Sam said, his voice calm and reassuring. But that was Sam. Not much ruffled him. There was worry in his eyes, but he kept his cool, and right now Nathan appreciated that because he was damn close to losing his shit. One of them needed to remain calm.

"They've made it to the rendezvous," Sam relayed to Nathan. "The chopper is there and waiting. We'll split up. We'll take you and Shea to Taos. The others can take the trucks and meet us there."

"Shea?" Nathan asked fearfully.

Sam's lips tightened. "No change."

They all went silent and increased their pace. While Nathan couldn't feel the pain, he could feel the *effects* of the stab wound. He was a little slower processing information. The ground seemed to move slower beneath him. Everything felt like some bad slow-motion replay.

And it pissed him off.

Not only was Shea bearing the brunt of her treatment, but now she was taking his pain.

Finally they burst through the trees where the helicopter waited. Garrett and Ethan eased Nathan down, and he strode forward, his hand cupped over his side. His entire focus was on Joe, who was standing by the helo holding Shea tightly to his chest. What scared him the most was the amount of blood that stained his brother's clothing. And the way Shea lay so very limp in his arms.

"Get in," Joe ordered.

When Nathan started to protest, Joe bared his teeth in a snarl. "Get the fuck in. I'll hand her to you once you're in and secure. I'm not going to lose either one of you, goddamn it."

With Garrett's help, Nathan crawled inside and propped himself on the far edge of the seat, where he could lean against the wall. Joe came in after, still holding Shea, and when he sat next to Nathan, he gently laid her in Nathan's arms.

"You've got to stop her," Joe said fiercely. "You're going to lose her if you can't get through to her, damn it."

Nathan gathered Shea in his arms and pressed his lips to her cool forehead. Everything that mattered was in his arms. Dying, because she was hell-bent on saving him. Tears burned his eyelids and he bit his lip to hold them at bay as he silently begged her to come back to him.

I'm here, baby. Right here, holding you. I'm okay. Can you

feel me, Shea? Can you feel how much I love you? Fight your
way back to me. Do it for me. Do it for us. I want forever
with you.

He stroked his fingers down the side of her face and followed them with gentle kisses. He completely ignored Donovan, who knelt in front of them and placed his hands over
Shea's side to slow the steady flow of blood.

Nathan pressed his forehead to hers. *Feel me, Shea. Feel my*
love. Hear me. Come back to me. You've got to break away.
You've got to give yourself a chance to heal. I can't lose you,
baby. You're so determined to protect me and to save me. Then
goddamn it, come back to me. I'm not dying and you're damn
sure not going to die for me. If you're so determined to shield
me, then you better goddamn well snap out of it because you'll
do a piss-poor job of it in your grave.

Nathan.

There it was. The faintest whisper in his mind, but he
heard it. More than that, he *felt* it. His grip tightened around
her and he could no longer hold back the tears.

I'm here, baby. I'm here. I'm okay. I swear it. I'll be fine.
Break off from me and talk to me out loud. You're scaring the
shit out of everyone. Give me back the pain, Shea. It's time
you let someone take care of you for a change.

She blinked. Just once, but the cloudiness left her eyes and
she stared up at him in confusion as if she couldn't quite comprehend that he was there.

"Nathan," she whispered aloud.

"Yes, baby. It's me," he choked out. "Now let go. Let go
and let yourself heal."

She took a deep shuddering breath, her features creased
with all the pain she'd been shouldering. And then just as
quickly, fire licked up his side. It took everything he had not
to react. To sit there like he didn't feel a thing. He knew if he
so much as flinched, that she'd be back, shielding him, taking
it so he didn't have to.

Donovan slid onto the seat beside him, and before Nathan
realized what he was doing, he plunged a needle into his arm.

"Painkiller," Donovan murmured low so only Nathan could
hear. "I know it hurts, man, and I know you don't want her to
know. If you start to go out, I'll take her."

Like hell that would happen.

Some of the tension that had knitted her brow eased and relief was stark in her eyes. Joe took Donovan's place in front of Shea and carefully peeled back the blood-soaked shirt so he could ascertain how much if any she still bled.

The others who'd hung back and remained silent during the entire flight leaned forward, their expressions ones of astonishment as Shea's side slowly began to return to normal.

Nathan knew it would take longer this time, but he was content that at least the bleeding had slowed and that she was no longer bearing the agony in his stead.

His jaw was tight as he battled the burn in his side. The medicine Donovan had injected was already starting to take hold, though, and wooziness stole over him, leaving him heavy and lethargic.

"How are you feeling now, Shea?" Joe asked gently.

She slowly turned to look at Nathan's twin. She licked her lips and attempted to smile, but she seemed far too tired to actually pull it off.

Her brow furrowed as she seemed to give his question a lot of consideration. Finally she sighed. "I don't know."

Some of the dullness had returned to her eyes and that worried Nathan. It was as if she'd gathered the last of her strength in her effort to help him and then to crawl back when he'd begged her to let go.

Exhaustion. He could feel her exhaustion and her confusion beating at her in relentless waves. She looked to each of the occupants of the helicopter but there was no recognition in her eyes, even though Nathan knew she knew who they were.

She turned her face into his chest and whispered so low that he couldn't hear what she said. He leaned down close and gently touched her cheek.

"What did you say, baby?"

She shifted just enough that her mouth was visible and she whispered, "Promise me you're okay. Promise."

He kissed her because at that precise moment he was too choked up to get out even the simplest of words. He sucked in ragged breaths and closed his eyes. He laid his cheek against hers and whispered close to her ear, "I'm never leaving you, Shea."

CHAPTER 43

"**WHAT** am I going to do about Shea?" Nathan asked as he sat on the edge of the exam table waiting his discharge.

His side hurt like a bitch, but the knife hadn't struck anything vital and had only penetrated two inches. The doctor had wryly told him that a higher being had guided the blade because it had every opportunity to strike a vital organ but had slipped past without so much as scratching anything but fatty tissue and muscle.

He'd been stitched up, but he'd refused more pain medication. If it got bad later, Donovan could fix him up. For now he needed a clear head because Shea needed help, but they didn't dare expose her to further scrutiny.

"I've called Maren," Sam said in a low voice. "Joe's with Shea now. As soon as you get out of here, we're going to fly Shea to see Maren."

"We're taking her to fucking Costa Rica?" Nathan demanded.

Maren Scofield was a doctor KGI had rescued from Africa a few years back. She'd been instrumental in Rachel's rescue or at least her recovery. She was someone KGI trusted and a damn good doctor. But the last Nathan had heard, she was still in Costa Rica. Not ideal. He wanted Shea home, not in fucking Central America.

"No. I've asked Maren to come to Tennessee. We're taking Shea home and Maren will meet us there," Sam replied.

"Then what the fuck are we waiting for?" Nathan hopped off the bed and started for the door. Pain jolted through his side, momentarily robbing him of breath. He stopped to steady himself and breathed away the rising nausea.

Sam made a grab for his arm. "You can wait a few more minutes to get your discharge paperwork. You'll need the prescriptions and you're going to take the meds or I'll shove them down your throat. Shea needs you."

"Yeah, I might have been a little hasty on that get the hell out of here," Nathan gritted out.

"Let them give you the goddamn injection," Sam snapped. "You've got to remain calm and pain free or Shea's going to pick up on that and start taking it for you."

"You're right, you're right. Look, let's just get out of here. Van can give me an injection. I won't argue. I'll do exactly what he tells me, I swear, but let's get the fuck out of here. I want to get back to Shea."

They were interrupted by the nurse walking back in. She handed Nathan a clipboard and pointed to the places she wanted him to sign and then she handed him the prescriptions. She didn't act particularly friendly and she beat a hasty retreat, but then Nathan supposed she likely thought they were some kind of criminals.

At least Resnick had kept the local cops out of the picture. The asshole did have his uses.

"Let's go," Sam said. "And you better take it easy. They're waiting at the airport. The jet just touched down a few minutes ago, so as soon as we get there, we're on our way home."

Surely there wasn't a better word in the world. Despite Sam's order to take it easy, Nathan walked as fast as he could down the corridor and out the emergency exit to the parking lot, where one of the SUVs was parked.

Garrett was leaning against the hood, and when he saw Sam and Nathan heading toward him, he shoved off and opened the passenger door so Nathan could get in.

"Any word on Shea?" Nathan asked when Garrett climbed into the driver's seat.

"Bleeding has nearly stopped. Wound is still open but seems to be closing at a slow rate."

"But how is she?" Nathan asked anxiously.

Garrett sighed. "Same, man. No change."

Nathan closed his eyes.

"She'll be better when you're there," Sam said.

Nathan hoped to hell his brother was right. What Shea had gone through was unimaginable. It hurt him to know just how much she'd endured. He'd never get over the fact that he'd promised to protect her and yet he'd been powerless to prevent her from being taken from him.

It seemed like an eternity before they roared up to the private airfield where the jet was waiting. Nathan opened his door before the SUV came to a complete stop and was already out and hurrying across the hot concrete to the plane.

Outside the plane, Steele, Cole, P.J., Dolphin, Renshaw and Baker stood guard. They may have looked relaxed, like they were waiting for someone, but Nathan saw that each was focused on an outlying area, watchful for any potential threat.

He mounted the few steps into the plane, and when he stuck his head in, he saw Donovan in the cockpit along with Ethan. He glanced to the right to see Swanny sprawled in one of the seats.

Swanny sat forward and motioned back to the sitting area. "Joe's back with Shea."

Nathan pushed down the aisle past the seats and into the lounge area, where there was a sofa, a table and two other armchairs. Joe was sitting on the couch, Shea cradled against his chest.

Her shirt was pulled up just over the wound on her side, and Nathan sucked in his breath at the shock of seeing his wound on her flesh.

Joe looked up and their gazes met. Joe's lips tightened and he silently shook his head. His heart about to split wide open, Nathan went forward and gently took Shea from Joe and then crossed to one of the armchairs to sit.

A moment later, Sam and Garrett walked back, and Joe spoke in low tones to them, giving them his report. Nathan tuned them out, his concentration solely on the woman in his arms.

He smoothed his fingers over the lines of her forehead, wanting to ease the strain. He touched the softness of her cheek, traced the delicate line of her jaw.

She was so much a part of him. As much as breathing, eating or sleeping. She was there in every thought, every part of his heart and soul.

"Rest now, baby," he whispered against her brow. He didn't want to drain any of her flagging strength by speaking telepathically to her. She was so fragile and infinitely precious. So very precious to him. "We're going home. I'm taking you home, where you'll get better. I'll take care of you. I'll be with you every minute of the day, and we'll put our demons to rest together."

She seemed to relax and he cradled her close, tucking her head underneath his chin. Her breathing evened out, and he sensed for the first time that she was actually resting.

Donovan pushed his way through Sam and Garrett and squatted beside the chair where Nathan sat. "You're getting this whether you want it or not. If we control your pain, we control hers. You both need rest, so don't fight the effects."

Nathan didn't offer any protest. His side was screaming, and for Shea, he'd do whatever it took to make her more comfortable.

When Donovan was finished, he stood and told the others to prepare for takeoff. Nathan remained where he was while the others took their seats and belted in.

The drug didn't take long to take effect. His muscles seemed to uncoil and he relaxed as the pain's edge was tempered. He held Shea tightly as the jet taxied down the runway and then lifted off.

Home. To Tennessee. He was bringing Shea home. He just hoped to hell that she trusted him enough to stay.

He dozed lightly, Shea's warmth as soothing as the drug that Donovan had given him. His eyes flew open when he heard footsteps.

Sam, Garrett, Joe and Swanny came through and sat on the couch and the other armchair.

"Is she doing any better?" Sam asked in a low voice.

"She's resting," Nathan said. "Really resting." He glanced down at her eyelashes resting on her cheeks and his chest tightened all over again. "They broke her. Whatever they did, they broke her."

"Bullshit," Joe said. "She's down but she's not out. I don't believe for a fucking minute that they completely broke her. She saw you through hell. She's fierce. She'll be okay."

Nathan smiled at his brother's staunch assessment of Shea.

"I've spoken to Resnick," Sam said. "Things are a mess right now. A lot of fingerpointing. A lot of denial. He's collecting evidence before it can be destroyed."

"What about Grace?" Nathan asked quietly.

Sam shook his head. "No one knows. She wasn't there. Resnick's putting out his feelers. Rio hasn't reported in, which means he's turned up nothing yet. My guess is she's lying low somewhere."

Nathan tried to control the rise of anger. Where the fuck was Grace? How could she leave her sister when Shea needed her the most? How could she just fall out of contact when the two sisters were so deeply connected?

He knew his anger was unreasonable. There could be any number of reasons why Grace wasn't communicating with Shea. But right now Shea needed to be surrounded with people who loved her. She needed her sister.

"Resnick feels like they've been unable to locate Grace and were focusing for now on Shea," Sam continued.

"Who is they?" Joe demanded. "Do we even know who the hell is behind this? It's pretty damn hard to fight a nameless, faceless enemy. Those bunch of damn science nerds aren't the masterminds of this. They're following orders. Even the security was lame. Someone is fronting the money and the manpower. The question is who and why?"

"That's just it," Sam said. "Everyone is denying involvement. We have to face the possibility that we'll never know. I don't fully trust Resnick. His ass is on the line. He won't be completely honest with us unless it suits his purposes."

"Do you believe that shit about why he took Shea?" Nathan asked. "Do we have any proof that he didn't make everything up so I didn't kill him?"

"How would we ever know differently?" Garrett asked.

"Let's put nerd boy on it," Joe said. "There isn't info Van can't find when he wants it."

Garrett chuckled. "I wouldn't let him hear you say that. He'll kick your scrawny little ass. He's got moves that I don't think there are names for."

"What about those two Russian scientists Resnick mentioned?" Swanny spoke up.

Sam frowned. "Resnick said they were back in Russia."

"What if he's lying? What if he doesn't want them to be found? Or maybe that's what he was told. Maybe he thinks he's telling us the truth. Either way, it bears looking into because they'd know a lot of answers to our questions," Swanny said.

Garrett suddenly grinned. "With Resnick so busy doing cleanup in New Mexico, he certainly won't be at his office. Van and I could take a little trip so Van can do some hacking. Van would cream himself over getting into Resnick's secure files. Can you imagine the shit that man has buried in his computer?"

"That's not a bad idea," Sam said slowly. "As soon as we land, you and Van take the jet and head for D.C. I want whatever information you can find and then we'll know exactly how straight Resnick is being with us."

Nathan eyed his older brothers even as his hold tightened around Shea. "What are we going to do?"

Garrett stared back, his blue eyes steely with resolve. "We do what we always do when there's a threat to the family. We close ranks. We protect. We built that compound for a reason. Resnick breached it because he damn well knew how to, but we won't make that mistake again. From now on, we trust no one. We're not going to let a bunch of crazy-ass nut jobs pick Shea apart because she's gifted. She belongs to you so now she belongs to us. We're going to protect you both."

"So eloquently said, Mr. Smooth," Sam teased. "But I couldn't have said it better myself. Stop worrying about us, Nathan. You focus on Shea. We'll do the rest."

"I don't know if I ever thanked you," Nathan said quietly. "All of you. Not just for Shea, though I'll always be grateful for the risk you put yourself through for her. She means everything to me. She's . . . my life. But thank you for not giving up when I was being such a hard-ass and so unreachable."

A glimmer of a smile lit Joe's face. "Now maybe we can stop tiptoeing around you and start beating your ass again."

Nathan held up his middle finger. "You can sure as hell try."

CHAPTER 44

IT was time to force herself back into the real world. She knew it. Embraced it. Sort of. But at the same time, lingering fear and terror paralyzed her whenever she made the effort to shake off the shadows that surrounded her.

Shea liked Dr. Scofield. There was a kindness to the young woman that put Shea at ease. At first, she'd been terrified that this woman was like all the others. There to study her. Hurt her. Treat her like a specimen.

But she was achingly gentle with Shea. She talked to her in soft tones as if she knew that Shea could understand exactly what she said. She'd smile and tell Shea not to hurry, that she'd come around when she was good and ready and when she felt safe.

It was odd, how disembodied Shea felt and how she could function and yet exist in a vacuum. She could process simple things like going to the bathroom. Eating. Drinking. Acknowledging simple requests. But it was as if her mind had been damaged, perhaps more damaged than her body, and both were taking time to heal.

The Kelly women fascinated Shea. Her quietness gave her the opportunity to study the women who'd married into the

Kelly family as well as spend more time with Marlene Kelly and even Rusty, who she understood wasn't a blood relation but a Kelly all the same.

Every day, one of the women visited her. Usually they'd sit on the back deck of Sam's home and enjoy the warm weather and the view of the lake. Sam had insisted that Nathan and Shea stay with him and Sophie, since the home where Nathan had been living was outside of the compound.

At night, Nathan would tuck Shea into bed and then wrap himself around her, holding her, just holding her. He was a constant comfort to her. Rock steady. Unwavering.

Each day he took care of her, seeing to her every need or just sitting quietly with her. He didn't push, but she could sense the growing disquiet within him. She knew he worried. She hated that she was the source of his unhappiness, but she didn't feel ready to bridge the gap that existed between the world she'd retreated to and the world where Nathan waited.

Fear was a powerful inhibitor.

Today Shea sat on the deck, huddled in a blanket despite the warmth of the summer afternoon. She vaguely wondered who would come today, since not a day had passed that someone hadn't come to sit with her since she and Nathan had come here.

Dr. Scofield would be back this afternoon as she was every afternoon. In the first days that Shea had come home, the doctor had been a constant presence, and Shea idly wondered if there was concern that she was a threat to herself. But then the doctor had told Shea that she was recovering nicely and that she'd look in on her in the afternoons.

Shea found herself looking forward to the company of the other women. She missed Grace, and worry for her sister weighed heavily on Shea. The other Kelly women and even Dr. Scofield filled an emptiness left by Grace's absence.

With a sigh, she settled into the comfortable chair and focused her gaze on the sparkling waters of the lake and let her mind roam free, blanking out everything but the present. No past. No future. Just this moment. She closed her eyes and inhaled, letting the sun dance across her cheeks and spread warmth through the lingering coldness in her veins.

"**SHE'S** not getting better," Nathan said, his voice thick with grief. He stood where he could see Shea through the window, watching as she sat, just as she did every day, staring over the lake.

Donovan and Garrett had returned from their fact-finding mission. There was a lot to process. There were plans to make. But he could do nothing until Shea recovered enough to sort out all that had happened. She was his priority. Always.

"I don't agree," Sophie said firmly.

"I don't either," Rachel said.

Nathan turned to where his sisters-in-law and Sarah stood a few feet away. Sophie was holding Charlotte on her hip. The baby was a miniature Sophie. All blond hair and big blue eyes. Beautiful just like her mother.

How he loved these women. They'd rallied around Shea, accepting her and sweeping in to care for her. Every single day they sat with her, talking to her, making sure she wasn't alone. They bullied her into eating. They treated her just like she was normal. Already a part of the family. It was as if she'd always been there.

His throat knotted because he wanted to tell them how much he loved them for what they were doing, but he couldn't even get the words out.

"She *is* improving, Nathan," Sarah said softly. She put a gentle hand on his arm and squeezed. "At first she didn't even acknowledge us. I wasn't even sure she knew we were here. But then I noticed that she'd look at us. She'd listen to what we were saying and even respond. Not overtly, but I could tell she knew what we were saying."

"She's waiting for us even now," Rachel said. "Look at her, Nathan. She knows we should have been out there by now. She keeps turning her head, just slightly, but she turns so she can see the door because she's expecting us to be here just like we have every day."

"With your permission, we're going to try something a little different today," Sophie interjected.

Nathan's brow furrowed and he looked questioningly at her.

Sophie shifted Charlotte to her other hip then exchanged looks with Rachel and Sarah before glancing back at Nathan. "We're going to take a more direct approach. I want you to stay away. Don't interrupt."

Warning bells went off in Nathan's head. He didn't like the sound of this at all. "Maybe we should wait to see what Maren thinks."

Rachel shook her head. "We've already discussed this with Maren. She agrees. We're not going to be hurtful to her, Nathan. We know how fragile she is. Promise us you'll let us try and that you won't interfere. Ethan will be over in just a few minutes to take you to the shooting range. He says it's high time you got off your ass and went back to work."

She finished the last with a cheeky grin.

"I don't want to leave her," Nathan said. "I don't want her to think for even a minute that I've left her. What if she panics? What if she thinks she's back in that hell she existed in? What if she needs me?"

Rachel's eyes darkened in sympathy and she took his hand in hers. "I know you don't want to leave her. You've been with her every day. She knows you're here. She knows you aren't going anywhere. She knows that, Nathan. I promise. You need to get out. Get some air. Spend some time with your brothers. Leave Shea to us. I swear to you we'll take good care of her."

They were right, but it didn't make it any easier to think of leaving her even for a little while. Rachel squeezed his hand and urged him with her eyes to do as they'd asked.

He leaned forward and kissed her on the cheek. "I know you will. I couldn't leave her in better hands."

"Then go," Sarah urged.

He let go of Rachel's hand and started toward the door but then paused and turned back one last time. "Call me if . . . if there's any change."

THEY were late. Shea would have frowned but there wasn't much to frown about and it took too much effort. It was too beautiful a day to exert negative energy, and she'd worked so hard to expel any and all blackness from her mind.

A surge of excitement danced up her spine, dispelling some

of the murkiness she'd embraced, when she heard the door slide open. She turned ever so slightly to see that Rachel, Sarah and Sophie had all come out. The baby . . . Shea pondered a minute, trying to remember the baby's name. Charlotte.

She loved it when Sophie brought the baby out to toddle around in the playpen that had been erected on the sprawling deck. A mat covered the wood so that Charlotte didn't get splinters in her hands or feet.

Toys were scattered carelessly around the area, and Shea thought the entire house and deck looked . . . lived in. Like a family shared love and laughter within its protective arms.

Sophie leaned over to put Charlotte down on the mat and handed her one of her favorite toys to chew on. She was teething and gnawed on anything she could get her hands on.

Rachel settled into the swing next to where Shea sat wrapped in her quilt while Sarah sat on Shea's other side in a wicker armchair. Sophie came away from the partitioned-off play area and sat with Rachel in the swing.

"You're looking better today, Shea," Rachel said, her sweet voice soothing over Shea's ears like music.

Sarah and Sophie both smiled and nodded their agreement. Shea knew they were lying, but she loved that they cared enough to want to make her feel better. And even if she didn't look better, she thought maybe she did indeed *feel* better.

Sophie rose from the swing and went to perch on the oval wooden table that rested just in front of Shea. Their knees were nearly touching. She reached for Shea's hands and for a moment simply held on and squeezed comfortingly. Rachel and Sarah both sat forward, their gazes focused solely on Shea. Shea could feel the warmth and the love in those stares. She marveled at how these women could care so much for someone they didn't really know. But then Shea already liked them so much and she drew great comfort from their company.

"Shea, it's time to stop hiding," Sophie said gently. "I know you're scared. I know you've been through such a horrible ordeal. But you're safe now. You're with people who love you. It's okay to let down the barriers and allow us in."

Rachel glanced first at Sarah and then to Sophie and finally back to Shea. "We understand what you're going through. We've all been there. I'm still working on getting there, but it gets easier every day. We're all here to help you. All of us."

"Nathan is so worried for you," Sarah said. "He's not sleeping well. He's not eating. He loves you so much, Shea. He's suffering too, and I know you don't want that. He hides it from you because he doesn't want to burden you and he doesn't want to add to your stress."

Shea's brow wrinkled and she blinked. They all looked so very sincere. And worried. Part of her wanted to push through. Shrug off the heavy veil of silence and the comforting white void. But the other part of her feared losing that barrier because, without it, she was without defense. Open, raw, memories clawing relentlessly at her.

Rachel leaned forward and added her hands to Sophie's as she stared earnestly at Shea. "You don't have to do this alone. You have the entire Kelly family behind you. I'll always be willing to listen. Or to help you. I still go to a therapist to talk about the time I spent in captivity. It does get easier. I promise you."

"And I go twice a month to a rape counselor," Sarah added quietly. "Garrett has been so wonderful. His—*my*—family has been unfailingly supportive. It feels so good to say 'my family.' I'm not even married to Garrett yet, but you are all truly my family. And that includes you, Shea. You've been a part of this family since you brought Nathan home to us."

"Our point is that we all have our share of fears, imperfections and issues to work through," Sophie said. "But we do it together. As a family. Because that's what family—or at least *this* family—is all about."

Tears burned Shea's eyelids. Emotion welled and expanded in her chest until she thought she might burst at the seams. She had no idea what to say or if she could say anything at all. She stared helplessly at these women who were for all practical purposes her sisters. Like Grace.

"Come home, Shea," Rachel said softly. "Come home to stay. It's safe here."

She raised her gaze to fully meet theirs for the first time. She saw excitement bloom in their eyes as she met each one in turn. And then she saw movement behind Sophie. Her breath caught as the baby toddled toward the multitude of steps leading down toward the lake.

One of the gates had come open and Charlotte was fast heading toward the steps. Shea tried to shout a warning, but the words stuck and she could do more than watch helplessly as the baby started to fall.

To hell with this. She was tired of being a coward, and this beautiful baby wasn't going to suffer because she was scared to face reality. Was this what she'd become? Some spineless, witless blob of insanity?

She bolted from her chair, knocking Sophie to the side as she flew toward Charlotte. The other women let out startled exclamations, but Shea could only see Charlotte and the imminent danger she was in.

Shea dove low, snatching her literally from the air as she pitched over the first step. She rotated so she'd take the brunt of the fall and she wouldn't squash the child. Then she braced for impact.

She landed on the fourth step with enough force to knock the air from her lungs, but still she hung tenaciously on to Charlotte, determined to protect her at all costs.

She slid down the remaining steps, head first, on her back, each bump jarring her entire body. When she hit the bottom, she lay there a moment and stared up in wonder as Charlotte gave her a huge gummy grin and promptly drooled on her.

Sophie, Rachel and Sarah flew down the steps, babbling, yelling, shouting "Are you okay?" and "Oh my God!" Sophie tried to take Charlotte from Shea, but Shea held on and hugged the baby to her as she gingerly rolled the rest of her body off the steps.

Her entire body hurt, but nothing felt broken. Still clinging to Charlotte, she settled on the bottom step and buried her face in all that sweet-smelling baby skin and hair. Charlotte, completely unfazed by the event, chortled in glee and grasped a handful of Shea's hair, pulling as she tried to maneuver it to her mouth.

Tears streamed down Shea's cheeks. She hadn't even realized she was crying. Her shoulders shook and she wept. Huge, aching sobs.

Around her, Sophie, Sarah and Rachel gathered, sitting in intervals on the steps so they could wrap their arms around both Shea and Charlotte.

"Thank you," Sophie whispered. "Oh my God, thank you, Shea. I don't know how you did it. I was so scared. I didn't see her. I don't know how the gate came undone. I'm always so careful. Sam is always so careful. If you hadn't seen her. Oh God, if you hadn't seen her."

Charlotte began to squirm, protesting the suffocating circle of women surrounding her. She pulled away from Shea and this time Shea let her go. Charlotte patted Shea's cheeks with both hands and let out a squeal of delight that Shea felt all the way to her toes.

And then Shea smiled back. God, it felt so good. Then she laughed. Tears still streaming down her cheeks, she laughed and let the sheer joy of the moment invade her soul.

One by one, each of the women hugged Shea fiercely and Shea hugged them back, grateful for that bond that had already begun forming. Family. Friendship. All the things that made life worth living despite the risks, the dangers and the unknowns.

Rachel wiped at Shea's tears with the pads of her thumbs and gave her a watery smile of her own. "I think there's someone who'd love to see you about now. Why don't you go over and surprise him?"

CHAPTER 45

HE wasn't shooting worth a damn. He was all over his target. He was ready to say to hell with it all and go back to Shea.

"Glad we aren't depending on you for cover," Garrett grumbled beside him. "We'd all get our asses shot up."

Garrett was the only one who'd hung around after Nathan started shooting. The rest of his brothers had beaten a hasty retreat and were a safe distance away.

"I can't do this," Nathan said in disgust. "My head's not in it. Furthermore I don't want my head to be in it right now. I just want . . ," He broke off and squeezed his fingers into a fist in frustration.

Garrett put his hand on Nathan's shoulder. "I know, man. I know. You'll get there."

"I hope to hell you're right. I feel so damn helpless. I feel like there's something I should be able to do to help her. To make her not so afraid. To help her forget the nightmare she's protecting herself from."

"She's been through a lot," Garrett said quietly. "But she's strong. She's a fighter. Right now she's just doing what she has to do to survive and cope. Think about all you did to survive the hell you endured. You're still dealing with it. And you will. Just like she will. Only you'll do it together."

"Is that what you and Sarah do? Deal with it?"

"Every damn day," Garrett said in a somber voice. "Some days are better than others. But the good ones? Are so damn sweet that they more than make up for the bad ones."

Nathan took off the safety glasses and then pulled the earplugs he'd draped around his neck and pocketed both. It was pointless to continue wasting ammo.

He nodded in Swanny's direction. "You and Sam thinking of taking him on?"

Garrett followed Nathan's gaze to where Swanny was involved in a push-up contest with Ethan. "Maybe. If he's interested. You know Van's putting together a team. The plan was always for it to include you and Joe. There's no hurry. You, Joe, even Swanny have a lot to sort out before you can be cut loose. We have time."

Sam and Joe strode toward Nathan and Garrett, broad grins covering their faces. Garrett stared suspiciously at them, but they ignored him and focused on Nathan.

"Take a look, Nathan," Joe said, pointing behind him.

Nathan swiveled, scanning the terrain for what Joe was trying to draw his attention to. Then he froze and he forgot to breathe. Or maybe he just couldn't.

Shea was walking toward him, slowly, her steps a little unsure. But it was her. And she was looking right at him.

He stared in wonder, his gut so knotted up that he couldn't even swallow. He'd never seen such a beautiful sight in his entire life. He wanted to laugh. He wanted to cry. He wanted to throw up a fist and let out a triumphant yell.

"Well, what the hell are you waiting for?" Garrett asked, his grin as big as his brothers'. "Go get her!"

Nathan started out with a stagger. As he got his feet under him and his knees stopped shaking, he increased his pace until he was running. As fast and as hard as he could, his only thought to get to her.

She stopped when she saw him coming, and then her smile lit up the entire world. His world. It hit him right where he lived and nearly took him to his knees.

When he finally reached her, he gathered her up in his arms and hugged her tightly against him and then spun round and round as she laughed her delight.

She threw back her head, spread her arms out as he spun them both. Her laughter rang out, the sound so beautiful and pure that no words could describe it.

Finally he stopped and let her slide down his body until their noses were nearly touching.

"I love you," he said hoarsely. "Oh God, I love you so damn much, Shea. Welcome home, baby. Welcome home."

She threw her arms around him and hugged him so fiercely that she had a stranglehold around his neck. "I love you too," she whispered. "I'm so sorry I worried you."

He pulled away and put a finger to her lips. "Shhh. You've come back to me. That's all that matters."

He kissed her and she tasted so sweet, felt so soft and warm and so very precious in his arms.

"I want a life with you, Nathan. I've been so very afraid. I'm still afraid. I didn't want to involve you or your family. I still don't know what the future holds, but I realized that whatever the future does bring, I want to face it with you. I want your family to be my family. I love them already."

He smiled and gently lowered her to the ground, but he didn't let go of her. He kept her close, touching him, pressed against him. His hands were everywhere, reassuring himself that she was here, with him, her beautiful eyes clear and comprehending.

"They already are your family, baby. And they love you too."

"Can we go see our house?" she whispered. "I never got to see the inside."

He gathered her in his arms again and just held on, absorbing the feel and the sheer joy that blew over him, wave after wave.

"Yeah," he choked out. "I think I can arrange a tour. I'm afraid your husband-to-be has been slacking in the building department, but he just happens to have a horde of very capable brothers, not to mention numerous friends, only too willing to help out. I'm betting we could have it done in no time at all."

She pulled away, her eyes sparkling mischievously as she slid her hand into his. "Are we getting married?"

He cupped her chin and pulled her toward him. "Hell yes, we're getting married. Today, tomorrow, next year. I don't care when. Okay, I do, but I'm willing to wait until you're ready and, more importantly, when you're feeling better. All I care is that you're going to live here with me. Always. Together. That you love me half as much as I love you. That's enough. You'll always be enough for me, Shea."

She smiled up at him, her eyes shiny with tears. "You've been so patient with me, Nathan. I'll get there. I've been assured by some very special women that it takes time, but that I'll never be alone. And you know what? You'll get there too."

He softened all over. She knew he still fought his demons, that like her, he still battled his fears and anxieties. But yeah, he'd get there. As long as she was with him, he could fucking take on the world.

"We make a pretty messed-up pair, you know that?" he said with a laugh.

"I think we're perfect for each other," she said softly. "We have each other to lean on and when we need them? We have family to lean on as well."

He pulled her into his side as they started toward the house he'd begun building months ago when he'd returned home, a mere shell of the man he'd once been.

Now? He felt reborn. Whole again for the first time in so long. He no longer looked to the future with uncertainty. What he saw filled him with such joy that it overwhelmed him.

A life with a woman who'd saved him from hell. Who'd put him back together when he'd thought he was beyond repair. Love could do amazing things. She was his miracle, and he thanked God every day for sending her to him when his need was so great.

Now he could do the same for her. He'd love her every single day of his life. He'd never take for granted just how precious she was to him, and if it took everything he had, he'd make damn sure she felt safe and loved every single minute of the rest of her life.

CHAPTER 46

NATHAN and his brothers looked up as they heard a knock on the outer door to the war room. Nathan sighed. "I'll get it."

The others chuckled as he went to let Shea in. She had an access code specifically assigned to her, but she always knocked, unable to get over her hesitancy of just barging into the KGI headquarters.

He opened the door and for a moment drank in the sight of her standing there looking so beautiful and . . . happy. There was a lightness to her eyes that had been absent for a long time. Her skin held the first bloom of a tan, a testament to how much time she spent outside.

Then he took her hand and pulled her inside. "You have to start using your code, Shea. We gave it to you for a reason."

"I know. I still feel like I'm intruding, though. Maybe I'll just knock and then use the code. That way you know I'm coming."

Donovan chuckled as Nathan and Shea joined the others. "I hate to break it to you, but we knew you were here when you got within twenty yards of the building. Just use the code and come on in."

"Has there been any word from Rio?" she asked anxiously.

Nathan slid his hand along her back in an up-and-down motion. Donovan's face softened with regret. "No, honey, I'm afraid not."

Shea tried to hide her disappointment, but she failed miserably. His brothers all grimaced because they hated to see her sad for any reason. They all went to great lengths to treat her with the utmost care even though she improved greatly with each passing day.

"We do have some further information and we've also fielded a request from Resnick. Why don't you have a seat and we'll fill you in," Sam said.

She smiled at Sam and then included the others in her acknowledgment before she went to sit on one of the couches. She perched on the edge and appeared serene, but Nathan could feel her nervousness as well as her deep disappointment—and worry—that Grace hadn't been found yet.

We'll find her, baby. We won't stop until we bring her home to you. I promise.

Her features softened and her eyes glowed. It was like a fist to his gut how she lit up when he spoke to her telepathically. They didn't often communicate that way in front of his family. Shea still wasn't entirely comfortable with how well her abilities were received, but she was getting there.

I know you will. I have faith in you and your brothers.

"If you two are finished sending telepathic kissy faces," Garrett said dryly.

Before, Shea would have likely blushed, ducked her head and felt horribly conspicuous. But she was growing more comfortable with his family all the time, which thrilled Nathan.

She raised her chin and smirked in Garrett's direction. "I was just telling Nathan that I needed to remember to tell Sarah how many F bombs I overheard you dropping yesterday."

Garrett sighed while everyone else dissolved into laughter.

Sam grinned and then dropped into the chair across from the couch while Nathan settled beside Shea. The others gradually chose spots to sit, but Swanny hovered in the background. He still hadn't reached his comfort zone but he was fitting in nicely. He was going home in a few days, but Nathan knew Sam had extended a job offer, and while Swanny had said he wanted time to think about it, Nathan figured he'd go home, settle things, and be back. He hoped so at least. Swanny was adrift. He needed KGI. He needed a purpose just as Nathan had when he'd returned from Afghanistan.

"Resnick asked if you'd be willing to meet him, Shea," Sam began.

Shea's mouth dropped open and she automatically inched toward Nathan until she was pressed tightly against his side. He slipped his arm around her shoulders and squeezed.

"Is he crazy?" she demanded.

"There's a lot you don't know, but know this before we get into all the whys and wherefores. You don't have to do anything you don't want to. Period. If you say the word, the man will never set foot in this compound. Understand?" Sam leveled a look, catching her gaze and holding it. "You're in the driver's seat. We'll only do what you want us to do, okay?"

She smiled and nodded.

"Now, he wants to meet you because he was conceived in the same lab where you and Grace were born."

Shea went completely still, so still that for a moment Nathan worried they'd upset her already.

"Then why?" she whispered. "Why would he do that to me? Why would he allow it? He knows. He has to know what went on there, doesn't he?"

Nathan kissed her temple and stroked a hand down her hair. But he remained silent so Sam could give her the details as unemotionally as possible. Nathan couldn't be objective. He still couldn't even think about Resnick without wanting to kill the bastard. He couldn't forgive the fact that, if not for Resnick, Shea wouldn't have been captured a second time.

"He wasn't the one who handed you over to the people who hurt you. I know it seems that way. He took you from us because he wanted to protect you. It was stupid. But I don't think he ever meant for you to be harmed. There's more. He believes there's a good possibility that he's your brother."

This time, Nathan felt her shock roll through him. Their pathway was open and he could feel all the conflicting emotions. Her anger. Sadness. And her confusion.

"He was an experiment too. A failed one, by his account. He doesn't have special abilities like you and Grace. He's the one who helped the Petersons when you moved to Oregon. He finally tracked them down after they disappeared with you and Grace years earlier. He funded their efforts and directed them to call on him if help was ever needed. He asked them to tell you and Grace the same but evidently they didn't trust him or maybe they just didn't want you to know the truth about their roles in your birth and the fact that they weren't your biological parents."

"Does he know who wants Grace and me so badly?"

"He hadn't given us all the information, but Donovan did a little hacking and we have access to all his files," Sam said with a satisfied grin.

Shea glanced to Donovan, her eyes wary.

Donovan sent her a reassuring smile. "I don't want you to worry. Okay? Promise me that."

"Tell me," she said softly.

"He spoke of two Russian scientists, so I went in search of information regarding them as well as anything else I could find out about the purpose of the experiments and their intended uses. I was able to track down one of the scientists, who still lives here in the U.S. despite Resnick thinking or at least saying that he'd returned to Russia."

Shea went still and leaned forward, her eyes narrowed in concentration.

"In the beginning this was solely a military-funded and -backed research subject. Highly classified. Furthermore, there were other successful test subjects besides you and Grace. There were other children born with psychic talents. But once they discovered that they'd been able to produce the ability to heal, the others were discarded, adopted out, dropped from the program."

"Grace," Shea whispered. "It was about Grace all along. Why keep me then?"

"Because you have that ability too, Shea," Donovan said gently. "Yes, it would seem that your abilities differ, but think about what you did for Nathan. Now consider how you and Grace could operate as a team. Remote healing. We talked about this before, remember? You could communicate with and take the pain and suffering from someone. Grace healed Swanny through you. Now think about how the military would use gifts like these. Indestructible soldiers. They get injured on the battlefield and are healed telepathically. They get captured and tortured for information? You take their pain and suffering and shield them from it. They'd be like machines. Never breaking. Imagine it from a rescue perspective. Just as you did for Nathan, you could communicate with the prisoner and lead a rescue team to him. These are talents that, yes, the military would kill for."

"But you work for the military. All of you. Or at least you did," she said in bewilderment. "Don't you still?"

"This is a part of the military that no one ever sees. Not even the enlisted themselves," Sam said. "'Funded by the military' is a code word for a top-secret project that only a few very high-ranking people even know about. The men and women out there serving aren't monsters. They're doing their jobs. Research like this is done for black op groups that don't officially exist. We're telling you this because you deserve to know. We aren't supposed to know all we do, but we're arming ourselves with knowledge so that if there's ever a need, we'll go public far and wide in order to protect you and Grace and any others who are targeted for this kind of research."

"So there's nothing we can do? I—we—just have to live with the knowledge and never be certain whether they'll come after me again?"

"Resnick is very determined to blow this operation from the top down. I don't entirely trust him anymore. But I also understand where he's coming from. He's playing the game just like we have to play the game. If he's successful in pulling the plug, this will all quietly go away. It'll be like it never existed."

"If only it were that easy," Shea murmured.

Nathan laced his fingers through hers. "You'll never be alone again, Shea. You'll never have to live your life on the run. We take a stand here. Together."

"Hooyah," Ethan softly called.

"Fuckin' A," Garrett said emphatically. "And the first one of you who rats me out to Sarah gets their ass kicked. That includes you, Miss Shea."

Shea smiled and Nathan nearly folded in relief. She was going to be okay. He felt it.

"Shea?" Sam said.

She turned her attention back to Sam.

"What do you want to do about Resnick? He wants to see you but he's determined that you feel safe, which is why he wants to do it here, with all of us present. It might be good for you to talk to him. He could probably answer a lot of your questions."

Slowly she nodded and then took a deep breath. "Okay. I'll see him. Maybe he has information that will help us find Grace." She hesitated a moment and then looked back up at Sam. "When?"

"Whenever you want. Whenever you're ready. You just say the word and I'll make it happen," Sam said.

"Thank you," she suddenly blurted out. She turned to look at them all, her eyes glowing softly. "Just thank you. You all have risked so much for me, and now that I've met your wives, I know I couldn't bear for anything to happen to you that would take you away from one of them because of me."

"You risked everything for our brother," Joe broke in. "How could we not do the same for you?"

"We should probably stop now, or I'll get really mushy," Shea warned.

That brought chuckles from the others, but they all stared at Shea with clear affection in their eyes.

Nathan smiled and pulled her tight against him, dropping a kiss on top of her head.

"That right there is why we'll risk what we have to for you," Ethan said as he stared at Nathan. "He's smiling again. He's himself again. You did that, Shea. You brought him home."

CHAPTER 47

SHEA snuggled deeper into Nathan's arms and watched as fire-flies danced through the air and hovered close to the ground. They blinked through the tree branches and sparkled like Christmas lights in the dark.

"I love it here."

"Hmm. I love *you*," Nathan said.

She smiled as his arms came tighter around her. They were sitting in the swing on Sam's deck as night fell around them. They rocked gently back and forth, aided by Nathan giving them a slight push every once in a while to keep them going.

"I wish Grace were here. She'd love your family. She'd love Sophie, Sarah and Rachel. Especially Sophie. Of all of them, I think she's most like her."

Nathan brushed his lips across her forehead. "She will be, baby. Rio will find her."

"This is so perfect that I worry I'll wake up and it will all be gone."

Not going to happen. You're stuck with me. If you ever do disappear on me, there isn't a corner of this earth I wouldn't look for you in. You're mine, baby. And I'm never giving you up.

She hugged him close and then leaned up to kiss him, her lips moving possessively over his.

"That's good because I hope you know that goes both ways. I'll find you, Nathan. You're mine."

He kissed her back, his hands sliding up her arms as he pulled her farther onto his lap.

"There's just one little thing we need to discuss."

She raised one eyebrow. "Oh?"

He settled her astride him so that her knees dug into the pad of the swing on either side of his thighs.

"Yeah. I'm going to be working with my brothers from now on. There's a possibility I could be injured. You and I talked about this, about the dangers I face working for KGI."

She nodded solemnly.

"You can't be butting in and taking my pain for me," he said sternly. "You have to promise me, Shea. No more."

She rolled her eyes. "You're so full of shit."

His eyes widened and then he grinned. "Feeling feisty tonight, are we?"

"If you'd shut up and take me inside, I'd show you just how feisty," she murmured in his ear just before she nipped at the lobe.

"Whoa, wait a minute. You aren't distracting me from my original purpose. I want your promise, Shea."

"You aren't getting it, Nathan."

He glared ferociously at her, but she merely smiled back and slid her hands down to cup him intimately. He was already hard and bulging against his jeans.

"So this is how it's going to be," he grumbled. "You distract me with sex anytime you don't want to do something I've asked you."

"Is it working?"

"Hell yes."

He abruptly got up from the swing, carrying her with him as he headed toward the door. She reached out to open it and he shouldered his way inside.

He carried her into their bedroom and dropped her on the bed, coming down over her, covering her with his warm, hard body.

She stared up at him, all the love she felt shining in her eyes. It swelled in her chest and overwhelmed her with its power. She loved this man more than anything. He'd gone to the wall for her. He'd known and accepted from the very start that they were destined to be together. Not a day went by that he didn't make her feel loved and cherished beyond measure.

Life was so very good, all the more sweet for everything they'd endured together.

She lifted her hands to his face and smiled up at him. "Just think. You'll get a reputation as a pushover."

He kissed her and then nibbled a path down her neck before pulling back to smile down at her with answering love and adoration. "I think I can live with that."

GRACE Peterson drew the blanket tighter around her and huddled in the dark. She stared blankly at the star-filled sky. The mountain air was cold. Not just chilly, as it had been as dusk had descended, wiping away the comfortable remnants of a sunny afternoon. It was frigid.

A low moan escaped as her muscles tightened and protested not only the cold but the weakness inflicted upon them by so much death and sickness. Pain had long since lost any meaning to her. What she felt couldn't really be considered pain. It was worse. She couldn't feel anything but the desolation of hopelessness and despair. The knowledge that she would probably die from the horrors inflicted upon her. And perhaps she deserved it, for she hadn't been able to help all who had been thrust upon her.

Her escape had been a fluke. The mistake of one of the men charged with her care. Though it couldn't really be considered care. They'd shown her no regard. She'd been treated like an inanimate object. Some magic wand they waved at a wound or an illness and expected her to make it all disappear.

She hated them for that. Hated them for their callousness. For using others as they'd used her. Pawns. Objects to provide them with information. They weren't even people. Just numbers.

Another shiver rattled her teeth and settled deep into her bones. She simply couldn't imagine ever being warm again. She curled her feet further into the blanket and tucked the ends securely under her chin.

She missed her sister, Shea. Ached for the comfort of her touch. The brush of her mind and the image of her smile. She hadn't ever really understood and hadn't ever taken seriously Shea's decision for them to separate. Until the day she'd been captured and she realized that if they'd been together, they would have both been taken.

Shea had always been determined to keep Grace safe, but now, Grace was equally determined to keep Shea as far away from her as possible. Grace was hunted. She knew her pursuers were probably in these mountains already. They could be a short distance away.

And so she'd slammed the door shut on her sister, and the void hurt every bit as much as the bombardment of sickness and pain she'd absorbed. Not having Shea there was the worst sort of loneliness. She'd severed the telepathic link between her and her sister, and her worst fear was that it was permanent. She'd never get it back.

In a way, she supposed it would be a blessing. If she lost her abilities, she could have a normal life. But so would she lose the ability to make a difference in someone else's life.

She closed her eyes, exhausted by the weight of responsibility, sorrow and regret. She hated that she wasn't stronger, that she'd crumbled under so much stress. But the ailments had been thrown at her, one after another. Broken bones, horrible bloody wounds, tumors, diseases, and the list went on and on. The most horrific experiment she'd undergone was when it had been demanded of her to reach inside the mind of a woman with a mental illness and heal her.

For three long days Grace had known what it truly was to be insane. She'd lived the woman's existence while the woman had gone away cleansed of the darkness in her brain. Twice, Grace had tried to kill herself, not because it was what she wanted, but because it was what the illness dictated. In the end, she'd been restrained, unable to do even the basic necessities for herself because the fear had been too great that she'd find a way to end her life.

She was hungry, but the thought of food made her stomach twist into knots. She drank water from nearby streams frequently, because she knew she had to do something to keep her strength up.

Quietly, she turned over, rearranging the blanket in the fruitless hope she'd somehow find greater warmth. Eventually she'd have to reach out to her sister, but if she did so now, Shea would see the horrific shape Grace was in. Shea would come. She'd put herself in grave danger. Grace would never be able to live with herself if Shea was sacrificed because in a moment of weakness Grace gave in and tried to re-establish the link with her sister.

Silent tears slid down Grace's cheeks, briefly warming her skin until the chilly air turned it to ice. She angrily scrubbed them away and hunched lower, furious with herself for allowing despair to control her.

She was stronger than this, and she'd be strong again. She just needed time to recover from her ordeal. Maybe she'd never be the same as she was, but she wasn't going to give in. If she died, she'd die running. She'd die standing up and fighting. She refused to die in some laboratory where rats were treated with less disdain.

A distant sound froze her to the bone. She went so still that even her breath sounded like a roar in the night. She pushed the blanket over her mouth, trying to quell the noise and she stared into the trees, trying desperately to see through the thick curtain of night.

Someone was coming.

Discover Romance

berkleyjoveauthors.com

See what's coming up next from your favorite romance authors and explore all the latest Berkley, Jove, and Sensation selections.

See what's new

~

Find author appearances

~

Win fantastic prizes

~

Get reading recommendations

~

Chat with authors and other fans

~

Read interviews with authors you love